PRAISE FOR KERRY ANNE KING

Praise for *Whisper Me This*

"Rich in emotions and characters, *Whisper Me This* is a stunning tale of dark secrets, broken memories, and the resilience of the human spirit. The novel quickly pulls the reader onto a roller-coaster ride through grief, mystery, and cryptic journal entries. At the heart of the story is an unforgettable twelve-year-old, who has more sense than most adults, and her mother, Maisey, who is about to discover not only her courage, but the power of her voice. A book club must-read!"

—Barbara Claypole White, bestselling author of *The Perfect Son*

"Moving and emotionally taut, *Whisper Me This* is a gut-wrenching story of a family fractured by abuse and lies . . . and the ultimate sacrifice of a mother's love. King once again proves herself an expert with family drama. A triumph of a book."

—Emily Carpenter, author of *The Weight of Lies* and *Burying the Honeysuckle Girls*

"Kerry Anne King writes with such insight and compassion for human nature, and her latest novel, *Whisper Me This*, is no exception. The families on which the story centers have secrets they've kept through the years out of concern for the damage that might be done if they were exposed. But in the end as the families' lives become intertwined and their secrets come inevitably to light, what is revealed to be the most riveting heart of this book are the gut-wrenching choices that were made in terrifying circumstances. One such choice haunted a mother throughout her lifetime and left behind a legacy of mistrust and confusion and a near unsolvable mystery. Following the clues is an act of faith that sometimes wavers. There's no guarantee the end will tie up in a neat bow, but the courage of the human spirit, its ability to heal, is persistent and luminous throughout the pages of this very real and emotive story. I loved it."

—Barbara Taylor Sissel, bestselling author of *Crooked Little Lies* and *Faultlines*

Praise for *I Wish You Happy*

"Laugh, cry, get angry, but most of all care in this wild ride of emotions delivered by Kerry Anne King. Brilliant prose inhabited by engaging characters makes this a story you cannot put down."

—Patricia Sands, author of the Love in Provence series

"Depicting the depth of human frailty yet framing it within a picture of hope, *I Wish You Happy* pulls you in as you root for the flawed yet intoxicating characters to reach a satisfying conclusion of healing. King's writing is impeccable—and her knowledge and exploration of depression and how it affects those it touches makes this a story that everyone will connect with."

—Kay Bratt, author of *Wish Me Home*

"Kerry Anne King's Rae is a woman caught between the safety of her animal rescue projects and the messy, sometimes terrifying reality of human relationships. You'll never stop rooting for her as she steps into the light, risking everything for real friendship and love in this wistful, delicate, and ultimately triumphant tale."

—Emily Carpenter, author of *Burying the Honeysuckle Girls* and *The Weight of Lies*

"Kerry Anne King explores happiness and depression [and] the concept of saving others versus saving ourselves in this wonderfully written and touching novel populated by real and layered people. If you want to read a book that restores your faith in humanity, pick up *I Wish You Happy*."

—Amulya Malladi, bestselling author of *A House for Happy Mothers* and *The Copenhagen Affair*

"It's the horrible accident that forms the backbone of the plot at the beginning of *I Wish You Happy* that will take your breath and have you turning the pages. The hook has a vivid, ripped-from-the-headlines vibe, one that will have you wondering what you would do, how you would respond in a similar situation. But there are so many other treasures to find in this story as it unfolds. From the warm, deeply human and relatable characters to the heartbreaking and complex situation they find themselves in, this is a novel to savor, one you will be sorry to see end. Sometimes funny and often very wise and poignant, *I Wish You Happy* is a reading journey you do not want to miss."

—Barbara Taylor Sissel, bestselling author of *Crooked Little Lies* and *Faultlines*

"Kerry Anne King has written a novel that will grab you right from page one and then take you zipping along, breaking your heart and making you laugh, both in equal measure. It's a lovely story about how we save ourselves while we try to save those around us. I loved it!"

—Maddie Dawson, author of six novels, including *The Survivor's Guide to Family Happiness*

Praise for *Closer Home*

"A compelling and heartfelt tale. A must-read that is rich in relatable characters and emotions. Kerry Anne King is one to watch out for!"
—Steena Holmes, *New York Times* and *USA Today* bestselling author

"With social media conferring blistering fame and paparazzi exhibiting the tenacity often required to get a clear picture of our lives, King has created a high-stakes, public stage for her tale of complicated grief. A quick read with emotional depth you won't soon forget."
—Kathryn Craft, author of *The Far End of Happy* and *The Art of Falling*

"*Closer Home* is a story as memorable and meaningful as your favorite song, with a cast of characters so true to life you'll be sorry to let them go."
—Sonja Yoerg, author of *House Broken* and *Middle of Somewhere*

"Kerry Anne King's tale of regret, loss, and love pulled me in, from its intriguing beginning to its oh-so-satisfying conclusion."
—Jackie Bouchard, *USA Today* bestselling author of *House Trained* and *Rescue Me, Maybe*

"King's prose is filled with vitality."
—Ella Carey, author of *Paris Time Capsule* and *The House by the Lake*

WHISPER ME THIS

ALSO BY KERRY ANNE KING

Closer Home: A Novel

I Wish You Happy: A Novel

WHISPER ME THIS

a novel

KERRY ANNE KING

This is a work of fiction. Names, characters, organizations, places, events, and incidents are either products of the author's imagination or are used fictitiously. Any resemblance to actual persons, living or dead, or actual events is purely coincidental.

Published by Lake Union Publishing, Seattle

www.apub.com

ISBN-13: 9781503901957 (hardcover)
ISBN-10: 1503901955 (hardcover)
ISBN-13: 9781503900769 (paperback)
ISBN-10: 1503900762 (paperback)

Cover design by Shasti O'Leary Soudant

Printed in the United States of America

First edition

For David—my partner in all things, my best and most trusted friend

Whisper me this, my darling, my love
The song of the moonlight, of stars up above.
Whisper me truth, love, and whisper me lies,
Warm days of winter, cold summer skies.
Whisper me anger, whisper me rain,
Whisper me flowers, then whisper me pain.
When I come to die, love, then whisper me this
The shape of a memory, the truth of a kiss.
Whisper me, whisper me, whisper me this
A lifetime of memories, and one final kiss.

COLVILLE, WASHINGTON

1982

Chapter One

My parents' bedroom has always been off-limits.

Not that anybody has ever said to me, "Do not enter this room without permission." There's no *Keep Out* sign on the door. The list of rules my mother wrote out and stuck on the refrigerator with a magnet does not say *Stay out of my bedroom.*

The bedroom rule is both unwritten and unspoken, but I know it as surely as I know the sky is blue and grass is green. It's one of those things I shouldn't need to be told.

Marley knows the rule as well as I do, but Marley doesn't care about the rules. "It's the Forbidden Kingdom," she says, squeezing my hand. "We must be brave."

Today we are playing explorers, willing to risk cannibals, lions, and even our mother in our quest for hidden treasure. Marley says we are fearless adventurers, but I'm scared. My knees feel funny, and I hear my heart beating in my ears. When I catch a glimpse of myself in the mirror hung above the long, low dresser, I look like a little kid, not a bold warrior princess in disguise.

"Maybe we should conquer some other land," I whisper, but Marley is braver.

"I wonder what's in there?" She waves toward the two big white doors that take up nearly one whole wall of the room.

I gasp. "We can't go in there."

"Sure we can. We just need the right magic words to say to break the sealing spell. And don't you even think about abracadabra or bibbidi-bobbidi-boo."

"Not a good idea, Marley."

I look over my shoulder. The bedroom door is firmly closed, but is not much of a barrier between us and parental wrath. I hold my breath. Listen for footsteps. I hear the hum of the electric heater out in the hall. Wind in the trees outside the window. The sound of the television, muted by distance.

Marley, unafraid, lays a hand on the closet door. Nothing happens. No electric zing. No lightning. No earthquakes.

"Behind these doors lies the Cavern of Secrets," she intones. "Treasures await, stored long ago by dragons. All we must do is speak the word of opening and the treasure is ours."

Curiosity builds in me. All my life I've caught only glimpses of this room, usually through the half-open door. It reminds me of the place in church where the minister stands, spotless and sacred and off-limits to kids.

The dark wooden furniture. The giant bed with its perfectly smooth bedspread. The curtains, always closed and blocking out the light. My own small self, reflected in the mirror, is the only thing out of place.

As for that closet, it could contain anything.

"Well, open it, then," I say, all my caution evaporating in a rush of need. Whatever lies behind those doors is important and necessary to my survival. I'm sure of it.

"You have to do it," Marley says, stepping back.

This is the annoying thing about Marley. She has all the best ideas, but once she's talked me into trouble, she always makes me take the necessary action. That way, I'm the one who gets in trouble while she is—poof!—nowhere to be seen. Certainly nowhere to be punished.

"I don't know the magic word."

"Yes, you do," Marley says.

And then, all at once, I do know. I leave my spot by the door, my feet sinking into the carpet with every step, little tufts of cream and gray fibers tickling the spaces between my toes. Raising both arms in the air, like the picture in my Bible storybook of Moses making a path in the Red Sea, I proclaim, "Adventure! Adventure's the word."

Again, it seems like nothing happens, but the incantation works. When I lay my hand against the closet door, it glides open with only the whisper of a sound, revealing a secret room that looks to my eyes more like a store than a mysterious kingdom full of treasure.

Rows of clothes hang neatly on hangers, all lined up by color. On one side, shirts and suit jackets. On the other, dresses and blouses. On the floor, shoes. Boxes, neatly stacked, all sealed shut with packing tape. More items are arranged on shelves above the clothes racks, too high for me to reach or even see clearly for the most part, but I recognize a badminton racket. And there's a stack of gifts, brightly wrapped in Christmas paper.

A spicy fragrance tickles my nose.

Marley is on her knees in the back corner of the dress side of the closet, in front of a suitcase.

It's just an old brown suitcase, but it makes my insides feel jiggly. All at once I don't want to play anymore. I want to run back to the safety of my own room and crawl under the covers. But I'm a brave explorer, so I slide the door closed and tiptoe over to join her.

"Open it," Marley says.

The jiggling in my middle spreads to my hands. I clasp them behind my back and shake my head. "It's an evil suitcase. We should leave it alone."

Marley gives me a withering glare. "Don't be chicken."

So I take a big breath and drop to my knees beside her. My hands are shaking, but I manage to press the buttons on both latches.

Click. Click.

I lift the lid.

Nothing jumps out to bite me. On top is a layer of blue tissue paper that crinkles as I set it carefully aside.

Beneath it, neatly folded, is a white dress. It's made of shiny, slippery fabric and is covered over with lace.

"Silk," Marley says. She knows all the words, even though she's only seven minutes older than me. "Or maybe satin."

These are words we learned from reading time with Mom.

At school they are teaching us reading, but only easy words and boring stories about mice and cats. We already know all the letters and the way they fit together to make words. We don't say this. If Mom finds out, maybe she'll stop reading stories at bedtime and tell us to read our own.

Bedtime is my favorite Mom time. She's not too busy to hug me then. She doesn't have a list of chores for me to do, and she doesn't quiz me about the names of countries I'm supposed to be memorizing or make me count to a hundred or recite Bible verses.

She snuggles up with me in my bed, both of us holding the book, and reads me stories by the light of my bedside lamp. She never reads to Marley, but it's still Marley who remembers all the words, even the hardest ones.

Last night Mom read "Cinderella," the one from a big, fat book with *Grimm* on the spine, not the one from the glossy picture book, where the stepsisters have pointy noses and Cinderella looks so light on her feet she might drift up into the sky.

I can only pick out some of the words in that book. Marley says *grim* means *dark*, and for sure, there are lots of dark words on those pages.

Silk and *satin* are there, but also *hideous*. And *orphaned.*

"What if we were orphaned?" she asked me, the night Mom read "Hansel and Gretel."

"They weren't orphaned," I told her. "Their father was still alive."

"Maybe they would have been better off orphaned," she says, "since he wanted to kill them and all."

Her words made me feel like I feel now, shivery and shaky. It's not the witch in the gingerbread house that scares me; it's the idea of my parents not wanting me anymore. When I wake screaming from nightmares and Mom comes to soothe me with hugs and soft words, it's always from the same dream. Always she asks, "What were you dreaming, little one? Tell me."

And always I tell her, "I don't remember."

And always it's a lie.

But I'm not dreaming now. I'm with Marley and we are safely hidden in the forbidden closet. The dress doesn't look anything like the pictures in the "Cinderella" book, but I do think the word *silk* suits it just fine.

"Put it on," Marley says. "You can be Cinderella."

"I don't want to be Cinderella."

"What about Princess Leia? That's even better."

We haven't seen the *Star Wars* movies. Mom says we're too young. But we've heard about them from other kids. Lacey at school has a picture book all about the story, and we've seen Princess Leia in her white dress, carrying a gun through the spaceship. Leia is much more exciting than Cinderella and balls and dancing.

Still.

"We'll get in trouble." My hands are already smoothing the material, though.

"Nobody will know."

Underneath the dress are two small pink blankets and one blue stuffed bear. The bear is a twin to the one sitting on my bed, the one that goes with me into dreamland every night.

Wrapped in one of the blankets is a picture. Marley and I stare at it, trying to make sense of the image. A girl holds two babies bundled in pink blankets. The girl has my mother's face, but she's wearing blue jeans and a T-shirt and has long, loose hair hanging down almost to her waist. She wears lots of blue eye shadow and thick mascara.

The girl looks like Mom, except that Mom always wears a dress or slacks and a blouse. Her hair is short. She never puts anything on her face except lotion and ChapStick.

The picture makes my stomach feel sick, so I wrap it back up in the blanket. I pull the dress on over my head. It makes a whispering swish and spills out around me on the floor, more like Cinderella's train than Leia's dress. Marley picks out a pair of high-heeled shoes, and I'm balancing on them, precarious, checking out my transformation in the full-length mirror, when the closet door opens, and the Evil Stepmother stands there, staring at me, hands on both hips, lips pressed tightly together in an expression that means I am in serious trouble.

Because it's not the Evil Stepmother at all, and I'm neither Cinderella nor the brave Princess Leia saving an empire. My own real, true mother has caught me snooping in things that do not belong to me.

"What are you doing?"

It's a trick question and I know better than to answer. She can see what I'm doing.

"Who were you talking to?"

"Nobody."

Her eyes burn me. I try to hold her gaze, but I'm balancing on high heels. My foot slips into the toe of the shoe and then sideways. I topple over, grabbing at an armful of dresses for balance, but they slide off their hangers and come with me, all of us in a heap at the bottom of the closet.

Mom moves between me and the suitcase, closing the lid.

"Get up. Take it off."

I scramble to obey, only I'm tangled in fear and fabric, and in the end, her hands lift the dress over my head.

"You are not to come in my room without permission. You are never to play in this closet. Do you understand? Look at me when I'm talking to you."

My eyes travel up to her face, the same face as in the picture, only not so soft. I can't look her in the eye, so I find the scar on her left cheek, a thin white line, and focus on that. The face in the picture didn't have this scar, and I find that comforting. The picture girl couldn't have been my mother, holding two babies wrapped in pink blankets.

"Now," Mom says. "Tell me again. Who were you talking to?"

"Marley." The name croaks out of me like a frog. I bend my head to hide my face, but Mom catches my chin in her hand and forces me to look up at her again. Her fingers are as hard and sharp as the gingerbread witch's. They hurt me.

"There is no Marley," Mom says. "Do you understand me? I've told you before, you're too old for an imaginary friend."

"She's not imaginary." I'm shocked and frightened by my own boldness.

"Look around you," Mom says. "Do you see any Marley?"

"She's hiding."

The fingers shift to my shoulders, both hands now, both shoulders, and she gives me a little shake. "She is not hiding. She is a figment"—shake—"of"—shake—"your imagination."

My shoulders hurt, enough to bring tears smarting into the backs of my eyes, but I won't cry. I won't. I know better than to say anything, and I set my chin, defiant.

"Promise me you will stop this silly game," Mom says. "Promise me. Now."

"No."

It's the first time I've defied her. That one word hangs in the air between us.

"You will give her up. You will give her up now. This is the end of this nonsense." Mom grabs one of Dad's belts from a hook in the closet. With her free hand, she clamps my wrist in an iron vise and drags me out of the closet and over to the bed.

I don't fight her. I'm too shocked to do anything but let her bend me over her knee. When the strap comes down on the backs of my legs, I start to struggle, but by then it's too late. She's got me pinned. The belt keeps coming, thwacking down on my butt, my thighs.

All my resolution not to cry is gone by the third hit, and I hear myself wailing, loud and sad.

"What's going on?"

Dad's voice stops everything: the thwack of the belt, Mom's torturing fingers anchoring me in place, the loud sobs bursting out of my throat. Both of us freeze, heads turning to look up at him.

"I'll take that," he says, very quietly, and tugs the belt out of Mom's hands.

"She was snooping in the closet," Mom says. "Into my stuff. Playing pretend."

"We weren't snooping," I whimper. "We were exploring. Marley is real. I don't care what you say."

"See?" Mom says. "She still hasn't learned. Give me back that belt."

"Leah," he says. This time his voice is a reprimand, a reminder, the tone of voice he uses on me when I run into the house without taking off my muddy boots.

Mom's fingers press harder into my skin. They are going to tunnel through flesh and meet each other, and then the bone will crunch in her grasp. Marley whispers in my ear that maybe Mom is an ogress and not my real mother at all.

"This is ridiculous," the ogress says. "This Marley nonsense has got to stop."

"Let me deal with it. Please, Leah. You're too angry."

Dad looks like the hero in one of my favorite fairy-tale movies, offering himself to the dragon in exchange for the princess.

The ogress's fingers are really starting to hurt. I keep my jaw clamped, but the whimper gets out anyway.

"Leah." Dad's voice is very gentle now. He's doing some sort of eye juju, his face only inches away from the ogress. He puts his hands over hers, and she lets go of my shoulders.

The Dad Magic melts something inside her. She makes a strangled noise that turns her back into Mom and hurts me more than the belt ever did. Dad sits on the bed and puts his arms around her. She hides her face against his shoulder.

"Go to your room, Maisey. I'll be there in a bit," Dad says. His voice is muffled, his cheek pressed against my mother's hair.

I go.

My butt hurts and my legs hurt and the sounds my mother is making hurt me even more. I lie on my bed, my face buried in the pillow. Marley is here, but she looks thin and tattered around the edges.

"I have to leave now," she says, and even her voice sounds thin.

"I know."

"Don't forget me."

My heart is a lump in my chest when she evaporates and leaves me alone. I'm cold. My room is cold. I climb into bed with my bear and hide under the covers.

I refuse to come out of my room for dinner.

"I'm not hungry," I tell Dad when he comes to check on me, but after he's gone, I eat the cookies and milk he left on my dresser.

Much later, Mom comes to tuck me in. I'm already in my pajamas and under the blankets, *Grimm* open in my hands, the lamp shedding a circle of light on the pages.

"I'm sorry," Mom says, perching like a bird on the edge of my bed. "I got too angry." Her eyes are red and puffy, and she talks like her nose is blocked with a cold.

"Can I have Marley, then?"

She sighs. "There is no Marley. I got mad, and I'm sorry for that. But you need to grow up. No more Marley. Now, are you ready to read?"

I look up from the book. "I can read it by myself." It's true. It's been true for a long time—I just hadn't realized.

"I could read to you anyway." She looks sad, sitting there on the edge of my bed. Part of me wants to hug her. But my legs are still burning from my whipping, and Marley's gone, and in that moment, I love my mother and I hate her in equal measure.

"That's okay," I say, keeping my eyes on the page, even though right now I'm not making sense of any of the letters. "But thanks anyway."

She lifts her hand as if to stroke my hair, then lets it fall onto the blanket between us. I pretend she isn't there, that I'm all alone with the book. When she sighs again and leaves me, I bite my lip to stop calling out after her. And when the door closes behind her, with a barely audible click, I know that if I have punished her for taking Marley from me, then I have also punished myself.

KANSAS CITY, MISSOURI

2017

Chapter Two

Time for me is not linear. It flows in random loops and swirls, and sometimes in huge, incomprehensible leaps. I have entertained the possibility that I possess my own personal wormhole that opens into an alternate time continuum whenever I'm engaged in an activity of interest. Reading, say, or messing around with paint.

Today, for example, I swear it has only been two minutes of normal human time since I sat down to delve into the lusciously fat, solid, fantasy novel I bought yesterday. It can't be more than two minutes, but the clock on the wall has mysteriously moved forward by fives and tens.

The bacon I laid in a pan on the stove before picking up the book has gone from cold and flabby and streaked with white to black and crusty and on fire in a time span that is a matter of mystery. I can't ponder the vagaries of time, though. I must face the shrill reality of a smoke-filled kitchen. Indecisive as usual, I'm torn between extinguishing the fire that has ignited in the spattering fat and doing something—anything—to stop the brain-blasting noise from the fire alarm over my head.

Fire first. Always.

Pinpricks of overheated oil spatter my hands and arms as I reach to put a lid over the pan and turn off the burner. My mother would have a fit. Thirty-nine years old and I can still hear her voice in my head, as clearly as if she's in the room with me. Can see her plant both hands on her angular hips, tilt her head to the right just enough to let her hair graze her shoulder, and pin me with the gaze of disappointment.

You must learn to focus, Maisey. One thing at a time. When you are cooking, cook. When you are studying, study. When you are cleaning, clean. You must learn this skill if you want to succeed.

It's an old lecture, one that follows me back as far into my childhood as I have memories. It's as pointless now as it ever was. I am incapable of this type of unified purpose. My mother's concept of success mystifies me as thoroughly as the idea of a straight line through time.

My daughter, on the other hand, was born practical. No hesitation there, no scattered thoughts and indecision. She arrows into the room, focused and efficient.

"Again?" she shouts, loud enough to be heard over the blaring screech.

She drags a chair across the kitchen and climbs up on it. It strikes me, as she stretches for the smoke detector, how much she's grown. The last time we played out this scenario her fingers barely grazed the plastic, and she had to stand on tiptoe. How long ago was that? Her T-shirt pulls tight against her chest, and I can see the unmistakable beginnings of breasts.

"What?" she asks into a sudden silence, the battery in one hand, the detector in the other.

I realize I'm staring, shattered by the realization that my baby is going to be a teen, only a few more months, and then the separation and the fighting and where will I be when she leaves me to follow her own life? *Don't leave me, Elle. Don't ever leave me.*

When I don't answer, she scrambles down and does all the things I should have done.

Opens a window.

Turns on the exhaust fan.

Gets out a cloth and the dish soap and starts cleaning up the greasy mess all over the stove.

"Seriously, Mom. You can't be trusted to cook and read at the same time. How many times have we had this conversation?"

She sounds exactly like my mother, which reminds me, belatedly, that I am the mother and Elle is still a child.

"Here, I'll do that." I take the cloth from her hand and scrub the stove top. I'm focused enough now, my senses full of acrid smoke and the burning patches on my arms and the lump in the back of my throat.

Elle makes a choking noise and opens the front door. Fresh, June-scented air flows into the kitchen, swirling the smoke.

"Why are you making bacon anyway?" she demands. "What happened to salad for dinner? I thought that was the new normal."

"The new normal is me being allowed to deviate from routine."

"Oh, please. That's the old normal." She snorts, a disgusted chiding sort of snort, and then, unexpectedly, she bursts into a fit of helpless giggles. "You are incorrigible. And I love you that way."

She dances across the kitchen and hugs me. I can't fit her head under my chin anymore, she's gotten so tall. Another inch and she'll be looking me level in the eyes.

"Where did you learn that word?" I mumble against her hair, holding on to her as if she's going to dissolve into the bacon smoke and be lost to me, a wraith, a memory.

"My English teacher wrote it on my last paper."

"Oh dear. You need to pass English, Elle Belle." I release the hug and tilt her chin up. Her eyes are the same changeable hazel as my mother's—mosaic eyes, pixels of jade and mahogany, eyes that could mislead a casual acquaintance into overlooking the single-minded iron will behind them. My eyes can be blue or green, depending on the light. My father's are gray. My genetics are as off-kilter as my sense of time.

"Mrs. Wilson needs to stop giving out such stupid assignments," Elle retorts. "I am not going to waste my time writing about my summer vacation." She makes air quotes around the last three words, her voice a mockery of her teacher's.

"What exactly did you write?"

"A short story. Can we go out for dinner?"

"Now who is deviating from normal?" She is evading me, and I know it. Mrs. Wilson will no doubt be emailing to let me know that my daughter is persisting in a path of defiance and attach a copy of the offending story.

But I also know that one of these days, inevitably, Elle will turn up her nose at the idea of dinner with her mother. Every day that she wants to be with me is a gift.

"All right. Let's go for dinner. Mexican?"

"What happened to losing twenty pounds before you turn forty?"

"I have a month. Close that window and get your shoes. Let's make sure the bacon fire is out, though."

When my phone rings, I glance at it, but don't answer. Nobody I know. The only people I ever really pick up the phone for are my parents, and not always even then.

Elle is not like me.

She answers before the second ring. "Yep, she's here. Just a minute."

Ignoring my exaggerated headshaking and my lips forming the words "I'm not here," she holds out the phone. "It's somebody called Mrs. Carlton," she says, and the world collapses inward, all in soft-focus slow motion, like an earthquake in a movie.

One of my bare feet is illuminated by light from the window; the other foot remains in shadow. Tiny blobs of bacon grease speckle the floor between them. A haze of smoke winds its way in a visible layer above my head. Elle's eyes are bright with curiosity. Her hand, holding the phone, looks strong and capable, and the smooth curve of her nails is the same as her father's.

I watch my own hand reach out for the phone. The fingers are longer than Elle's, more tapered, the nails coated in glittery black. There's a burn from a grease splash right next to the first knuckle. It's red around the edges, forming a perfect fluid-filled blister at the center. All those little body cells, rushing around to do damage control, histamine alarms blaring, white blood cells rushing in.

Elle shoves the phone into my hand, reminding me that I'm supposed to do something besides stand here. The phone feels heavier than it looks, and my voice, when I say hello, floats upward to join the smoke above my head, a cartoon bubble of a question that doesn't want an answer.

I'm going to get an answer though, whether I want it or not. A long, detailed, scorching one, because this is Mrs. Carlton calling. Mrs. Stay-Off-My-Lawn Carlton. Mrs. I'm-Telling-Your-Mother Carlton. Mrs. Shouldn't-You-Be-Doing-Homework and Why-Is-That-Boy-Kissing-You Carlton.

"Maisey?" I hardly recognize her voice. It's gone soft and quavery. She sounds like she's eighty. But then, she was already old when I was sixteen. She might *be* eighty now. She might be pushing a hundred.

"How did you get my number?"

"It was on your mother's fridge. I'm calling because I don't think your father should be alone just now."

"Why not?" That's the first question. It's followed by the crushing and more obvious one, the question that transforms my lungs from spongy air reservoirs into solid, impermeable plastic, incapable of retaining oxygen. "Where's Mom?" That's the second question, the one I don't want to hear the answer to.

"The ambulance just left. The police are still here, but it doesn't look like they're going to arrest him. Heaven knows I can't stay with him. I have things to do at my own house, and besides, I'm not sure I'd feel safe. You know?"

I don't know. I don't know anything. None of this conversation makes sense.

I can hear voices in the background. Male. Authoritative. Voices with answers.

"The police are there?"

"They came with the ambulance. I think they might call Adult Protective Services if they don't arrest him, but you should probably—"

"Let me talk to the police."

"You want to talk to the police?" She sounds scandalized, like I've asked to talk to somebody at ISIS headquarters.

There's a sound of heavy breathing and shuffling feet, and another voice comes on the phone.

"Maisey?"

"Dad? What on earth is going on over there?"

"The police are here."

"I heard that. Why? Why are the police there? What happened to Mom?"

"Your mother—" Silence. More heavy breathing. "They took her in the ambulance. She didn't want to go, Maisey. And I can't find the—"

"This is Officer Mendez. Is this the daughter?"

A new voice. Male. Confident. The slightest hint of a Latino accent. The question mark is only for the purposes of confirming my identity, and I know that I am now talking to the police.

The daughter.

As in, the next of kin. The now-responsible party for a disaster so high on the clusterfuck scale there is no number sufficient to mark it.

"What's going on? What happened to my mother?"

"She's alive," he says, but his tone doesn't offer much hope that she's going to stay that way. "The neighbor—Edna Carlton—called, after your father refused to let her speak with your mother. She states that she got worried when she didn't see anybody enter or leave the house for the last three days. She states that your father appeared edgy and was unshaven and confused, which is not normal for him. There was dried blood on his shirt—"

"That's ridiculous. Edna Carlton is a busybody. Are you sure she's not embellishing facts?"

My father has never missed a shower or a shave in his entire life, or at least not for as long as I've known him. Partly because he's neat and particular and partly because my mother would never permit it.

My mother. Rushed off in an ambulance.

Mendez and I suck in simultaneous deep breaths.

"Your father presents as described. He neglected to lock the door. Mrs. Carlton, worried about your mother, entered the home when he did not respond to her knocks. She found your mother in bed, unconscious. She then called 911. Your mother is severely dehydrated. She has suffered a blow to the back of the head. There is blood on the kitchen floor."

I put my free hand on the counter behind me for balance.

"Mom?" Elle asks. "What's wrong?"

I turn my back to the fear on her face, leaning my forehead against the kitchen cupboards, and make one last Hail Mary for denial. "She's fine, right? Nothing a little IV fluid won't fix?"

"Is there somebody with you, Maisey? Maybe you should sit down."

I hate this voice, with its accented vowels and competent professional sympathy. I don't want to hear anything he has to tell me, no matter what words he uses to say it.

"I'm not alone. I don't need to sit."

He clears his throat, and I press my forehead harder against the cabinet, feeling the edge press a line into my skin, focusing on the pain. Elle comes up behind me and takes my hand, the trembling that runs through my muscles transferring to hers, and I visualize this Officer Mendez person frozen into a block of carbonite, like Han Solo in *Star Wars*. But I am not Darth Vader or Jabba the Hutt or even an incompetent young Padawan. I lack even a glimmer of power, and Mendez keeps talking.

"She's in a coma," he tells me. "Most likely from the blow to the back of her head. Your father is looking at domestic violence charges, along with criminal negligence and possibly others."

My breathing shifts from autopilot to a difficult obligation.

"Mom?" Elle asks, tugging at me. She sounds younger, no longer her bossy self. I squeeze her hand, a reminder that I haven't suddenly shifted into some alternate reality.

"Listen, Officer. My father does a capture-and-release program for spiders and stinkbugs and mice that get lost in the cupboard. He would never hurt her. Maybe she fell. Or had a stroke or something."

"That will be for the judge—"

"You said there was blood in the kitchen. Maybe she slipped. Hit her head on the counter. Did you ask him?"

"We asked. That's what he said, that she fell. He reported that after she fell, he did not call 911 because, I quote, 'She wanted to die.' He states that he then dragged her into the bedroom and up onto the bed."

"If that's what he said, that's what happened."

But none of this can be right. Elle lets go of my hand, and I feel myself on the edge of a long free fall.

"Those are the charges we're looking at," Mendez says. "Domestic violence. Criminal negligence. He didn't call for an ambulance. Three days, if your neighbor is right."

"Edna Carlton is old, in case you didn't notice. Maybe she's just confused—"

"The blood in the kitchen is dry, as is the blood on your father's shirt. There are flies. Nobody has picked up the paper from the porch for three days."

Elle shoves a chair into the back of my knees. I collapse into it.

"To your knowledge, has he ever hit her?"

"No. God, no. I told you—"

"What about you, ma'am. Has he ever hit you?"

The absurdity of my father hitting anybody, ever, sends my mind on a scavenger hunt through my childhood, seeking out instances. I meet my mother's hand repeatedly—a smack on the butt, a tap on the cheek—but my father's hands are always gentle.

"Maisey?" The cop yanks me back to this moment.

"No," I say. "Never."

"Is your father . . . unbalanced . . . in any way?"

"My father is the kindest, most gentle soul on the face of the planet, and I can't believe you are even—"

"What about dementia?"

"What?"

"Dementia. Alzheimer's. Has he been having difficulty with memory? Sometimes there are mood swings, dramatic changes in personality—"

"No. He does not have dementia. There are no mood swings. She fell. That's the most direct—"

"And he didn't call an ambulance. Was there an advance directive, do you know? He claims these were her wishes, to not go to the hospital."

"No, I don't know. If she made a directive, she never told me."

"And you're sure he isn't suffering from dementia?" Mendez persists.

"No! No, he's fine. We talked last week. He was perfectly lucid."

"Sometimes people with Alzheimer's can hold it together for a while, at least for short stretches of time. When was the last time you were here, to observe him over an extended time period?"

The words pull out the lynchpin of a towering pile of accumulated guilt that crashes around me and buries me to the ears. How would I know? I haven't visited home in three years. I talk to my parents every week, but the calls are brief and superficial. If my father's been slipping, I didn't notice, but then I've not discussed anything more difficult than the weather and the Seahawks with him. As for my mother, she'd never submit to something so demeaning as Alzheimer's, or allow anybody she loved to suffer from it.

"You are the only immediate family member we have been able to locate. Is there another relative closer? You are in Kansas City, is that right?"

"Yes," I tell him. "I'm in Kansas City. No, I have no siblings and Mom has no living relatives. Dad's only sister died over a year ago."

"So you don't know of any terminal illness or advanced planning? Would she want to be on life support, if that's required?"

"No. I don't know. She might not have told me."

An image flashes through my head: my mother lying senseless and helpless, stuck full of tubes like a semi-animate pincushion, my gentle father, suddenly red-eyed and hunchbacked, leaning over her with a bloody knife.

"I'll be on the next plane."

"Perfect. Please call the hospital. I can give you the number. Do you have something to write with?"

I can't be this person. I can't make decisions between wheat, rye, and sourdough. How the hell am I going to sort out what to do with my parents?

"Do you have a pen? Are you ready?" Officer Mendez is persistent.

"Elle, get a pen."

She's back in a heartbeat, writing down the numbers I repeat to her. Mendez hangs up.

My world takes on an air of unreality. This is someone else's smoke-filled kitchen. The tile pattern on the floor sucks me into a geometric tangle of blue and tan and a bile-colored, putrid green. There are scratches bitten in to it by the legs of chairs.

"Who puts tile like that on a floor?" I ask. "It's beyond hideous."

"Mom." Elle's voice, taut with anxiety and frustration, draws my eyes. Now that I'm sitting, she's taller than me. It's wrong to be looking up at her like this; it changes the angles of her face, makes her look older.

If I say any of the words out loud, it's going to make what Mendez told me true. Just a few more minutes is all I want, a little more time to sit here in a comfy cocoon of denial, but Elle won't give me that. So

I tell her. Not all of it. Just part of it, the part I can manage to get my mind around.

"Grandma's in the hospital. It's serious. I need to go and help Grandpa."

This is the reframe of the century, and Elle is too smart to buy my story. "You were talking to the police."

"Grandpa's a little . . . confused. They want to put him in the psychiatric ward. Or maybe jail."

Irrational laughter bubbles up at the image of Dad in jail. I doubt very much that my father has ever incurred so much as a parking ticket.

"You're scaring me," Elle says.

Her voice sounds far away, but these words are the key to whatever strength lies at the core of me. I am the parent. I am the responsible one.

"I'm sorry. Don't be scared." I put my arms around her and rest my head against her chest. She grounds me, and I manage to get the deep breaths going, and with them my brain starts to function again in fits and starts of coherence, punctuated by long oceans of drifting memories and daydreamed fears.

"I need to book a flight. You'll have to stay with your dad—"

"No way."

"Elle."

"I'm coming with you."

"You are not. You have school."

She shrugs that off. "I can make up a week of work in, like, a day. You know I can. I'm coming."

"What about English?"

"I'll write Mrs. Wilson her stupid vacation thing and send it to her. Come on, Mom. It's not like she's going to *fail* me."

When Elle thinks she's right, she's as unshiftable as a block of granite, and I can tell by the particular firmness at the corners of her lips that this is one of those times.

"Look, sweetheart, I'm going to be busy."

"Right. You'll need help." She's no longer looking at me, her fingers tapping away at her phone. "We fly into Spokane, right? Wow. We could still catch an eight o'clock that would get us there by midnight. How long is the drive into Colville, again?"

"Elle."

"Do you want to get a hotel or drive up that night? You're gonna be awfully tired, although you can sleep on the plane."

"Elle. You can't go."

"Why can't I?"

Because. That's the best answer I've got, and it's not an answer that has ever worked on this child. I have no logic-based reason to tell her no. She's right about school. She can pull off straight As without any effort when she sets her mind to it. Even Mrs. Wilson, for all her unhappiness about Elle not following directions, won't fail her.

As for taking care of Elle, the reality is she's more likely to take care of me.

I don't want to go through the heartbreak ahead. I don't want Elle to go through it. So I offer her the only thing I've ever been able to offer her: the truth.

"I want you to remember your grandparents the way you know them now. Grandma's . . ." I choke on the words, take a breath, try again. "Grandma's had a very serious accident. She's in a coma. And Grandpa is apparently not himself, maybe getting senile. I don't want you to see them that way."

Elle fixes me with what I call her old-soul look, an expression that encompasses compassion for me and wisdom far beyond what any sheltered child should have gathered in a short life.

"I want to say good-bye," she says. "I don't care if it hurts."

This, as she knows, I can't deny her, and she goes back to her search. "So you should grab these flights, quick. And book a hotel if you want one. We can rent a car at the airport and talk to my teachers tomorrow."

I cave. Leaving her with her father would be the right thing to do, maybe, but I want her with me. "We need to pack," I tell her.

"I'll pack. Good thing yesterday was laundry day."

"Good thing. You know what else is a good thing?"

She looks back at me over her shoulder, already halfway out of the room to complete her part of the mission. "What?"

"You, Elle. You are the best thing, ever."

Chapter Three

In the fifteen years he's worked as a fireman and a paramedic, Tony has seen strange things, sad things, and outright disturbing things. He's witnessed deaths accidental and purposeful, traumatic and peaceful. He's played a part in so many dramas of tragedy and salvation that sometimes he thinks he's seen everything, but then a case unexpectedly gets under his skin.

Like this one.

An old man, so frail in appearance that a tiny puff of wind might blow him over, sits on the bed beside a comatose woman, holding her hand. She lies motionless, pale as death, the only sign of life the painful rasping of her breath.

On the dresser, a series of photographs shows them younger, animated. There are photos of the two of them, arms around each other, her head leaning on his shoulder. There are school portraits documenting the growth of a young girl into a woman and pictures of her together with her parents.

Tony recognizes the daughter, but it takes a minute to bring back her name. Maisey. That's it. He hadn't known her well, but that cloud of red-gold curls is unforgettable. She'd been a year ahead of him in high school and moved in different circles. All AP classes and smart kids for her, while he had been relegated to basic and shop and didn't really hang out with anybody.

Not that he wasn't plenty bright himself, only there were a couple of dark years in middle school where he didn't care—about school or anything else—and he had to repeat seventh grade. It put him behind both academically and socially, and he'd always felt like he was scrabbling to dig out of a hole.

He'd envied Maisey a little. Had thought her life must be easier than his.

But appearances, as Tony knows all too well, can be deceiving.

In this case, the shrill-voiced neighbor tells a tale very different from that of the happy family photos: one of late-night arguments and a disruption of routine. Three days, she says, since the woman, Leah Addington, has left the house.

The blood on the kitchen floor, black and tacky, and the flies buzzing around the remains of something unrecognizable in a frying pan on the stove corroborate her insinuations.

The blood in the kitchen triggers inevitable flashes of memory, and Tony braces himself, knowing they will pass, as they always do.

His mother on her knees, a bruise darkening on her cheek.

His father's hand raised. His voice shouting curses and insults.

The sound of blows, of weeping.

Cara's voice brings him back to the moment. "Sir," she is saying to the man. "Sir! We're here to treat your wife."

The old man blinks at the intrusion of strangers into his private world.

"Who are you?"

It ought to be pretty obvious, given their uniforms and the stretcher, but the old guy doesn't seem to be firing on all cylinders.

"Ambulance," Tony explains. "Your neighbor called 911. I understand your wife is ill."

The old man's face remains blank, uncomprehending. He blinks again, then turns away and pats the woman's hand.

"It's all right, Leah," he murmurs. "I won't let them take you."

Cara, ten years younger than Tony and new to the job, raises her eyebrows in a question and looks to him for guidance. Tony draws a deep breath and immediately wishes he hadn't. The room stinks. A laundry hamper by the bed is filled with soiled towels. A trash can overflows with incontinence pads.

"It's all right," the old man says again. He runs his free hand through his hair and then over his eyes. "She's dying. Here. This is where she wants to die." His words are slow, heavy.

"How long has she been ill?" Tony asks, circling around to the far side of the bed.

The old man follows him with his eyes, lips moving soundlessly, as if counting. "I don't know," he whispers. "I've lost the count. Leah, how many days?"

The woman in the bed is clearly not going to answer. Her rasping breath pauses for a moment, as if she's listening, waiting, and Tony's adrenaline flares, ready to start the resuscitation protocol. But then she sighs and begins again, each breath labored and difficult.

"Sir," Tony says, "is there an advance directive somewhere? Did she write up her wishes of what she wanted?"

The old man's face clears. For the first time, his eyes focus. "Yes. Yes, that's it. How could I forget a thing like that? She made it. We both signed it."

Relief flows through Tony, warm as sunshine. Maybe this woman wasn't shoved or hit or neglected. Maybe she has cancer or some other incurable disease. If she has written up her end-of-life wishes, then this lost old man is exactly what he seems, the loving guardian of his wife's last hours.

The relief fades as rapidly as it came.

"I don't know where she put it," the old man mutters. "She told me. I don't remember. I looked and looked . . ."

"I'll check the fridge," Cara says, and vanishes down the hall. The refrigerator is a common place for people to leave medical information—advance directives, last wishes, contact numbers. Tony already checked it with his peripheral vision on their way past: fridge magnets, photos. Nothing that looked like an advance directive.

But Cara is right to have a more thorough look. Tony's grateful—the last thing he wants to do is spend more time in that kitchen.

A siren wails in the distance, coming closer. That will be the cops, and he's grateful for that, too.

As long as he lives, he will never shake the memory of the time he helped resuscitate a woman only to discover later that she was a hospice patient, dying of terminal cancer. If an advance directive can't be found for Leah, the cops can be the ones to make the call about whether to take her into protective custody for treatment or not.

"I looked." The old man's voice rises in frustration. "I looked in all the places. Nothing."

"Is there someone we could call? Your daughter, maybe? Maisey, right?"

Reaching out, slowly, so as not to agitate the old man, Tony rests his hand on the woman's forehead. Her skin is dry and hot with fever.

"Don't touch her. You're not supposed to touch her. It's not in the plan."

"I'm not taking her anywhere," Tony soothes. "Just checking on her, okay?"

He slides his hand under the back of the woman's head, finds the swelling, the cut, the blood-matted hair. "What's your name, sir?"

"Walter Addington."

"Well, Walter, I can see that Leah is certainly ill. Why don't you let us take her to the hospital, give her some fluids—"

Cara's voice cuts across his words. "No directive. Just the daughter's phone number."

Heavy footsteps signal the arrival of an officer. Mendez. He's a good cop, and Tony's glad to see him.

"What have we got?"

"Dehydration, a head wound. We've been unable to assess and treat, as Mr. Addington here says there's an advance directive and she wants to die at home."

He watches Mendez assemble the pieces. The old man, unshaven and lost-looking. The unconscious woman in the bed. The dirty, stinking towels in the hamper. The glass of water with the spoon in it on the bedside table.

"What happened, Mr. Addington? There's a fair amount of blood in the kitchen. And on you. *Old* blood. Can you explain that?"

"She fell," Walter says. "She hit her head. I brought her in here to rest, but she won't wake up." He shakes his wife's shoulder, very gently. "Leah. Wake up. Tell them."

"I've seen enough," Mendez says. "Take her in. Mr. Addington, come with me, please."

"No!" Walter protests. "You can't. She doesn't want to go." He leans over on the bed, covering his wife's body with his own. "I promised."

Sickness twists in Tony's belly, a revulsion for this whole mess. Maybe he'll go back to school, find another job. One that doesn't expose him to loss and despair on a regular basis.

"Come on, Mr. Addington," Mendez says, apparently unmoved and matter-of-fact. "Don't make this harder than it needs to be."

The old man resists, but Mendez pulls him away as easily as if he were a child. "If I have to arrest you, then you can't go see her in the hospital."

"I can't—you can't . . ." Walter's resistance stutters to a stop, his brain grappling with a problem that shuts him down. Mendez propels him out of the room.

Tony and Cara kick into gear, a smooth, synchronized team. EKG. Blood pressure. Cara gets the IV started—not easy, given the blood loss and dehydration. As they roll the stretcher down the hallway toward the ambulance, Walter's protests follow them.

"Listen, Officer. She didn't want this. Wouldn't want this. Please, you have to listen . . ."

The words, the desperation in the old man's voice, worm their way under Tony's skin.

What a sordid, ugly, twisted mess. He's glad to be out of the house, will be glad to turn Leah Addington over to the ER staff and walk away. But he knows he won't shake this case off easily. He feels the restless itch of his own trauma heating up.

When his chief calls to say somebody has phoned in sick and asks if Tony can work a double shift, he's more than happy to volunteer. Anything is better than the nightmares that are waiting for him if he tries to sleep tonight.

Chapter Four

On Elle's advice, I wait to call Greg until we're at the airport. Easier to ask forgiveness than permission, she says. Since we're already through TSA and waiting at our gate, there's not much he can do besides layer on the guilt.

Linda answers, sounding frazzled. I can hear the baby crying into the receiver and find myself wondering how Greg is adapting to this unexpected interloper in his perfectly ordered life.

"Maisey," Linda says, "everything okay with Elle?"

"Elle is great. I just need to talk to Greg."

"Are you sure? He had a hard day. I don't like to bother him."

"It's kind of important, Linda. Please."

I hear the sigh, can almost feel her fatigue through the phone line. "All right. I'll get him. Greg? Greg! It's Maisey. No, I have no idea what she wants."

"You're where?" Greg demands, predictably, when I tell him.

Elle grins at me, a momentary flash of conspiratorial mischief that lightens my heart.

"Elle and I are flying out to see my parents. We'll be boarding in about fifteen minutes, so I need to keep this short."

I can hear him breathing, and I know he is pinching the bridge of his nose and closing his eyes the way he does when he's frustrated.

When he speaks it's with an exaggerated calm. "Would you care to explain why you are flying out to Washington State, with our daughter, on a school night?"

No, I wouldn't care to explain. As it turns out, I don't have to. Elle grabs my phone.

"Hi, Daddy."

His voice might as well be on speakerphone. "I'm talking to your mother."

"Grandma's dying and Grandpa needs us. Don't worry about school. We've got it covered."

A silence. "Elle. Give the phone back to your mother."

"Whatever, Daddy. Love you. Kiss baby Jay for me."

She hands me back the phone. I take it reluctantly, bracing for the lecture I probably deserve. It's Greg's unexpected kindness that undoes me.

"Are you okay?" he asks, and those three words melt the shield of ice that's carried me from my kitchen into the airport.

No, I am not okay. I may never be okay again. If I answer, my voice will break. The tears will flow. I'll be a sobbing lunatic in the middle of this overcrowded gate, and everybody will stare.

"Right," he says, on the other end. "Stupid question. Of course you're not okay. Oh my God. You could have called me, Maisey. If you'd only let me, I . . ." His voice trails off, but not before those words dump me into a memory so vivid I can taste the rancid bitterness of the stale gas station coffee rapidly cooling in a paper cup.

The first big decision I ever made for myself was on a summer night twelve years ago. The night I told Greg I wouldn't marry him, despite the baby growing in my belly.

"God," he says. "Your mom. Is she even allowed to be sick? You must feel like the universe is turned inside out."

"I'm okay. Just in shock. We'll let you know when we get there."

"All right," he says. "Keep me informed. Give your mother my love, will you?"

If I had made a different choice way back then, Greg would be flying with us. Him, me, and Elle, the three of us, a traditional family. I try the idea on for size and shrug it off, like a coat that doesn't fit. Elle is all the family I need.

~

My old hometown looks dark and deserted when we roll in halfway between midnight and dawn. No lights. No cars. Even the gas station by the traffic circle is deserted. A slow, bleak drizzle of rain intensifies the effect.

My brain, short-circuited by fatigue, anxiety, and the energy drink I bought to help me navigate the seventy miles of dark, deer-infested highway between Spokane and Colville, goes straight to apocalypse. I imagine the entire population sizzled into nothing by an electronic pulse or sucked up into a spaceship, the buildings left standing.

Plague.

Zombies.

Maybe I'm driving Elle into a trap. I could let this traffic circle swing me right back around, let it fling the rental car free back onto the highway, back toward Spokane.

Small towns sleep at night, I remind myself. *It is two a.m., and we are not in Kansas City anymore.* I've got enough to worry about without adding imaginary dangers into the mix.

Dad, for example. He hasn't responded to any of my calls since our brief and disturbing conversation. At least the hospital has people to answer the phone to tell me my mother is still alive and breathing. They also can tell me that they have not seen my dad, that he hasn't come up to visit her, and that in itself is the most ominous news of all.

I try to blink some moisture into my eyes, but the lids grate like sandpaper. My face feels like it might crack if I dare yawn or smile or do anything other than stare at the road. My hands are fused to the steering wheel, and my whole body thrums with the vibration of tires on pavement.

All the way through town, I entertain the hope that everything is a huge misunderstanding. Dad and I will laugh about Mrs. Carlton, the wicked witch next door, the way we did when I was a child. Every one of her stinging remarks to me, about me, were softened by the stories Dad would tell.

Me, the fairy-tale princess. Her, the spiteful but powerless witch, bound by a magic spell that kept her from inflicting any true harm.

I tell myself that the real fairy stories are the ones the cop was spinning on the phone. Dad was in shock, that's all. Who wouldn't be? And there's no way he let Mom lie unconscious for three days without calling for help.

But then I turn onto our street and all my make-believe falls into ashes.

The house is lit up like a carnival, every window glowing. Smoke pours out of the chimney—black, copious, and all kinds of wrong.

My parents, for as long as I can remember, have been in bed every night by ten. All the lights off, except the dim one over the kitchen sink. And the fireplace is used only for ceremonial purposes. Small, decorative fires at Christmas. An occasional blaze on a Saturday night to go with hot cocoa and whipped cream.

I skid into the driveway far too fast and slam on the brakes just in time to avoid crashing into the garage door. Elle bolts upright, eyes wide but glassy with sleep and confusion.

She follows me out of the car and up to the front door, which is locked.

I beat on it with my fists, shouting, "Dad! It's Maisey. Let me in!"

Nobody comes to the door. Acrid smoke drifts down from the chimney and into my nose. Panic freezes my brain, and it takes me way too long to lift the fake rock sitting right beside the door for any would-be thief to see. My hands are shaking, and I drop the key not once but twice before I manage to turn it in the lock and open the door.

The entryway is blue with smoke.

"Get back in the car," I order Elle. "Call 911. If the house explodes, run for it."

"If you're exploding, so am I," she protests. "But I'll call."

No time to argue. I dash through the entryway, down a short hall, into the living room.

"Dad!"

A haze of smoke drifts along the ceiling, but the only flames I can see are in the fireplace. Dad is on his knees in front of it, the poker in his hands. A sheaf of half-burned paper, some black and smoldering, some flaming, spills out onto the hearth. He pokes more paper into the fireplace, and with a whoosh it ignites. Hot paper ash floats out into the room, sucked by the current of air from the open door. Some lands on the carpet. A spark lands in Dad's hair, and he drops the poker and swats at his head.

A wad of flaming paper stuck to the poker continues to burn perilously close to his pant leg. He's as oblivious to the danger as he is to our arrival.

"Dad! What on earth are you doing?"

I rush across the room and stomp out the flames on the paper, grinding ash into my mother's carpet. The stink of hot chemicals and singed hair fills my nostrils.

She's going to kill me, I think, before I remember that she may never know or care what happened. That is the thought that sends a spike through my chest, skewering my heart.

Dad turns his head, so terribly slowly, and looks at me. His eyes are blank, his face so expressionless I'm afraid that he doesn't even know who I am.

But it's even worse than him not knowing. He is not happy to see me.

"Maisey," he says. "I figured you'd turn up." His tone is one of final resignation, not joy or gratitude or relief. And then he turns his back on me, picks up the poker, and starts turning over the unburned papers in the fire.

I hear the town siren begin to wail, a lonely, terrifying sound that has always made me want to dive under the furniture and hide.

I drop to my knees beside him, careless of the soot and ash, and take the poker out of his hands.

"It's plenty warm in here, don't you think? Maybe we should let this go out."

Something fierce passes through his eyes, and I actually think, *Oh my God, I'm about to be smacked with the poker,* before his hands let go and he melts, as if he's made of wax and the fire has softened him. His shoulders round. His back curves. His chin sinks down onto his chest.

"There's more," he says. "I know there's more. I've forgotten something."

He's not talking to me.

My whole body feels stiff and strange and without sensation. Plastic. I don't know how I am supposed to behave if my father has forgotten that he loves me, if my mother isn't here to tell us both what to do.

So the two of us stay where we are, kneeling in front of the fireplace, like supplicants before an altar. Outside a siren wails, coming closer and closer until it's nearly deafening.

"Must be a fire somewhere." Dad turns his head toward the sound.

"You think?"

I look at the soot spread around us, the dusting of ash in his hair, on his shoulders, like dandruff.

It's too late to call off the fire brigade, and they come stomping in through the front door. Two firemen in full gear, extinguishers at the ready.

So much antifire power to leverage at one small fireplace. Fatigue has made me giddy. I put my hand over my mouth to push back rising laughter, but it leaks through my fingers and into an unwelcoming silence.

"Fire is not a joke, ma'am," one of the suited figures says. He sounds like my elementary school principal that time I put earthworms in Catrina Larsen's desk, and she had hysterics worthy of black widow spiders or rattlesnakes or something.

Mr. Myers used the same tonal inflection, stood in the same stiff, disapproving way. And I'd had an identical attack of the giggles that got me suspended from school for a day and earned me a spanking from my mother.

"The consequences for a prank call to 911 include jail time," the fireman says, in the same sanctimonious tone. I realize all at once that I'm the one holding the poker. I'm going to jail or hell—one or the other or both—and still, I can't for the life of me stop laughing.

"I called," Elle says. "There was smoke. And burning papers flying around the room. Am I going to jail?"

"I don't think this was a prank," the other fireman says. I like his voice better. It has a warm, comforting sound to it, like chocolate or a good red wine. He sets down his extinguisher and takes a step into the room. "Mr. Addington? Are you all right?"

Dad is not all right. He's tilting sideways, a human Tower of Pisa, only his tilt is accelerating at a visible pace. His mouth is open, his breathing loud and harsh.

My laughter congeals to something gelatinous and cold in my throat, and I'm unable to breathe or move. Is Dad going to have a stroke now, too, both of my parents checking out of life together?

"Can't. Get. Up," Dad gasps. "Need a hand."

The fireman moves to act as a reinforcement so Dad doesn't topple off his knees. "Are you hurt? Should we call an ambulance?"

"No. Just . . . I've fallen and I can't get up," Dad says. A wheeze escapes him; I'm not sure if it's a laugh or some sort of predeath breathing pattern.

The fireman pulls off his gloves and reaches down, respectfully allowing Dad to use him like a ladder to climb to his feet instead of picking him up like a child.

"Old men and floors," Dad says. "Not compatible."

I stare up at the two of them, the idea of getting onto my own feet suddenly daunting.

My fireman extends a rescuing hand down to me, still steadying my father with the other. It's a large hand. Square fingers, evenly cut nails. Warm when I take it, both strong and gentle. A pair of very blue eyes look down at me. His mouth has smile lines around it.

The hand is attached to a muscular arm that lifts me effortlessly up onto wobbly feet.

"Maisey, right?"

"How do you know my name?"

"High school."

I scan his face, trying to remember, but draw a blank. "I'm sorry. I don't—"

"Tony," he says. "No worries. You wouldn't remember."

My gaze drifts from the fireman to my father, who sways like a drunk. There is, as Officer Mendez told me, dried blood on his shirt. He hasn't changed his clothes. He hasn't shaved.

I realize I'm still clinging to the fireman's hand and let go to steady my father's arm.

"You need to sit down, Dad?" He doesn't seem to hear me.

The other fireman, the self-righteous one who is probably happy there's an actual crisis in motion, finally takes a step in our direction.

He's too slow.

Dad collapses from the bottom up, like a demolition charge has gone off. Knees first, then hips, then spine, all the bones and joints turned to jelly.

My fireman is behind him, though, holding him, sinking down to the floor with him so he doesn't fall. The other guy radios for an ambulance.

As for me, I can't seem to summon up the requisite amount of panic. I used to make little jokes about how my parents were so joined at the hip they'd probably go out together.

I didn't mean it, I pray, silently, just in case God or the fates or the universe or whatever it is that drives the boat is listening.

My fireman, kneeling across from me with Dad between us, is busy checking for a pulse. "He's breathing easily; his pulse is a little fast, but strong. I'm also a paramedic," he explains. He pats Dad's cheek, shakes his shoulder. "Mr. Addington. Walter. Can you hear me?"

Dad's eyes roll under closed lids, then flicker open. He stares up at the fireman, obviously dazed.

"There you are," my paramedic fireman says. "How are you feeling?"

"I've been better," Dad says. His voice sounds weak. His lips are dry and flaking, the bottom one split and bleeding slightly. He's old, but he shouldn't look this old, with fragile skin stretched tight over his cheekbones, his eyes faded and sunken. "Who are you?"

"My name is Tony. We met earlier, and here we are again."

Dad just blinks at him, clearly not remembering.

"Can you move your legs for me?" Tony asks. "First the right, then the left. Good. Now, your hands. Can you touch your nose with your right hand? Your left?"

Dad goes through the motions obediently, and Tony raises his eyes to mine. "I don't think it's a stroke or a heart attack. My guess is he's dehydrated and probably hungry. Maybe he's not been eating since your mom got sick. That ambulance coming, Marco?"

"On its way. About ten minutes out."

"Don't need an ambulance," Dad says. "Help me up."

"You need to lie here and wait," I tell him. "Do what the fireman tells you."

"He's not a doctor. Let me up."

Dad's voice sounds stronger, and he starts scrabbling at the floor, trying to push himself up to a sitting position.

"I think it's fine," Tony says, and helps Dad sit up there on the floor. "Do you think you could drink a little water, Mr. Addington? Maybe take an aspirin? Just in case it is a stroke." He looks at me. "Are there any aspirin in the house?"

"I don't know. I just got here."

"I'll go look!" Elle says, and dashes off toward the kitchen. There's a sound of running water, of slamming cupboard doors, and then she's back with a small bottle and a glass of water.

Dad looks at the outstretched hand holding the pill with a frown of concentration. His bleary eyes follow the hand up the arm to Elle's shoulder and finally to her face.

"Hey, there," he says. "What are you doing here?"

Elle is unfazed. "Getting you aspirin, Grandpa."

"You all think this little pill is going to fix what's wrong with me?" He surveys our faces, and then his shoulders start to shake with dry, nails-on-a-chalkboard laughter. "That's the first funny thing I've heard all week."

But he reaches for the pill, and we all wait patiently while his stiff, old-man fingers fumble to grasp it. Finally it's in his mouth, and he's swallowed half of the water in the glass.

More sirens in the distance, drawing ever closer. More uniformed bodies stomping all over my mother's floor with their boots on.

Dad, who has always been a marshmallow in my mother's hands, decides to reveal a latent streak of obstinacy.

"You can all go home and go back to bed," he says, with great dignity. "You are not putting me in that ambulance."

"Daddy . . . please." My voice wobbles a little, a small betrayal that surprises me. I'm not given to tears. My hand goes to my throat, covering the lump that has been quietly accumulating since I walked into this house.

He shakes his head. "You're here. You can keep an eye on me."

I want to tell him I don't have a caretaking bone in my body. I want to tell him I need to go see Mom. I want to tell him that parents are for leaning on, not the other way around. Not a single word is going to fit past the obstruction that has replaced my voice box.

Tony, crouched on the floor, still supporting my father, takes off his fireman's hat and lays it on the floor beside him. "Tell you what," he says. "We let you off the hook with the ambulance, but you agree to let your daughter drive you up to the ER, just to get looked over. Can we make it a deal?"

By the time Dad finally nods agreement, I'm dizzy and realize I've been holding my breath.

The ambulance team turns around and tracks out of the house.

So much for leaving Elle to sleep, but she doesn't look like she needs it. She's bright-eyed, bushy-tailed, and ready for action, as my mother would say. The thought that my mother might not say anything ever again flits through my consciousness, and I swat it away. I can't go on functioning if I'm having those kinds of thoughts.

The self-righteous fireman goes out to wait in the truck while Tony helps get Dad into a coat and shoes. We support him between the two of us and walk him out to the car, Elle opening and closing doors and acting as gofer.

When we're all settled in the rental, Tony knocks on my window.

"You've got your hands full," he says, when I roll it down. He hands me a phone number, scribbled on the back of a Walmart receipt. "If you need anything, unofficially, buzz me."

I nod. My smile muscles are in a state of paralysis and refuse to make even a token effort.

As I turn the key and start the engine, my mind runs through a list of disorders that might be causing my facial paralysis.

Bell's palsy.

MS.

Lou Gehrig's.

Parkinson's.

Brain cancer.

How about grief and shock, Maisey? Have you considered these as possibilities? Questions start bubbling to the surface, and the first one spills out, even though Dad's face is a blank that should have warned me off.

"What really happened to Mom?" I ask him.

His head turns toward me, slow and creaky, like an automaton in need of new batteries. His eyes are blank. He doesn't answer.

"Dad. What happened to Mom?"

He blinks three times, rapidly, his electronic wiring on the fritz, and then his eyes light, and he sees me—*me*—again.

"She fell."

"Three days ago, the police said."

I wait for him to contradict the absurdity of this, to clearly and unequivocally tell me that Edna Carlton is full of bull hockey and the police have lost their minds.

But he just swallows and doesn't answer.

"Dad!"

"She didn't want to go to the hospital." His eyes go dark again, and he stares not at me, but past me, out into the night.

It takes Elle and me both to get him out of the car and into the ER reception area. Fortunately, the staff are not only expecting us, but know the story already. We don't even have time to sit in registration before the doors open and a tech comes out to get us.

Somebody fetches snacks for Elle and me from the staff room. Homemade cookies. Crackers and cheese. A cup of real coffee with half-and-half. I can't choke down food, but the coffee is a lifesaver.

"I heard your mom is up in ICU," the tech says, his voice comfortingly matter-of-fact. "If you want to go see her, we'll start working up Walter here. It will take a bit, and we can call you when we know anything."

Dad doesn't seem to even hear. He lies on the exam table where they put him, staring up at the ceiling. His expression is blank. He looks old and fragile, and my heart feels swollen and sick. Feverish.

"I'll stay with Grandpa," Elle says.

At the sound of her voice, he turns his head, and the blankness in his eyes dissipates a little. "What are you doing here?" he asks, as he did at the house. As if he's only just seen her for the first time.

"Waiting," Elle tells him. I hesitate. She's only a child, and he's so terribly lost. Elle makes a shooing gesture at me with her hands, and I step out of the door and head upstairs, leaving pieces of myself behind all the way, like a trail of breadcrumbs.

Chapter Five

A curtain is drawn around my mother's bed.

At first glance she seems to be sleeping. But I've seen her sleep before, and this is different, a terrible absence rather than slumber. She looks smaller than I remember. Her body, always thin, seems insubstantial, barely a bolster-size bump beneath the hospital blanket and sheets. One arm lies on top of the covers. An IV tube connects to the back of her hand. On the inside of her elbow a bruise blossoms, probably from a blood draw. I find myself wanting to cover it. A sleeve. A Band-Aid.

Lacking that, I cover the blemish with my own hand, startled at the heat of her skin.

The room smells like disinfectant. It reminds me of scraped knees and the sting of hydrogen peroxide and my mother's voice telling me I am brave, I am strong, I can handle this temporary pain.

But I am not brave, and I have never been strong enough to carry the weight of my mother's ambitions and expectations, to bear the brunt of her obsessive love.

Since my earliest memories, Mom was in control of everything. She ran the house with precision. Calendars, schedules, lists, and more lists. Routine was her religion. When I came home from school, she allowed me a half hour of homemade cookies and milk to sweeten what I came to think of as interrogation about the school day. What did I learn? Who were my friends? What could I do better or smarter tomorrow?

This was followed by homework, from first grade on up. If I had no homework, she gave me some.

"You're smart, Maisey. You have opportunities. But that will get you nowhere without discipline."

My father came home every day at 5:15. If he was a minute late, she got restless. At two minutes, she was pacing. At 5:20 she'd be looking out windows and standing on the porch. The advent of cell phones was God's great gift, and she embraced them with fervor. To this day, when my cell phone rings and I answer, I expect to hear her voice demanding, "Where are you? Do you know what time it is?"

"Where are you?" I whisper now, sitting by her bedside. "Do you know what time it is?"

Her breathing is loud in the room, loud enough to cover the whirr of the IV pump. It rasps and rattles in her chest.

A nurse comes in, checks the IV, straightens the sheet over my mother's thin chest. Her eyes pass over me and away, like I'm wearing an invisibility cloak. I can see that she doesn't want to engage, but I need information.

"Is this normal? Her breathing? And she feels hot to me."

My questions hit the nurse right between the shoulder blades. Her body turns to face me, stiff, like it's all one piece and none of the joints move on their own.

"None of this is normal." Her jaw is as locked as the rest of her, and the eyes suddenly leveled on me are ice-cold.

I stare back at her, bewildered by her clear hostility. "Can we do anything about it? I mean, should she be on oxygen or something? Is she getting antibiotics?"

"She's dying," the nurse says. "Do you really want to prolong the process?"

Her words connect squarely with my solar plexus and knock all the breath out of me. She's right, of course. The doctor I talked to on the phone yesterday was much kinder and did not use blunt words. But the message was the same.

My mother is leaving me.

The room door opens wider and another nurse comes in. This one is older and heavy with her years, her breasts and hips straining the bounds of her scrubs. She lays a hand on the younger woman's shoulder. "Can you answer the light in 205? I've got this."

Nurse One looks like her face is going to crack under the strain of holding back whatever it is she wants to say, but she pivots and stalks out of the room.

"I don't understand," I whisper at her retreating back.

"She's young," the new nurse says, as if that explains everything. "She's offended by death and it makes her angry. You must be Maisey. I'm so glad you're here." Her voice is warm and welcoming. She actually sounds glad.

It's a good thing somebody is. I sure as hell am not.

Nurse Two frowns as she listens to my mother's breathing. She pulls a thermometer out of her pocket, and her frown deepens as she runs it across my mother's forehead.

"It's 102.6. And her oxygen level is dropping."

"Can't we do something?"

"We took an X-ray. I'm afraid she's acquired pneumonia. It's a common complication in people who are unconscious for any length of time."

She lowers herself into the folding chair directly beside mine, so close that her shoulder, her thigh, press against me. Normally I would pull away from the contact, but her bulky warmth feels good, comforting. We sit there, side by side, listening to my mother's terrible breathing.

"Is she suffering?" I whisper the words.

"Oh, honey, no. Very peaceful. She's deeply asleep." She pats my hand. "It's not really my place, but I'm going to bring this up now, since the doctor isn't here. When the ambulance picked her up, your father told them she wanted to be allowed to die. But he seemed a little confused, so now I'm asking you. If she should . . . stop breathing . . . do you want us to resuscitate her? CPR? A breathing machine?"

Panic. My feet and hands go ice-cold. My feverish heart wants to escape my rib cage and go scuttling out the door and out of the hospital.

"I know it's difficult," the nurse says. "What would your mother want?"

"I don't know," I whisper, but of course this is a lie.

My mother would want to make her own decisions—to be in control of this situation and tell her body and everyone else in the room what to do. That's what she would want.

"According to the ambulance team, your father said Leah put together an advance directive in which she specified all of this."

Warm relief comes flooding in. I don't have to make decisions, after all. My mother came through, planning it all out in advance. Of course. That's exactly what she would do.

"Well, good. Then do whatever the directive tells you."

The nurse sighs. Maybe out of frustration with me, or the whole situation. "They tell me he wasn't able to find the directive. So we have only his word for it, and he's apparently in no state to be making decisions."

"Because he's a little confused?"

"Mental Health was out to see him yesterday evening, after your mother came here. They didn't call you?"

"Maybe they missed me. I was traveling."

I think guiltily of the phone in my purse. When I pulled it out to call the hospital, there were five missed calls. Four from Greg. One from an unknown number. I didn't listen to any of the messages.

"Mental Health can't determine competence in the legal sense. Only whether individuals with mental disorders are dangerous to themselves or others. They felt your father was okay to stay home by himself for a few hours until you got here. But no, he didn't do well on the mental status test."

The words sink in, slowly, punctuated by Mom's rasping breaths. Words and breath grate on my skin, threatening to uncover a nerve center I can't afford to expose.

"You don't understand. I can't make decisions like this. I don't *do* decisions."

The nurse pats my hand again. "So hard, so hard. In part because your mother is so young. Let's hope you have a few hours to think about it. But you should know that with the extent of the bleeding in her brain, she won't be coming back. If she lives, she won't be the woman you know her to be."

With that, she heaves herself up out of the chair with a grunt. "This hip," she says. "It's going to be the death of me. You just sit here and think on things. I need to get back to work."

And she leaves me alone with my mother's loud breathing and a litany of guilt.

Mom wanted me to be rich and successful, to carve some sort of mark in the world instead of skating over the surface. I should have been a real journalist, preferably the sort of perfectly coiffed woman who could smile at the cameras from behind the desk of a major news corporation and intelligently interview world leaders. Not a fly-by-night lightweight skipping from job to job at small newspapers and supplementing her income taking Santa photos at the mall during Christmas.

I should have visited more often. I should have known my father was declining. I should have been there the minute my mother fell ill.

I have failed her every which way from Sunday, and now maybe I have to decide whether she's going to live or die.

The very last hope I have of redeeming myself is making the right decision now.

I lean forward and bury my face in the cool sheet, trying to let the tension go out of my spine and shoulders, but they feel about as pliable as a sheet of particleboard. My eyes still refuse to close. I try to focus on the decision I'm supposed to be making, marshaling lists of pros and cons to the idea of life support, but my brain hops around from my father's bizarre behavior and fainting spell to my mother unconscious here beside me.

My cell phone buzzes, and I check the text messages with dread, but it's only Elle.

elle: vampires here for grandpa's blood

maisey: the lab, you mean?

elle: don't be so boring. this one is totally a bloodsucker. he doesn't sparkle but I bet he's a hundred years old anyway

elle: IV started. gpa wants to go home

maisey: tell him to stay put. Do I need to come down there?

elle: he's sleeping now. i'm bored. cn i come up?

maisey: gma's also sleeping. I'm also bored. Stay put. Both of you.

A surge of irrational anger hits me. How dare my father disintegrate like this! He is supposed to be taking care of my mother. Why didn't he call me? Where is the advance directive he was talking about?

Why the hell was he burning papers in the fireplace?

My cell is almost out of battery. I stare at the missed calls alert and think about listening to the messages but just tuck the phone back in my purse. Not now.

The clock on the white wall across from me says 8:00 a.m., which puts me over 24 hours without sleep. My eyes have reached a whole new level of dry. Mummified. Stiff. Desiccated. The salt from my tears has served only to suck out more moisture.

When the phone dings again, the screen blurs in and out of focus, and I blink five times and squint in order to see.

elle: Mom?

elle: There's a cop here.

elle: Mom?

Chapter Six

I skip the elevator and take the stairs, adrenaline pushing me to run faster, faster. My brain has helpfully supplied me with an image of my father in handcuffs and Elle weeping, a dramatic musical score playing in the background. But when I reach the ER bay, Dad is snoring on the gurney. IV tubing snakes from a pump into the back of his hand.

Elle is wide-eyed and a little breathless, but it looks more like excitement than fear.

An officer stands on the other side of the bed. His pleasant face is counterbalanced by a duty belt bristling with a holstered gun and a Taser.

"If this is about the fire or the call to 911, I don't think he was trying to burn the house down," I say, before the cop can say anything. "I'm the one who called it in, I'm afraid, before I'd realized we could easily handle the problem. It wasn't a prank."

"I'm the one who called it in," Elle corrects. There's a spot of color in each cheek, and her eyes are clearly full of uniform and dark hair and deceptively sensitive lips. Lord have mercy.

"I don't know anything about a fire, ma'am. I'm here about allegations of criminal negligence and possibly attempted manslaughter."

My lips feel too stiff to answer. I put one hand protectively over Dad's. His fingers twitch. His eyes move beneath the lids, but he doesn't wake.

"I'm Officer Mendez. I believe we spoke on the phone. You are Maisey, yes? Walter and Leah Addington's daughter?"

I nod. There doesn't seem to be any air in my lungs.

"Obviously I don't want to arrest him. Will you be able to stay with him? Mental Health doesn't think he's dangerous, but they don't think he's able to stay alone."

Air rushes back into my lungs with a whoosh, too much of it now, making my head spin.

"He didn't hit her," I protest. "He didn't shove her. He's never hit anybody."

"We're looking at him for criminal negligence, not assault. Although, in light of the new X-ray evidence—"

"What evidence? What are you even talking about?"

He fumbles in his shirt pocket for a small notebook and flips through it. "Excuse me for a moment. I'm not a medical professional, and I need to consult my notes. This is what we know. The cause of the brain bleed is undetermined, but her doctor was able to confirm the discovery of an aneurism in your mother's brain several months ago. It is her opinion that the most likely cause of your mother's current condition was a rupture of this aneurism, although she probably struck her head on the counter as she fell."

I stare at him. My mother had an aneurism? A weak balloon of an artery, slowly growing in her head, and nobody bothered to tell me? No. Of course she wouldn't tell me. I might try to talk her into sharing the control, giving me a copy of this now-mythical advance directive.

Mendez coughs. "So far, we only have Walter's word that he was acting on her wishes. And with the X-ray evidence of multiple broken bones—"

"What broken bones?"

"The doctors performed a chest X-ray to confirm pneumonia. They found—let me see—three old rib fractures and a fractured clavicle.

They then did additional X-rays and discovered an old fracture of the humerus—"

"And you think *my father* did this?"

"It fits the pattern for domestic violence. There is also an old fracture of her left eye socket."

"Oh, don't be ridiculous. I told you on the phone—he's not capable of hurting anybody. Does he look like he could inflict deliberate injuries?"

I wave my hands over my father, who looks ancient and pathetic at the moment. His comb-over has come undone, long strands of gray hair trailing across the pillow. His cheeks are sunken. Under the thin cover of the sheet he looks gaunt and skeletal.

"You'd be surprised, ma'am, what can happen in domestic violence situations. I had an elderly female who eliminated her husband with her cane—bashed him right across the head."

"You're making that up," Elle accuses.

Mendez clears his throat. His voice is softer when he speaks again, almost sympathetic. "Perhaps he is not a violent man. Alzheimer's can dramatically alter the personality. Gentle people become violent. Very proper ladies suddenly begin to swear."

I shake my head to clear it. None of this makes any sense. I feel like I've walked through a mirror into a darker version of Alice's wonderland. Leave it to Elle to articulate the gist of the thing.

"Grandpa's a wife beater? That's crazy!"

Crazy doesn't begin to describe it. My oxygen problem is beginning to balance itself out, only now my knees are wobbly. Letting go of Dad's unresponsive hand, I wrap both of mine around the bed rail, squeezing as tight as I can, trying to find sensation in my fingers.

"Listen, Officer. I can tell you that there have been no beatings. Even if my father has . . . dementia. Which he doesn't. My mother bosses him, not the other way around. She would have taken care of the problem. Trust me."

"Evidence is evidence," he says, consulting his notes. "Three old rib fractures. Left clavicle. Left humerus. Left eye socket. The pattern is suspicious."

"And I'm telling you nobody has been beating my mother. Especially not my father."

"I'm glad to hear that. Maybe an accident, then? She fell down the stairs? Ran into a door?"

If I were a snake, I would strike now. Bite him right on the nose. I picture poison pumping into his body. His face turning purple and black, maybe a nice spasm or two.

"Ma'am?"

Elle presses her arm against mine. She has reason to know that my affliction of indecision is balanced in the scales of character flaws by a true redheaded temper.

Warnings disregarded, I welcome in the anger, gather it.

Heat floods through me, right down to my once-cold fingertips, bringing energy behind it. Even my hair has energy; I can feel all the tiny roots tighten in my scalp. I picture my hair flying out in a cloud of electric sparks all around my head.

"I don't know what you've been smoking, Mr. Mendez, or who decided to let you play dress-up in that police uniform, but this is ridiculous."

His face flushes. A hit. My anger responds with a surge of vindictiveness. Before he can say anything, I let it carry me forward.

"Let me guess. This looked like low-hanging fruit to you, and you volunteered. Nobody else wanted to come over here and grill an old man while his wife is dying upstairs."

"Mom," Elle protests, putting a hand on my arm. If I so much as glance at her, I know little tiny cracks will start running through my lovely rage. I keep my eyes fixed on Mendez.

A vein bulges on his forehead, and his jaw is clenched so tightly the muscle bunches.

"Ms. Addington—"

"Don't try to placate me. Do you have a warrant? Are you going to arrest him?"

"I'm merely investigating—"

"*Merely?* I don't think you're *merely* doing anything. You're expanding the boundaries of your specified investigation. That's what you're doing. Go fight some criminals or stop some speeders or something. Hey, I'll give you five bucks, and you can go buy some doughnuts to take with you."

I'm on a roll. Somewhere inside, a tiny voice of self-preservation tries to make itself heard, but I know that the next thing out of my mouth is going to have the word *pig* in it.

Dad saves me. Not for the first time.

His eyes open, surprise and confusion crossing his face.

"Maisey," he says, tremulously, reaching for my hand. "Why are you angry? What's going on?"

He peers up at Officer Mendez, squinting as if trying to focus, and the fear smacks me yet another whack over the top of my head. Dad's not acting. He's genuinely lost. If this is true, if it's true that my mother is upstairs in a coma, then anything could be true. All the horrible things this officer is saying Might. Be. True.

My body sags at the knees, the railing digging into my ribs as I collapse against its support. I've got no more stuffing. There's a loud buzzing in my ears. Somebody should fix the fluorescents; they're way too dim.

"Mom?" Elle's voice sounds far away.

I can't seem to turn my head. The floor is disappearing under my feet, and the buzzing drowns out further words.

Something solid behind my knees; hands lower me to sitting and push my head forward so I'm doubled up over the emptiness in my belly. My own breathing grows louder than the buzzing in my ears. My heart is beating in my head now, instead of in my chest where it belongs, and it's beating way too fast.

"She hasn't slept in forever, and I don't think she's eaten anything. Plus she's worried." Elle sounds frightened. I need to comfort her, but I can't move.

"I can't imagine being grilled by the police has been helpful," a woman's voice says. A warm hand rests on my shoulder, steadying, gentle. Another slips onto my neck, checking my pulse. "Don't worry, sweetheart," the voice says. "She'll be fine."

My heart begins traveling in the right direction, out of my head and back toward my chest. I can feel all my fingers and toes, along with a growing sense of embarrassment. It's tempting to pretend I'm unconscious, but of course I can't.

"I'm okay," I croak. "Sorry."

"Take your time," the voice says. "No rush." And then to Elle, "Maybe you could go ask the nurse if they have some juice or something for your mom?"

I manage to get my eyes open.

Dad has drifted back to sleep. A woman in a white lab coat stands beside his bed, looking at the monitors, then placing a stethoscope to his chest and listening. She drags the other visitor chair close to mine and sits, holding out her hand. "You must be Maisey. I've heard a lot about you."

When I take her hand, it feels small and fragile in mine, bird bones, but what I read in her dark eyes more than makes up for her physical stature. This is not a woman you want to tangle with.

"I'm Eliana Margoni," she says. "I'm your mother's doctor. The nurses told me you were here with Walter. I'm sure you have many questions."

Her calm compassion undoes me. Tears well up, and I'm powerless to hold them back.

"If it helps," Dr. Margoni says, "I'm certain that the bleeding in your mother's brain is from a ruptured aneurism. We discovered it about three months ago and knew her death was just a matter of time. The idea that your father hit or shoved her is ludicrous."

"Why didn't they tell me?"

Through my tears she's a distorted blob of black and white, the expression on her face unreadable.

"That is a question I'm afraid I can't answer. It was a ticking time bomb. Your mother opted not to try a repair, which had a high probability of leaving her brain damaged and incapacitated. Your father disagreed. As long as there was hope, he wanted to try. But you know how she is."

"I know."

Dr. Margoni squeezes my hand. "I understand that we've been unable to find her advance directive. I can tell you that she told me one had been done and that they would bring a copy to the clinic. That didn't happen. But I can attest that she told me she would like to die quietly at home and was not interested in extraordinary measures. I have that note documented. I would need a subpoena to release it to the police, of course, unless Leah's next of kin gives permission."

Even though I am the next of kin, and this means making a decision, a warm ray of sunshine pierces the frosty coldness inside me. Her tone is incisive and authoritative, turning the world right-side up.

"If it would be helpful, then I would totally support releasing that to the police. Of course."

Dad makes a louder snoring sound and jolts awake. His eyes are wild, scanning the room, but before I can get up, the lids drift closed again, and he falls back asleep.

"We've given him a sedative," Dr. Margoni explains. "He was exhausted, poor man."

"I understand there is a matter of broken bones," Mendez says, stiffly. "Can you explain those away?"

"How did you hear about that?" Dr. Margoni sounds severe now. "I'm quite sure you don't have a warrant."

"Sources," he says. "Small town. People talk."

"Small town is no excuse for a breach of client confidentiality."

"Look. I heard about it. I'm investigating. It's my job. You think I want to be here? Walter's done my parents' taxes. He goes fishing with my uncle."

Dr. Margoni glares at him, then turns back to me. "I'm here because I just heard myself. Small-town news travels faster than radiology to a doctor, apparently."

Elle comes back, carrying a can of Coke. "Vending machine," she says. "It's ice-cold."

I'm not thirsty, but I take the can because Elle brought it for me. The curve of the can in my hand, its weight, the cold against my palm, all serve to calm and ground me. I take a swig, the sweet fizz ending in a bitter taste. I want Elle to leave the room again but can't think of an excuse.

"What's up?" she says. "Is it Grandma? You all look like a funeral or something."

Dr. Margoni gives me a questioning look.

"Elle already knows," I say, giving permission to carry on the conversation. I glare at Mendez, the one who is responsible for her knowing, but he ignores me and talks directly to the doctor.

"I heard there are a lot of old fractures. Highly suggestive of domestic violence."

"All *old* fractures, as you say. Healed."

"But how old is old?" Mendez persists. "Six months? A year?"

"Ten years. Twenty. Once the fracture has formed a callus, there's no way of knowing how long ago it happened. She's been a patient at the clinic for ten years, and there are no documented injuries during that time frame."

"How would you know?" Mendez asks. "An abused woman won't often tell you, am I correct? Maybe the injuries had time to heal between visits."

"Leah was not an abused woman," Dr. Margoni says, dismissively. "She had an appointment to see me, by the way, to create a POLST form. That's an official document outlining her wishes for treatment, Maisey. Based on our office conversations, I think it's highly likely Walter acted on her wishes by not calling for medical assistance."

"Three days," Officer Mendez growls. "That's a long time to let somebody lie around unconscious."

"Three days in which, I understand, he somehow managed to get her into a bed, despite his significant arthritis and degenerative disc disease. Three days in which he bathed her, spooned water into her mouth, and watched over her."

"Serial killers have done the same for dead bodies."

While they are discussing my parents—my mother's desire to die, my father as a demented killer—the tension and incomprehension within me keeps growing.

"I don't want her to die," I blurt out, cutting short the legal discussion.

"Nobody does," Dr. Margoni says. "Death does not always comply with our wishes. I understand that you must be completely overwhelmed, but we need to decide what to do when she stops breathing. Or when her heart stops beating. She didn't want any lifesaving measures; she didn't even want to come to the hospital."

I look at my father again, asleep, drugged, unaware of us. A thin line of saliva trails from his open mouth, down over his chin. It makes me feel ashamed, like I'm looking at something I shouldn't see.

Dr. Margoni pats my hand. "This is hard, I know, and very sudden for you. But you need to understand that your mother is not coming back from this. The most you can hope for is that she'll be able to sit in a wheelchair and stare out the window. Her cognitive function has been destroyed."

"You don't know that." My voice sounds desperate to my own ears. "People come back. There are all those stories. People who are in a coma for, like, years, and then they wake up."

"Maisey." She drags the chair sideways so she's sitting directly in front of me. "Think carefully before you decide. I agree that the decision is going to ultimately be yours, given your father's current state. But I'd urge you to think of the kind of woman your mother was and what you think she would want."

This kind, competent doctor wants me to let my mother die. I can feel the pressure, a vise clamping my chest, probing at my brain.

I close my eyes to shut her out, to shut out my father and the cop. My world has turned inside out. I feel like I'm floating above the chair. My butt has no sensation. I need to talk to my mother. I need her to be here to talk to. She can't die; not now. Not yet.

I know what the doctor wants me to say. What my father wants me to say. Definitely what my mother wants me to say.

For once, I don't care about what anybody else thinks I should do. I open my eyes and try to make my voice authoritative. It comes out as a pathetic little squeak. "Keep her alive. Whatever that takes. God. She's too young for this."

Dr. Margoni rubs the back of her neck. Up close, I can see fine lines around her eyes and dark shadows beneath them. She looks older than I'd originally thought. My age, at least. Maybe more.

"We've already started her on antibiotics and oxygen, but I want you to think carefully about the other things. She's unable to eat, and that's not likely to change anytime soon. If the antibiotics kill the infection and she's able to keep breathing, she will begin to starve."

"That's horrible," Elle says. "You can't starve her."

It's not right for Elle to be here. She shouldn't even know about this. But I can't send her to go stand in the hall.

Dr. Margoni includes her in the conversation as if she has every right to be involved.

"Your grandma is unconscious, so she wouldn't suffer. However, we can insert a central line into an artery and give her some highly nutritious liquid called total parenteral nutrition. Or we can put a tube in her stomach and feed her that way."

There are no words for how much my mother would hate this, but even so I say, "Do that, the tube thing. Feed her. Don't let her starve."

"And if she should stop breathing? You want us to bring her back? CPR and shock her heart? Intubate her and put her on a breathing machine?"

And there I'm stuck. That's a call I'm not able to make.

"We really do need a decision," Dr. Margoni says.

I want to put my fingers in my ears and hum, the way I did when I was a defiant little girl and didn't want to listen to one of my mother's lectures.

My stomach twists on itself and begins to rise. I feel acid in my throat. I'm going to puke, all over this nice doctor's shoes.

"No," I manage to whisper. "If she . . . if she dies, let her . . . don't bring her back."

She pats my hand, approvingly. I'm a good girl again. I've complied. Inside, I'm screaming.

No. Don't let her die. Bring on all the tubes, all the machines, all the treatments. Whatever it takes. Don't let her go away from me.

Dr. Margoni pushes back her chair and gets to her feet. "Dr. York, the ER doc here this morning, says your father is dehydrated and exhausted. His blood sugars are way too high, and so is his blood pressure. I'd guess he was too distraught by your mother's condition to eat or take his medicine. Dr. York would like to admit him. Is that a problem with you, Officer?"

"Insufficient evidence to make an arrest," Mendez says. He gives me a human smile, the kind that makes it hard to hate him, and leaves the room.

A nurse bustles in, a guy this time. "So, we're going to admit, then? Can I have your signature here?"

He hands me a clipboard and a pen, talking all the while. I nod, numbly, staring at the papers he's given me. All the words run together into a blur on the page, and I sign without any understanding of what it says.

Dad's eyes stay closed. For a fraction of an instant, I think he isn't breathing, but then a low buzz, a snore, vibrates through his slack lips. The nurse puts a hand on his shoulder and shakes him, gently. "Mr. Addington. Walter."

Dad's eyes fly open. "Where's Leah?" He scrambles to sit up, arms and legs jerky and uncoordinated.

"Take it easy, Walter," the nurse says, pressing back on his shoulder.

Dad's eyes dart around the room and light on me. "Maisey. God. I have to find Leah."

"Easy," I tell him. "We'll find her in a minute."

He fumbles with the rails, trying to find the catch, but his hands are shaking, and his fingers are stiff. He rattles the railings and starts shouting. "Lower these goddamn rails and let me go."

Blood starts backing up the IV tube in his left arm. The contraption on his finger pops off. An alarm starts beeping.

Dr. Margoni puts her hand over his clenched fist and looks directly into his wild eyes. "Walter, it's Dr. Margoni. Leah is being taken care of. I promise."

"She's dying. Oh God." He gasps for breath. His right hand releases the railing and goes to his heart. His skin looks gray. "I can't—she's all I've got."

"Dad. Breathe. We're not going to let her die. Okay? I don't know what she made you promise, but I'm not going to let her die."

"I need to be with her," he says. "Where is she? Leah? Leah!"

"Daddy. Please. Lie back down."

The nurse pushes a button that sets off another alarm. I grab Dad's left hand and try to pry it off the railing, wanting to hold it, wanting to salvage the IV, needing him to transition back from wild man to my calm and predictable father.

A woman in scrubs runs in, followed by a man and another woman.

"I'll get the nitro," one of them says.

"Give him two milligrams of Ativan," Dr. Margoni directs. "And let's get him in restraints."

"On it!" One of the nurses bustles back out.

"Walter. Mr. Addington. You need to calm down."

But Dad is beyond reason. He swings at Dr. Margoni, who just barely evades the blow. She wrestles Dad's arm and starts wrapping it in a soft restraint that she ties to the bedrail.

"Mr. Addington," Dr. Margoni says again. "Listen to me." Dad turns his head in her direction, and the nurse uses the distraction to pry his free hand from the bedrails and start wrapping it in the restraints.

"You'll hurt your heart. You need to calm down. Leah needs you to be calm, okay? She wants you to breathe and just wait here for her."

A nurse returns with a syringe and a plastic cup harboring three tiny little pills. She injects medication into his IV. Within minutes he stops fighting the restraints, his eyes drooping.

"Open," the nurse says, as if he's a child. Dad opens his mouth, and she plants one tiny tablet under his tongue. "Nitroglycerin," she explains to me. "For his heart."

Dad sighs. His eyelids drift closed.

"Is he having a heart attack?" My hands are pressed over my own heart, feeling its pounding.

Dr. Margoni smiles at me. "I don't think so. He gets chest pain when his heart is stressed, like now. Nitro opens up the vessels."

I stare at the man tied to the bed, quiet now under the influence of the sedatives. If I hadn't seen him take a swing at Dr. Margoni, I wouldn't have believed him capable of it.

The doctor seems to read my thoughts. "It's amazing what even a small illness can do to the mental processes in an elderly adult. I suspect he'll be much better tomorrow."

"God, I hope so."

Watching him like this is worse in some ways from what is going on with my mother.

"You might take a look around to see if you can find an advance directive for either of your parents."

"Do I need an attorney?"

"It wouldn't be a bad idea. For right now, though," she says, "you and your daughter need to get some rest."

I'm about to object. I need to check on Mom. And there's no way I can leave Dad like this, trussed up like a Thanksgiving turkey. But then I look at Elle, who has retreated into the visitor's chair, her knees drawn up to her chin, her arms wrapped around them. Tears pour silently down both cheeks.

Shit.

I am in over my head. This is an understatement. I am miles below the surface, in the deepest, darkest canyon of the ocean floor, and I'm not in some special little diver bell contraption, either.

The EKG nurse has the wires all hooked up, and a reassuring, steady beeping fills the room.

Dad has already passed out cold. Whatever was in that syringe, I want some. Only, of course, I have to go on being responsible and get Elle to bed and, horror of horrors, call on Greg for legal advice.

Chapter Seven

As it turns out, I don't need to call Greg. Two minutes into the drive home from the hospital, he calls me.

"What's going on?" he demands—barks, really, like a drill sergeant with a whole new batch of green recruits.

"Hello to you, too."

"Why didn't you call me?"

"I've been a little preoccupied."

"I'm not asking you to be glued to the phone. I'm asking that you let me know that you—and my daughter—arrived safely. That your plane landed, that you made the drive okay, whether everybody is still alive. It's noon already, and I assume your plane landed at midnight. I've been worried sick."

Now I feel guilty, on top of everything else, and that makes me stabby. His voice is loud enough that I know Elle can hear him. I hate fighting in front of her.

"Elle is fine. If you were so worried, why didn't you call her cell phone?"

"I did. Straight to voicemail."

"I turned it off," Elle says in a small voice. "In the hospital. Like the sign said."

"Here." I hand her the phone. "You tell him."

Washington State has laws about driving and talking. Besides, I'm exhausted and distracted, and there are deer in Colville. There are also a lot of intersections without so much as a yield sign. It would be fantastic if Elle and I crashed and ended up in the hospital. Maybe we could have a group room for the whole family.

"You should cut Mom some slack." Elle is lecturing her father. "What with the fire, and the police, and both Grandma and Grandpa in the hospital—I'm not sure, it got sort of complicated—okay, here she is."

She holds out the phone. "He wants to talk to you."

The explanation is unnecessary. I can hear him shouting without putting that phone anywhere close to my ear. "Let me talk to your mother."

I can totally understand why he's throwing a fit. At the same time, I don't want to cope with him right now. As if it's operating independently of my oversight, my thumb gets decisive all on its own and presses the disconnect button.

Silence invades the car. My hand drops to my side, still white-knuckled around the phone.

"You hung up on Dad."

"I'm driving."

"I still can't believe you did that."

I can't believe it, either. I don't think I've ever hung up on anybody in my life. Greg will not take this well.

Elle starts to giggle.

"I don't see what's so funny."

For some unknown and incomprehensible reason, my words add fuel to her hilarity. The giggle grows into trills of delicious laughter. She used to laugh like this when she was a baby, a sound of pure, astonished delight, untroubled by thoughts of who might be listening or whether the stimulus was worth the response.

It's contagious.

When Elle's phone rings, we're both laughing so hard the tears are pouring down our cheeks.

"It's Dad," she says, looking at the caller ID. A snorting noise comes out of her nose, like a pig, and that sets her off again.

I picture Greg's sternest courtroom face, the one he uses to admonish the jury. This elicits a snort from me, which sets Elle off again, just as she's composed enough to say hello. I can hear the voice of frustration on the other end.

"Hello? Elle! Hello? Let me speak to your mother."

Elle straightens her face to serious. She takes a breath and busts out laughing again.

"I can't." She holds the phone out to me.

I'm not sure I can, either, but years of following Greg's directions sobers me enough to pull the car over to the side of the street and answer. My *hello* is breathless and a little strangled. Greg is not amused.

"What the hell is so freaking funny?"

Elle presses both hands over her nose and mouth to stifle her laughter, staring at me with wide eyes and raised brows. I shift my body away from her to look out the window and take a breath.

"Damn it, Maisey. Explain."

"Nothing is funny. Not a single thing. Either that or everything is funny—the whole great, wide, absurd universe. At the moment, we are unsure."

"Maisey."

"It's a laughter experiment? Therapy. One of my counselors was into it."

He's breathing heavily through his nose. I recognize the sound. I've heard it in the courtroom. I've heard it in the bedroom. It's the sound of a fight brewing. I know the words that are going to come out of his mouth next, and I say them for him. "I'm serious, Maisey. This is serious. When are you going to grow up?"

And now I've gone too far. The silence on the other end of the line is deafening. Elle has stopped laughing.

"You are going to put Elle on a plane—"

"Listen, Greg. She's fine. I'm sorry. I need some legal advice."

More silence. A heavy sigh. "What have you gone and done?"

"Me? Nothing. It's Dad."

"Walter? How could Walter be in legal trouble?"

I ignore the fact that Greg has no problem at all believing I've stepped into trouble with the law and explain all about the criminal negligence charge, Mom's broken bones, and Dad's confused behavior. I refuse to use the word *dementia*, although it's taken up prime real estate in my brain. It squats there, an ugly blot of a word, spelled out in capital letters, in Gothic font, dark and threatening.

The legal problem distracts Greg from my irresponsible behavior, and his tone shifts to a dispassionate, intellectual consideration, as if I'm a client and not his crazy baby mama. "I'd suggest that you get a psych eval done ASAP."

"I'm fine. Really. Just a little tension-breaking laughter—"

"On your father, Maisey. Focus."

"But he's not rational at all right now, Greg. Fighting restraints, trying to climb over the rails of a stretcher—"

"That's the point, Maisey. We want him to be confused."

"We do?"

"If you can prove he didn't have the capacity to know right from wrong, that would be helpful. Also, if your mom really did fill out an advance directive, then we can argue that he was just following her wishes. Maybe it was ill-advised to keep her at home for so long, but if he was confused and unable to make decisions, then they can't convict him of anything. See if you can get a dementia diagnosis."

I want to smack my forehead with the phone. Greg has unleashed the monster by speaking its name out loud.

"Maisey?"

My throat feels too tight to squeeze words through, but I manage, although I sound squeaky. "I'm here."

"Action plan. I'll make it simple enough for even you to follow. Although maybe you should write this down."

"Okay. Writing."

In reality, I'm not writing anything.

Greg's reminder that I'm incapable of focused, goal-directed activity has triggered my obstinate streak, and in this moment I'm not about to do anything he tells me.

"Are you ready?" he asks. "Do you even have a pen?"

"Just give me the fucking plan, Greg. I'm not completely stupid."

"I hope you are not swearing in front of our daughter. First, find the advance directive if there is one. Second, find a psychologist to do psych testing."

"The mental health guy did a mini mental status exam on him already."

Greg sighs, his superior, do-I-really-have-to-explain-this sigh. "A mini mental status test isn't going to be sufficient to prove that he's not competent. You need a battery of tests. Administered by a psychologist. You got that?"

"Got it."

"Write it down. Psychologist, not psychiatrist. There's a difference. Third, call me the minute cops start talking to either you or Walter. The very minute. Okay? No more free interviews. I'd think you'd know better than that by now."

His scolding showers over me in a familiar pitter-patter. I don't need to hear the individual words. I know the message, which generally boils down to "all the ways Maisey has screwed up again." I set the phone in my lap and pull back out onto the street, waiting for the change of intonation that signals he's moved on.

"Maisey? Maisey! Let me talk to Elle."

I pass the phone over. Elle talks for a few minutes. "Dad says to tell you to remember to charge your cell phone," she says when she hangs up.

Words that I resent all the more because he's right. This is a thing I would never have remembered.

~

My parents' house is a much bigger problem than I am prepared to deal with.

It's empty, for starters. Not the sort of emptiness you get when people are gone for a couple of hours on a trip to town. It's the same echoing emptiness I felt sitting beside my mother's bed and realizing that whatever it is that makes her my mother is missing. Every noise we make, from turning the key in the lock to wiping our feet on the doormat and obediently removing our shoes in response to the little wooden sign that says *Shoes that remain by the door will be blessed*, seems like an intrusion.

In case the desire for blessing might be missing in some rogue human breast, there's a picture of a tiny black demon with a pitchfork eyeing the tempting buttocks of a cartoon man who is walking into a house with shoes still on his feet.

If the curse exists, my friendly fireman and a whole slew of ambulance and legal personnel are in for some pitchfork jabs. The new carpet that Mom is so proud of is trampled with muddy footprints and ashes. I stick my head into the kitchen with some thought of finding Elle something to eat and draw it right back, like a startled turtle. More footprints. A dried pool of blood by the island. A buzz of flies, busy with a frying pan on the stove. The stink of something rotten.

"Not hungry," Elle says from behind me.

My stomach squeezes in on itself, pushing a wave of nausea up my throat, and I back away, breathing through my mouth.

"You didn't eat breakfast," I tell her. It comes out as "You diddun ead breagfasd," and she does that snort-laugh thing, and again we're giggling, only this time even through the insane laughter, I can feel a noose tightening around my throat.

"Too tired to eat," she says. "Also, ewww. What was in that frying pan, besides flies?"

I don't want to know. But I know damn well I'm the one who is going to have to clean it up. First, I tuck Elle into bed. My old bed. It doesn't look like my room anymore, and I'm glad of that. Mom has repurposed it. Impersonal modern computer desk. Ergonomic chair. A couch/daybed that might have come from Ikea. In the closet I find blankets and a pillow, and Elle snuggles down and is well on her way to sleep before I make it out of the room.

With Elle off to dreamland, the next thing on my agenda is to look for Mom's advance directive, a document that is beginning to seem as mythical as the holy grail. Still, I make my way to Dad's study, which is mercifully neat and orderly, all as it should be. I sit down in his chair, gathering warmth and strength from my memories of his steady, gentle presence.

A large planning calendar sits in the middle of his solid wood desk, the squares filled with notes made in his precise, tiny handwriting. The Dad Font, I've always called it. A notation for next week catches my attention: *Dr. M./POLST*.

All the warmth flies away. If Mom was planning a POLST, like Dr. Margoni said, then it's probable that there really is an advance directive somewhere.

If I were my mother, where would I keep such a thing?

The most logical spot is the four-drawer cabinet that has stood behind locked closet doors in this room for as long as I can remember. Dad takes his clients' confidentiality seriously.

Finding the keys is too easy. The inside of the middle desk drawer is like an advertisement for one of those little plastic organizer trays.

Everything is neatly stowed. It's the complete opposite of my desk, in which items are piled so high you can't even see the plastic organizer.

But when I go to open the closet door, it is already unlocked. Behind it, file folders and papers are strewn helter-skelter all over the floor. The top drawer of the cabinet is open. Even the picture of Jesus and the little children that hangs in front of the safe is on the floor, and the safe door is also hanging open.

My heart slams against my chest.

That small, twisted shame I felt watching drool trail down Dad's chin while he slept resurfaces. I'm not supposed to see this. It's sacrilege of a sort. My father has made this mess. He left the file cabinet unlocked. The safe open. The closet unlocked.

I put my hands on either side of my head and squeeze them together. This is not my father's behavior. He doesn't do this. He wouldn't do this. That *dementia* word comes crawling back into my brain, a snake of a word this time, poisonous.

I can't think of any other explanation for a calm, methodical man to be burning papers in a fireplace, scattering files around like this. I want to sink to the floor in the middle of the scattered files and wail like a frightened child, but I can't. There's too much to do. And I am the only person anywhere around to do it.

I begin cleaning up the mess, all the while asking myself what he might have been looking for. The safe contains passports, both his and Mom's. Stocks and bonds. A copy of their will, which noticeably is lacking any mention of an advance directive. Nothing of any particular interest, like gold or expensive jewelry or some terrible secret.

The files strewn all over the floor are client income taxes, mostly. Mom's old medical records. A year of utility bills and car repairs and home maintenance. Receipts. Nothing that would indicate a reason to start burning things.

An overwhelming sense of exhaustion creeps over me as I contemplate trying to guess where these files are supposed to go under

Dad's careful organizational system. And then I realize that it doesn't matter, and I just shove them in any which way, using the Maisey Organizational System, which consists pretty much of "I know it's in there somewhere."

If his mind has deserted him, he won't know or care. If he comes home okay, he can fix it himself.

Curious now, trying to track the unusual workings of my father's mind, I pick my way through the muddy mess in the living room and crouch down by the fireplace. I saw a movie once where some guilty soul had burned papers, and the words were still visible. No such luck here. The papers are too blackened for me to read any words. A manila folder lying on the hearth looks like a thousand other folders. Beige and noncommittal.

What makes it stand out from all the other beige folders on the face of the planet is my name. There's a sticky label, printed, that says *Maisey*.

I have a folder at home labeled *Elle*. Per the Maisey Organizational System, it has all things Elle in it. Her birth certificate. Social Security card. Vaccination records. Certificates of excellence from school. A funny picture of her with her hair all disheveled, cuddled under a blanket and sitting on the heat vent, one of her favorite places to be.

Mom doesn't organize things the way I do, by which I mean to say she actually organizes them. Social Security cards will be in a file so labeled. Vaccination records will be under vaccination records, probably with a separate folder for each family member. I can't imagine what would be in a folder with my name on it, unless it's childhood drawings or school papers.

The folder feels empty, but I open it anyway. All I find is a tiny little sticky note that reads, *Shred this*.

A hollow space opens in my chest where my heart is supposed to be. This—whatever this is—is about me. My mother had Maisey secrets and told my father to destroy them.

I blaze a trail back to Dad's office. The shredder under the desk is jammed with a wad of paper stuck so tightly that I can't pull it free. Unplugging the electrical cord to prevent any accidental shredding of my fingers, I anchor the base between my feet and tug with both hands. No dice.

There are scissors in the desk, and I use those to saw away at the paper, cutting and tearing it free just above the shredder blades. I'm holding eleven half-sheets, their bottoms mangled, the top halves legible. Eight of them are my mother's old medical records. The tops of the pages hold only demographic data: her address, date of birth, allergies, medications. Whatever she saw the doctor for is missing, and I move on.

Page nine is a different kind of paper, smaller, the sort that comes on one of those refrigerator magnet to-do list pads. It's pink and has a butterfly and flower on the right. A cute little header says, *Life Is Short, Do It Now.*

A list is written in my mother's decisive script. Half of the page is missing, presumably lodged in the shredder. The part I can read says:

Don't forget to shred this when you're done.

1. The medical records

2. Birth certificates

I'll never know what was meant to be number three.

Page ten is a different type of paper yet again. Loose-leaf, college-ruled. At the middle of the page, neatly centered, my mother has written in bold black ink:

Shred this first.

Chapter Eight

My heart is in my throat, interfering with my breathing. My hands are shaking as I shuffle to page eleven, where my mother has written these words:

> *My poor Walter. You deserve answers to all your questions. I wish, for both our sakes, that I could give them to you. I think it would be comforting for you to know the truth. But I don't think you could keep the secret, and it must never be told.*
>
> *And yet, the closer I come to death, the more difficult it is to keep silent. I want to talk about my past. I need to talk about it. Memories are bursting me at the seams.*
>
> *Maybe if I write it all out here, that will help. Maybe if I write it as if I am telling it to you, after all, that will grant me some absolution for my sins. I am convincing myself, here, that it is safe to write what is hidden. If it's not safe, it seems a risk I must take because guilt and remorse and regret are gnawing away at my insides just as surely as that treacherous vessel in my brain is eroding under the pressure of my own blood.*
>
> *Justice of a sort. What Maisey might call karma, although I've never believed . . .*

And there it ends. No page twelve. No clue as to what she might feel remorseful about.

A quaking starts in my belly and spreads into a full-body tremble. My thighs feel as substantial as jelly in an earthquake, and no amount of willpower from me will steady them. In my empty chest, a dark fear blossoms, and with it, a memory, sudden and stark.

Me, exploring my parents' closet, and my mother's rage at catching me there. I feel the sharp sting of a belt whipping across my buttocks and the backs of my thighs. Rebellious tears burning my eyes against my will. Mom yelling at me.

I have small gaps in my memory. I've forgotten events before. Usually they come back to me gently, sliding into place as if they've never been away. Sometimes memories get temporarily buried under other things, but then life shifts, and they surface as a small reminder, no more.

This memory is not like that. It is neither subtle nor quiet; it enters my awareness with all the violence of a detonation, blowing my world sky high. It breaches an emotional dam at the center of me, allowing words and images, sensations and emotions to tumble around and around, all mixed up together.

My breath rasps in my throat. My heart threatens to beat its way out of my rib cage.

Did I have a friend over? I have a sense of not having conducted my exploration alone.

Marley. My God. How could I have forgotten?

Marley was my constant companion, more real to me than my actual schoolmates. We read books and played games, and on that fateful day, explored the no-fly zone of my parents' closet.

That day was the end of Marley. Not because of the beating, but because I heard my mother weeping.

"This Marley business has to end," she'd sobbed, clinging to my father. "I can't endure it. I can't."

What had we done that was so terrible? Played princesses in the closet. Dressed up in what must have been Mom's wedding dress. Uncovered an old suitcase . . .

Oh my God. The suitcase. The two pink blankets. That picture.

The short hallway between me and my parents' room feels like a mile at least. I run, bumping into the wall with my shoulder, fumbling with the door knob.

A wall of smell assaults me as the door swings open. The bed is unmade, covers tossed back in a rumpled mess. A blue bed protector pad covers the sheet, and a trash can by the bed overflows with more. I try to picture my mother lying here, unconscious, my father bathing her, changing her. My mind recoils, and I press both hands over my nose and mouth, holding my breath, fighting my gag reflex.

Trying not to look at the bed, I make a dash for the walk-in closet. When I enter, I pull the door closed behind me. The closet smells spicy and secret—cedar and another unnamable fragrance made up of Mom's perfume and Dad's cologne—but my mother's illness has also invaded here. There's a big open box still half-full of bed protector pads. Two sets of brand-new sheets, still in the plastic, with a note in her handwriting that says, *You may need these.*

Later, I tell myself. I will deal with all this later.

The suitcase still occupies its accustomed place in a back corner. I fall on my knees in front of it, my heart beating in my throat. My trembling fingers fumble with the latches, and I hold my breath as I open the lid.

The pink blankets are still there, but they are wadded up, no longer perfectly and precisely folded. The picture of a young girl wearing my mother's face, holding two babies wrapped in pink blankets, is missing.

All these years I have forgotten about this picture. Now it seems like the most important thing in the world, a priority beyond restoring order to this house or figuring out what to do about my parents. Retracing my steps to the study, I dump out the shredder basket on the floor. Mostly the papers are standard white paper. The remnants of the to-do list are jammed around the shredder teeth.

And mixed in with the ordinary paper, thicker pieces of a photograph.

Sorting these out from the others, I carry them to Dad's desk and sit down, forcing my blurring eyes to focus as I reassemble the picture. I expect it to take forever, but it's easier than a jigsaw puzzle, and the strips line up with little effort.

My memory has proved accurate. Two pink bundles. Two babies.

Logic, Maisey. Don't jump to conclusions. There could be any number of explanations. Maybe she's holding someone else's babies. Sure, Dad shredded the picture, but he's not rational. It doesn't have to mean anything.

I go back to the filing cabinet and search it, methodically, one file at a time, looking for my birth certificate.

It's not there.

Memory shows me my father, burning papers. If the fireplace was his recourse when the paper shredder failed him, my birth certificate is likely ashes, along with the rest of whatever my mother was writing.

But why?

Hoping that some pieces of this mystery have escaped the flames, I use the ridiculously inadequate decorative shovel hanging on the hearth to scoop the ashes out of the fireplace and into a trash can. Maybe, just maybe, there are some intact bits of paper that will tell me a story.

There's nothing, though.

By the time the fireplace is emptied, the hearth swept, the ashes dumped outside in the trash bin, my body is exhausted, but my brain is possessed by an almost frantic energy. I try to sit for a minute, but I can't rest, and I move on to cleaning the rest of the house. I vacuum the carpet in the living room, scrub the kitchen floor clean of my mother's blood, and dispose of her beloved cast iron frying pan, still holding what once might have been pork chops.

A call up to the hospital to check on my parents lets me know that Dad is sedated and sleeping. Mom is the same, no better, no worse. "Get some rest," the nurse says. "You need to take care of yourself."

I check in on Elle. She's sprawled on her back, one arm above her head, palm open, the way she used to sleep when she was a baby. She stirs, as if she feels me watching her, but then settles back into her sleep. I'd had a thought of crawling into the bed beside her, but she has expanded into the entire space and I don't want to wake her.

Which leaves me with a choice between the bed in my parents' room and the couch. I've already stripped the bed, thrown my mother's pillow in the trash, and put the laundry in the machine. But the thought of trying to sleep in the bed where she lay unconscious and maybe dying for three long days brings a bitter taste of nausea into the back of my throat.

Couch it is. I lie down and drop almost instantly into sleep.

~

Some noise startles me awake. I've been sweating. My clothes feel simultaneously stiff and clammy. My mouth tastes disgusting, and my lips are cemented together. When I pull them apart, a little piece of skin rips away, and I can taste the salt of blood when I touch the stinging spot with my sandpaper tongue.

It's still light outside the living room window, but the shadows are long and slanted. Late evening, then. I should get up. Check on Elle. Have a shower. Try to scrounge up something for us to eat.

Disoriented and still only half awake, I sit up and swing my feet onto the floor. My right ankle brushes against something soft protruding from under the couch. I bend down to investigate and come up with my mother's knitting bag.

Nothing fancy, just a soft fabric bag, faded by years and multiple washings to a dull, nondescript graying green. Surely some essence of my mother clings to it. She never could just sit, and all my memories of family movie night or entertaining visitors are infused with the soft click of her needles.

This, finally, is a talisman for the mother I know. The normal mother, who goes to church every Sunday and runs the PTA and organizes everything. Not the mother who has secret fractures of multiple bones, who tells my father to shred things and keeps a secret journal, who hides pink blankets in her closet.

But even the humble knitting bag goes all wrong. I hug it to my heart, wanting to bring her closer to me, and feel a dull weight swing against my ribs. Maybe a book, I tell myself. A lot of people carry a novel around with their knitting. Mom never did, but that's the sort of habit that could easily change. Curious, I set the bag in my lap and feel my way past several skeins of yarn until my fingers run into something that is most definitely not a book.

Smooth. Cold. Metallic.

This can't possibly be what I think it is. An odd-shaped flashlight, maybe. A novelty item.

But when I bring it up into the light, there is absolutely no doubt that I am holding a handgun.

It's black. Sleek.

Lethal.

And completely incongruous.

Violence in any form was forbidden both in and out of our house. Even during my high school years, Mom banned me from watching thriller-type movies or TV cop shows. I snuck detective novels, even Agatha Christie, into the house under stacks of textbooks and hid them under my mattress, the way some kids hide cigarettes or porn. When I was fifteen, she grounded me from hanging out with my best friend for a month after we snuck into a theater to watch *Pulp Fiction*.

Now that I have Elle, I don't blame Mom for the *Pulp Fiction* bit. I want to shelter my daughter from all the darkness in the world, in movies as well as in real life. The point is, I've never seen a gun in person. I've certainly never held or fired one. I don't know if this specimen is loaded. What if Elle finds it? Elle wouldn't play with a gun, surely, but there are those stories of people accidentally discharging guns. What if Dad finds it in a state of mental derangement and accidentally shoots somebody?

My heart is trying to beat a hole through my rib cage.

I sit there on the couch with the gun in my clammy hands, pointing the dangerous end away from me.

I can't think what to do. I could put it away somewhere. Tuck it into the bottom of Mom's cedar chest. The top shelf of the closet. But I can't stop thinking about the crazy way Dad was tearing at the restraints in the hospital. I can't stop the *what if* thought of Elle getting shot. I've seen enough movies to know I can't just drop it into a shrubbery or something. A kid might find it. Or a criminal.

The phone number the fireman gave me is still crumpled in the pocket of my jeans. I pull it out and look at it. Tony Medina. I try to summon a memory of him from high school, but again come up blank. He seemed nice enough. If he's lived in Colville all this time and works for the ambulance and fire department, surely he's not a lunatic or a serial killer or something.

I haven't stayed in contact with anybody from home, other than Greg. I don't even know who might still live here, and I certainly don't know who else I could call.

Before I have time to be frozen by my usual indecision, I grab my cell phone and try to dial.

The thing is dead. I've forgotten to charge it, despite Greg's instructions. I stare at it, blankly, my thought processes about as active as slugs in a tub of salt.

Clearly I need to get my shit together before I'm functional enough to even call for help.

Very carefully, holding my breath in case the thing accidentally goes off, I tuck the gun into my purse. Taking purse and gun into the bathroom with me for safekeeping, I take a shower. Brush my teeth. Lubricate my eyes with eye drops.

Out of both ideas and excuses, I pick up my parents' landline phone.

It's 8:00 at night. I hope that's not too late to call. Part of me—a big part—is hoping the call will go to voicemail. I'll hang up. Maybe I'll leave a message. Maybe I won't.

"Hey, who's this?" It's a woman's voice, and there's a hint of laughter in it that negates the apparent rudeness of her greeting. There's the sound of TV in the background. Voices, music.

Still. It's a woman. I feel my face heating and know if I look in the mirror I'll be red with shame. I've called a desirable man to help me, and he has a girlfriend. Or a wife. Of course he does. What was I thinking?

My thumb hovers over the End Call button, but her voice stops me. "Wait. Don't hang up. Shit. I bet this is some sort of work call. You're looking for Tony, right? I can get him. Especially if this is about work stuff. Do not hang up. I repeat, do not hang up your phone. I shall produce Tony momentarily. Wave of the wand and shazam!"

Shuffling, muted voices, and then a male voice comes on. I think it's familiar, although I'm so upside down by now I can't be sure. "Hello? If you have not yet fled to a galaxy far, far away, speak to me."

"If this is a bad time . . ."

"This is a perfect time."

"This is Maisey. From the fire that wasn't."

"I know who you are."

"How on earth did you know?"

"I recognize your voice. How are your folks?"

"They kept him, my dad. Up at the hospital. He's all confused."

Tony's voice is calm and sympathetic. "He's been through a lot. Can't imagine. How long have your parents been married?"

I don't honestly know the answer to this. "Longer than I've been around. Look, my folks aren't the reason I'm calling. I mean, sort of, but not exactly."

"How can I help?"

Just like that. Straight-up. No winding twists and turns, just a question requiring an answer.

So I tell him. My face red with embarrassment, sitting on the counter in the steamy bathroom, feeling helpless and stupid and almost out-of-body.

"I'll be right over," he says. No difficulty with decision-making for this guy.

"Look, I realize you're with family and probably don't want to—"

"No, it's fine. I was wanting to get out of the house for a bit anyway. I'll be right there."

He hangs up.

I'm still standing there with the phone in my hand, appalled by what I've just done, when the damn thing rings. It scares the bejeezus out of me, skittering out of my hand and into the sink. When I grab for it, it's now just wet enough to be slippery and squirts out of my grasp twice before I bobble it and manage to get it in both hands.

I figure it's probably Tony calling back to cancel, having had an earful from his girlfriend, but it's Greg.

"Did you find the advance directive?" He doesn't even ask about Mom and Dad. He is Attorney Greg, and I am now his client.

"Hey, I'm just out of the shower . . ."

"You didn't, did you?" he says. "You didn't even look."

"Dad burned papers, Greg. And he shredded things. Why would he do that?"

Mom told him to. I don't tell Greg that part, that strange, absurd part. I also don't tell Greg about the pink blankets and the two babies or my sudden memory of my childhood imaginary friend.

"From what you're telling me about his current mental state, *why* doesn't seem like a valid question. Do you think he burned the advance directive?"

"He might have. I've been all through the filing cabinets and haven't seen it anywhere."

Greg says nothing. I say nothing. Both of us say nothing for long enough that I think maybe he's drifted off to sleep, but he's just thinking.

"And the neighbor?"

"What about her?"

"What does she say about your dad? Is she still making noises about domestic violence? Does she think he has dementia? What exactly did she say to the cops?"

"I haven't talked to the neighbor."

"Talk to her. Invite her over for coffee."

"You're kidding, right?"

"Maisey. This is not about your comfort. You want to get your dad clear or not?"

I sigh. I would like this to be about my comfort, but most things in life are not. "I want to get my dad clear."

"Good. Tomorrow morning. Coffee with the neighbor. And search—I mean really search—for that advance directive."

"It's not here, Greg."

"Try the bank."

"What?"

"Some people keep important papers in a safe-deposit box. Try that."

"Which bank? And don't I need some sort of document to be able to access a box? Like a power of attorney designation or something?"

"I'll email you a form. Get it printed and get Walter to sign it."

"I can't believe you just said that. How can that even be legal?"

He sighs so heavily, I swear I feel the wind move through the phone and into my ear. "This is to keep him out of jail, right? And to take proper care of your mother. It's not like you're defrauding somebody out of money."

Shades of truth. That's the legal system in action. I don't like it, don't want to be part of it. I'm saved from any commitment by the ringing of the doorbell.

"Gotta go, somebody's here."

"If it's that neighbor—"

It's not the neighbor, though.

It's rescue, in the form of a decidedly attractive paramedic fireman by the name of Tony.

Leah's Journal

I've never believed in journaling or in visiting a counselor, for that matter. It's one thing to send a child to therapy and quite another to go yourself. I didn't tell you about my counseling session, as I didn't tell you about so many other things. I only went the one time. There was no point going back—the words are lodged too tightly in my chest to be able to speak them to a stranger. So even though I know full well you won't be reading this, it makes it easier if I pretend that I'm writing it for you.

Dying isn't easy, as it turns out. Not that I thought it would be, but I did not expect this clamoring of old ghosts, rattling their cages and demanding consideration. Was I right in what I have done? Was there a better way? I need to face up to these questions and the answers if I am to die with any sort of peace.

When I told the counselor I would not be coming back, she suggested that I try a journal. I scoffed, but memories are hounding me now, night and day, and something must be done to lay them to rest. You will never know how much I long to speak them to you, but I don't have that kind of courage. I've asked myself if maybe once the story is written out I could ask you to read it, but even that is beyond me.

No. My first plan is best. When I am done exorcising my demons (if this is even possible), these pages will need to be destroyed.

Still, I find that it is comforting to picture you reading over my shoulder.

My past has been locked away so completely and so long that it had come to feel like it wasn't mine, my memories no more relevant to me than a book I'd read or a movie seen and forgotten long ago.

No more. Emotions well up inside me at odd moments, as powerful and fresh as if they were brand-new. You are my only defense, that and pure willful stubbornness. I can't speak to you of this, and my will, it seems, is failing.

How will I keep from spilling it all out to you? Can I persuade you that it's just grief over my own early demise or maybe pain from a headache? Maybe writing it here will be a means of damage control.

Still, I am evading what I must write. You see how it is? Talking around the edges of things. Never speaking the truth of it. Because if I speak of it, if I speak of any of it, then one of two things will happen: The disaster fended off by my silence will come crashing down on us. On Maisey.

Or nothing will happen, and all my heartbreak will have been for nothing.

I'm not sure which fate would be worse.

Chapter Nine

Tony fears only three things in life: guns, women, and the nightmares that fracture his sleep.

Standing on the Addingtons' front porch in the not-quite-summer twilight, awaiting a confrontation with two of these items combined, he has a ridiculous urge to race back to his truck and peel rubber right out of here. But his mother has raised him both to honor promises and to assist those in need, and he's not about to let a little anxiety deter him from his duty.

Maisey is only in town for a week or two to check on her parents, he reminds himself. Hell, she has a kid and is probably married. As for the gun, he's a crack shot and a gun safety expert. He can handle this.

Still, when the door opens and Maisey looks out at him, her abundant hair wild and untamed and framing those changeable blue-green eyes, his heart kicks up a notch. Sweat dampens the back of his T-shirt, despite a cool breeze.

You can do this. Just keep it light. Disable the weapon. Be polite. Then get the hell out of Dodge.

"Gun squad, reporting for duty." He touches his fingers to the brim of his cap in a fake salute. "Where is the offending weapon?"

Maisey hesitates, briefly, crossing her arms over her belly, her eyes flickering over him full of questions. Nervous, he thinks. Probably having second thoughts about inviting him into the house now that he's out of his official capacity. He smiles at her, tries to make his six-foot-three bulk look small and nonthreatening.

"I can wait here, if you want to go get it."

An unexpected smile, pure mischief, lights up her face. "Wouldn't Mrs. Carlton just love that? She's already watching us from her window. Come in. Guessing what we're up to will totally make her day."

She steps aside to let him into the entryway and leads him into the living room.

"Hang on, I'll go get it."

Funny how a uniform and a crisis change everything. Out of his uniform now, with no official business here, it feels strange and wrong to him that he knows the floor plan of the house, has been in the master bedroom, has seen the blood in the kitchen. He's here by invitation, he reminds himself. He's here to do a favor. Such a small thing, really, and he hates the way the inevitable anxiety creeps into his body.

Maisey is blessedly quick, returning in less than a minute with a shapeless leather handbag. She holds it gingerly in outstretched hands. "It's in here."

"I thought you said it was in your mom's knitting bag."

"It was. I couldn't just leave it there." She presses the purse against his chest, and he can't do anything other than grab it. His hands are starting to tremble. He can feel it, though thank God it isn't visible yet.

Turning his back to her, he carries the purse over to the couch and sets it down, feeling his way through the clutter of items for the gun, which he knows will have settled to the bottom.

"My mother caught me snooping in my sister's purse when I was six," he says, offering an explanation for his reaction, a story that is true, although far from the truth. "I caught a spanking for that one. She said a woman's purse is private business, and a man should keep his hands to himself."

"Must have been a pretty effective spanking."

"You'd think so, right? You'd be wrong. Jessica caught me snooping in her purse again later. Hey, I was curious about the ways of women. Jess wasn't bound by any maternal principles of responsible discipline. She beat me up. Bloody nose. Black eye. When I tattled to my mom, she just looked at me. 'Bet you don't do that again,' she said, and she was right. Now, thirty years later, you're forcing me to scale the fortress. I'm terrified."

He lifts the gun out of the handbag, keeping the barrel down while he ejects the magazine and clears a 9-millimeter round from the chamber.

"Your mom is a badass. It was fully loaded with one in the pipe."

"No."

Maisey's tone makes him look up. Her eyes, wide with alarm, dominate her face. She shakes her head, emphatically. "My mom is the queen of the church supper and the PTA. She is vociferously antigun. When I was a kid, she tried to start an organization for mothers against firearms. It didn't fare well here in Colville, but I can't imagine what would change her like this."

"Maybe it belongs to your dad? A lot of women opt for a .22. This is a Glock with a high-capacity magazine. It's a lot of gun."

A laugh bubbles up out of her. "My dad? Not exactly a gun man."

"It must belong to one of your parents," Tony persists. "Nobody else lives here, right?"

Maisey's face crumples at his words, and she chokes on a sound halfway between laughter and tears. "I can't ask either of them," she whispers.

Hell.

He wants to comfort her, to make her laugh again, but that's not why he's here. *Secure the gun, make sure everybody is safe, get out. That's the plan.*

He lays the emptied gun down on the coffee table and thumbs the ammo out of the magazine. "Maybe you can ask your dad tomorrow. I've seen people come clear overnight with rest and hydration."

"Maybe." She looks like a defiant child, hands clenched into fists, blinking against a flood of tears. A choked sob escapes her, and then another. All at once she reminds him of his little sister, Mia, and his resolve is all undone. "Hey," he says. "Hey."

He puts a hand on her shoulder. Her body stiffens, and he thinks he's made a mistake, but then all the tension goes out of her, and she rests her forehead against his chest. Tony strokes her hair, murmuring, "Hush, now, it will be all right," as if she's a child.

Her arms go around him, and she buries her face in his shirt, her body shaking with sobs.

He holds her. Just like comforting one of his sisters, he tells himself. But it isn't. Not remotely. Her hair isn't smooth and black; it's soft and fine as silk. A red-gold curl catches on his hand and winds around his fingers. Her back is a long, smooth-muscled arc, and his body responds, against his will, with an inconvenient arousal.

Thinking desperate thoughts of cold showers and accident scenes doesn't do much to help.

When her tears slow, and she draws in a shuddering breath, he drops his hands with a mixture of relief and regret and waits for the fallout. "Don't be mad now," he says.

Maisey scrubs the tears from her eyes with the palms of both hands and blinks up at him. "What? Why would I be mad?"

"I have sisters, remember? They always get bitchy after I see them cry. Especially if I'm nice." He grins at her, trying to look big-brotherly and nonchalant and having no idea if he's succeeding or not.

She snorts, and a little snot bubble comes out of her nose.

"Oh my God," she says, clamping both hands over her face.

Tony laughs. Despite his body's demands, despite the gun waiting on the coffee table, despite everything, it's genuine, clear, delighted laughter. He fetches the box of tissues sitting on the end table by the couch and brings them to her.

"Tears are damned messy," he says.

She grabs a handful and turns her back to blow her nose and dry her face.

"How many sisters?" she asks.

"Five."

She spins around and goggles up at him, jolted out of her embarrassment. "Five? Five sisters?"

"Yes, ma'am. Four older, one younger. Not a brother in the bunch. You?"

"I'm an only."

"Lucky."

"Am I? It seems like it might be fun to have sisters." There's a wistfulness in her voice.

"Yes. Well," he says, wondering what it might have been like to grow up alone, without the tangle of girls alternately tormenting and taking care of him, "sisters are a mixed bag. Trust me. That was my little sister who answered the phone when you called. Mia. We share a house."

Maisey's mouth opens, then closes again. A slow flush darkens cheeks already red from her weeping.

"What?" he asks.

"I thought she was your girlfriend."

She says it like maybe it matters to her, whether he has a girlfriend or not. His heart skips a beat, and he's quick to tame it. "Girlfriend? Ha! Too many women in my life already. Seriously. Mia's good people, but I should warn you that she'll want to meet you now. You sure you're not mad?"

"Not the tiniest bit. A little embarrassed. Very grateful. For the gun, and for . . . can you keep it for me? The gun? I don't know what to do with it."

Tony's heart jabs sideways. His belly tightens. Whatever he does tonight, he won't be taking the gun with him. He needs a solution, and he needs one now.

"Tell you what. You hold on to the gun. I'll take this." He tucks the magazine into the front pocket of his jeans. "That way it can't hurt anybody. Can you get me a ziplock bag for the ammo?" He looks up at her, questioning.

Her eyes are focused on the gun, her forehead creased with worry. But then she draws a deep breath, and her face clears. "Deal." She picks the weapon up with the tips of her fingers and drops it back into her handbag. For a minute she just stands there, as if she doesn't know what to do next, and then she sort of crumples down onto the couch.

"You okay?" he asks.

"Exhausted," she says, sliding down so she can rest her head. "I feel like I've gone boneless."

"When did you last eat?" He hears the words come out of his mouth and wants to call them back. *What are you doing, idiot? Get out of this house. Bail.*

"I don't know," she says. "Yesterday? Maybe the day before."

"Maybe it would help to get a little food into your body."

She laughs in a way that is perilously close to another bout of tears. "No food in this house worth eating. Aside from dry cereal. The milk has gone bad."

"Fine," Tony says. "I'm ordering pizza."

"I don't know . . ."

"You need to eat. Your daughter needs to eat. I can't imagine either of you are up to cooking. And, if I may say so, I am always hungry. So I'll order pizza, and if you send me away, I'll take a slice to go."

He realizes he is holding his breath, waiting for her answer. So much seems to hang in the balance of pizza. Maybe she'll say no. Maybe she'll thank him for his assistance and usher him politely out of the house. This is the safe solution, the thing that ought to happen.

But instead, Maisey covers a yawn and gives him a small half smile. "Let me go wake Elle. She'll never forgive me if I let her sleep through pizza. But first, I'll get a bag for *that.*" She gestures at the heap of rounds on the coffee table.

As if from a distance, Tony watches himself reach out a hand to help her up off the couch, hers so small and pale compared to his. An unfamiliar emotion expands inside his chest. He feels protective toward his mother and his sisters, but that feeling pales compared to this. He's had plenty of crushes on women, but again, that feeling is different.

He watches her walk out of the room—the glorious hair, the slim hips, the easy way she walks even when she's clearly exhausted—and knows he has opened the door to a whole heap of trouble.

Chapter Ten

Exhausted as I am, sleep lurks just outside the boundaries of consciousness and refuses to come closer. The old couch has a lump right under my shoulder blade and is about an inch too short to let me stretch out my full length.

Awake, I feel like I'm standing on the edge of a precarious slope of secrets. One tiny misstep and I'm going down in a rattle of loose shale. Truth is more likely to kill me than set me free. My subconscious grasps this theme, and every time I manage to drift off, I wake with a start and the sensation of falling.

My brain goes over and over and over all the problems I need to solve. My dad, so lost and confused and accused of unthinkable atrocities. My mother. Her injuries, her missing advance directive, her *gun*. Which leads me to Tony. I can't decide whether he counts as problem or solution. Either way, the memory of my face pressed up against his hard-muscled chest, his hands smoothing my back, does nothing to relax me into sleep.

At the first sign of the coming dawn, I give up the battle and get up. Breakfast is leftover pizza, cold out of the box.

I take a bite, but the congealed cheese and flabby crust make me gag. I'm too worried to eat.

I've already called the hospital. My father is *resting comfortably*, whatever that means in medical speak, and my mother is *stable*. Neither of these terms reassures me.

"Can we please go to the grocery store?" Elle asks. "Not that I'm opposed to pizza. But maybe we should have a vegetable for lunch."

"You've got a point." My brain is running on Mom's missing advance directive and whether I really want to find it or not, and if so where it might be and how to access her safe-deposit box. But a stop by the grocery store might just be more immediately important.

When the house phone rings, I figure it's Greg again and don't answer, but Elle picks it up.

"Hey," she says, "do I know you?"

This is her standard initial response to telemarketers. What happens after that varies depending on her mood. Sometimes she'll lead them on by pretending to be me and having great interest in whatever is being offered. Sometimes she'll ask the sort of questions that would make a preacher run for the hills.

Listen, Steve, my mom won't talk to me about this. Since I've got you on the phone, can you explain why women were stoned in the New Testament if a man slept with them during that time of the month?

So I'm only half listening before I realize that she's actually making plans with some unknown caller.

"Sure, that would be awesome. Ten? Yep, hang on, I'll ask her." She mutes the phone. "Hey, Mom, can I go to the gym with Mia? And then maybe shopping and the afternoon movie?"

I stare at my daughter, bewildered. She's been with me the whole time we've been here, and somehow she's managed to make a friend.

"Who?"

"Mia. Tony's sister. Here, you can talk to her."

She unmutes the phone. "Here's my mom."

"Hey," a female voice says, as casual as if we've been BFFs forever. "How are you doing this morning? Sorry about last night, by the way.

Tony said you thought I was his girlfriend. Now that's the funniest joke, like, ever." And she laughs as though she means this, then stops, just as abruptly. "Oh God, I'm doing it again, aren't I? I can't help myself. You haven't said a word yet, and I'm still going on. You are actually there, right? Hello?"

"Yes. Hi. I'm here."

"Cool. So anyhoo, if I haven't scared the pants off you yet—I promise I'm not a nutcase. You can ask Tony. I just talk. A lot. Anyway, I wanted to help if I can. So I thought maybe you'd like to have me pick up Elle and keep her busy today so you can take care of family stuff."

"Um . . ."

"I'm good with kids. I'll be by in about twenty minutes. Okay? She's in good hands, I promise. Nothing on my driving record. Or my legal record. Oh, wait. Better come clean on that. There was that shoplifting charge when I was eleven, but I'm all over that. Scout's honor."

She pauses for a breath, and I dive in with, "Look, I—"

"Right? It will be so much better this way. And don't worry—I'll enjoy it. I happen to have the day off and not a single plan. Colville is incredibly dull this time of year. See you in a few."

"Listen, Mia, I don't think . . ." But she's already gone, and I'm talking to dead air.

Elle squints her eyes and wrinkles her nose. "Don't you look at me like that, Mom. I know what you're thinking. Do you really want to drag me around with you doing boring stuff when I could be having fun?"

"Elle, we don't even know this woman."

"She's Tony's *sister*." This declaration is delivered as if we've known Tony for thirty years, rather than a few hours.

"Right. And Tony responded to our 911 call and bought us a pizza. That doesn't exclude him from the predator pool. He could be a serial killer, for all we know."

A damned attractive serial killer, I add to myself.

"Mom. Please. You've been watching way too much TV. Maybe she could take me to see Nana. I should visit her, right?"

Guilt again.

I'm not fond of Greg's mother and she isn't fond of me, but she is still Elle's grandmother, and they don't get to see each other often. I hadn't even thought about Elle wanting to visit her. And I really do have some things I need to do that would be better accomplished without the assistance of a twelve-year-old Sherlock Holmes.

"Well," I say, considering, and Elle knows she's won.

She hugs me, a quick, tempestuous squeeze around the neck. "You worry too much," she says. "It will be fine."

Mia shows up at about double her estimated twenty minutes, out of breath and apologetic. "I'm so sorry. I couldn't find my shoes. And then I left my phone at home and had to go back for it. There was actually traffic. Can you believe it? Like, when is there a traffic problem in Colville? Only today."

She looks like Tony, minus the crooked nose. She has huge blue eyes accented with black eyeliner and shimmery shadow, waves of nearly black hair falling over her shoulders, and an expressive face reflecting every emotional shift suggested by her rapid speech. I'm relieved to see she's not a fashion plate and neither is she Goth nor punk, although the beaded bracelets at her wrists and the huge quartz crystal swinging from a chain around her neck hint at some New Age voodoo. None of that is likely to hurt Elle.

"I'm ready," my daughter says, as if she has just accomplished this state of readiness and has not been fidgeting at the door for the last twenty minutes. She drops a kiss on my cheek. "Say hi to Grandma and Grandpa," she says, and she's out the door.

Mia lingers. "I'll take good care of her, I promise. I'm more responsible than you'll be thinking I am. Honest. Here's my cell number, but you should know that around here sometimes I'm out of range, so leave a message and I'll call back a-sap."

She hands me a business card, and with that, the two of them are down the sidewalk and climbing into a Jeep of indeterminate age. When Mia starts the engine, it belches out a cloud of black smoke. I have one foot out on the porch, ready to run after them, but the vehicle is already moving. Elle waves enthusiastically.

Mia drives carefully, using a turn signal even though the street is empty, and I take a deep breath and try to let go of my worry. The business card is professionally done, advertising her services in massage therapy and Reiki. Maybe I'll have to make an appointment. God knows I could use both a massage and an energy alignment, both on a cosmic scale.

Before I head up to the hospital to check on my parents, I swing by the bank—the grocery store can wait. There's a short line, giving me just enough time to work up sweaty palms and an accelerated heart rate.

The bank teller has to call out twice, and when I step up to her window, my first thought is that she should still be in high school. Short spiky hair, vivid eye shadow, a tiny diamond lodged in her left nostril. There's also a slight bulge in her cheek that makes me think she's got gum stashed there, the way Elle does sometimes.

When I tell her what I need, she stares at me for a minute and then picks up her phone and speaks into it. When she hangs up, she points to an office cube behind me. "Bethany can help you. I can't do safe-deposit boxes."

Bethany is not still in high school. In fact, she went to school with me. She dated Greg before I did, which gives us way too much in common. Despite the fact that we were sworn enemies the last time I saw her, she sweeps me into an enthusiastic hug.

"Oh my God. It's Maisey! How long has it been? You look fabulous!"

I know full well I look anything but. I've had a shower and donned clean clothes, but skipped the makeup. There are tears in the emotional weather forecast for today, and it would only end up smeared all over my face. I'm well aware that I'm pale and baggy, that my eyes are red and swollen. Bethany, on the other hand, does look fantastic. I'm trying to figure out what work she's had done—that Invisalign thing to her teeth, maybe a little Botox—when her face assumes the expression of sympathy.

"I heard about your mother. How is she doing?" she asks, head tilted enough that her dangly earrings graze her shoulder, her penciled eyebrows lifted in the questions she has yet to ask. Her eyes have a gleam in them that is a little too avid for a question about safe-deposit boxes, and I can only guess what sort of stories are circulating around town about my parents.

"She's in the ICU. She's still unconscious. She's got pneumonia."

"Oh no. I can't believe it! She was in here only two weeks ago. She seemed so healthy. I guess we just never know, do we?"

I don't like being part of this *we*. I don't like this conversation. I don't even want to be here.

"Listen. I need to have a look in my parents' safe-deposit box. Can I do that?"

"Let me see. Do you have the key?"

I produce a key, hoping it is the right one. It was in an envelope in Dad's file cabinet, marked as important financial records, the name of the bank written across the front in Mom's handwriting, not his.

Bethany approves the key with a nod, setting it down on the desk between us while she taps away at the computer with red lacquered nails. "Here we go," she says, which sounds promising. A furrow appears between her eyebrows as she scrolls down the page, and that does not look promising at all.

"Oh dear," she says. "You are not listed as one of the parties granted access. Only your parents."

"What does that mean, exactly?"

"According to the law, you can only access the box if both of your parents die and you bring in the key and a death certificate."

I stare at her. "No. There has to be another way."

"Get your dad to sign for you. I'll give you a form." She catches my expression and leans forward, lowering her voice. "Or, if he's not fit to sign, you might be able to get a court order."

"No. You don't understand. There isn't time for this. I'm looking for Mom's advance directive. We need it yesterday. Or last week. If we wait until she's dead, that kind of negates the purpose of any directives she might have specified."

"Oh dear." Bethany stares at me, and this time there's pity in her eyes. "Well. Bring your dad down, maybe?" But her tone of voice makes it clear she's heard all the rumors about Dad.

"He's in the hospital." A traitorous quaver wobbles my words, and I dig my fingernails into the palms of my hands in an effort to steady myself. If I cry now, every bank customer for the rest of the day is going to know about it. The stories are just too good not to share. On the other hand, I really need to get into that box, and maybe if Bethany feels sorry for me, she'll play magnanimous heroine and help.

So I dab at my eyes with my fingertips and let the wobble stay. "He's in the hospital, too. All confused. He can't tell me anything, and I can't bring him here. What am I going to do?"

I lift tear-filled eyes to hers.

You'd think we were long-lost friends, the way she places one hand over my arm and pats me, leaning forward to whisper, "Oh hell. It's you. We're friends, right? But you have to promise not to tell."

"Of course."

Decision made, she's shifted into Nancy Drew. "Bring the key. We'll just look, okay? And if the advance directive is there, we'll make a copy, and you can say you found it at home."

"Right. In Dad's filing cabinet. Under legal documents. With the will."

Bethany nods. "Come with me."

I follow her over to the side of the bank, through an open steel door that looks like a giant safe. We stop in a small room that's lined on all sides with keyed, silver panels. My skin prickles as I think about all the secrets contained here. Who knows what people hide away, out of sight? But there's no time to daydream.

Bethany walks directly to box number 45. She puts the key in the lock but then hesitates, drops her hand, and says, "You do it. It's not really my business what's in there."

Given the burn of sleuth fever in her eyes, this is nothing short of heroic. I turn the key and draw out the box, as cold and foreign in my hands as my mother's gun. There's a table to set the box down on while it's opened. Bethany comes up behind me as I open the lid, her stint of martyrdom overcome by curiosity. I just look at her, hands on the lid, until her eyes fall, and she turns her back.

I'm prepared to find nothing, and at first that's what I think I've found.

Some stocks and bonds. Copies of my parents' wills. A legal-size manila envelope. Sealed. I pick it up and hold it, but the fact that one of my parents sealed it and put it here gives me pause. All those lectures from my childhood, through my adolescence, into my adult life: "Mind your own business, Maisey. Snoopers get their fingers caught in mousetraps."

"Aren't you going to open it?" Bethany asks, eyeing me over her shoulder. "That's probably it."

She's right. Regular rules don't apply here. I have no scissors, no letter opener, and my skin quivers with the violation of tearing the flap.

Inside are two sheets of paper. I see right away that this is not an advance directive, but I pull them out anyway, turning my back to screen my birth certificate from Bethany. If I'm adopted, the whole town will know before nightfall.

Only, it's not my birth certificate I'm looking at. Or else they've changed my name. It says *Marley*, not Maisey. Mom's name is on there, and that's the only recognizable piece of information.

"What is it?" Bethany asks, behind me.

"Nothing. Just a birth certificate." My voice sounds wrong to my own ears, as if it belongs to somebody else. I have just enough rational thought process left to know that Bethany must not see this. Can't know about it. I shuffle it behind the other piece of paper. Also a birth certificate, and this one is mine. I stare at it, blindly, frozen into a statue. My inner warning system is blaring all kinds of alerts. Hide it. Shred it. Put it back in the envelope.

My fingers refuse to respond.

"That's it?" Bethany asks. "Just a birth certificate?"

"Yep." My voice rings tinny and false, but speaking corrects whatever was wrong with my brain-to-muscle connection, and my hands slide the documents back into the envelope. "Looks like the directive isn't here."

"Bummer," she says. "Well, it was worth a try, right?"

"Right."

I need to get out of here. Panic scrabbles at my rib cage. My heart feels like it's vibrating, it's beating so fast. I can't get enough oxygen.

Somehow or other, I manage to put the envelope back in the box and lock it with the little key. Bethany slides the whole box of secrets back into its little slot. I don't feel like my body belongs to me anymore, but the pair of legs I seem to be borrowing hold up to the challenge and carry me out of the suffocating space into the open area of the bank.

Every eye in this space seems to be focused on me, aware of the dissolution that has just occurred.

"Sorry that didn't work out," Bethany says. She sounds like she means it and pulls me into a hug.

My arms feel weighted and numb, like they've been injected with novocaine, and I don't hug her back. I have to say something, and the automatic "Thank you so much for your help" that passes my lips comes straight from Mom's indoctrination into politeness and manners. That's one good thing about a thoroughly learned lesson—it doesn't require any brainpower. Fortunately, there's another customer waiting on Bethany's services, and when she turns away, I take advantage of the opportunity to flee.

Once through the doors, I keep moving. Sidewalk under my stranger feet, bits of sand and gravel crunching. Amazing how these feet—my feet, even though they feel so awkward and numb—know exactly what to do. I can't think. Can't feel. Instinctively, I keep walking, away from Bethany's sympathy and the weight of her curiosity. The sunshine is bright and blinding, but I don't feel any warmth. Don't feel anything at all.

I forget to check for traffic before stepping into the crosswalk, and a horn blares at me.

That wakes me up enough to draw a breath on purpose. Sensation rushes back in with that conscious breath and the next one. My feet, my hands, are all pins and needles. I realize I've been hyperventilating, and I slow myself down, counting in and out breaths in my head and coordinating the count with my footsteps.

This is not my first attack of panic, not the first time I've felt like the entire fabric of reality has unraveled and left me floating and terrified. It's just the first time that there has been a legitimate, identified reason.

Usually, what Mom always called my "anxious fits," as if they were nothing more than a childhood meltdown over bedtime or a denied treat, come and go without rhyme or reason. The raft of counselors I've seen for this have offered a variety of explanations, my favorite of which is that sometimes the body just does things for no reason whatsoever, and my anxiety has no basis in my psyche.

As I walk, focused on my breath and my feet, my body becomes fully mine again. And every solid step, every conscious breath, cements the new reality in place.

I am not an only child, and all those false memories are not false after all.

Marley.

The name stops my feet, right in the middle of the sidewalk.

My mother lied to me. Deliberately. Repeatedly. She told me Marley was the product of my overactive imagination. Sent me to a counselor so the counselor could tell me I was delusional. "No more looking for Marley," Mom said. "No more asking about her. No more telling stories about her. She is not real, Maisey. Grow up and let this childishness go."

But the birth certificates don't lie, and at my parents' house I have the shredded picture of my mother holding two babies. I don't need to have the copies in my hands to revisit the details. My brain retains the evidence. I can see the legal seal, the important information in three-dimensional font.

Mother: Leah Lenore Garrison.

Father: Alexander Lloyd Garrison.

Which means not only was Marley real, but my father is not my father. How is it possible to live thirty-nine years on this planet and never guess that your parents are harboring secrets of this magnitude?

The first clear emotion I feel is anger. Not a slow-blossoming, warming anger, but a solid wall of rage that hits me like a sledgehammer and nearly knocks me over sideways.

How dare my parents—both of them, not just my overcontrolling mother but my beloved father, too—lie to me like this? Because now I have a secret, a secret I don't want and never asked for. My entire middle-class upbringing has been a lie, and the people I need to confront with that are not available for questioning.

Leah's Journal

Let me begin with the smallest of my regrets, and that, my dearest Walter, is you.

When I first found you, even when I married you, I confess I did not love you. I wormed my way into your life and your heart like a parasite into an apple, and for most of the same reasons. From the first minute that I sat in your office and looked at your kind face and your honest eyes, blurred by those finger-smudged lenses in those old-man glasses you used to wear, I knew that above all things you were safe.

And that is all I was looking for. A shield. A new identity. A father for Maisey.

That, and somebody I could manipulate into letting me keep my secrets.

Any guilt I feel over those old machinations is small and fleeting, because I fell in love with you after all, beyond my expectations or intentions. You—us—the love we found together, that was a surprise, my Walter. The rest of my life has been rigorously planned, I suppose. Maisey thinks me rigid and obsessive. She uses softer words, but I hear the tone behind them. I saw it in her eyes the last time she visited, and I know why she never comes home.

The truth is, I don't know any other way to be.

I always thought you never knew I had been splintered and glued back together, but I wonder now if I've underestimated you. I'm not going to ask. We are what we are, after all these years. Some things should be allowed to slumber undisturbed.

Chapter Eleven

When I get to the hospital, I charge up to Mom's room. I have some things I need to say to her.

She's lying there, eyes closed, an oxygen mask covering her nose and mouth. Her breath rattles in her chest. She looks tiny and shrunken, like an unearthed mummy, and the better part of me regrets the pain I've caused her by keeping her alive.

The better part of me is small and weak and completely subsumed by grief and betrayal and rage.

I put my lips close to her ear and whisper, "How could you lie to me like this? What happened to my sister? What did you do to Marley?"

She stirs for the first time since I've entered the room. Her head rolls side to side on the bed. Her right hand lifts an inch above the covers.

An impossible hope blossoms. She's going to wake up, just like that, and talk to me.

But then her breath catches. There's a horrible gurgling sound in her throat.

And then everything stops.

Her hand falls back to the bed. Her head stays where it is, turned toward me so I can see the closed eyes, the slackness of her mouth.

She doesn't breathe out.

I hold my own breath, waiting for her, willing her to start back up. She can't just lie there, like a wind-up toy that's stopped in midmotion.

A clock ticks.

Nothing happens.

I erupt out of my chair and burst out into the hallway, looking for somebody—anybody—to help. There's a button or something I should have pushed, but I can't remember where it is, and I'm not going back now.

"Help me! She's not breathing!"

A thin, sparse-haired man wielding a mop in the hallway looks up at me. "What room?"

"I don't know. I can't think. Just get somebody!"

"Be right back," he says. "Just hold tight."

He sets off around the corner. I run back into Mom's room, hoping hoping hoping this is all part of my faulty imagination, and she's breathing again.

She hasn't moved.

Her skin has taken on a dusky-blue color.

I grab her hand, which already feels colder, and start babbling a stream of incoherence. "I didn't mean it. I'm sorry; please don't die now, not like this. Give me a chance to make it right . . ."

Sharp voices come through the speakers out in the hall.

"Code blue, ACU."

A nurse comes in, on the run. My nurse, the one who listened and patted my hand. She's at Mom's bedside, feeling for a pulse in her throat, then leaning over to listen with her stethoscope.

"What are you waiting for?" I demand. "She's not breathing."

The nurse straightens, slowly, and meets my gaze. "Her heart's not beating."

"Aren't you going to do CPR? What are you waiting for?" I'm stuck in a horror movie where nothing makes sense. I put my own hands on

Mom's chest, as if I'm going to do CPR myself, only I haven't a clue what I'm supposed to do.

"She's a no code, honey," the nurse says, pronouncing each word carefully. "You agreed to that. It's in the doctor's orders and hanging above her bed."

I shake my head.

"No. Whatever I said before, it was wrong. I was wrong. You have to bring her back. I'm not ready . . ."

Running feet pounding in the hallway. A rattling sound.

Three staff members hit the room, one of them pushing a cart.

My nurse holds up a warning hand. "She's a no code."

"No, she's not," I say. "Thank God you guys are here."

The man looks from the nurse to me, and then to the *No Code* sign posted above Mom's bed.

"I'm her daughter. I agreed to the no code, but I didn't know—I didn't mean—I changed my mind. Please, help her."

"Family wishes," the man says to my nurse. "No time to argue. We're on or we're off."

"Is she the decision maker?" another nurse asks.

My nurse nods, and the three go into instant action. I step back to the corner of the room, forgotten and out of the way. The male nurse kneels on Mom's bed, puts his hands on the center of her chest and starts CPR compressions. Her body jolts like a rag doll.

One of the nurses rips off Mom's gown, slapping pads on her chest, hooking her up to a machine. Another administers medication into her IV with a syringe. Somebody else holds a mask attached to a bag over her nose and mouth, pumping air into her lungs.

I can't even see her anymore, she's so surrounded by people.

Then, just like on TV, somebody shouts, "Clear!" The man doing CPR lifts his hands. Everything stops. Mom's body jolts. They all wait.

And then it starts again.

A hand grasps mine, and I glance up into blue eyes luminous with compassion. "Come away. You don't need to watch this."

It's tempting to let this kind person lead me away, but I twist free of her and shake my head. This is my fault, all this noise and chaos. I insisted on trying to bring Mom back; if she chooses to come back, the least I can do is be here when it happens. To listen if there's a miracle of last words. To tell her, if she regains consciousness, that I'm sorry.

And still, through all this overwhelming grief and fear and loss, my anger is an ever-present demon. It tangles itself in all the other emotions, stealing the sweetness from my love, poisoning my fear. I watch from the doorway, until finally everything stops.

"I'm calling it," somebody says. "It's 9:56."

Shoulders droop. Heads bow. But only for an instant. Then gloves and gowns start coming off. Leads are disconnected. Machines are turned off. Somebody rolls the crash cart out of the room.

A pair of eyes finds me; the man who called time. "Oh my God. What is she doing here?" he asks a nurse who is pulling a sheet up over my mother.

But nobody stops me as I drift from my corner over to the bed. Mom is naked under the hastily pulled-up sheet. There's a tube taped to her mouth. IVs in both arms. Pads stuck to her chest. Her hair sticks up wildly on her head.

The room is deathly silent.

"No loved one should have to watch this," the man says. "Let us clean her up, and then you can come to say good-bye."

"I'm the one who wanted this." My voice breaks on a sob. Tears start pouring, and it feels like they're coming from somewhere other than my eyes, somewhere deep at my center, where a vital part of me has broken open. I double up around the damaged place, both arms folded over my belly, trying to suck in air. Breath refuses to cooperate. I'm too broken inside. Blackness traces the edges of my vision. A loud roaring fills my ears. My knees are going loose, and I'm just about to fall when breath finally comes rushing into my oxygen-starved lungs.

My body makes a noise I didn't know I was capable of, a loud keening wail of loss and betrayal. "No. No, no, no, no, no."

There are voices telling me to breathe. Hands pushing and pulling, compelling me away from my mother's still form laid out on the bed. Away from the terrible silence caused by her lack of breathing. I have no clear awareness of where we are going until I find myself sitting somewhere dim and quiet, all the voices gone.

When my vision clears enough to see, I'm looking directly at an angel. White wings, outstretched hands, face all kindness and compassion.

Only a statue, and I'm glad it isn't real. Any angel coming to me now will be an avenging being. My last words to my mother contained anger and accusation, and then I brought down a whirlwind of torment on her.

I'm as shocked by this as I am by the suddenness of her death, the way she could be breathing one moment and not breathing the next.

Here.

Not here.

My mother.

Some stranger with a lifetime full of secrets.

These conflicting realities sit side by side, and I can't summon an emotional connection to either of them.

"Here. Drink this."

Not the angel talking to me, but a mere human, more boy than man, sporting a still-adolescent beard. He offers a glass of water and a sympathetic smile. To me, the smile looks pasted on. A solicitous mask that he's learned from somewhere and donned.

Comforting Expression Number 3, for a grieving woman in shock.

He pushes the glass of water into my nerveless hands. "Drink a little. Really. It's good for shock."

Shock. Is that what this is? I feel like I'm encased in a shell of ice. If I move, if I drink the water he's extending to me, the ice will crack, and I will feel . . . something. I'm not at all sure I want to do that, but my hands move of their own accord, accepting the glass and bringing it to my lips.

He's right.

The sensation of ice-cold water flowing down my throat, into my stomach, serves to wake up the rest of my body. My arms and legs feel weighted, and there's an elephant sitting on my chest.

"Better?" the man asks.

I nod, not speaking yet, and take another swallow.

"I'm Chaplain Ross. Would it be all right if I pray for you?"

It's phrased as a question, but it's not meant that way. He is hell-bent on prayer. I can feel it. And at the moment, I'm not on the sort of terms with God where this is a comforting idea. But my childhood beliefs are deeply ingrained, and saying I don't want his prayer feels like sacrilege.

He pats my hand. His is clammy. He smells sweaty, nervous. If I were a better person, maybe I'd feel some kindness toward him, but as it turns out the very first emotion to really hit me here in the chapel is irritation.

"I know you're heartbroken right now," he says, still patting, "but I assure you, there is comfort in God."

"How old are you?" I ask him.

He blinks rapidly. His eyes are pink-rimmed, the lashes so pale they are barely visible.

"I don't think that is relevant—"

"I think it is. You want to tell me about the comfort of God. I'd like to know if you're old enough to have ever needed comfort."

"Age has very little to do with the need for God." He says it politely enough, but with an edge that is a reprimand. Point taken. I don't know his life. Maybe he was an abused and battered child. Maybe his entire family was killed by a drunk driver when he was six.

I don't know. I don't want to know.

"What is your faith base?" he asks.

"I don't know what you mean."

"Do you attend a church?"

I don't. I haven't been inside a church in years. "Lutheran, I guess," I tell him, giving him the church of my childhood, the church my parents still attend. Or have attended.

"Our Father," Chaplain Ross intones, his voice dropping into a soulful register, "we know that you are the source of comfort for all who mourn. Our help, our rock, our solace . . ."

If he'd gone for a genuine heartfelt, please-bless-Maisey sort of prayer, I might have stayed. It is quiet and peaceful here in the chapel. But I'm not going to hang around and listen to this fledgling boy–man use prayer as an opportunity to tell God what he already knows.

Without apology, I get up and slip away. The chaplain, eyes firmly shut, continues to pray. Maybe it will do him some good. There's precious little hope for me.

Leah's Journal

In fairness to myself and all my decisions, I will allow myself to invoke my childhood as a defense. Is it strange that I don't miss my parents? I never missed them. Not once since I fled my old life to manufacture this one have I even been tempted to contact them. Probably they are dead by now.

Does this make me a bad person, Walter? I can see the sorrowful expression on your face if I were to tell you this. Never judgment from you—never that—but still. Deep in your eyes, a change in your opinion of me. You, who would never abandon anybody.

You cared for both of your parents until they died. Supported your sister through cancer, talking to her every day, never shying away from her pain. How different my life would have been if I were more like you. But I am who I am, and I have done what I have done.

Does it help if I say that the presence of both my mother and my father in my childhood was superficial and had less impact than my favorite books? Dad was an alcoholic, and Mom was a shell of hopelessness. I don't blame them for this, mind you. Both of them were carrying out longstanding family traditions. I don't imagine it occurred to them that there might be another way to be.

Neither one of them beat me or was even verbally abusive. They didn't have the energy to spare for that. I didn't matter enough to them for that. I vaguely remember that Mom might have worked when I was little, before the baby brother came along, only to be snuffed out in a meaningless crib death. After that, she did nothing but watch TV and smoke, endlessly. One or the other of them bought groceries, at least until I was old enough to be sent to the store. Nobody cleaned house in any meaningful sort of fashion.

My grandmother, my father's mother, was the salvation of my childhood. All that I remember of hugs and stories and security came from her. I remember her apartment, overwarm and cramped but clean. It smelled of lemon and vanilla, not tobacco and whiskey. She baked cookies for me. She would make the dough, and we would lay them out on the cookie sheet, her crooked old hands and my young ones side-by-side, working together.

She died when I was fourteen, and the empty hole she left in my world was the portal into what happened next.

Chapter Twelve

The doorway of Dad's hospital room stops me like a force field. I stand there, watching him, my body and my emotions trying to encompass this new shift in reality.

Walter Addington. The man I've called Dad all my life, the parent I've always been the closest to.

Whether he is really my father or not, whether he lied to me or not, my love for him is deeply rooted, and it's my job, now, to tell him that Mom has left us both.

He's sitting up in a chair today, no longer tied to the bed. His hair is combed. But he still looks frail and old and so very much alone. A wave of grief swamps me. How can I do this? How can I be the one to walk in and tell him?

I find myself hoping he's still confused, that the truth about Mom's death won't sink in.

His eyes, focused on the TV mounted above his bed, finally swing around to me, and I don't have to say the words at all.

"It's over, then," he says. "Was it peaceful?"

No, it wasn't peaceful. It was a final battle of wills between her and me, and I've lost again. Shame shoulders its way into my already toxic mixture of grief and anger and betrayal. Maybe I'm a coward; maybe it's the better part of me trying to protect him, but I can't tell him the truth.

"It was peaceful," I tell him. "She died in her sleep."

"Ah, Maisey," he says, and opens his arms to me.

It's not the time to tell him what I know. To ask questions, to express my betrayal. That one small gesture from him turns me into a frightened, wounded child, and I fall on my knees and wrap my arms around him, resting my head against his chest.

For a long time he holds me there, stroking my hair. I melt against him, my ear pressed against his chest, listening to his heartbeat, letting myself believe that he is strong, that he will take care of me.

"I need to go home. Please, Maisey. Take me home." He looks lost, more like a frightened child than an old man, despite the lines carved into his face and his thinning hair.

"We need to talk to the doctor first."

Both of his hands go up to the sides of his head, as if it hurts him, and he squeezes. "Can't think. Need to think. She made a list."

"Dad."

His bloodshot eyes focus in on me. His hands clamp around mine so tightly, I gasp with the pain of my rings digging into my flesh.

"Where is she, Maisey? What did they do with her?"

I think he's already forgotten, and now I have to say the words. "She died, Daddy. I got mad at her, and then she died."

Please. Please listen to me. Please be here for me. Please understand what I need. And then maybe you can tell me all about this massive fairy-tale life you and Mom concocted. Maybe you can explain the why and wherefore.

My knees ache from contact with the hard floor. My body feels like it's been worked over by a meat hammer. Everything hurts, from the roots of my hair down to the tip of my baby toenail.

"She wanted to die," he whispers, easing up on my hands. "But where is she? Where have they put her?"

"I don't know. It just happened. I asked her about Marley, and then she died."

His body stills. His hands go slack. I think he's heard me, that he's going to answer, that despite his grief and confusion maybe he will tell me the truth. But then his jaw wobbles. Tears fill his eyes and drip down over his cheeks.

"Where's Leah?" he whispers. "What have they done with her?"

"Hey," another voice says from behind me. "I heard. How are you holding up?"

Dr. Margoni rests a cool hand on my shoulder. "How are your knees? Let me get you a chair."

"Maisey," Dad says, again. "Where is your mother?"

"Daddy, I've told you. Please don't make me tell you again."

"Going in circles?" Dr. Margoni asks. She sets a visitor's chair down beside Dad and extends a hand to help me to my feet.

"It's like that *Groundhog Day* movie, only worse."

"I like *Groundhog Day*," Dad says. "What's his name, that actor? And Andie. She's wonderful. Leah gets jealous, how much I like Andie. Hey, even an old man still has eyes."

"Bill Murray," Dr. Margoni says. "The part with the puddle. I like that. I stepped in a puddle on my way here. Would have been nice to know it was there."

"Happy endings," Dad says. "The ending is good."

Not this ending, I want to tell him. *This ending really sucks.* But he already looks sad, and I can't tell him about Mom again.

Dr. Margoni seems to read my mind. "This isn't the end yet," she says, softly. "We're at the messy middle."

Boy howdy, does she have that right. She has no idea how messy.

"So you do have a decision to make," she says, after we're all quiet for a minute, reminding me that I am now the responsible adult in the family. There will be plenty of decisions. God, I hadn't even thought about the funeral. Maybe if my long-lost sister were here, she'd help me plan it.

Dr. Margoni isn't thinking about the funeral. "What are you going to do when your dad is ready to discharge from the hospital?"

"What? Oh. I hadn't even thought that far."

Dad has slipped away from us altogether, eyes closed, chin on his chest.

"I'm going to keep him another day. Per Medicare, if he's admitted for three days running, we can transfer him directly into another facility."

No, no, no. I can't have heard her right. "You mean a nursing home?"

"I was thinking more of assisted living. He'd have more privacy and autonomy than in a nursing home. I know it's hard," she goes on. "But he can't stay here. He's certainly not able to care for himself at home. Even if his altered mental state is just due to grief and being off his medications, it would be pretty hard for him to manage on his own."

A memory comes to me, of Dad staying up with me one long night when I had an ear infection. The doctor's office was closed, and Mom was not about to incur an emergency room bill. She dosed me with Tylenol and sent me to bed. It was Dad who heard me sobbing with pain at midnight and came to comfort me. All that long night, he sat on my bed with my feverish head in his lap, stroking my hair, distracting me with funny stories, feeding me more Tylenol every four hours around the clock.

"He'll get better, though, right? This is just grief and shock and not taking his meds."

"Possibly," Dr. Margoni says, but there is too much hesitation in the way she shapes the word. "It's hard to tell. Sometimes it takes weeks for an elderly person to bounce back from an illness."

Dad jerks awake, startling my heart into a gallop. "Leah," he says. "We need to tell Maisey. You can't—" And then his eyes fall on me. "Oh dear. Oh hell. Do you know?"

Where is he in time, and which question is he asking? The aneurism in my mother's brain? Her past life? Marley?

"Yes, I know," I say. "I know everything. It's okay." I keep patting his hand, my heart free-falling over and over, no safety net to catch it. It's not okay. He's not okay. Some things time cannot fix.

"I told her we should tell you," he says. "Over and over, I told her, 'Just call her, Leah. Or let me call her. Let her come to say good-bye.'"

"I was here, Daddy. I was with her when she died."

"I need to see her. Take me."

He presses against the chair arms with his hands and leans forward. His whole body is vibrating, though, and this time when he tries to stand, he only clears a couple of inches from the chair before he falls back. It doesn't stop him. He tries again.

A vivid image of my mother the way I left her makes me hold him back.

"Not a good idea. Not now."

"It might help him," Dr. Margoni says, very gently. "To see her body. It might help him retain the finality and let her go."

I shake my head, but I can't say anything. If I open my mouth, I'm going to vomit, and I clamp my lips tight together and drag deep breaths in through my nose, trying to settle the stormy seas in my belly.

"Let me see if they've got her cleaned up," Dr. Margoni says. She squeezes my shoulder, gently, and leaves the room.

Dad tries to get up, and again I press him back.

"We'll go in a minute, okay? Just hang on. We'll go see her."

It seems longer than a minute before Dr. Margoni shows back up, this time with a wheelchair. "Let's take a ride," she says. Her calm, professional compassion helps me calm my own body. The two of us help Dad up onto his shaky feet and into the chair. But the reluctance to go back to that war zone of a room, to confront the body of my mother—after I defied her wishes and tried to make her live, after the things I said to her and knowing the lies she told me—is overpowering.

I sink into Dad's chair, still warm with his body heat. "Maybe I'll wait here."

"You might find it helpful to see her one more time," Dr. Margoni says. "Otherwise you're going to be stuck with that last visual."

I press my hands against my eyes, making black spots dance, but I still can't shut it out.

"I need you," Dad says, stretching out a tremulous hand. "Be with me, Maisey."

Which does it, of course. I've lost my mother and my entire framework for reality. He's lost the woman whose secrets he's kept for almost forty years, whoever she was. So I get up and follow the wheelchair down the hall. We go to a different room, for which I'm grateful. It's a corner room with windows on two walls, letting in sunlight and the reminder that outside there are blue skies and timeless mountains.

Mom lies in a hospital bed, a sheet pulled up over her chest, her hands folded over it. She wears a clean hospital gown. Her hair is neatly combed, her face washed, the horrible tube removed from her mouth. Except for the color of her skin, which is all kinds of wrong, she almost looks like she's sleeping.

Still, I hang back at the door while Dr. Margoni rolls Dad up to the bed.

"Leah," he whispers, touching her hand. "Oh, Leah. It should have been me."

I'm braced for an emotional storm, but it doesn't come. He just sits there, almost as still as she is. When he pushes himself up to standing, Dr. Margoni doesn't stop him. Dad smooths Mom's hair, touches her cheek, leans down to kiss her lips.

"Soon," he whispers. "It won't be long." He lets out a long, tremulous sigh that leaves him smaller, older, frailer, if such a thing is possible, then falls back into the chair.

Dr. Margoni looks at me, eyebrows raised in a question.

The answer is no. No, no, a thousand times no. Mom looks peaceful enough from where I'm standing, but closer-up death will get me with a bitch slap. I don't want to smell it on her. Don't want to touch her skin now that the soul is gone. Don't want to risk her eyes snapping open, her finger rising to point at me, her dead lips opening to croak, "You are in so much trouble, Maisey Dawn."

I don't need her to put any more guilt on me.

So I stay where I am, feet planted, spine stiffened by stubbornness and fear. The tears betray me, though, running down my cheeks, warm and alive where the rest of me feels as cold and dead as my mother looks.

Dr. Margoni crosses the room, takes my right hand, and uncurls the fingers I've clenched into a fist. She tugs at me, gently, and my feet obey, taking me to the bed, to my mother.

Her skin is as cold as I expected when I touch her hand, and her face looks subtly different, like one of those wax museum figures. I shiver at the idea that maybe she'll start to melt if I touch her.

"Just tell her good-bye."

I don't want to tell her good-bye. I'm not ready to let her go. Not yet, not like this. But I feel compelled to tell her something, and I lean down and press my cheek against her cold one. I mean to tell her I love her. That I'm sorry my last words to her were angry. But what comes whispering out of my lips is not at all what I thought I wanted to say. Not angry words this time, but lost and bereft, with the bewilderment of a child.

"What happened to my sister?"

Leah's Journal

And here we are. The pivot point where this story turns, the balance point of my sins, the advent of the man who spread a shadow over the rest of my life.

I don't want to talk about him. I don't want to invoke his name. It feels like summoning the devil.

Here I sit. Five minutes after writing those first lines, my hands are shaking. Heart racing. I want to burn this page, tear it into tiny pieces, scribble out the ink, and I haven't even written down his name.

My rational mind tells me you won't see this, Walter. He won't see this. Nobody will see it, and contrary to what my imagination is wanting to tell me, he has no magical powers that would let him see what I'm writing here.

He is not a devil or a god. He is not all-knowing or all-powerful.

Alexander Garrison. The father of my children. Nickname: Boots.

There, I've done it. The world is still standing. Wouldn't it be ironic if confronting my fear and my past was the thing that ruptured my aneurism? But it hasn't. And I shall go on.

"Boots" sounds like a diminutive, doesn't it? Something you would name a cat or a hamster.

There was nothing diminutive about him. He was nobody's pet anything, not even his mother's. He was always dangerous, and there lay half of the attraction. That hair, red-gold masses of it down onto his shoulders. Green eyes. That in itself would have been enough to make all of us girls swoon, but then there was the music. Put a guitar in his hands, and he was elevated from swoon-worthy to a young god.

I was invisible to him at first. Four years younger and hiding in the shadows at school. A little too smart for my own good. A little too poor, a little too adrift.

He noticed me first at a homecoming dance. I was fifteen and in tenth grade. He was nineteen and in the graduating class. I'd borrowed a dress from a friend. Saved up money to buy department store makeup. I had my first date, with another invisible kid like me. God help me, I can't even remember his name. Can barely remember his face.

Boots swaggered in late, a rebel. Always a rebel. Everybody else all dressed up, tuxedos and ball gowns, and him in a black T-shirt, faded Levi's, and those shiny leather cowboy boots, the ones that gave him his nickname.

I'd seen him before, of course, in the hallways at school, had heard whispers and rumors.

But that night, I was awestruck. I'll admit it. I coveted the way he walked, those boots clumping down as if he owned the floor they walked on. The bold way his gaze cut through the crowd. The way his chin tilted, the slight smirk of superiority that said he knew damn well he was better than the rest of us.

That night, those eyes fell on me, standing alone by the snacks table.

I wish to God I had been standing elsewhere. I wish I had been smarter or been less vulnerable or had a parent who might have intervened in what was to come. But what is the point of wishing? What is done is done, and there is no going back.

Writing this, today, I feel the weight of that stare, as if he can see me still from so many years and so many miles away. I can't help feeling that he knows I am writing this. His eyes say that I've broken my promise, and now he has license to break his. He can't possibly know, of course. I am just a coward, caught in a hard place between death and a memory. Would you think less of me if I told you that death seems the friendlier option?

I have grown weak, it seems. This is too much for me tonight. Tomorrow I will gather the shreds of my courage to go on, but for now I will say only this. His gaze fell on me. And young fool that I was, I welcomed it. Welcomed him. Offered him a cigarette from the pack I'd stolen out of Mom's purse, even though I didn't smoke. The appearance of coolness was everything.

So I offered up a smoke, and he offered up . . .

Tomorrow, tomorrow. I'll write it tomorrow. I am a coward still, after all these years.

Chapter Thirteen

I tell Elle that I'm just running next door to see if I can borrow a couple of eggs for a late breakfast, but what I'm really planning to do is pump Mrs. Carlton for information.

Elle has super sensors when it comes to evasion and doesn't let me get away with it.

"I'll come with you," she says.

"Wait here. I'll only be a second."

"Mom—"

"Elle, for once, listen to me. She's not the fun sort of neighbor. Stay here. I'll be right back."

I close the door firmly between us. The air is cold. Rain slants down out of a gray sky. I should go back into the house for a coat, but then I'll have to fight Elle all over again.

Ducking my head, I race across the wet lawn, fat drops of water bouncing off my head. The steps of the Carltons' porch are sagging. Spiderwebs wrap around the support posts.

The paint on the front door, once a definitive mallard green, is faded and peeling, and when I knock, a flake comes loose and drifts down toward my toes. A straw broom leans up against the door, but judging from the little drift of dirt and debris lodged against it, sweeping hasn't happened in a while.

"Is she a witch?" Elle asks, behind me.

I swing around, bumping my elbow on the doorframe. "I told you to stay in the house."

"But what if you never come back? Like if she puts you in the oven or something?" She keeps her tone light, but her hand creeps into mine the way it used to when she was a little girl.

Memory strikes. Mom reading "Hansel and Gretel." Marley afraid of the witch, wondering whether Mrs. Carlton has a big enough oven to roast a little girl in. Not really Marley, I remind myself. I only imagined her.

Before I can detach Elle and send her back, the door swings open, loosening an assault of bleach fumes out onto the porch.

Edna Carlton has been old as long as I can remember, but the walker is new. The tight gray bun, spiked with black hairpins, is the same, as are the glimpses of pink scalp on the top of her head. Her eyes, black and clever like a crow's, are as bright and sharp as ever. I feel awkward and about ten years old; it's all I can do to keep from shuffling my feet and twirling the hem of my T-shirt around my fingers.

"Mrs. Carlton. Hi. Good morning."

"Maisey Dawn. It's been long enough. A woman should visit her aging parents, I always say. Might have prevented this current disaster, in fact." Her eyes shift to Elle. "Well, well, well. Almost grown up already. She favors you more than her father, I think."

"Listen, Mrs. Carlton, I just came over to tell you that my mother . . . passed . . . yesterday." I hate the word even as I say it. What does *passed* even mean? Some sort of entrance exam to the next life?

It's impossible to read the expression on the old woman's face as she takes in this news. She tilts her head to one side. "And where's your father? Jailed for murder? Oh yes. I heard the cops talking. Terrible thing. Unbelievable."

Elle's fingers tighten around mine, and I squeeze hard, half comfort, half warning not to engage. "Dad's in the hospital; he was severely dehydrated and ill. Listen, we can't stay long. I was wondering—"

"If I'd help plan the funeral. Of course. Your mother was a wonderful, God-fearing woman, and she should have a wonderful send-off. You won't have a clue who her friends are or who should be part of the service. I'm so glad you at least had the sense to ask me."

More guilt. Mrs. Carlton is right, of course. I don't know who to ask. I'm not even sure what a church funeral looks like.

"Well, are you coming in? Heat's not getting any cheaper," Mrs. Carlton says, interrupting my thoughts. I take one last breath of cool, rain-fresh air and enter the house, Elle right behind me. Bleach fumes set my eyes to watering and sear the lining of my nose. Sauna-level heat intensifies its effects, making a bleach-nebulizer that burns my lungs. Elle sneezes, loudly, and earns a glare from Mrs. Carlton, who produces a tissue from one of her pockets and tucks it into my daughter's reluctant hand.

"Come and sit a spell." Mrs. Carlton turns her back and shuffles down the hall.

Elle holds the tissue with the tips of her thumb and forefinger, *ewww* written all over her face, and I gesture maniacally for her to just put it in her pocket.

Oblivious to Elle's antics, or at least I hope so anyway, Edna stays on course and doesn't turn around. She doesn't seem to lean on the walker, and as we follow her down the spotless hallway, I catch her picking the thing up and carrying it for a step or two before remembering that she's supposed to lean on it, not use it as a fashion accessory.

The sitting room hasn't changed at all since my childhood. The blinds are closed tight to keep the sun from fading either the carpet or furniture. Same stiff old couch and chairs, same dull beige lampshades, all still covered in plastic to keep off the dirt.

Elle and I lower ourselves gingerly onto the sofa, planting our feet to keep from sliding forward off the slick surface.

"I used to babysit your mother," Mrs. Carlton says to Elle. Her voice is grinding and harsh, out of keeping with a tiny frame so aerodynamic that she seems to hover above the armchair, still gripping the walker to keep herself from drifting away. I keep sneaking glimpses to see if her butt is touching the chair.

"I remember."

Mrs. Carlton wasn't my mother's first choice of babysitter, but she couldn't argue with the convenience of having childcare right next door, or with the price, which was free. There were days, mostly during tax season, when both of my parents stayed late at the office. On those days, when the school bus dropped me off, I would do my homework at Mrs. Carlton's kitchen table, while her venomous gossip poured over me and gave me insights a kid definitely didn't need into the behaviors of all the neighbors.

I remember tasteless dinners, and the misery of washing dishes afterward and never getting them clean enough to satisfy.

"It won't hurt you," Mom said when I complained. "Life isn't all fun and games, Maisey."

"You were just a bitty thing when your folks moved in," Mrs. Carlton is saying now. "Maybe three and so precocious. Watchful, you were. All big eyes. You had a way of hiding in plain sight. You'd be sitting right there, and all the adults would forget about you. Freakish for a child that age, I always thought."

My ears perk up. This is exactly the direction I want this conversation to go. If anybody knows the secrets my parents have been keeping, it will be Edna Carlton.

"Life is truly a vale of tears. Your mother was far too young. How old was she, now? She can't have been more than twenty when she moved in here with your father. When I asked if her mother knew she'd moved in with an older man, she just about tore a strip off my hide. Total spitfire, I tell you. Informed me that she was of an age, thank you very much, and that who she'd married was none of her mother's business and certainly none of mine. Then she slammed her door in my face, and it was two weeks before she consented to speak with me again, and then only because she was in need of a babysitter."

"She'd been sick," I say, as soon as I can squeeze a few words into the torrent. "I don't suppose they told you."

"Hmmmph." Edna actually says this, pronouncing all the phonetics. I've always thought when I saw *hmmmph* in books that it was an exaggeration of a sigh or a *hmmm*. Nope. There's actual spittle involved; an errant ray of sunlight sneaking in past the closed blinds highlights the tiny drops and turns them into rainbows.

"What are you looking at, Maisey? You always were the strange child, staring off into nothing like you could see the dead wandering about. Can you?"

Startled out of my musing on rainbows and spittle, I stare at her, blankly looking for the right answer to her question.

"Can I what?"

"See dead people."

I blink back a vision of my mother's dead body as I saw it before she was cleaned up and made presentable. If she were to haunt me, she would come to me like that, vengeful and trailing IV tubes and EKG wires. I wish I'd let her go peacefully. I wish I could go back to that instant and make a different decision. Regret sits like a boulder where my stomach used to be.

"She means like ghosts," Elle says, helpfully, scuffing her feet in the perfect carpet and then catching herself as she starts to slide forward off the slick plastic. "Obviously you can see dead people."

"Right." I scrub my sleeve over my eyes and swallow to steady my throat. "No. I don't see ghosts. I was probably daydreaming. I did that."

"Looks like you still do."

My right hand curls into a fist, and I force it flat and slide it under my butt where it will behave itself. *I will remain calm. I will remain calm. I will not rise to her bait.*

"Did you notice anything different with my parents in the last few months?" I ask, steering the conversation toward what I really want to know.

"Besides the part where he hit her over the head and let her lie there for three days without calling for help? If I hadn't come over to check on her, the poor dear would have died right there in her bed."

"She had an aneurism. She fell."

"Or maybe he pushed her."

And that's it. My tolerance is done. I don't care that she's an old woman. I don't care that my father isn't technically my father. I don't care that I'd planned to try to weasel information out of her about my childhood and my parents and whether she knows anything about Marley.

I'm on my feet, the air crackling around me like I'm about to burst into flames.

"Give me one reason to believe my father would hurt her. Just one."

Edna cowers back away from me, both hands raised in front of her face as if she thinks I'll actually hit her. She's tiny and ancient and bitter. Shame infiltrates my rage, but I don't back down. Not yet.

"Well?"

"I was just theorizing," she quavers. "It's the way of men."

"Not all men. Not this one." Another childhood memory rises from the depths, summoned by her words. Edna had a husband once. He's long dead, but I remember him as lean, stringy, and oddly yellow. I asked my mother about the color of his skin, the yellowed whites of his eyes.

"Too much beer," she'd said, and that was all. At that age I'd imagined the beer actually settling into his skin and eyes and wondered why it didn't turn him brown. Now, seeing her hunched up and trembling in the face of my anger, I wonder if the story she's manufactured for my parents is born out of one of her own.

I make an effort to soften my voice. "Did you hear anything, see anything? Was he shouting at her?"

"You want to know the truth? I'll tell you. *She* shouted at *him*. I heard yelling a couple of times, so loud it came into my house through closed windows. Not to speak ill of the dead."

"What was she saying?"

Edna settles her face into calm propriety, folding her hands in her lap. "I am not an eavesdropper."

Right. And birds don't fly.

On the rare occasions I heard my parents fight, it was always because Dad refused to follow some directive or other. Despite his quiet nature and his abhorrence of fuss and emotional outbursts, if he didn't agree on something, he would tell her. He went along with her on most things, but every now and then, she'd run up against a streak of iron in him that would not budge or bend. And then the sparks would fly until she accepted the inevitable and either found a way around him or acknowledged that he was right.

Maybe it's dementia, but the out-of-character things Dad has been doing—burning papers, not calling an ambulance—could also be the result of my mother's planning. Dad would have fought her at first and then would have given in because what else are you going to do when the woman you love is about to die? And once Dad makes a promise, he keeps it.

"Could you hear what they were fighting about?"

"Mostly I couldn't make out the words. But the one time I just happened to be standing on the lawn, and I heard him say, 'God damn it, Leah, don't you make me do this!' Just like every abusing lowlife scum ever says, blaming the woman for his behavior. And then she said, 'And when I'm dead, then how are you going to feel?'"

My stomach twists and twists, putting my own spin on these words rather than the one Mrs. Carlton has manufactured out of her own perspective. I can picture my father, pushed to the breaking point. Mom hammering away at him with a combination of logic and manipulation, with that final, masterful thrust of guilt to finish him off.

"Well," I say, "I suppose you told this to the cops? That's why they believe he's been beating her. Did you ever see her injured? Did she have a black eye?"

"I'm not stupid," Mrs. Carlton retorts, confirming my suspicions in the way her blue-veined arms unconsciously hug her rib cage. "Men hit where the bruises don't show."

I initiate a silent count to ten, trying to rein in my temper, but I've forgotten about Elle.

She bounces up off the couch and unexpectedly turns on me, rather than on Mrs. Carlton. "Seriously, Mom? You're going to just let her say this shit? Grandpa would never hit Grandma. Right? Tell her!"

"Elle—"

"What? This is all so stupid! And they think *Grandpa's* crazy." She bursts into tears and runs out of the room. In the stunned silence that follows in her wake, the slamming of the door is loud and clear.

"Well. I never," Edna exclaims, but there's no venom in her words.

"Excuse me. I'll check in later about the funeral," I manage, and then I'm down the hall, out the door, and after my daughter. I catch up to her before she makes it across the lawn.

"Elle." I grab hold of her arm, but she jerks it out of my grip.

Tears track down her cheeks. "How could you let her say all of that . . . *shit*? She's a horrible old woman. I hate her!"

"Elle. Elle!"

Back ramrod straight, she marches up the steps and into the house. I follow, all the way down the hall to my old bedroom, where she flings herself facedown on the bed in an abandon of dramatic misery.

Memory of the thousand and one times I pulled a similar move almost makes me smile, despite my own heartbreak and confusion. It never helped me when Mom followed and tried to talk me out of a fit of despair, so instead I just sit there and stroke Elle's hair.

She allows this, which is a good sign, and after a few minutes she asks, "You don't really believe that bullshit?" Her voice is garbled by the pillow, but I'm skilled at deciphering.

"I don't believe it. No."

"Then how could you *let* her?" She rolls over and stares up at me, flushed and tearstained and utterly beautiful in her outrage.

The decision to tell her sort of makes itself. One minute I'm trying to think up an evasive half-truth and the next my mouth is moving.

"I was gathering intel. Like a spy. So I wanted her to keep talking."

"What kind of intel?" Curiosity has trumped her grief. I recognize the tone of her voice. I consider, for the umpteenth time, sending her home to her father. And then I figure, what the hell? She already knows half of it and will put the rest of the pieces together all by herself if I don't bring her in.

So I tell her about what I found at the bank. About the fact that my father is apparently not my father. By the time I'm done, she's sitting up cross-legged in bed, looking like she's never shed a tear in her life. Her eyes glow with enthusiasm and curiosity.

"We have to find out," she says, bouncing a little on the mattress.

"Grandpa is not exactly a good source of information right now."

"Google," she says, off the bed and rummaging in her backpack. "What was your sister's name again?"

"Marley."

"Last name."

"Garrison. I hardly think we can just type in a couple of names and presto, magically find people who have probably been dead for years."

Elle plops back down with her iPad in her lap. "I can see why they wouldn't tell you about your father. I mean, if Grandma left him, then there's a reason for that, right? And I can see why she wouldn't want to talk about that. But why wouldn't she tell you about your very own sister?"

This is a very good question. Elle is not content with asking questions; she's already on a hunt for answers.

"Do we even have wireless? Oh, never mind, there it is. WalterandLeah. Not exactly imaginative. What's the password?"

"A12345."

She stares at me. "You're kidding."

"It's been that ever since they first got wireless. Neither one of them are—were—big on creativity. I told you."

"All the neighbors are probably getting a free ride on their wireless," she says, tapping away.

"Especially Mrs. Carlton."

Elle giggles. "Probably using their wireless to watch porn."

"Elle!" My reprimand is spoiled by laughter of my own. The concept is so ludicrous.

"Holy shazam," Elle whispers, staring at the screen. "I mean, I thought we'd find something. But this?"

"What? Show me!"

I climb up on the bed beside her, and she turns the tablet so I can see, not some sad old obituary for a baby, but an advertisement for a country and western band called Forsaken. Three men with guitars and a woman holding a violin. The picture was taken in front of a crumbling barn, a red sunset vivid in the background. The effect is apocalyptic and unsettling.

"What does this have to do with anything?"

Elle stabs her finger at the woman with the violin. "Meet Marley Garrison."

"Oh, come on, Elle. That's just way too easy. How many Marley Garrisons are there in the world?"

"She lives in Washington. In a place called . . . Finley. Where's Finley?"

"Right outside of Pasco. This is insane, Elle."

"Wait. Let's make her bigger so we can see if she looks like you." She moves her fingers apart and Apple does its magic, enlarging the woman's face. "Whoa. That's freaky."

"What? Let me see."

Elle has the tablet up close to her face, squinting at it with one eye and then the other. "This Marley person looks more like Grandma than you do. She could be Grandma. Well, if Grandma wasn't dead, I mean."

The word *dead* splatters over me like a bucket of ice water over the head, breaking through the numbness of my shock and raising a terrible, empty ache at the center of my chest where my heart is no longer beating. I can't get a breath either in or out, and for one eternal moment I think maybe I'm going to die here and now.

Heat comes rushing back in, and with it breath whooshes into my lungs. My heart makes up for lost time, running way too fast.

"Look," Elle says, turning the screen. She's magnified the photo of the woman so that her face fills the screen. I feel like I'm looking at a ghost.

This is my mother's face. The same lips, the same cheekbones—even the way the hair swirls up and off her forehead in a smooth wave. The hair is blonde and curly, not dark and smooth, but a perm and some bleach could pull that off easily enough.

What haunts me most is seeing my eyes in my mother's face, wearing an expression that could never be mine. They are the same wide-set, blue-green eyes that look at me out of the mirror every day. But where mine always seem to be asking questions, hers have all the answers.

The screen wavers in front of me, and I realize my hands are shaking. I close my eyes to break the spell, to shut out this face, and immediately see the child version, the imaginary friend Marley of my childhood. I can't begin to understand what happened here. How my over-responsible, zealous, helicopter parent of a mother could have somehow forgotten a child.

Waves of dizziness wash over me, and Elle barely rescues the tablet from a plunge to the floor. I fall back on the bed, staring up at the ceiling.

"We have to go see her," Elle says. "We can listen to the band. And then you can talk to her after."

My lips are numb, and my voice sounds foreign to my own ears. "We can't go anywhere right now, Elle Belle. We have Grandma's funeral to plan. And we have to figure out what to do about Grandpa."

"We don't have to go anywhere. They'll be here. Well, almost here. Kettle Falls at the Northern Ales on, let's see, Friday night. Family friendly, it says, so don't even think about not taking me with you."

"Elle. We can't go."

I say it with conviction, but I'm torn. Marley. After all these years. The possibility of seeing her, of connecting, of doing something about those ragged threads of incomplete memories that keep snagging my current reality and tugging me backward is deeply alluring.

"Why can't we go?" Elle demands.

"Because Grandma. People don't go to concerts right after somebody dies."

"I don't see why not." Her face retreats out of my field of vision, leaving me alone with the ceiling. There is a tiny spider up there, moving around on spider business. I let my gaze fixate on him, one small black speck in an expanse of white, or almost white. It comes to me that if Dad goes into a nursing home, I'll need to sell this house to pay for it. And then I get sucked into wondering how I can possibly navigate everything that needs doing here while still maintaining my apartment in Kansas City. I can't afford to fly back and forth. I've already maxed out my credit card to pay for this trip. I can't afford to take more time off.

The truth is, the time I've already taken is going to make it pretty near impossible to cover my bills this month. I live way too close to my margins. The temp agency I'm currently working for doesn't provide benefits, so I'm not getting vacation pay. My only savings resides in the account where Greg deposits child support, a fund that I dip into only when Elle needs something I can't otherwise provide. A familiar web of worry and indecision grounds me in my accustomed reality. The worry points are different, but the feeling is the same. I'm still me, even if my mother is not who I always thought she was. This is strangely comforting. My breath eases, my heart slows. My eyelids grow heavy, and I am sorely tempted to drift off into sleep. Elle, oblivious, keeps up a running commentary, her fingers still moving.

"What's the father's name? On the birth certificate?"

"Alexander Garrison."

"Hmmm. There are a bunch of Alexander Garrisons. Who knows which one it is? But maybe Marley could tell you about him. We are going, right? To the concert?"

I need to tell her no. No, we are not going. But I'm so sleepy now that it's hard to form words. Her chatter is familiar and comforting. I let it circle around me, just the cadence and the music of it, taking pleasure in her enthusiasm without latching on to the meaning. I'll worry about Marley and the concert later.

The next thing I'm aware of is Elle shaking my shoulder. I mumble something and try to roll over. My tongue feels hot and dry, stuck to the roof of my mouth.

"There are people here. You have to wake up!"

"What people?" At least that's what I meant to say, but I hear it come out as "Mmm?"

"You've been sleeping for hours. And I'm hungry, and we're out of pizza. Mom!"

This time, the shake of my shoulder is energetic enough to hurt. My eyes blink open and then squint against the light directly overhead. I bring up my forearm to shield my eyes. In my entire history I've been hungover exactly once, and it's manifestly unfair that I feel that same way now but haven't had the benefit of a single drink. Inventory of my body isn't promising.

Mouth: fuzzy.

Stomach: rebellious.

Brain: sluggish.

Head: pounding.

"Mom. Seriously. You have to get up. There are church ladies in the living room. They are asking an awful lot of questions."

Rolling over onto my side, I push up into a sitting position and sit there, blinking at Elle. She goes in and out of focus, but it's impossible to miss the exasperation. Hands thrown up in the air and that toss of the head are pretty much a universal language.

When she stalks out of the room, I let my throbbing head drop into my hands, rest my elbows on my knees, and try to engage my wayward brain.

Much as I would like to escape out the bedroom window, I need to deal with this.

Elle, still stiff with disapproval, returns with my hairbrush and a dripping washcloth. She holds the cloth out to me, and while I scrub it over my face, she starts brushing out my tangled hair.

"You're a good kid," I mumble, and it's true. She's a great kid, in fact. I don't deserve a kid like this. "Okay. I guess I should go face the music."

"Clothes."

"Elle. It will be fine. What makes you think they're church ladies?"

"They said. They have casseroles. They asked for coffee."

"Oh God." I change into a clean pair of jeans and a nice shirt. It's wrinkled from the suitcase, but there's nothing to be done about that. In the living room, the two armchairs are occupied by Elle's church ladies. One of them is thin, perfectly coiffed, and dressed in a tailored jacket and a pair of gray pants. The other wears a ball cap over shoulder-length hair, a T-shirt, and grass-stained jeans.

Safe-deposit-box Bethany perches on the edge of the couch. The instant she sees me, she's up onto her feet, clacking across the floor on high heels to envelop me in a hug. "You won't tell anybody, will you?" she whispers in my ear. "That I broke the rules about the box?"

"Our little secret," I whisper back, thanking the goddess of silence. I don't need anybody speculating about Mom's advance directive or anything else that might have been stashed in that box.

The woman in the ball cap is waiting for her turn at the hugging. I can't place her at first, and it takes me a minute to peel back the layers of memory and see her as younger, slimmer, and dressed for church. Alison Baldwin. She used to play the piano for church services. Taught a Sunday school class.

Alison's hug is bony but heartfelt. She smells of sweat and fresh-cut grass and gasoline.

"You poor dear. So tragic. Were you able to say good-bye? You got here in time?"

"Yes, I was with her when she died."

Talk about evasions. I was with her, all right. Saying good-bye wasn't exactly what I was doing.

"I apologize for my appearance," Alison says. "I was out working on the lawn when Nancy came by for me. I'd completely lost track of time."

Nancy must be the name of the other woman. I still can't summon up a memory of her. She's got a timeless face and style and was probably wearing a skirt and jacket when she was twelve.

"Your mother was an admirable woman," Nancy says, getting up much more slowly from her chair and not attempting the hug. "A fine Christian and such a strong and giving person. We won't know what to do without her. She will be irreplaceable."

"Truth," Alison says. "Head of the clothing drive. Church board member. She'd recently begun playing piano for the choir. Which reminds me—what are we going to do? There's the July Fourth concert coming up, and we'll have to find someone to fill in." Her gaze swings round to me and lights up. "What about you? You had piano lessons."

I had piano lessons, all right, but even my mother recognized the futility of that endeavor and they were short-lived.

I snort. I don't mean to, but it just happens. It's an unladylike pig snort, and all eyes in the room land on me at once. There's a little dampness on my upper lip on the side of my left nostril, and I hope to the God I don't quite believe in that I haven't ejected a spray of snot. I cross the room for a tissue, which gives me the opportunity to hide my face.

"Not a musical bone in my body. I'm sorry. What about Bethany? You were always much better at piano than me."

"Oh, I couldn't possibly! It's been years and—"

"I didn't know you played the piano!" Alison exclaims. "What a precious gift from the Lord! Why did you never say anything?"

"Like I said, I don't even have a piano and—"

"You could practice at the church," Nancy cuts in. "That piano doesn't get played enough."

"How's your dad doing?" Bethany asks me, a little desperately.

Her ploy works. "Yes, tell us all about your poor father," Alison says. "How is he holding up? This must be so difficult for him."

"Life is truly a vale of tears." Nancy shakes her perfectly coifed head, but her eyes are sharp with curiosity, not soft with grief, and I am on my guard.

"How about I go make us some coffee and put the casseroles in the fridge?" Bethany asks, brightly, and vanishes before anybody has a chance to object or bring up the piano again.

"Where *is* your father?" Nancy cuts her eyes around the room, as if expecting to see him hiding behind the recliner or the drapes.

"In the hospital. He's been very . . . confused . . . since Mom died. The doctor wants to put him in a facility."

"Oh, surely not!" both women exclaim at once.

"Jinx," Elle whispers, but either they don't hear her or have no idea what she's talking about.

"I heard—forgive me if this is difficult, but I heard that the police were involved?" Alison's eyes have an avid gleam of curiosity that wipes out my polite conversation circuit.

"Mrs. Carlton called them. From next door. I'm sure she's told you all about it."

The quick flush rising to Alison's cheeks tells me I'm right. Conjecture and gossip will have run through the church like wildfire in a drought and spilled over into the rest of the town. I wonder whether they all believe the tales about Dad or if there is a stream of sympathetic church ladies flowing into his room up at the hospital.

"Well, now, that's just unfortunate," Alison says. "Such a nice man, he's always seemed. I've not seen any symptoms of confusion. Have you, Nancy?"

Nancy shakes her head slowly. "He's always seemed fine, the little I've seen him. He's not as faithful in his attendance as Leah. But then, remember Don Plummer? He'd been deep in dementia for years, and we never knew. He could still shake hands and say, 'Good morning, God bless.'"

Alison can't stop herself. "Are they . . . going to send him to jail?"

"He hasn't been charged. Just to set the record straight, Mom had a known aneurism. She fell. He knew she wouldn't want to be kept artificially alive, so he didn't take her to the hospital."

Alison gasps. Nancy blinks. "I can't imagine why she wouldn't have told us such a thing. We could have helped in so many ways."

Which is exactly why she didn't tell you, I think but do not say. *Because she would have hated your sympathy and your pity and your help.*

"What's going to happen with your dad, then?" Bethany asks, coming back from the kitchen. "You can't take care of him. I mean, you don't even live here. Do you have room for him back in Kansas City? If he's not able to be home alone, then a facility is the only way. My mom's at Parkview. She loves it!"

"I haven't decided yet."

"Of course not," Nancy says, taking charge of this conversation and getting back on track. "You have a great deal to think about. We are here to discuss the funeral plans, if you're up to talking about that? Edna called us for help, and we need some biographical information for the eulogy."

"We need to pick a day—next Saturday, we were thinking, if that's okay with you. You are having the funeral in the church, of course."

Alison says this as if there is only one church in town, and I suppose, for my mother, this is true. And if they want to plan the funeral, that's also fine with me. Mom's eulogy, her memorial, all should be for the woman the church and the town believe her to be.

Any extra biographical material I may have uncovered or will uncover in the next few days will be off the record.

I haven't talked to anybody other than Mrs. Carlton about funeral planning, but I'm willing to bet there's a message on my phone, along with several messages from Greg. I fumble for the damn thing. Sure enough, Greg times six.

I look at my daughter. "Have you talked to your father today?"

"He called."

I recognize that tone. "Did you answer?"

Her lips press together into the Line of Stubborn Resistance.

"Oh, holy shitmeister. He'll be having a royal cow."

My exclamation is punctuated by an audible gasp from Nancy. Alison tugs the brim down lower over her eyes as if to block out the sight of me, or maybe she is thinking she can cover her ears. Bethany winks, as if my language is a part of the secret between us.

At least my indiscretion has served to break up the logjam, and the three of them drift toward the door.

"Don't forget about the casseroles," Nancy says, turning heroically back as if it might be worth braving a few demons in order to save the food.

"Thank you so much. Why don't you just connect with Edna about the funeral, and I'll get the details to her? Perfect." I keep talking, herding them toward the door. "I'll tell Dad you said hello."

"Tell him we are praying for him."

"Of course."

"And for you. And your daughter."

"Right. Thank you."

The door closes between them and me, and I lean my forehead against it, just breathing. Part of me, albeit a small part, is appalled by my own behavior. Mostly I'm just grateful to have that out of the way. They can catalogue me as the apostate I am, and maybe they will leave me alone.

Elle is giggling maniacally. "I can't believe you said *shitmeister* in front of the pastor's wife!"

"Elle. You can't—"

"Where did that word even come from?"

"I am a bad person and a terrible mother."

"No, you're not. You're just—incorrigible." And then she bursts into giggles again.

Her laughter is irresistible. I catch myself smiling, despite my confusion and grief and anger and everything. Laughter follows, and I let it happen, bubbling up and cleaning out emotional toxins. A few real tears follow the laughter tears, but that's okay. I get another tissue and wipe my eyes.

"The church ladies are good people," I tell my daughter. "They mean well. I don't want you to think—"

She hugs me. "I know, Mom. I know."

Leah's Journal

And now you know about Marley. You were never meant to have this information, and you didn't even get it from this journal. Maybe I'll stop writing and burn the whole thing now, as it certainly didn't serve its purpose in helping me keep my mouth shut. All these years I've kept that secret close, but I hadn't thought I might blab her name during my sleep.

And then when you asked me, in the middle of the night while I was shaking from the nightmare, "Who is Marley?" I told you the truth of her. Yes, Marley is real, not an imaginary figment of Maisey's active mind. She was my child. Is my child. Maisey's twin. And yes, I left her behind.

You think differently of me now that you know. I see it. You love me yet, my Walter, because you are a loving man. You want to make excuses for me, but I have refused to give you any material to build them out of. This is a torture for you, and I see that, but there is nothing I can do.

You want me to find her, reach out to her. We actually fought about this—you, who have never really fought with me on anything. Oh God. You can't know how this tears me apart. Do you know how much I want to see the girl? To try to explain to her what happened and how a mother could do such a heinous thing? But I can't. I can't even explain it adequately to myself, or to you.

Thank God Maisey and Elle are well away. I'm going to die anyway, so my safety is a small thing. But you, Walter. I won't allow my past to hurt you, if I can stop it.

That's why I went to town today and bought a gun. Who knew it could be so easy? The nice man at the pawn shop showed me how to use it. How to load and unload. How to aim. Tomorrow, while you're at work, I'll go to the shooting range and find somebody to teach me.

Chapter Fourteen

Tony stands in place at the shooting range, ear protectors on, his Sig held loosely in both hands. He doesn't shoot. Not yet.

He's waiting for the flashback to hit and clear before he starts his practice. It will come. It always comes. Sometimes it's slow, and he thinks it's gone and not going to happen. This is something he dreads more than the flashback itself.

The memory is his punishment, purgatory, and salvation. It keeps him on the straight and narrow. Reminds him of the price he's sworn to pay and the path he is set on. If the memory doesn't hit him hard enough to shred his guts and threaten to drop him, then he knows he is in danger.

Every Sunday afternoon he comes to the shooting range to go through this ritual. It's been ten years now, once a week, fifty-two times a year. All the other regulars know his routine. They assume he's meditating before he starts to shoot. They think he's a badass for this, a sharpshooter. Some of them think he was a sniper in Iraq.

Nobody knows the real reason he comes here, regularly, every week. Nobody asks.

Once, there was a new employee, a little too nosy, who started in with questions.

"Hey, buddy. Whatcha doing? Praying your shots don't miss?"

"Tallying my sins," Tony says. "Making peace with my dead."

And the guy had laughed, as if this was high humor and Tony was a joker. But the next week when Tony came in for his ritual, the owner walked over and told him the kid had been fired. "Not a place for asking questions," he'd said. "My apologies."

Today the free fall into memory is delayed. Instead, Tony remembers a different gun and a pair of wide eyes not quite blue or green, as if they can't decide what color they ought to be. God have mercy. He has no space in his life for this, for the way a small thought about Maisey accelerates his heart and sends his blood rushing to places it has no business. And now his brain has followed, and he wrenches it back.

Here. Now. The gun in his hands.

As if it is aware of his betrayal of attention, the memory ambushes him from behind and very nearly drops him. One ragged breath gets away from him before he's back in control, because that is part of this exercise.

To let the onslaught take him back to that day, that hour, that minute, that second when his finger pulled a trigger. It is his penalty to himself to relive it, fully and completely, once a week for the rest of his life.

His awareness fragments into two: the man standing here at the shooting range and the child he once was in another place far from here.

To his child-self, the gun is heavy, an unfamiliar weight. His hands are shaking, heart pounding, but he knows what he's doing. Knows, when he pulls the trigger, what will follow.

And still. His finger tightens, curls back toward his thumb. There is a recoil. A sharp crack that hurts his ears. His eyes are clamped shut, so he knows only what his body feels and what his other senses tell him. Shrill voices screaming. A gasp. Moaning. The weight of something heavy hitting the floor.

Hands trying to pry the gun from his locked fingers. Fingernails tearing at his skin. Frenzied. Frantic. His mother's voice.

"Give me the gun, Tony. Give it to me. Let go. It's over."

The gasping, whimpering, pitiful, blubbering breaths of a dying man. The stink of gunpowder not quite overpowering the tang of blood, the putrid gaseous stench of shit and piss.

I did this, he reminds himself. I pulled the trigger. The bullet hit him. He is dead.

Ritual completed, guilt and retribution program firmly reinstalled, Tony pulls himself out of the flashback. He knows the drill. Focus on what is. The feel of the floor beneath his feet. The gunpowder smell of the shooting range. The ongoing blitz of rapid-fire shots. He drags air in and out of his lungs in steadying breaths.

Only then does he open his eyes, fix on his target, and begin to shoot. As usual, his bullets hit the target in tightly clustered groups at head and heart. He's a deadly shot. And this is why he does not, cannot, will not carry a gun or have one in the house. Why he couldn't take the gun away for Maisey.

He is not to be trusted with women any more than he should be trusted with guns.

On the way out, he secures his weapon in the locker he rents for that purpose and then says, casually, to Brent behind the desk, "I hear Leah Addington passed. Know anything about the funeral?"

"Wondered where she was," Brent says. "Damn. She was just getting good. Hope nothing bad went down?"

"Some kind of stroke or something," Tony says. "May she rest in peace."

Following a hunch that a woman with a gun like that, loaded and ready, might want to know how to shoot it, he'd asked the question. He'd like to ask how long she'd been coming to the range but knows better than to show curiosity. Still, he's earned a couple of important pieces of intel. Leah Addington has not been shooting guns for her entire life, and Brent has reason to believe her death might be from something other than natural causes.

Tony isn't sure if he should tell Maisey—what would be the point? She was obviously shaken up by the fact that her mother even had a gun. What he wants to know is why a woman like Leah had a gun in the first place.

"Her daughter and granddaughter are at the house," Tony says. "Any reason to believe they're in danger?"

"Nothing specific. Look, since she's dead, I'll tell you this. She came in here a few months back and asked if someone could teach her how to shoot. Determined little woman. Didn't talk much. Certainly didn't look like the gun-owning type. But something had made her twitchy. Asked questions about shooting to kill."

"Thanks. I'll keep an eye out, then."

He wonders, though, as he walks out to his car. What kind of threat could appear out of the blue to spook a woman like Leah? Briefly he weighs the possibility that Walter is the danger, but just as quickly discards this. You can tell a lot about a man by the way his daughter treats him.

Tony will have to keep an eye on the family, just in case. A wave of pleasure sneaks up on him at the idea of spending time with Maisey. It's tempting to entertain it, to justify it, to tell himself it will do no harm. But he doesn't believe this. Not really.

A real relationship is a thing he cannot allow. He will help her as if she was one of his sisters, but that will be the end of it.

Chapter Fifteen

Dad sits in a chair, looking mindlessly toward the window, clearly lost inside himself. When we arrive his gaze comes around to us, but there's no light in his eyes. Elle hugs him, installs herself on the edge of his chair, and begins the sort of chatter only a twelve-year-old girl is capable of. Every word draws him back to us, away from whatever mindless zone he's been drifting through.

When an aide brings in a dinner tray and sets it up for him, he actually eats most of it. Every time his hands forget what they're doing, Elle reminds him.

It's the dessert that does us in.

He takes one bite of hospital apple pie and makes a face. "What is this supposed to be?"

"Pie," Elle says, poking at the rubbery crust and crunchy apple pieces with the fork. "At least, I think it's pie."

"That's not a pie," he protests. "We'll get Leah to make you a real one, just as soon as I get out of here."

My mom's pies are legendary. With his words I taste an intoxicating bite of salty, tender crust, tart but buttery sweet apple, cinnamon, and brown sugar. It melts in my mouth but sticks in my throat.

There will be no more pies. Not one. Not like that. Nobody else, anywhere in the world, makes pies the way my mother made them.

Dad sees it. I watch the knowing steal a little more of the strength from his face, as if the very bones of his cheeks and jaw are being eaten away by my mother's absence.

"I'll make you a pie, Grandpa," Elle says into the suffocating silence that follows his words.

His eyes travel toward her voice, hover, and then find me.

"I want to go home," he says, for all the world like a lost child.

I have to tell him that I live in Kansas and don't have room for him. I have to tell him I'll be selling the house. That there is no home to go to.

But the words are a giant, prickly cactus lodged in my throat. My heart hurts, in a truly physical way, an ache that frightens me with its intensity.

A long silence falls. Tears track down his cheeks, but he doesn't weep, and the silent agony does further damage to my own heart. I cannot begin to comfort his grief; it's too massive for me to even touch.

Elle feels no such limitation. She settles herself into his lap, wraps her arms around his neck, and leans her head against his chest. "I love you, Grandpa," she says, and the words shake loose both his pain and my own, so that before I even know it's hit me, I'm bent over at the waist, torn apart by weeping I can no longer hold back.

I cross the space between us and kneel in front of his chair, burying my face in his knees. His weeping and mine make a rhythm, two pieces of a whole. The third and final piece is missing, will always be missing, but in that moment we begin to heal around that loss, bringing Elle in to complete the circle.

Little by little the intensity of my grief eases. My sobs soften and slow. I hear my father's breath following this same pattern, and soon I am aware only of our breathing—mine, Elle's, and my father's.

I push myself back and sit on the floor, wiping my face with my sleeve and looking around for much-needed tissues. Dad's arms are around Elle, his cheek resting on the top of her head. His face is wet, his eyes red. She, too, is smudged by tears, and if my heart was not so newly emptied, I would feel a fresh pang at the weight of knowledge and maturity I see there.

Too late I wonder if I should have sheltered her from this. Greg would have. My mother would have. But then I feel the warm tug of connection between her heart and mine, mine and Dad's, and for the first time in my life it occurs to me that maybe my own weird way of being in the world is right after all.

I'm mulling all of this when the door opens and Dr. Margoni comes in. Her eyes roam over the three of us, and there is no judgment in her expression. If anything, her expression softens, and she offers a gentle smile and also a hand.

"You look like you may be stuck," she says.

Her fingers are slim and cool, but she is strong. I let her help me back up onto my feet. My body feels different, as if something has shifted. A different center of gravity that makes me feel not weighted, exactly, but grounded. As if I'm not about to fly away next time a puff of wind or emotion hits me.

"So," she says, once I'm on my feet and have found my way first to the tissues and then to the sink to wash my hands. She passes the box of tissues to Elle, who quietly dries her eyes, and to Dad, who honks his nose loudly, clears his throat, and shifts restlessly in the chair.

"Walter, your blood work is much better. Your blood sugars are better controlled. The dehydration is resolved. Your blood pressure has come down. How are you feeling?"

"I feel like my wife just died." There's no bitterness or irony in his tone, just flat acceptance of the fact.

Dr. Margoni nods. "Of course. In a way, that is good and exactly as it should be. That means your emotions are working. Do you know what day it is today?"

She leads him through a catalogue of basic reality. Where and when we are. Which president is currently in the White House. She makes him copy a drawing, pick up and fold a piece of paper, repeat the names of three objects.

Today, he knows some of the answers. He gets the month right, but not the day. He knows he's in a hospital, but not which one. He picks up a piece of paper as instructed, but forgets to fold it. When she asks him to count backward from one hundred by sevens, he refuses to even try.

For me, this would make total sense. I can only do backward sevens if I have a calculator. But Dad's always been a whizz at math, especially calculations. We did a contest between his brain and my calculator once. He won.

I watch his face as he realizes he's getting more and more things wrong, and by the end of the ordeal his hands are shaking.

Dr. Margoni looks grave as she writes a note on her clipboard. Then she sets it aside and gives an assessing look that lights on every one of us. "So, there is no reason to keep you here any longer, and the question becomes this: What next?"

This is the place where I need to dive in with my plan for him to go into supported living.

I can't do it.

Speaking the words is a physical impossibility, and I realize, in one shaft of illumination, that my life is never just going back to how it was. Whether Walter is my father in blood or not, he has been my father for as long as I can remember. He's already lost my mother. I won't be a part of him losing everything else.

"He comes home," I say.

Dr. Margoni looks up at me, startled, her brows rising into smooth arches of question. "With you? To Kansas City?"

I shake my head. "No. To his house. Here."

"I don't understand," she says, and then, "Let me clarify. I understand that he wants to go home, and that you want that for him. But he's going to need a lot of help, at least for a while."

I look at my father and try to picture him as one of those forsaken-looking old people in a wheelchair, dozing in front of the TV in a nursing home. As much as I try to tell myself that they're not really forsaken, that assisted living is not a nursing home, that maybe he'd be happier hanging out with a group of old people instead of mourning at home, it seems impossible.

But then, the idea of Mom being dead is equally impossible.

Dad doesn't say anything. He doesn't need to. His request to come home is still ringing in my ears. He looks small and unmoored and defenseless. A page from one of my childhood books flashes into my head, a Dr. Seuss extravaganza of gratitude not to be an abandoned sock, mistakenly left behind in a dark cave.

Dad looks like the picture of that abandoned sock. Limp. Forgotten. Doomed to disintegrate and unravel, thread by slow, lonely thread, without my mother. Without his home.

Greg and my mother have always said I need to start thinking with my head instead of my heart. My head is ready to supply all sorts of reasons why Dad can't come home. My heart is whispering something else altogether. I didn't do what my mother wanted and needed for me to do. If I make the same mistake with my father, I won't be able to live with the regret.

"I'm taking him home. We'll figure something out."

Dr. Margoni beams a smile at me that lights up all my own dark and dusty corners. "You should know that if you take him home now, and then decide you can't handle it, it may be harder to find him a placement," Dr. Margoni says. "But he can go home today, if you're sure that's what you want to do."

"I'm sure."

"Let me go write the orders. A nurse will be in to sign you out in a little bit."

As soon as Dr. Margoni is out the door, Elle rushes across the room and squeezes me breathless with a giant bear hug. "This is why I love you," she says. Then laughs and squeezes me again. "Well, one of the reasons. How long can we stay?"

"I hadn't thought," Dad says, very quietly. "This will disrupt your life too much."

"Not much of a life to disrupt," I tell him, realizing as I say it that this is true. My job is disposable. My apartment contract is up next month. I'm not dating anybody, and none of my friends will miss me much. More importantly, I won't miss them. Apart from being a mother to Elle, I've been skimming the surface of the Life Pool.

And now my skimmer has been confiscated. I don't have a life jacket. I'm being dunked unceremoniously into the deep end, and I sure as certain had better learn how to swim.

Leah's Journal

Boots. He is all the reasons why I wanted Maisey to marry Greg, who is all the things I didn't know to look for. How would I have known? You taught me what a good man is, Walter. Responsible, polite. Successful. Kind.

Boots was none of these things. His contempt for society and authority was so thick, you could spread it with a butter knife. What was he still doing in school at nineteen? I've asked myself this question. The answer, I'd guess, is that he found it fun to torment the teachers in the same way he liked to torment small creatures. Besides, he had a school full of girls who had stars in their eyes every time they looked at him and boys who tried to emulate him.

He was a god in school. In the real world he was only a wannabe god, and that makes for a dangerous man.

That night at the dance, he swaggered in late, in his leather jacket and Levi's. His eyes swept over the gym, the couples dancing, the little knot of girls chattering, the teachers who were supervising, and for some reason, landed on me. My date was elsewhere. Hiding in the bathroom or bailed out the side door, maybe. I wasn't exactly at odds with the other girls, but not friends, either, which left me very much alone.

Easy prey. I see that now.

But when he crossed the room to me, when those glorious eyes zeroed in on mine, I was exalted. Boots had singled out me. Chosen to talk to me. I don't even remember what he first said. My heart was flooded with the wonder of his attention, my brain misfiring in all directions.

And when he patted his pocket and said, "Shit. I left my smokes at home," I was in a position to help him out. My intention was to give him a cigarette. That would be enough from a lowly mortal girl like me.

But he smiled as if I were suddenly the most beautiful girl in the room.

"Well, come on then," he said. And right then and there, he grabbed my hand. Just like that. In front of teachers and students, at the snacks table, he claimed me.

Me.

He led me outside in the warm dark, back around behind the school, my hand encased in his. We smoked a cigarette together. He was free with his hands, touching my hair, my shoulder, slipping an arm around my waist. He didn't kiss me. Not yet. I would have let him, I was already so far gone, but he was smarter than that.

He led me back into the gym and sealed the deal by dancing with me. My social status climbed through the roof in a single evening. Before the night was over, I'd been invited to parties by people who had previously ignored my existence.

I was in love. And he was—who knows what he was. Of all the girls at his disposal, why me? What did he see in me that made him choose me? I wondered then. I wonder now. I suppose it doesn't matter. All that matters is that he did and that I was happy to be chosen.

And that, dear Walter, is the first of my many sins.

Chapter Sixteen

When we get him home, Dad wanders through all the rooms like a visitant ghost, insubstantial and looking for something that no longer exists. He stares at the fireplace, all cleaned up now and emptied of ashes. He shuffles into the kitchen and looks at the place where Mom fell, running his fingers over the edge of the island where she hit her head. I fill a glass with water and hand it to him. He accepts it, but doesn't drink, looking from the glass to me and back again as if he doesn't know what it's for or what to do with it.

He lurches into movement again, this time into his study. He sits at his desk and carefully sets down the glass, but his hand is shaking, and water sloshes over the edge and forms a puddle that he doesn't seem to see. He opens and closes the center drawer without touching anything. Gets up and opens the closet that holds the file cabinets. I've locked them back up, and he rattles the drawers but seems content just to know they are secured.

Wordless, he brushes past me. Down the hall to the bedroom he has always shared with Mom. At the doorway he hesitates, draws in a ragged breath, and sways like a tree in the wind. Elle and I both launch ourselves toward him, ready to break his fall, but he steadies before we reach him. One low, wretched sound strangles in his throat as he walks to the bed, pulls back the covers, and climbs in without bothering to take off his shoes.

I can't help noticing that he's chosen Mom's side, not his own, or the way he turns and buries his face in her pillow. Feeling like an intruder all at once, I back out and close the door behind me. Elle's eyes are glassy with tears.

"Is he okay?" she whispers.

My best answer is a shrug. "He's just . . . lost, I think. Has no idea how to be without her."

I remember feeling that way myself when I first moved away from home. As fiercely as I craved my independence, my right to be myself and create the margins of my own life, my mother's competent fingers had been in every corner, every piece of my personal pie. Existence on my own had loomed like an uncharted wilderness. My salvation, then as now, was the country known as Elle.

"We need a plan," I tell her. "Get a pen."

She scampers off in search of pen and paper. Elle loves lists. I don't need them, but there's still something comforting about writing things down in black and white. Of course, her lists are given to great detail, and mine are random jottings, but we've been making these documents together since she learned to print her first words.

When I arrive at the kitchen table, she's already there. In front of her, geometrically arranged, is a notepad and a pen, two glasses of water, a calendar she's unearthed from somewhere, and both of our phones. Phones are useful during these planning sessions, since they hold our calendars, our address books, and all the other apps that make life both easier and more complicated all at once.

"Ready," she says. "I suggest we do a Maslow."

In case I'd forgotten that Elle is way too bright, this is a reminder. Of course, Maslow is partly my fault. I mentioned him once when she was four, talking to myself, really.

I'd been contemplating taking a college class, had actually signed up and everything, all in a quest for self-actualization. Meanwhile, there was barely enough food in the refrigerator to get us through the week, and I was a month behind on the rent.

"Who's Maslow?" Elle had asked, plunking her sturdy, warm little body down in my lap and staring at my computer screen. "Is he a computer game?"

I'd pictured Maslow traveling around like Pac-Man, snarfing up self-actualization diamonds. First I thought it was ridiculous. Then I thought maybe it was genius. Probably an idea that somebody will come up with in the future and use to make a shit ton of money.

"Maslow is dead," I'd told my daughter, completely unprepared for dewy eyelashes and a trembling lip.

"Like Goldwing?"

"Yes, like Goldwing." Elle's very first goldfish had passed just the week before, and her grasp of the permanent reality of death had been immediate and thorough, leading to a spate of nightmares that had just begun to taper off.

"Did somebody flush him?"

"What? No. No, he was buried. Long before you were born. In California, far, far from here."

"Did you know him?" She was all curiosity, which was infinitely preferable to inconsolable child grief, so I told her about Abraham Maslow and his hierarchy of needs.

"He was famous," I told her, "for figuring out something that is actually pretty simple. We need food and shelter first, before we need anything else, because without those things we will die. Then we need people to love. Once we have people to love, then we can learn to love ourselves and start working toward the things we are good at, the things that make us happy."

"I love *you*," she'd announced, kissing me on the nose. "And you love *me*. So now we can go do happy things." And then she'd run off singing to play some invented game involving all her stuffed animals and a box of Legos.

Ever since then, though, we've engaged in what she calls "doing a Maslow" every time we have a problem to solve.

"Food," she says, writing it down in neat block letters. "We are all going to starve if we do not get some food in this house."

"The fridge is full of casseroles. Or you could eat oatmeal. I saw some in the pantry."

Elle makes gagging noises, sticks out her tongue, and lets her head drop over onto her shoulder like she's dead. "Lentils, Mom. And I swear one of them is tofu."

I should insist on casserole as nourishment. They were a kind gift; the least we could do is eat them. But I also had a peek in the refrigerator and was equally uninspired by lentils and another dish with pale, nondescript chunks that jiggled when I pulled the pan out for a better look.

"Your point is made. Number one task is buy groceries. Got it. Next up—a roof over our heads. And that's not going to be quite so easy, Elle Belle."

"What's hard? We live here. With Grandpa. Roof. Done."

"Sweetheart."

"Mom, don't you dare even start."

And here we are, already, right at the heart of the difficulty. Maslow had it all wrong with his neat little pyramid, because the levels are all kinds of mixed up and interwoven. In this case, shelter is all tied up in love and belonging, meaning the tug-of-war between me and Greg over Elle.

"You have school. Even smart kids can't just skip out indefinitely."

"School is out in, like, a week."

"This might be a forever thing, Elle. He could be sick for a very long time."

"Then I can go to school here. Or—I know what! You can homeschool me." Her face lights up as she says this, glowing like a mini sun.

She's been after me to homeschool her ever since she discovered, all the way back in first grade, that she already knew most of the curriculum.

It's not that I'm opposed to homeschooling. It's that I'm opposed to the ridiculous concept of me as anybody's teacher. Plus, I would have had to do battle with Greg, who has been pushing for the gifted program. At his urging, I went to one informational meeting, which was full of zealous mothers who reminded me too much of my own, and point-blank refused.

Greg has acquiesced, for now, as long as I've kept up my end of what he calls enrichment and I call having fun with my daughter. We take adventurous trips to museums. Run small chemistry experiments. Bake cookies, which totally counts as math. Visit the zoo and talk to the zoo staff. We've watched caterpillars turn into butterflies, raised praying mantises and pollywogs, and even dissected a cow heart obtained from the butcher shop.

Maybe I would be better at homeschooling than I've given myself credit for, but I shake my head. "There won't be time. I'm going to need to find a job, Elle. Add that to the list as part of shelter."

"And while you're at your job, who is going to stay with Grandpa? See? It's perfect. I do homeschool and take care of him. You go to work. It's not like you have to teach me things—there's online school."

"Your father will never go for that."

"We could ask him."

This is not a new discussion, and both of us automatically assume our battle stations, shields up, weapons ready.

Elle has both hands flat on the table, palms down. Every line of her body is alive with focused energy. Her eyes are target-locked on mine. I counter with my relaxed, confident Mom stance, the one that is meant to indicate there is not even an issue to address.

Nothing to see here; move along folks.

Not that this ever works, but I try.

"What about your friends?"

She shrugs, the one-shoulder version that says she's hiding emotions.

It strikes me that it's been weeks since anybody has been over or since she's asked to hang out somewhere.

"Elle?"

She sighs. "Erica's moving to California. And Jaimie hasn't talked about anything but boys for a year."

"You have other friends."

"Well, here I've got Mia."

"I mean kids your own age."

"Why? I like Mia. She actually talks about things besides boys and TV. Besides, it's not like Kansas City has an exclusive on kids."

And with that, all my resistance crumbles. It's an epic collapse and feels just like one of those videos where a large building is blown up with a demolition charge. I remember well enough feeling like I didn't fit in at her age, how hard it was to navigate the relationships with the other girls.

Besides, selfish or not, I need Elle to be with me.

"Okay," I tell her.

Her mouth flops open and she gasps like a stranded fish. "Wait, what?"

Suddenly giddy, I grin at her. "Great idea. Solves all kinds of problems. Add researching online homeschool to that list. And homeschool support groups in Colville. Oh, and Washington State homeschool regulations. Anything we need to present a case to your father."

Elle's mouth closes, her eyes well up, and she melts down in her chair. Her arms go on the table, her face buried in them, her shoulders shaking with sobs.

I freeze, an electric Taser jolt going straight to my heart. Paragraphs of intact text from the parenting books I've read laser through my brain. Kids need stability. Structure. Boundaries. They don't really want change. They push against the boundaries, but they don't really want them to give way. Elle needed me to hold the line, and instead I've restructured our whole world order.

"Elle, honey. We don't have to. I thought that's what you wanted."

She launches like a rocket up out of her chair, sending it skittering backward across the tile. "Of course it's what I want." She flings herself into my lap with enough force that my chair nearly goes over backward. Both of her arms wrap around my neck so tightly I can hardly breathe. "Thank you. You don't know." Her voice breaks off into sobbing.

I pull her into my lap even though she's nearly as tall as I am, rocking her like I used to when she was a little girl.

"Honey, don't get your heart too set on this. We've got to get through your father first."

She sniffles and scrubs her wet face on my shoulder. "You're the custodial parent."

"And he's an attorney. We don't want to push him too far."

She sits back then and looks at me, her expressive face transitioning rapidly between joy, tears, fear, and consternation.

"He wouldn't go all legal on you. Would he?"

"He never has, but I wouldn't want to push him. He might win, Elle. If it came down to a custody battle."

"So you're just going to cave? You're not even going to try? Homeschooling is the dream of my heart, and you're going to snatch it away before it has a chance."

These lines are delivered in true drama queen fashion with one hand over her heart, a performance worthy of an old-time silent movie heroine being tied to the railway tracks. Warring parts of me want to smile, weep, and smack her.

"No, we're going to create and present an airtight case. That's your assignment."

"Got it." She flings her arms around my neck and hugs me again. "I love you."

"I love you, too, baby girl. Now, are you going to keep writing things down? Because we are not done with Maslow yet."

She rubs her face on my shirt, leaving wet splotches behind, and then grins at me, impish and irrepressible. "Yes, but make it quick. I have a legal brief to write."

"God have mercy," I mutter. "Okay. So we'll live here and let Grandpa pay for our room and board. Our apartment lease is up next month, so we'll let that go. But I'm still going to need a job."

Dutifully she writes, *Find Mom a job.*

My prospects of finding a job in a small town are a little dismal, but if we live here with Dad, our overhead will be minimal. Greg pays healthy child support for Elle, enough to cover anything she needs. But my mother will roll over in her not-yet-grave if I take a job at McDonald's or some other fast-food establishment.

"You can do better, Maisey." This has been her response to any job I've ever held. She's right, of course. A gig taking Santa photos at the mall during the holiday season isn't exactly a resume builder. It was fun, though. I loved every minute. Every job I've ever embarked upon was a learning experience or an adventure or just plain fun. Even the newspaper reporter job that took me to Kansas City in the first place was fun, until my editor retired and was replaced by a soul-sucking asshat who wanted to leap the corporate ladder in a single bound.

About two weeks into his tenure, I quit and took a job with a temp agency, which has landed me stints doing everything from answering phones in a veterinary office to writing community articles for small newspapers. I love the variety, even though I know this is a phase I should probably have grown out of about twenty years ago. I keep waiting for some great life purpose to rise up in front of me and declare itself, but I don't seem to be wired for greatness.

Elle is staring at me, tapping the pen on the table.

"What?"

"You were daydreaming. Are you really going to just let the church ladies plan Grandma's funeral?"

"I am. What's next?"

She grins. "Tony."

"I don't think I follow you."

"We've got safety and basic needs and shelter taken care of. Love and belonging come next."

"Could we skip that and get straight to self-actualization? Besides, I have you and Grandpa. All the love I could possibly need."

Elle makes a scoffing noise. "Not the same. Tony's cute. Don't you think?"

Cute isn't the word I would use for Tony. At all. Too masculine. Too much muscle. Too much shadow hidden beneath his grin and his gentleness. I'm not about to share any of these thoughts with my daughter.

"Can we get back to work?" I ask her. "I don't have time for boys right now."

This doesn't get me off the hook.

"Oh, fine," she says. "Aunt Marley, then. She definitely fits under love and belonging. Don't you miss her? We can go to the concert, right?"

Marley.

I don't remember her as anything more than an imaginary friend, and yet her name is at the center of everything—all this mystery. It is also the heart of the breach between my mother and me. My desire to find my sister is equally balanced by a desire to stay as far away from her as possible.

I take a breath, curl my toes, tap my fingers on my thighs. One of my counselors taught me this trick for staying grounded—one of the counselors who reinforced my mother's continued statements that Marley was made up of my imagination, that I needed to make real friends and live in the real world.

Elle is waiting for an answer. I give her an evasion.

"So she's Aunt Marley now? Just like that?"

"Well, she is my aunt, right? So what else would I call her?"

I drop my head into my hands and rub my temples. "Elle, this isn't going to be some exuberant family reunion. She might not even want to know us. Maybe she's a terrible person, and we don't want to know her. *If* we go to that concert. *If.*"

"She's family," Elle says, as if that is the answer to everything. "It doesn't matter what kind of person she is; she's still family."

Leah's Journal

I married Boots when I was sixteen, a bona fide shotgun wedding. My father sobered up long enough to be outraged and make some empty threats. Boots didn't need threatening. He was into me and loved the idea of himself as a father, that he was recreating in his own image. He wanted me by his side all the time, everywhere. I loved the way he wanted me all to himself.

"We don't need anybody else," he would say. I agreed. My few friendships fell away, one by one.

Mom was just too beaten down and tired to raise a fuss.

She tried. I'll credit her with that.

"You don't have to do this," she said to me. "Being pregnant isn't the end of everything. Have the baby. Give it up for adoption. You're a smart girl. You should finish school."

I thought this to be stupid advice. She hadn't done that. Why should I?

Logic, with a sixteen-year-old girl, doesn't always exist. I ought to have seen it then, where her own shotgun marriage landed her. With me and an alcoholic husband and no real life whatsoever. But I was madly in love.

At that point, I had no clue I was carrying twins. The idea of a baby (let alone two!) was sort of nebulous and unreal. My body hadn't changed much. Apart from a little nausea in the mornings, I wasn't even sick. Boots looked like an escape. Like salvation and a dream. He was going to be a rock star. And he'd chosen me—me! We were going to live in a mansion and have a castle in France. Travel all over the country, where he would perform before adoring fans.

And me? I would travel with him, of course. Me and a baby. One happy family.

It wasn't a church wedding. The pastor of our church refused to perform the ceremony. I thought at the time he was judging us because I was pregnant. I wonder now if it was his attempt to save me, or at least his refusal to be part of the devil's deal I was making.

So we were married at the courthouse, by a justice of the peace. I couldn't afford a wedding dress, and God knows Boots couldn't afford to buy one for me. He told me not to worry about it.

"We are not the dress-up sort of people, you and me," he said. So I wore my usual blue jeans, with a long shirt to conceal the snap I could no longer close.

I didn't have a friend to be my witness. For one, they were all too young to be legal. And I'd been so completely absorbed in Boots since that very first night that I really had no friends left who were interested.

My mother signed for me.

Boots brought two of his band members to bear witness. One was his buddy, Irv somebody. I never did know his last name. The other was a girl, Jolene Avery. Her name I knew too well. Boots talked about her a lot. What a fantastic singer she was. Her accommodating nature (this to highlight my own stubborn willfulness). How thin, how active, how sexy.

On our wedding day, Boots bought me flowers. A bouquet of genuine red roses. Nobody had ever done that before. He told me I was the most beautiful girl in the world and that we were going to be ecstatically happy. He didn't even look at Jolene on that day, his eyes only for me.

Chapter Seventeen

Of course we go to Marley's concert on Friday night, even though Mom's funeral is scheduled for Saturday. How can I not take advantage of an opportunity to talk to my *sister*? To finally find out what happened? To see if she's anything like the Marley my imagination conjured up for me as a child?

But it seems so wrong to go out to a brewpub for a concert, no matter what the reasons are. I worry about what people will think. I feel guilt and anticipation in equal measure.

As for Elle, she just keeps on arranging everything, and I keep on letting her. One of the things she's arranged, unbeknownst to me, is for Tony and Mia to go with us.

"Good for you," Mia says, engulfing me in a warm hug when they swing by to pick us up. "So many people get all stuffy about grief. Life doesn't end when somebody dies. I think it's fantastic that you're trying to go do something fun."

Even Tony's mother, who volunteered to stay with Dad while we are out, is totally on board with the program. She bustles in, radiating competence, kindness, and goodwill, another casserole in hand. This one gives off a heavenly aroma of tomato and cheese that makes my mouth water. She introduces herself as Hannah, but I can't bring myself to call her anything but Mrs. Medina.

The first thing she does after introductions is dish up a plate of food for Dad. He tries to tell her he isn't hungry, but she won't hear it. It only takes her about five minutes to cajole him into his chair at the table, a plate full of food in front of him.

So I don't need to worry about Dad, but I still have plenty of qualms about this outing.

If you are going to venture out to a concert the night before your mother's funeral in a small town where everybody knows everybody, then the last thing you want to do is go with a tall, dark, sizzling-hot fireman. In his black leather jacket and well-fitting blue jeans, he looks like he belongs in one of those Hot Fireman calendars they put out. Probably naked and holding a cat. This image does things to both my imagination and my body that are not safe for public consumption.

The brewpub inhabits a warehouse. There are two levels, but it's open all the way to the roof, and the upstairs is more of a railing-enclosed mezzanine. The downstairs part of it, where the stage is set up, has long trestle tables and chairs. Only a couple of the tables are occupied when I arrive, fortunately not by anybody I know. A group of teenagers is playing pool, completely oblivious to our arrival.

I select a table upstairs, near the railing, where I figure I can get a good view of Marley without being in her direct line of sight.

"Are you sure you want to sit all the way up here?" Mia asks. "We're early. We could sit front and center."

Tony rescues me. "I think she's doing incredibly well to just be out of the house. Maybe front and center isn't the best idea for tonight."

I go with this. It's true enough. The very thought of loud music and laughter sends a full-body cringe running through me. And I want to avoid being seen by anybody in town who might recognize me. But the real reason I've chosen this particular spot is that I want to watch Marley without her watching me.

"I'd like to be closer," Elle says. "Probably. Maybe we should hear them first. They might suck."

They don't. Elle has been playing YouTube videos all week. I'm not crazy about country music, but as far as I can tell, this band is tight and smooth. And Marley has a voice that could be described as smoky and sultry, a whiskey voice. The sort of voice that stirs the emotions in your belly like a spoon stirring cream into a coffee cup, but then maybe that's because she's my sister.

The waitress who comes around apparently went to school with Mia, and the two of them chatter about the fact that the band set up and did a sound check earlier, then zipped out to grab a bite to eat somewhere else. They left their sound guy to watch the equipment. She points him out, a man leaning against the railing to the left.

I glance in his direction, trying not to stare. Buzzed head. Bulging biceps and pecs stretching the limits of a black T-shirt with a skull on it. Full tattoo sleeves on both arms. I wonder what this says about Marley, whether he's a part of her life or a hired hand who happens to be good at his job. Tony orders us pizza and a pitcher of ale, with a root beer for Elle.

"Anybody want to play pool?" Mia asks. "Since we're going to be waiting."

"Me!" Elle says, bouncing up as if she's been ejected from her chair. "I always wanted to play. Can you teach me?"

"Absolutely. I'm fantastic at pool. Anybody else? Maisey?"

Her dark eyes sparkle, and she holds a hand out to me. It's a genuine invitation, and somewhere, beneath my layers of shock and grief and anxiety, I'm touched by it and want to respond.

But I shake my head. It's bad enough to be here at all, and I don't think my knees would hold me if I tried to walk right now. Ale is probably a bad idea, but the waitress arrives at this exact moment, setting a pitcher filled with foaming amber ale on the table. She pours a mug for me and sets a glass of water down in front of Tony.

"Thanks, Cass," he says.

"You got it, babe." She smooths her hair as she smiles at him, and then sashays away with a sway of the hips that tells me she has not failed to notice his hotness. Hell, they know each other. Maybe they've dated. Maybe they are dating now.

And why should that matter to me? Still, I watch her with a tiny shard of envy pricking at my heart, wishing I'd been born with those sorts of curves, that easy ability to smile and chat and be amusing.

Tony lifts his glass. "Cheers," he says.

"She forgot your mug." I gesture at the pitcher and his half-empty water glass.

"She remembered just fine." He says it casually, but there's a flat finality in his tone that means this topic is closed for conversation.

I ask anyway. "Not a drinker?"

"Not so much." He smiles, but it's not a real one this time. His eyes drop to the table, and he grabs a handful of peanuts and starts shelling them, making a little pile of shells on one side, peanuts on the other.

I pick up a peanut of my own, but just turn it over and over in my fingers. The vibe between us has shifted into a minor, discordant key. My fault for persisting with the nosy question. I keep telling myself it doesn't matter whether I've pissed him off or why he doesn't drink. But the people I know who swear off alcohol are all either former alcoholics or severely religious. If I'm going to have Tony around Elle, I tell myself, it's important to know. For Elle. Not that it matters to me.

"My father was a drinker," Tony says, glancing up and meeting my eyes with an intense blue gaze. "A very good drinker. Meaning he could consume more than his temper could handle on a regular basis. Kind of put me off the stuff for myself."

"I'm sorry." Whether I'm apologizing for my having asked, for his father having been an angry drunk, or for the messed-up state of the universe altogether, I'm not entirely sure.

And then it doesn't matter because the door opens down below and a group of people come in, carrying instruments.

The band has arrived.

I'm on my feet and leaning over the railing before I realize that my body has decided to relocate. There are two men, one with a dark ponytail down the middle of his back, the other wearing a baseball cap. But I have eyes only for the woman.

I get only a quick glimpse of her face before she sails up the steps onto the stage. She walks like my mother, with the same quick, confident steps. It's instantly clear that she's the boss. The men defer to her, listen, follow her lead like sunflowers follow the sun.

Marley waves to the tattooed guy at the sound booth. A smile changes his face from thug to lover in a heartbeat. And then her head turns, and her eyes scan the rest of the balcony, casually assessing.

What if she recognizes me? What if she doesn't? I hold my breath, waiting, but her eyes pass over me as if I'm invisible. She says something to her companion. He laughs and opens his guitar case. My legs have turned to mush, and my fingers have grown roots into the railing. I can't move. Can't breathe. Can't anything.

And then I feel Tony beside me. Breathe in the scent of leather and shampoo and a hint of wood smoke. "Excited?" he asks. "You must have access to way bigger bands than this, coming from Kansas City."

"We don't get out much," I tell him. Maybe later I'll tell him the truth. Maybe I won't.

Mia and Elle join us, surrounded by an energy cloud of enthusiasm and excitement. Mia is holding a glass half-full of ale, clearly not following in Tony's path of abstinence.

"I put the eight ball in the corner pocket," Elle says. "Oh wow. There she is. Right up close and personal. She looks fantastic, don't you think?"

There is no doubt that my sister looks amazing.

She's wearing a sparkly black shirt, form-fitting, and spandex pants with cowboy boots. Either she's spent more time at the gym than I have, or she has inherited better genes. Her blonde hair is braided in a thick rope. She has one of those expressive faces made for the stage.

The lights come up behind her, the band starts checking the tuning on their guitars. Marley doesn't say anything. Doesn't introduce the band. Just plays a chord, makes eye contact with each of her band members in turn, and starts to sing.

The band is tight, polished, but she dominates the stage. Her voice is conviction. The room is hers. The world is hers.

She is the daughter my mother always wanted, the person I forever failed to be. She is also, inexplicably, the daughter my mother abandoned.

I am utterly undone by the reality of this perfect sister. My knees, jelly before, become nonexistent. They are going to drop me.

I'm saved by a strong warm hand at the small of my back, a voice in my ear telling me to come and sit. Tony supports me back to my chosen table and into a chair. His attention, unlike every other human in this room, is not on Marley but is fully focused on me. He sits across from me, arms resting on the table, blue eyes and all his attention mine.

He is an anchor, a bulwark. My breathing adapts to his, the slow breath in, the easy breath out, and little by little bees stop buzzing in my ears. My heart settles into an easier rhythm.

"Better?" he asks.

"Better."

He shoves his water glass across the table, and I accept the hint and drink, slowly, letting the sensation of cool liquid on my tongue ground me in my own body even as the music keeps trying to sweep me away.

"Maybe this wasn't such a hot idea," he says, between songs. "You've had a rough week. Can you eat something?"

No. The answer to that is vehemently no. My stomach is raising a rebel army. There will be no eating. And no more drinking of anything but water. When the pizza arrives, I start mouth-breathing, unable to tolerate the smell of garlic and tomato sauce.

Mia and Elle drift over to inhale a couple of pieces, then disappear down the stairs to be closer to the music. It doesn't take long before the two of them are right up front and center, dancing. I can't help wondering how Marley can miss the fact that the adoring tween beaming up at her is family. Blood. Maybe she feels the draw, because for a minute there, she seems to be singing directly to Elle.

For me, the concert lasts an eternity. A thousand times I flow back and forth between the decision to talk to Marley after it's all over or just slip away without saying a word.

Not that Elle would let me. In the middle of the last song, she runs upstairs to get me, face aglow with excitement, her hair sweat-curled around her face, cheeks flushed.

"Come on! They are almost done! I can't wait to meet her."

Tony raises his brows in a question.

"We are going to introduce ourselves to the singer, apparently. If you don't mind waiting?"

I'm hoping maybe he'll tell me that he can't wait, that he has an urgent appointment or has to be at work and we need to leave right this minute.

Instead he smiles at Elle. "Cool. I'll wait here. Mia is going to be forever anyway."

Chapter Eighteen

Marley, coiling up cables on the stage, hears us walk up behind her. She turns, ready with a professional smile, probably expecting a fan.

I open my mouth to tell her who I am. Some version of, "Hey, guess what? I'm your long-lost sister!" but my voice box freezes.

Her eyes travel from me to Elle and back again. Her lips flatten out into a thin, compressed line. It's Mom's displeased expression, perfectly replicated on a stranger's face.

I swallow. "Hi, my name is Maisey and—"

"What do you want, an autograph?" She turns her back and continues coiling up a power cord, looping it around her hand and elbow.

"No, I—this might sound weird, but I'm your sister."

"I know who you are. The fabled Maisey. And Maisey Junior, if I'm not mistaken."

"You know about me?" Somehow, this seems worse than my not knowing about her.

"Trust me. I know plenty." Her voice is hard, dismissive, as far from the warm friendly tone she'd used on the crowd as I am out of my comfort zone. "What I don't know is what you're doing here."

Elle stiffens beside me and my anger sparks. "Go find Mia," I tell her.

For once she doesn't argue.

I follow Marley across the stage. "How?" I ask her. "How could you possibly know about me?" Dropping the cord into a box, she swings around to face me. Her feet are planted shoulder-width apart. She's a little shorter than me. Her eyes are the same shade of blue-green as my own, but manage to be decisive and calculating.

"I've always known about you, from Grandma and from Dad. You were always my mother's favorite. Spoiled and cosseted. She left us and took you with her, and there we are. He still keeps a picture of her on his bedside table, God only knows why. What do you want from me?"

"What? Nothing! I just—"

"This chick bothering you Marl?"

It's the sound guy. Up close he's a mighty muscle machine, all testosterone and tattoos and intimidation. He plants himself beside her, feet spread, arms crossed. And then his face changes as he gets a good, long look at me.

"She looks like you, Marley," he says. "Same eyes, anyway. The rest of her, not so much."

"She's my sister. My twin sister, to be precise."

His tough-guy persona dissolves with these words, and he forgets all about me. "You have a sister?" He sounds like a little kid who has just figured out Santa Claus is a lie.

Marley doesn't even look at him, her eyes still burning a hole into me. "It's no big thing, JB. Trust me. Go help the guys pack up. I'll just be a minute."

He hesitates, then walks away from us, but he looks back over his shoulder at her, at me, and what I see is more hurt than hostility.

"When I was a little kid, I had an imaginary friend," I blurt out. "Her name was Marley. We did everything together. Played games. Read books. I used to set a place for her at the table."

Marley's face could be carved from stone for all the softness I see in it.

"When I was a kid, I'd have been beaten half to death over stupidity like an imaginary friend. I made towers out of empty beer cans and stole books from the library. Glad to know I was having fun somewhere."

The words pulse between us, ugly and full of rage.

"What are you pissed at me for? I didn't even know you were real."

"And now you know. What were you expecting? Some sort of happy family reunion?"

"Answers, maybe," I tell her, which is true, but not the truth. I wanted my sister. I want the imaginary Marley, the one who loved me. The one who knew all the good words and had all the good ideas. The Marley who would know what to do about Mom's secrets and Dad's disintegration.

This Marley barks a harsh laugh. "You're in the wrong place if you're looking for answers. All I've got is a lifetime of questions. Ask your mother. What do you think I can tell you?"

"She's dead. I can't ask her anything."

Marley freezes in the act of turning away.

I feel the tears coming and do everything I can think of to stop them. Squeeze my hands into fists and dig my fingernails into my palms. Blink. Swallow. Look at the ceiling. I will not cry in front of this hard, sarcastic stranger who is also my only sister.

But, of course, the tears come anyway, a humiliating river of them. I choose to ignore them, rather than wipe them away, keeping my chin up, trying to hold a modicum of dignity.

"Oh hell," Marley says. She turns back to face me. I can't read the expression on her face because she's all blurry with my tears. Her breathing sounds loud, but maybe that's just my own. "Listen, Maisey. Some stones are better left unturned. We've never been family before; we're not going to start being family just because your mother died."

"Our mother," I whisper.

Marley shakes her head in denial. "Not my mother. I don't have one. Look, I've got to go. We're driving back tonight, and none of us are eighteen anymore. As for you and me? We've met. You've done your due diligence and tracked me down. Write it in your journal or whatever makes you happy, and let it go. Don't come looking for me. Understand?"

"I hear you." Her words feel like sucker punches to my gut. One-two. One-two. Add a right hook to the jaw, and Maisey is down for the count. I manage to get my unsteady feet moving away from her, but then she calls after me.

"Hey, Maisey!"

I turn back. Her bandmates are staring now. The sound guy comes back. Touches her arm.

"Marley," he says. "Easy."

"I told you," she says, softer now. "I warned you. Go home. Leave me alone."

I was going to tell her about the funeral. I was going to ask her what she remembers from our childhood, who our father is, if she knows why—*why*—Mom would have left her there and taken me.

Every muscle in my body feels shredded. My brain keeps spinning round and round, trying to make sense out of what makes no sense at all. What my mother could have been thinking. How my only sister can sing so beautifully while packing around so much venomous hate. My thoughts and feelings are so jumbled and bruised, I can't begin to know what I think or feel.

Elle, who didn't go find Mia after all and has been witness to this whole exchange, comes running up and flings her arms around me, clinging. "I don't understand," she says. "Like, at all. I thought she'd be happy to meet us."

"Not so much, apparently."

I can't stop shaking. My hands, my legs, my insides, keep shivering like it's twenty below zero.

Elle and I climb the steps together, and I fall numbly into my chair.

"What was that all about?" Tony asks, aiming for casual and missing by a mile. "The singer doesn't like fans? Couldn't hear what she said, but she didn't look so happy."

"Marley is . . ."

My voice fails me. I suck in a breath and try again. "Marley is my sister."

The words feel strange and familiar at the same time. I used to talk about Marley all the time, before my mother chased the words away from me with spankings and scoldings and trips to the counselor. She told me I was imagining things. That it wasn't healthy.

Even now I sneak a peek over my shoulder to see if Mom's behind me, ready to administer a quick swat to my behind for saying the forbidden words.

Tony blinks and looks confused. "You two are sisters?"

"Twins."

"Whoa," Mia says. "I need another drink." She pours one from the pitcher and gulps.

"Easy," Tony warns, in a big-brother tone.

She sticks her tongue out at him.

Now that the cat's out of the bag, I can't stop talking. "I've never met her, that I can remember. I didn't even know about her until a couple of days ago. I found a birth certificate in my mom's legal papers. I thought she must have been dead or something, but here she is. In the flesh. And for some reason she hates me."

Tony and Mia both stare at me like my nose has suddenly misplaced itself and is wandering over my face. "Still boggled," Tony says.

"Grandma probably left her because she's such a bitch," Elle says.

"Elle! Don't talk like that."

"Well, it's true."

"Marley would have been a baby."

"Bet she cried all the time. Mean crying. On purpose."

I feel an oppositional desire to defend my sister, the one who just told me to get lost in no uncertain terms. The one who appears to blame me for her childhood. Down below, Marley has her back to us. Sound Check Guy has his arm around her waist. Her head rests briefly on his shoulder, and he pulls her in for a hug.

How would I feel if my mother had left me when I was a baby? Especially if she'd chosen another child over me?

Guilt almost suffocates me, but I welcome it in. This, of all my emotions, is the most familiar. The most comfortable. As it settles its heavy weight into my belly, I'm able to breathe again. My legs and hands steady, although the internal quaking goes on.

"Let's get out of here," Mia says, her hand on Elle's shoulder. "Anybody else for ice cream?"

"There's nothing open," Tony protests.

"Safeway," she says. "A tub for everybody. Four favorite flaves coming up."

Maybe literally, I think, as my stomach does a little heave. But Elle perks up at the mention of ice cream, and I don't have to eat mine. As the four of us shove back our chairs and get up, I can't help one more glance down at Marley.

She looks up at the same moment. Our eyes lock. Neither of us waves.

I turn away first, quickly before my face crumples again. Tony's hand engulfs mine, and I let his strength flow into me, steady me, get me across the room and out the door. He goes serious, though, and as soon as he deposits me safely in the front passenger seat and shuts the door behind me, he closes in on himself.

In the backseat, Mia launches a full-scale effort to entertain Elle. Left alone to my own devices, I lose myself in a futile search of my memory banks for any sign of remorse or regret from my mother. Any mention of another child. Any hints about what happened. But all I find is another instance of how hard she worked to eradicate Marley from my world.

I'm five, and Mom has caught me with two cookies, instead of the one I'd been given permission for.

"I said only one."

"I only have one."

"Maisey, I know perfectly well you know the difference between one and two."

"Yes. There are two cookies. But only one is for me." And then my five-year-old brain catches up with my five-year-old tongue, and I stop short. A lie would have been better. I'm not allowed to play Marley games.

"And who is the other one for?" Mom asks. Her voice sounds curious, but it's a trap.

"No one."

Mom's hand, the one that can be so gentle when it brushes my hair at night, clamps around my jaw and tilts my head back so I have to meet her eyes. "Don't mumble, Maisey. Tell me, who is it for?"

"Marley." I squinch my eyes shut, prepared for a slap.

It doesn't come. She releases me. My adult eyes looking back into the memory see that her hands are trembling. That her voice, when she tells me to go to my room, is taut with tears, not anger.

I jolt out of the memory as Tony pulls the car into the Safeway parking lot. "Okay kiddies, go get your ice cream."

"Wait," Elle says. "Phone."

Even from the front seat I can hear that, first, it's Greg, and second, he's pissed. I cringe, hearing her explanation that we've just been out to a concert with Mia and Tony.

And now Greg is shouting. I can't make out the words, but the tone is clear.

"He wants to talk to you," Elle says, holding out her phone.

"Tell him I'll text him."

She shrugs and relays the message. "Don't shoot me, I'm just the messenger," she says. "Sorry. Fine, I apologize for my rudeness. Yes. I know. I'll tell her. Night."

"Whoa," she says, after she hangs up. "Dad seriously needs to chill. Too bad we can't send him ice cream. Are you coming in, Mom?"

I rest my head against the seat and close my eyes. The car is safe and warm. All the windows are open, and a cool, lilac-scented breeze wafts in through the windows. All at once I'm too exhausted to even open my eyes, let alone go into the store.

"I'll wait here. You know what I like."

"Maybe I'll surprise you instead."

"You are full of surprises, Elle." I force my eyelids open and dig in my purse for my stash of bills. "I'm buying. Get one for Tony."

The car doors slam. One. Two. And Elle and Mia race away across the parking lot.

"Mia is never going to grow up," Tony says, but there's the warmth of love in his voice.

"She's lovely. She's been wonderful with Elle." A lump comes up in my throat again. I had a sister for all of about five minutes before I lost her again.

"She loves kids," Tony says. "My sisters' kids are always hanging out with her. Mia says it's perfect because she gets all the fun of kids without the hard work and sleepless nights. Or the husband."

My phone buzzes and buzzes again with incoming text messages.

"Elle's father?" Tony asks.

"Yep." I flick through a series of messages. Greg has been texting all day, each one increasing in intensity. "He is not a fan of our activities."

"He's probably worried. Maybe you should call him."

"Are you kidding? If I catch him up, then he'll be really worried."

"You don't talk much, then?" Tony's voice is neutral, his face in shadow. It's impossible to tell whether he's making polite conversation or really cares about the answer.

"Generally only about Elle."

Relationship or no relationship, the idea of calling Greg while I'm sitting here with Tony feels wrong in my belly. I'm staring at his questions on the text screen, thinking about how to word a summary that won't send him into a meltdown, when the phone starts buzzing again. This time the screen lights up with a call.

Accepting the inevitable, I answer.

I needn't have worried about trying to be tactful; Greg is already having a supersonic meltdown.

"Where the hell have you been?"

"Take a breath, Greg. There's no cause for—"

"There is cause! There is plenty of cause! There is so much cause I could fill a corporate brief with it."

"I'm fine. Elle is fine. We've just been—"

"Out. At a concert. With a guy you don't even know. Are you out of your senses?"

He's shouting. I know Tony can hear every word, but it's too late to get out of the car and keep this private. Greg, to my knowledge, doesn't shout at anybody else. He's quiet. Controlled. Polite. The rages I rouse in him have always been a secret between us.

Not the good kind of secret, like birthday presents and surprises. Ours is a cloying, stifling, suffocating secret.

Normally I retreat in the face of his anger, but the distance between us and the presence of a strong protective male in the car with me is ridiculously liberating. Instead of hurrying to soothe, smooth, and calm the storming beast, an unruly little part of me perks up its pointed ears and takes control. Without conscious intent, I find myself mimicking his usual ultracalm, annoyingly rational tone of voice.

"We have actually and factually been out on family business. I'm confused as to why you're so angry."

"Are you freaking kidding me? Family business? Is that what you call going out on a date? You didn't answer your phone, so I tried to call Walter, and some woman answered. She told me you were out at a concert and who you were at the concert with. Elle affirmed the facts just now. So don't bother to lie to me."

"I hadn't realized that a concert is anathema. It was country music. Not even hard rock. No bats, no kittens, no blood."

Greg's voice lowers, but every syllable is emphasized for effect. There is probably spit on his phone. "A concert is fine under normal circumstances. You are there for your mother's *funeral*. You left Walter home *alone* with a *stranger*. You took *Elle* out with people you don't even know."

Each one of his phrases fans the already blazing fires of guilt in my psyche. I'm about to lapse into a standard apology, when he ruins his whole rhetoric with the one-liner guaranteed to fuel my rebellion.

"What are people going to think?"

My mother used to ask the same question. And my answer to her has been the same for years. "I don't know. What *are* they going to think?"

I imagine saying these words to Greg. Imagine his face congested with responding fury, that twisty blue vein on his left temple all puffed up like it gets during rush-hour traffic. I see his fingers twitch at the top button of his meticulous shirt, adjusting his perfectly coordinated tie.

I think of the way he constantly natters vague disapproval about my lifestyle, my parenting, my choices, and my lack of choices. The way he followed me after we broke up, first to Seattle, and then to Kansas City, with the eminently reasonable rationale that it's best for Elle if we parent her together. No matter where I go or what I do, Greg is always there to highlight my insufficiencies and failures.

But I'm here now, for the foreseeable future. And I'll be staying here as long as Dad needs me. Greg has Linda now, and the baby. It won't make sense for him to pack up his family and his thriving practice and move back to Smalltownsville to keep an eye on me.

This thought emboldens me to ignore the warning signs, to shush the guilt, to push on.

I match his tone, inflection for inflection. "I don't know, Greg, what are they going to think? More importantly, what are they going to think when they find out that Walter isn't actually my father, and that I have a twin sister named Marley who lives in the Tri-Cities and sings in a country band?"

Silence on the other end of the phone. Carefully controlled breathing.

When he speaks again, he's reverted to his courtroom voice, the one he uses on unreliable witnesses. I can picture him sending meaningful glances to the invisible jury presiding over my case. Perhaps a slight headshake before leaning toward me, a calm, condescendingly sympathetic expression plastered to his face.

"Listen, Maisey. I came down hard on you. I know you're under a lot of stress. Do you think maybe your imagination is running away with you?"

What he means is, *Have you finally lost your marbles? Are you batshit crazy insane? Would a little R&R in a mental institution help to restore you to reason?*

I take a steadying breath and press on. "I found two birth certificates, one mine and one made out for my sister, Marley. Walter wasn't the parental name on either of them. Oh, and I found a gun in my mother's knitting bag, and I think that, yes, going to my sister's concert and trying to talk to her counts as family business."

Again with the silence and the controlled breathing. "I'll have my mom come over, shall I? To check in on you? Just to be sure . . ."

"I'm not crazy, Greg. I resent the implication. Your mother disapproves of me, and she wasn't precisely friendly with my mother. So please don't."

"Maisey . . ." His voice rises again.

Tony is quick, too quick for me to stop him. He grabs the phone from my shaking hand.

"Greg? Hi. This is Tony. You are not helping. Maybe call her back when you're calmer." Tony pushes End Call, cutting off Greg midsplutter. "You could block him," he says.

"I could—what?" The idea is incomprehensible and foreign.

"Block him. If he's harassing you."

I shake my head to try and clear it. "It's not harassment, really. He's worried about Elle. We share custody. I can't exactly not talk to him."

The atmosphere in the car, despite the calm night outside, feels electric. My hair rises on the back of my neck.

"Give me my phone, Tony. I have to call him back and explain."

"You don't have to do anything."

"You don't understand! He's an attorney. He could take Elle." My voice breaks. I fan my face with my hand, waving back tears and trying to stop a weird gasping for air that my body has started, as if all the oxygen in the world will never be enough.

Tony deflates. "I'm sorry," he says. "I'm so sorry. I just—God, I hate guys who do that shit to women. Can't ever learn to keep my mouth shut."

"It's okay. I—it was nice to have somebody stand up for me. And I can see why you'd think that about him. But he's a good father. And he doesn't usually shout like that."

"It's just that tone he was using, making you feel stupid. You don't deserve that."

Which is when the memory hits me, right between the eyes with enough force to knock me backward against the seat.

It's no longer Tony sitting behind the steering wheel. It's Greg.

It's late, winter late, and already dark by at least three hours. Snow gathers on the windshield faster than the wipers swish it away.

Chuff. Chuff. Chuff.

We're parked at the corner of the lot, and the glare of the gas station lights stops short of me, in the passenger seat, illuminating only Greg's face so that he looks disembodied, insubstantial.

"When, Maisey? You keep putting this off and the baby will be our flower girl."

My hand goes automatically to my belly. In response I feel the flip, flip, of the baby growing in my womb. She feels like a fish, a tiny fish growing in a dark, private place that belongs, so far, only to me.

Greg wants halvsies, and I'm not sure I want to share.

"I don't know when. Soon. Just . . . not yet."

Every other day he asks about the wedding, the one he's been talking about since high school, the one he gave me a ring for months ago, the one he wanted before we moved in together, before we got pregnant. The wedding he wants because he says he loves me.

I have no good reason to put it off, and yet I do. Over and over and over again. Of course I love him, how could I not? He buys me flowers and takes me places. He's handsome and smart and going to be rich. But my love is a pale thing compared to the love he expresses for me. His feels too hot, too bright, like a fire that might consume me if I stand too close.

Whatever I give him, it never seems to be enough.

He wants all of me, including the bits that I've managed to keep for myself, hidden away from my mother. I've learned from her how demanding love can be, with all the expectations I can never live up to, and something inside me rebels at the idea of surrendering my inner self—or the tiny baby growing inside me—to Greg.

Mom wants me to marry him, and she doesn't even know about the baby. My secret. Still a part of me and nobody's business but my own.

She wants me to marry him because he's solid, whereas I am flighty. Focused, whereas I am scattered. Successful. Safe and law-abiding and going to earn more than enough money to support me in comfort. She says he will help me grow into the woman I'm capable of being. What she means is that maybe I'll finally stop being flighty and indecisive and irresponsible.

All my life my mother has made my decisions for me, not trusting I can make my own. And I've let her do it. I've let her decide everything from the color of the ribbon in my hair as a child to my choice of university and my journalism major. We all know I am terrible at making decisions, so why am I resisting both her wishes and Greg's now?

But whenever Greg asks me to marry him, I choke on the word yes. *I say maybe, and later, and of course "I love you," because I do, I must, what is wrong with me if I don't?*

But now there is a baby, or at least the promise of one, and that changes everything.

Greg takes a long quavering breath, and then another, and his shoulders begin to shake. In quiet horror, I realize he is crying, that I have caused him to cry.

My hand butterflies onto his shoulder and rests there, tentative. He stiffens beneath my touch, the muscle going from soft to rock-hard, and my hand flies back to the comfort of my belly and the baby swimming secretly within.

"I can't do this," Greg says.

I think I've heard him wrong, but he straightens up and turns his head to look at me. His face is wet with his tears, his dark lashes glued together, his features taut with pain and determination.

"This is the last time I'm asking, Maisey. Give me a solid answer tonight. Say yes. Say when. Hell, tell me the word, and I'll drive us all the way to Vegas, and we can tie the knot tomorrow."

My throat is dry, but the sensation of tiny wings flitting against my ribs is not grief or fear. I don't answer. Can't answer.

"I mean it," he says, desperation hardening his voice. "Tell me now, or it's over between us."

Fear comes barging in, a big old clumsy bear of it, crashing and rattling the corners of my life. I moved in with Greg before I finished college. I've never lived alone. I don't have a steady job. I sure as hell don't want to move back in with my parents. How do I think I'm ever going to be qualified to take care of a baby when I'm not capable of taking care of myself? I have to say yes. I'm going to say yes. What other choice do I have?

I open my mouth on the words that want to choke me.

"I . . . can't."

Greg's face turns a mottled shade of red and white. His hands clamp around my shoulders, the fingers digging into my flesh so hard they feel like they're going to meet, going to separate my bones.

I try to twist away. "Stop it. You're hurting me."

He doesn't stop. Instead, his fingers tighten more, and he shakes me. "You can't do this. It's my baby, too. Just as much my baby as yours. Say yes. Say it."

"No." My voice is small. It's hard to get my breath. I say it again, louder, using all my strength. "No!"

He lets me go, and I draw a quaking breath, thinking it's over. My eyes are closed and I don't see what's coming. An explosion of pain jolts my head sideways, lights flashing behind my eyes.

I hear myself sobbing before I'm aware enough to stop it, to clamp my teeth together and breathe against the pain.

"You can't raise a baby by yourself, Maisey. Let's face it. You're a ditz. And nobody else is going to want my seconds, so if you think you're going to find another father for her, you can forget that idea. You're pretty enough for a small-town girl but not pretty enough to bank on. This is your last chance."

"Maisey?"

Not Greg's voice. Tony's.

I take a breath, and then another. My hand goes to my face, remembering the shape of the bruise that lingered there for weeks, the one I accounted for by my general tendency to walk into doors.

When I open my eyes, I recognize the expression on Tony's face. I've seen it a hundred times plastered over other sets of features.

"Don't," I say.

"Don't what?"

"You're about to deliver some sort of lecture or advice or whatever."

"Are you a mind reader or something?"

"I just know that look. Go ahead and tell me. What did I do now? Or fail to do?"

"You?" Tony looks genuinely befuddled. "You haven't done anything. I'm just . . . worried. About you and Elle."

"Greg isn't going to fly up here and beat me up. He doesn't do that."

He only hit me once.

The words flash on my visual screen like one of those LED signs. I cringe, recognizing a phrase I've heard on TV, on Facebook, from some of my friends, but never recognized as a resident in my own psyche. I press my back to the door, one knee drawn up on the seat. My arms are folded tight around that ongoing quivering so deep inside me I can't touch it.

Tony clears his throat. "Good to know. But I was going to tell you about something else. I asked about your mom and the gun at the shooting range on Tuesday. Owner said she started coming in a few months back. Showed up every day and asked questions about stopping intruders and shooting to kill."

"And?" He's had this info for a couple of days and hasn't told me.

"And, put that together with your sister's hostility—"

"Marley? You think Mom was scared of Marley? She was cold, I'll grant you that, but I doubt she's a mass-murdering psycho."

"You talked to her for all of five minutes. How would you know? You said she knew about you. What if she just now found your mom and was coming after her? Don't you think it's a little too coincidental that they played a concert here tonight? That band is too good for Northern Ales. They've got bigger gigs to play."

I can't think of words to respond to this. The first thing that comes to mind is that Tony is paranoid. What he's suggesting is something out of a movie script, not the sort of event that happens in a well-ordered, structured life like my mother's.

But then, maybe her life wasn't so well-ordered and structured after all.

Tony shifts in his seat. "Look. All I'm saying is, be careful, okay? Lock the doors. Sleep with the phone by your bed. If Marley shows up at your door out of the blue, call me before you let her in."

"I can pretty safely promise you that, since I'm more likely to get a visit from the pope than from my sister. If either one of them knocks on the door I'll call you, too."

"I'm serious."

He is serious. I can see that. He's wound up tighter than an over-tuned guitar string. One more turn and something's going to snap. His jaw is so tight, the muscle bunches. There's a slight sheen of sweat on his forehead. His breathing has sped up to a rate that almost matches my own.

This retriggers my memory of Greg and the night he hit me. Whatever possessed me to talk to him the way I did on the phone just now? I'm terrified by my own audacity, and Tony, my safe protector, seems lethal all at once. Too big. Too male. Too full of untapped possibilities. Where on earth are Mia and Elle? Surely they've had plenty of time to inspect every carton of ice cream in the store. A group of teenagers spills out of a car, laughing, shoving. The automatic doors at the front of the store open but disgorge only one old man, bent and shuffling, clutching a brown paper bag.

No Mia. No Elle.

My breath keeps catching on a sharpness in my throat. Greg's right about one thing at least—I don't really know anything about Mia or Tony. I've trusted him, partly because of his occupation, partly because up until this minute he's made me feel safe and protected. But abusive men can be firemen. Stalkers can be policemen. Maybe, for all I know, Tony is the guy my mom was scared of. My hand digs in my purse for my phone and I clutch it, ready to dial 911 if I need to.

"I'll sleep with two phones by my bed," I say out loud, hearing the strain in my voice and hating it. "Cell and landline. I'll make sure all the doors and windows are locked. I'll call 911 before I let anybody in."

"Good." He relaxes a little. I watch him do it, one muscle group at a time. Jaw. Shoulders. Hands. "I didn't mean to scare you," he says. "I get a little intense. It's just—something about this situation has me all tied up in knots. Your—Greg—ignited the whole mess."

"He's not my Greg. Hasn't been my Greg since before Elle was born. He's married."

We sit there in a tight, awkward silence, both staring straight ahead. He drums his fingers on the steering wheel. I clutch my phone. Two more minutes, then I'm going in looking for Elle.

At precisely one minute and twenty-five seconds into my countdown, Mia and Elle emerge from the store, each carrying a shopping bag. Elle is laughing. Mia is talking nonstop and is still talking when she opens the car door.

"So then, George says a bear ran into him. Can you believe it? He didn't hit the bear. He was just sitting there on his four wheeler, and the bear came bolting out of the woods and plowed right over the top of him. Never even stopped to look back . . ."

A cool breeze enters the car with the two of them, a fresh hit of mountain air and trees with undertones of gasoline and exhaust. It clears my head. Grounds me.

"We've got a carton for everybody," Elle says. "Even for Grandpa and Mia's mom."

I think about the way Tony treats his mother, the way she kissed him on the forehead before he left. The way Mia clearly adores him. He's done nothing but be helpful. I have no more reason to believe he's dangerous than I do to believe that Marley is going to show up at my door with intent to kill.

Leah's Journal

The first time that he hit me, I was six months pregnant and already awkward and ungainly. I'd always been light and quick on my feet. Now I felt like a wide-load trailer on a two-lane highway. The doctor explained that I was extra big because of the twins. "Take it easy," he told me. "Slow down. There are extra risks with twin pregnancies, and the babies usually come early."

"No more sex," he'd said, at the last visit.

I was relieved by the prohibition. The babies were more than a fantasy now. They moved around inside me like secret subterranean creatures, the three of us forming a world of our own. Sex felt like an intrusion, like we might disturb them, hurt them, sully them somehow.

Boots did not share my relief. We fought after that visit, his rages growing in intensity. It wasn't just about the sex. He started pushing me to do other things I'd stopped doing on account of the babies. Smoke a cigarette. Have a drink.

"It's one party," he'd said to me, that night. "We're going. Can you find something to wear besides that tent? You look like somebody's pregnant granny."

His words stung me. He'd been on about my appearance all week. The weight I'd gained. The ugly red marks forming on my growing belly. I agreed with him. My jeans had long since stopped being an option, and I'd started wearing maternity dresses as the easiest thing. I'd been to the Goodwill and brought home what I could find. The dress was hideous. I was hideous.

I'd always had a sharp tongue in me, something Boots appreciated as long as it wasn't directed at him. I was hurt, and I retaliated, poking at his weak spots. "Maybe if you'd get a good job instead of lying around all day, I could buy something pretty."

"You've turned into a nag," he said. "I don't like it." His eyes had gone cold. He was looking at me the way he looked at teachers and police officers.

I should have taken the warning. Instead, I stood my ground. "Well, I don't like the way you're looking at me. It's not just you and me anymore—"

Those were the magic words to unlock his fists.

No slapping for Boots. It was a straight-up right hook to my cheekbone. Dropped me to the floor. I was heavy, and the fall wrenched my back. My head hit the floor, and there were lights flashing. He stood above me, looking down, breathing hard through his nose.

"Maybe you'll be good for something again someday," he said, but with scorn. "I'm going to the party. You can stay here."

And then he kicked me in the belly. It wasn't even a vicious kick. At that point, I wasn't worth the energy that would have taken. It was a gesture of disdain, the way someone might kick aside a bit of garbage on the road.

But those beautiful, shiny, cowboy boots had pointy toes, and my skin was stretched tight like a drum.

It was my soul and my heart that hurt worst. Something broke in me right then that has been broken since. All these years with you, my Walter, you'd think it might have been put right. But some things, I guess, can't be mended.

I was afraid more for the babies than I was for myself. What if that kick had broken something inside me? Harmed them? If it had been just me I'd like to think I'd have either stood up to him again or walked out. But I was young and frightened and so very pregnant. Where would I go? What would I do?

I had learned my lesson. When he came home, drunk, blubbering his apologies and begging my forgiveness, I held him and swore over and over that I would never leave him, that it would always be the two of us against the world, that even the babies would never come between us.

All of it lies.

I knew, right then, that I would figure out a plan to leave him.

Chapter Nineteen

When we pull up in the driveway of my parents' house, all the lights are on. My fear sensors start blaring like a fire alarm. Dad should be in bed. He should be sleeping. Surely Tony's mom wouldn't let him start burning things again, but what do I really know about her?

I am out of the car before it comes to a full stop. No evidence of smoke or fire, thank God, but I still cross the space between me and the door in a series of giant leaps, superwoman without a cape.

Dad and Mrs. Medina are as comfy as can be at the kitchen table, both nursing mugs of hot tea. She is a plump, comfortable-looking woman, with the same blue eyes as Mia and Tony, but her hair is lighter, a mousy-brown color, streaked with gray. She sits close beside Dad, one hand resting on his shoulder. His eyes are red and swollen, as if he's been crying.

Relief that he's okay gives way to a sucker punch of guilt.

My mother is being buried tomorrow, and the stranger I've left Dad with is doing a better job than I have of comforting him.

He tries to smile at me, though. "There's my girl," he says. "Hannah told me you were fine and not to worry. But I couldn't sleep."

"I'm sorry, Daddy."

"We brought ice cream." Elle breezes in and plunks her bag up on the kitchen counter, beginning to unpack. "I hope you like chocolate,

Grandpa. We didn't know what you would want, so we went simple. If you don't, though, you can have some of my cookies and cream."

Mia joins her at the counter, the two of them setting out a row of ice cream cartons and pulling out spoons and bowls and digging through Mom's spotlessly organized silverware drawers for an ice cream scoop.

Ignoring the ice cream, I drag a chair to where I can look directly into Dad's eyes. He's sad and lost, and I should leave him alone, but my need for answers is stronger than my better self.

"We went to a concert, Dad. To hear my sister, Marley, and her band. She was too pissed to talk to me. I can't say I blame her."

Dad's body jerks like I've shocked him with a Taser. Tea sloshes over the edge of his mug and onto the table as he draws his hands back and puts them in his lap.

"I've made a mess," he says.

"No worries, I've got it." Mrs. Medina bustles over to the counter for paper towels, but I don't think the tea is what he's talking about.

"You burned papers. You shredded documents. You said you'd forgotten something. What do you know that you're not telling me?"

He just shakes his head, avoiding my eyes.

In my peripheral vision, I'm aware that the ice cream preparation has stopped. Everybody is staring at us, waiting. I feel like a bully, an interrogator, but I can't stop. I have to know.

"I found the birth certificates. I found the pink blankets. I found the part of the list that tells you to shred all the papers. I found the first page of Mom's journal. Did you burn that, too?"

He draws in a tremulous breath. "Leave it at that, Maisey."

"I can't. Don't you see? You knew. All along you knew Marley was real. You let Mom convince me I made her up. That I was imagining things. She dragged me to counseling, made me think I was crazy."

He makes a small choking sound in his throat and drops his head into his hands.

"I don't blame you for any of it; I know how she was. She made you promise something, but she's not here now. You can tell me. You've been fantastic at being my dad. I know she made you do it. I know how she is—was—"

"Stop." His head comes up. His eyes focus on me, laser clear.

"I'm not going to stop. She lied to me. She controlled you. She—"

"I said, stop!" Dad slams his hand on the table. His mug rattles. My stomach makes an elevator trip up into my throat. He has never raised his voice to me. Never slammed a door or made a threatening gesture. I freeze, like a terrified bunny.

"You don't know anything about your mother, Maisey. I won't hear it. I won't talk about her. I won't talk about this. Not tonight. Not ever. What's done is done and stays done. Do you hear me?"

I stare at him in shock. We all do. Tony looks like he's carved from stone. Mrs. Medina puts an arm around Mia and pulls her in close. Elle the irrepressible actually has her mouth open.

As for me, I want to simultaneously collapse into a bubbling little heap of apology and grab Dad's shoulders and shake them.

"Just tell me this. Are we in danger? Mom had a gun. What was she afraid of? You have to tell me that at least."

He blinks and rubs his eyes, looking at the faces in the kitchen as if he's never seen them before.

"Are we having a party? I'm very tired. Would it be rude if I just go to bed?" Without waiting for an answer, he shoves back his chair and starts to get up.

He only clears the chair by a couple of inches before falling back, heavily.

"I've turned old, Maisey," he says, gently, as if he hadn't just been shouting at me. "Help an old man to bed?"

And so I do. I give him both my hands, and he grips them, tightly enough to squeeze my bones against each other. Using my weight, I lean back as he leans forward and drag him to his feet. He sways a little, and

I see Tony moving in my peripheral vision, ready to catch him if he falls, but then the swaying stops.

Red-rimmed eyes look down into mine, and Dad sighs, deeply. He plants a kiss on my forehead. "You're a good girl, Maisey. You always have been." And then he starts shuffling across the kitchen, and I move with him, holding his hand.

All my childhood selves move with us, across the kitchen, down the familiar hall, into my parents' room. How many thousands of times have we walked this way, hand in hand? Only then he was the strong and comforting anchor in my life. The man with the answers. The calm to my mother's passion.

Now he is frail and I am strong, and if he is the man with answers, he's not about to share them with me.

He sinks down onto the bed, fully clothed. "I'm too tired to undress," he says. "Will it matter?"

"It won't matter, Daddy. So long as you're comfortable."

I pull off his shoes, and he collapses back onto the bed, rolling over into my mother's spot once again. "I keep thinking she's coming back," he says. "I keep waiting."

"She's not coming back, Daddy."

"I know." He starts to cry then, and I lie down on the bed beside him and put my head on his chest. I have no more tears of my own, not tonight, only a deep and abiding ache in my chest that seems like it's always been there and will never go away.

I lie there until he stops crying. Until his breathing eases and slows and turns into a soft snore. He's fallen asleep on top of the covers, so I fetch a spare blanket from Mom's cedar chest and tuck it around him. I kiss him on the cheek and turn out the light.

Out in the kitchen, Mia is washing bowls and spoons in a sink of soapy water and Elle is drying. Mrs. Medina and Tony sit at the table. Nobody is talking. The energy in the room feels more like the aftermath of a bombing than an ice cream party.

All the eyes turned on me seem accusing and judging.

"Is he okay?" Elle asks.

"He's asleep."

"Maybe we should check his blood sugar," Tony says. "In case it's gone off again."

"I think we should let him sleep." I sound downright bossy. I don't care. The energy for pretending anything I don't feel right now is missing in action.

Tony pushes back his chair. "You're right, of course. We should go. Tomorrow is going to be a difficult day."

I look at the clock. God. It's nearly midnight. Mom's funeral isn't until eleven, but there will be so much to do.

"Thanks for staying with him, Mrs. Medina."

She smiles at me, despite my behavior, despite everything. She puts her hands on my shoulders and kisses me on one cheek, and then the other. Her lips are soft, her cheek cool against mine.

"I know it's not my place to give advice," she says. "I think if your mother were here, she might tell you this. Give Walter a little time. Give yourself a little time. You're in shock, the both of you. It will all come right in the end."

I want to believe her, but I can't imagine any of this ever coming right. Still, I nod.

"You don't believe me," she says. "Why should you? But I, too, have been through hard times. It will all come right. You'll see."

"Let's go." Tony circles her waist with his arm, and she releases me and walks with him to the door.

Mia hugs Elle. "We'll go bowling. Or shopping at Walmart. Or a movie."

"Will you be there tomorrow?" Elle asks.

"Wouldn't miss it," Mia says.

Elle yawns. Her eyelids are drooping. "Go to bed, Elle Belle," I tell her, and she doesn't argue.

"Night," she mumbles.

Once Elle is safely off to bed, Mia embraces me in a tumultuous hug. "I can't even imagine what you're feeling," she says. "What a clusterfuck, right?" And then she hugs me again.

"Mia!" Tony calls from the door.

She laughs. "Once a big brother, always a big brother."

Mia is like a breath of wind on a foggy morning, clearing the air, revealing sunlight. I hug her back, tight, and then follow her down the hall.

Tony waits by the door.

"You okay?" he asks.

I nod, unsure if my voice is going to work if I try to speak.

"Lock the door behind me," he says. "Check all the windows. Sleep with the phone. Just to be sure."

This is not comforting. I swallow back a sour taste rising in the back of my throat. "Maybe you should give me the ammo back? For Mom's gun?"

It's like a curtain drops over his face. All the softness is gone between one breath and the next. That hard, clenched look comes back. "I'm not sure that's a good idea."

"You got me thinking. Mom had the gun for a reason. Maybe I need one, too."

"You don't know how to use it. Guns are dangerous—"

"Just give me the ammo. Okay? If I use it, trust me, something more dangerous is going on."

He hesitates. "Tell you what. I'll just stay."

I have no idea how to take that. Before I can protest, he gives me his easy, disarming smile. "You'll sleep better if you don't have to worry. I'll sleep in the recliner. If there's any trouble, I'll take care of it."

This doesn't solve my problems, really. Any of them.

"You need to sleep."

"I can sleep in the chair. Besides, I'm used to taking night shifts."

There's no tactful way to tell him I don't necessarily feel safer with him locked in on my side of the door.

He misreads the pause and goes on. "Look, it's not anything about you being a woman and needing a man to protect you. Mia's almost better with a gun than I am. But you're not in the best of shape to be learning about guns. You're too shocked, too tired. After the funeral, how about I take you, the gun, and the ammo out shooting? Show you basic gun safety, teach you how to take a basic shot. And then I'll give it back to you. Okay?"

"Yes? I don't know. I've never been to my mother's funeral before. Don't know how I'll be after."

His face softens, then. He reaches out, hand curved, as if he's going to cup my cheek, but then lets it drop with a small slapping sound against his thigh.

"Not tomorrow. In a couple of days."

"And you're going to play bodyguard that many nights running? I thought you had a job."

"There's always Mia," he says, "only you'd never get any sleep because she can't stop talking."

"Tony, I don't know . . ."

"Please," he says, in the way I picture a starving man requesting a piece of bread. And then that smile, lightning swift and unexpected, totally disarms me. "Mama will have a fit if I don't do my part. Please don't put me in the way of a butt-smacking."

His words present an image of his gentle mother, five feet tall and very round, waving a belt at her tall and burly offspring. Laughter bubbles up before I can stop it. "Is she as dangerous as Mia? Because that sounds terrifying."

"Every bit. Hang on—I'll just give Mia the keys. That way you don't have to wait up to let me in. Okay?"

"I'm sleeping on the couch."

"I'll be extremely quiet. You won't even know I'm here."

My last bit of resistance is destroyed by a gleefully rebellious thought of Greg's disapproval.

I wait on the porch while Tony jogs down the sidewalk to hold a conference with Mia. She waves at me through the open driver's side window and slams the car into reverse, spinning the tires as she backs out of the driveway.

Tony walks back up the sidewalk toward me, and I lean against the railing for support. The reality of his maleness is nearly overwhelming. Just the idea of sleeping on the couch while he sits a few feet away in the chair, maybe watching me, sends blood flowing to all sorts of places it shouldn't.

It doesn't help when he holds the door open and gestures for me to enter the house first. I duck my head to pass under his arm and catch a whiff of musk and deodorant and sweat. He's all muscle and testosterone, and oh my God it's been so long.

Self-conscious, still wearing my T-shirt and my jeans, taking off only my socks, I lie down on the couch and pull the blanket up to my chin. Tony turns out the light, plunging us both into darkness. When my eyes adjust, I can make out shapes and shadows, thanks to the cracked-open drapes in the living room window. Tony is invisible in the dark rectangle that is my father's armchair. I picture him in my mind like a movie sheriff, with a star pinned to his shirt and a shotgun laid across his lap.

For a long time I lie there, wide awake, my body exhausted but thrumming with energy that won't let me sleep. My consciousness flits around, homing in on small sounds. My breathing. Tony's breathing. The occasional creak of a floorboard.

"Can't sleep?" Tony asks, after a long while of lying there, eyes wide open, staring up at nothing.

"Kinda wound up." Three breaths. And then, "You were right, about Greg. He did hit me. Only the once. Under provocation." The memory feels as fresh as if it happened today, not over twelve years ago.

My face actually hurts, although it's probably because I have my jaw clamped so tight it's hard to swallow.

"Bastard," Tony says.

Silence again. My breathing. His breathing.

The heater kicks on with a low hum. Outside, a car drives by.

Just when I begin to accept that I am not going to sleep tonight, that I might as well get up and make coffee and do something useful, Tony's voice floats out of the darkness.

"My sisters and I used to play a game when we couldn't sleep. I could teach you, if you want."

Something in his voice, wistful, hesitant, makes me sit up and stare as hard as I can into the shadows to try to read his expression. But all I can see of him is his silhouette, a solid shape in the dark.

"Okay," I answer, cautiously. "Because apparently I am not sleeping anytime soon."

"It's a kids' game," he says. "So bear with me. There's a verse to go with it. Like a nursery rhyme, sort of."

"Like 'Peter Peter Pumpkin Eater'?"

He laughs. "More like Truth or Dare. No. Wait. God, no. Not like Truth or Dare at all. There's a lullaby and . . . oh, never mind. I'm not helping much, am I?"

"Sing it," I tell him, wrapping the blanket around me like a shawl and huddling into its warmth.

"What? Now?"

"I can't sleep, and you are holding out on me with this lullaby."

"You're serious." A silence stretches between us. Another car drives by on the late-night street and then is gone, and we're back to the sounds of breathing. Tony's. Mine. The rustle of my blanket as I shift my weight and lie back down on the couch. Of course he's not going to sing. The idea is ridiculous.

My mouth is already open to tell him to just explain this game to me, when he takes a breath and does begin to sing, after all. The melody is haunting, his voice a clear, sweet tenor. And before he gets through the first two lines, my heart is vibrating to the tune of grief in E minor.

Whisper me this, my darling, my love
The song of the moonlight, of stars up above
Whisper me truth, love, and whisper me lies
Warm days of winter, cold summer skies
Whisper me anger, whisper me rain
Whisper me flowers, then whisper me pain
When I come to die, love, then whisper me this
The shape of a memory, the truth of a kiss.
Whisper me, whisper me, whisper me this
A lifetime of memories, and one final kiss.

Silent tears well up and spill over, tracking down my cheeks, but it's a beautiful pain, half grief, half pleasure. When the last note fades away, the silence that follows is alive with emotion. His. Mine. I want to cross the room, settle down in his lap, and rest my head on his chest.

It's all too much. Too much sadness, too much beauty, too much intimacy with a relative stranger. I blot my face with the blanket and try to settle my shaky breath.

"That is a *lullaby*?" I ask, breaking the mood.

He clears his throat. I hear his weight shift in the chair. "My mother used to sing it to us. I always thought it was. I never realized what a sad song it is."

"And there's a game that goes with this happy song?"

"Whisper Me This. That's the name of the game."

"How do you play it?"

"Whisper me truth, whisper me lies. You whisper two things, one truth, one lie—and I decide which is which."

"You go first."

Tony laughs softly. "All right. Here you go." He drops his voice to a whisper. "The moon is really a giant spaceship. Grasshoppers have ears on their bellies."

"Wait, what? That's not fair. Neither one of those can be true."

"You have to whisper," he replies. "And pick one."

"All right. I choose the grasshopper thing."

"Good choice. Your turn."

"Okay, but really with the grasshoppers?"

Tony laughs. "Nights on call as an EMT or firefighter means finding weird things on the internet. And yes, really."

"Hmmm." I lie back, pondering my turn. "No man has ever sung any song to me in my lifetime. The moon is not a spaceship; it really is made of cheese. Camembert, I think."

"Definitely camembert," Tony says. "I think there's a moon cave somewhere full of bottles of wine to go with it."

My laugh is a whisper. All the tension is drifting out of my body, up and away, like tendrils of mist rising off a morning lake. My limbs, my eyelids, grow heavy with sleep.

"My turn," Tony says, but his voice sounds far away. "I was a contestant on *America's Got Talent*. My favorite TV show ever was . . ."

I drift off into sleep before he finishes.

Chapter Twenty

Tony sits wide awake in the dark, listening to Maisey's soft, even breathing, asking himself what the hell he was thinking. The song, the game, the vulnerability of sharing them after all these years, has flayed him wide open.

Logic tells him that the bone-deep trembling that starts in his gut and radiates out through his body is just adrenaline, nothing more than the PTSD he's been dealing with since forever, but it's worse than usual.

So much worse.

Every nerve, every memory circuit is lit up like a neon sign. His heart feels exposed, the tracery of his nerves visible and glowing in the dark like the project of some mad scientist. Even though he knows full well it's not logical, he checks his hands and is relieved to find they're normal.

He tries to hold himself in the present. This room. This task he's set himself, to act as some sort of bodyguard for Maisey and her daughter. Who is he kidding? He's no hero, has never been. He's not even brave enough to tell Maisey the truth about the Whisper Me This game.

Truth is, he hasn't thought about the game in years and doesn't want to think about it now, but he has opened the door and the memories are determined to run through his mind, his body, dragging the emotional debris of fear and shame and loss along with them.

What he told Maisey about the game wasn't a lie, but it wasn't the truth, either. Playing had nothing to do with sleep and everything to do with soothing frightened children and keeping them quiet. The game was played in closets, behind locked doors, always as a counterpoint to his father's rages.

Tony grounds himself with his feet on the floor and grips the arms of the chair, but nothing he can do will hold back the tide of memory.

He huddles together with his sisters, all of them on one narrow bed. Vanessa and Jess have burrowed under a blanket. Theresa and Barb sit cross-legged, Barb hugging a pillow. Baby Mia is asleep in Theresa's arms.

Downstairs, in the kitchen, his father is shouting. His mother's voice, low and soothing, answers. Something crashes and all of them jump. The baby startles awake and begins to whimper, but Theresa hushes and rocks her, and she settles back to sleep.

Barb, always braver than the rest of them, tiptoes across the room to close and lock the door. Tony knows there is no real safety in this; the door to the room he now shares with Mia is cracked and hangs on its hinges, a reminder that locks can be broken and doors can be kicked in.

"Let's play Whisper Me This," Theresa says, cuddling the baby. "Vanessa, you first."

"Okay." Vanessa's whispered voice is so soft it's hard to hear through the muffling blanket. Tony doesn't even try to listen. He tunes in on the downstairs noises. He squeezes his eyes shut, remembering the last time fists flew, of the sound they made striking his mother's body, of her sobs, of the slap to the side of his own head that rattled his teeth and made stars flash in front of his eyes.

"Your turn, Tony." Theresa touches his shoulder. "Whisper me truth, whisper me lies."

He flinches at a dull thud downstairs, which is followed by a whimper and then the sound of weeping and more shouting. His body starts to shiver. "Boys don't cry," his father always says, but Tony's eyes don't care. Tears pour down his cheeks. His nose is running.

To his own surprise, his hands clench into fists. "When I'm big, I'm going to beat Dad up," he whispers, and he means it for his truth. "I'll make him stop."

His sisters meet this statement with silence.

Barb reaches over and smooths his hair. Vanessa and Jess peek out over the top of the blanket, eyes wide. Theresa squints her eyes at him.

"That better be your lie, Tonio," she says.

Another thud from downstairs. More shouting. A sharp cry of pain.

"I will," Tony says, louder now, feeling that his sisters don't believe him. "I'll punch him in the nose and make him bleed."

"That would make you like him," Theresa whispers. "Do you want to be a man like that?"

Tony isn't sure he wants to be a man at all. It's all women in his life so far, his mother and his big sisters and now baby Mia. Dad is the only man he knows.

"Come over here," Theresa says, and Tony crawls over Vanessa and Jess to sit directly beside her. She's been bossing him since his earliest memory, and he's used to following her commands.

"Hold out your arms," she says, and Tony does so.

Theresa shifts the baby into his lap, and he automatically wraps his arms around her so she won't slide off. He's only held her once, the day she came home from the hospital. There are so many willing arms with all the girls that he hasn't been offered the chance.

Which is fine with him. He hasn't wanted to hold her again. She cries too much and takes more than her share of everybody's attention. Her crib is in his bedroom, and she wakes him at night. He has to be extra quiet whenever she's sleeping, too, and she's stinky, all sour milk and poopy diapers.

Sometimes, he wants to shake her, even though he knows that's bad.

Now, he's surprised by how much heavier she is, how much she's grown. Maybe she knows he doesn't like her much, because she screws up her tiny face and makes a sound like she's going to cry.

"Rock her," Theresa says. "Pretend you're a tree in the wind."

Tony sways back and forth, pretending to be a tree, tuning out the sounds from downstairs.

Mia gives a little sigh and nestles against him. One tiny hand curls around his finger.

Something happens inside Tony's chest right then, a sort of melting that he's felt before when he's petting his neighbor's kittens. He doesn't want to shake Mia anymore, or send her back to the hospital. He wants to hold her, and rock her, and make sure that she is happy and safe.

Theresa nods at him. "That's the kind of man you want to be, Tonio. Don't you forget it."

Tony isn't sure exactly what she means. He still wants to beat up his dad, maybe even more now than ever, because the baby needs protecting . . .

Maisey cries out in her sleep, and it jolts him back into the now.

This room, this chair, this man-size body that still trembles like it did when he was a child. He didn't do a very good job of protecting Mia, he thinks now, or the others for that matter. How many times did Mia get hit after that night? Theresa and Barb, Vanessa and Jess? His mother? All of them, over and over and over again. And how many of those times was he cowering in a corner, behind a chair, even under a bed when the fists were flying?

How many of those times was he harboring rages of his own? Slamming doors, punching walls. His anger has always felt like some sort of evil science experiment, oozing out of containment into the corners of his life and exploding without warning. He remembers as if it had happened five minutes ago the first time he put a fist through the wall in his bedroom. The shock of that moment, of realizing that despite all his efforts he was growing into a man, and an angry one.

A man like his father. Not the man his sisters wanted—needed—him to be, but a violent man, capable of atrocity.

The gun in his hands. The recoil. The wet tearing sound of a bullet entering flesh.

God. He should not be here, should not have accepted Maisey's trust. The last thing she needs in her life is a man like him.

But it's too late to run. One thing he has always done throughout his adult life is keep his promises. And so he stays where he is, keeping watch, as the long slow minutes tick away. He's still there, watchful and wide awake, when the morning light seeps in around the curtains.

Maisey stirs as the light touches her face. He wants to block it, to shelter her from what this day holds, but he sees the memory of grief move across her face as her eyes open.

"You're still here," she says, her voice husky with sleep.

"I promised," he answers. Their eyes meet and hold, and the unbearable, beautiful intimacy of the night before is still right there between them.

Despite all the promises he made to his better self during the night, he's about to cross the room and kiss her, when the sound of an opening door and light footsteps in the hallway freeze him in his tracks.

Elle wanders in, yawning, and flops down on the couch beside Maisey. Tony's mind scrambles for words to answer the question that's surely forming in her mind, but she doesn't ask questions. "Hey, Tony," she says, as if it's the most normal thing in the world that he spent the night. "You want some cereal? Grandpa's got Froot Loops."

"I think Tony might want a real breakfast."

"I can make eggs," Elle says. "Mom burns everything."

Elle's presence has brought Tony back to his senses. He takes a breath and a simultaneous step toward the door. "Thanks for the offer, but I should go. I have things to do before the funeral. I'll call Mia to come and get me."

"The least I can do is drive you home," Maisey protests. "Don't bother Mia. She's probably still sleeping."

Which is true enough. Mia is not an early riser. Of course, any one of his sisters will come get him if he asks, but then there would be explanations and innuendos and conversations he doesn't want to get into.

"Are you sure?" he asks. "You've got a big day."

"I'm sure. Give me a minute to get ready."

She yawns and stretches, then shuffles out of the room, loose-jointed with lingering sleep. Tony can't help watching the way she moves, can't stop imagining the feel of her drowsy body molding against his, of allowing himself to deliberately bury his hands in her tangled hair, pressing his lips against her neck . . .

"You could ask her out," Elle says. "I wouldn't mind."

Tony opens his mouth to utter some sort of denial, but no words come out.

"I'm not stupid," she goes on. "I see the way you look at each other."

He clears his throat. "This is hardly a time to think about dating—"

"Why?"

"It's your grandma's funeral today, remember? I think your mother has enough to worry about. What is that look supposed to mean?"

The child sits cross-legged on the couch, resting her chin on both fists and eyeing him with an expression that is entirely too knowing. He decides not to wait for her answer. "I'll be outside on the porch."

"You're coming to the funeral, right?" Elle calls after him. "And bringing Mia?"

"We'll be there."

He breathes a sigh of relief when the door bangs shut between them. His whole careful system of controls, checks, and measures is unraveling at an alarming pace, and Elle has just sped up the process.

What if? he asks himself. *What if I did ask her out? Later. After the funeral.*

You're forgetting who you are, his memory answers. *You'd better find a way to remember.*

Leah's Journal

I'd promised myself I would leave him, but as it turned out, the leaving wasn't easy. I had two tiny unborn babies to consider. I was a high school dropout. My only skills were a smart mouth and a stubborn streak.

I missed a visit to my doctor, waiting for my bruises to heal. At the next visit, he put me on bed rest. Through the long, boring weeks from then until the babies were born, Boots pretty much left me alone. He said he was busy making money for us. If so, I never saw a penny of it. His mother would come over and help. She wasn't much for cleaning, but at least she washed the dishes and did the laundry.

She didn't talk much, but one day when I was lying on the couch, feeling sorry for myself, lonely and tired enough that the tears got away from me, she put her hand on my forehead for just an instant. It was a hard hand, callused and rough, but the gentleness eased me. Her words did not.

"Poor child. You're good and in for it now, I suppose."

I didn't ask her what she meant. I think I didn't want to know.

Chapter Twenty-One

I have never been to a funeral.

It's not that there haven't been deaths in my life; it's just that for one reason or another I've never actually attended the service that marked them. Dad's only sister, Aunt Del, succumbed to cancer when I was ten. One of my classmates died tragically just before high school graduation, the casualty of four-wheeling on rough terrain. Various acquaintances of Mom's church family also "went to sleep in Jesus," as she always said.

As a child, this phrase confused me hopelessly, especially since at least one of the deceased died at the wheel of his pickup truck. When Mom, busy discussing arrangements with the other church ladies, brushed off my questions, my imagination did its usual thing. I still carry in my mind today a picture of Mr. Peterson praying while driving, eyes closed out of respect to God, and accidentally drifting off to sleep. This is a state of consciousness with which I was well versed, something that happened fairly frequently to me during long church prayers.

So I had a clear image of Mr. Peterson falling asleep in Jesus, but my imagination failed at the magnitude of this event called a funeral. I wanted to go, that one time, having some sort of idea that maybe Jesus would be at the funeral and I could actually see him. Mom nixed that idea.

"Funerals are not for children," she said. It was her case-closed tone of voice, the one I never even tried to argue with. So I stayed home with a sitter while my parents went to say good-bye to Mr. Peterson. When Aunt Del died, my parents flew to Orlando and left me with a friend. At the time of my classmate's funeral, an event I would surely have attended, we were out of town on a family vacation.

So I've seen funerals on TV, read books, but it's my first time in attendance, and certainly my first time as a direct relative of the deceased. I don't know how to behave, and a dull anxiety mixes with my grief and fatigue.

My brain refuses to function, and by the time I get Dad put together and Elle rounded up, we arrive at the church a full ten minutes past the time appointed by Edna Carlton.

She is waiting for us in the parking lot, flanked by Nancy and Alison, who has discarded her ball cap and blue jeans in favor of a shapeless black dress. Nancy, on the other hand, is decked out in funeral fashion attire: a slim, perfectly fitted pencil skirt and black jacket over an ivory silk blouse. Her silver hair shines in the sunlight. Mrs. Carlton, between them, wears a timeless black dress and a hat with a net veil that has been in existence longer than I have.

I turn off the engine and remove the keys, but not one of us makes a move to get out of the car.

"When shall we three meet again?" Elle whispers.

A burst of laughter pushes past my barricaded lips, and I cover my mouth with my hand, partly to hide my lapse from the welcoming trio, partly out of guilt. I've always thought grief would be one uniform texture of sadness, but mine is so many layers of guilt and anger and now laughter.

I've just gotten myself under control and am formulating an admonishment for my daughter when Dad starts to sing, in his tone-deaf way: *There were three ravens sat on a tree, Downe a downe, hay downe, hay downe . . .*

"Dad!"

We are definitely the crazy car. If the three black crows out on the sidewalk had the powers of Macbeth's witches, all three of us would turn into toads on the spot.

"I'm just a crazy old man," Dad says, with an exaggerated shrug. "Who can blame me?"

Then, just as suddenly as he started to sing, his face falls. "I don't want to get out of the car. I suppose we have to go through with this?"

I reach for his hand. It has gotten so bony over the years, the knuckles red and swollen, the skin fragile and transparent. Elle leans forward from the back and puts her strong, young hand on top. "All for one, one for all," she says. "And all of us for Grandma."

We sit there, the three of us, linked by the bond of our hands and our grief.

Mrs. Carlton, tired of waiting or else convinced that we're too inept to open the doors, takes matters into her own hands. She breaks ranks with her sisters and yanks open the passenger door. "You are late," she scolds. "If we don't hurry, you'll miss the viewing."

"I've already seen her," Dad says. "She was dead before they took her from the house."

The scandalized expression on Mrs. Carlton's face goads my rebellious black heart into action. I get out of the car. Elle follows.

"I've already seen her as well. And Elle will pass."

In my heels, I'm a whole head taller than Mrs. Carlton, and I use my height to stare her down.

"Fine. But you're still late. Follow me."

She stumps off into the church. Alison glances my way, takes a step after Edna, then turns back and hugs all three of us in turn. Her body is warm, but the cheek she presses against mine is cool and damp with tears. "We're all so broken up. Edna means well. Are you ready?"

My throat swells in response to her kindness. "Ready as I'm going to be," I say, as she steps back.

"This way." Nancy leads us in a sad little procession, Elle, Dad, then me, with Alison guarding the rear. We walk through a side door into a hallway that smells of old carpet and air freshener and holiness. Thin strains of an inexpertly played organ seep through the walls and the ceiling and up through the floor.

Elle jams a wrench into the works and brings the whole program to a halt when she stops and turns to face me. "What if I want to see Grandma?"

I stare at her, heart in my throat. "You don't want to remember her this way, Elle Belle. Truly."

She stares back. Chin lifted, feet planted, centered like a discus thrower. "I'm not scared of feeling things. I want to see her."

I open my mouth to tell her no, absolutely not, under no condition, and then stop. Isn't that what I've always hated myself? Other people protecting me from what they think I shouldn't see or know? Things like having a sister, for example.

"She's not pretty to look at, sweetheart. Death wasn't easy."

"You were there. You saw her die. I haven't seen her for three years, and I want to see her now."

"I'll take her," Alison says. "If you'd rather not."

"No," I hear myself saying. "I'll go."

Elle wilts and bites her lower lip. Maybe I've made a wrong decision yet again. Maybe she wanted me to say no so she wouldn't have to feel guilty. Psychology is not my strong suit.

"Me, too," Dad says. He takes my hand. Elle backtracks and does the same on the other side. The hallway is just wide enough for the three of us.

"Off to see the wizard," Elle murmurs. I squeeze her hand.

"I don't know that there's time for a viewing now," Nancy says. "Listen."

The organ music has shifted from hymns to a semiclassical dirge. "That's the signal for the family to come in and sit down," she says. "Everybody will be waiting."

It's a reprieve. Elle and Dad both look at me. I open my mouth to comply, but I swear to God all at once I'm channeling my mother. "It's a funeral, not a party. They can wait."

Nancy's mouth opens, then snaps shut. There is lipstick on one of her teeth. This fact makes me feel better, sure and certain that I am mean-spirited and destined for hellfire. Her back is even straighter as she marches ahead of us, and I'm pretty sure that if she had an imaginative bone in her body, she'd be picturing herself as Joan of Arc right now, heroically walking to her death.

The hallway passes classrooms and a study, where an elderly gentleman stands in the doorway, clasping a well-worn Bible. From the look he exchanges with Nancy, I'm pretty sure he's her husband, Pastor McLean. My father confirms this with a nod and a murmured, "Pastor."

McLean is man of God enough to set aside his Bible and clasp my father's hand warmly in both of his, despite the fact that we are inconveniently late and messing up the program. The organ comes to the end of the song. There's a long hesitation, and then it starts all over again at the beginning.

Just past the study a set of narrow stairs leads to an open door, and through that door I know there is a platform and an open coffin with my mother lying inside it. Everybody in the church is already seated, and they will be staring at us, the best of them pitying our grief, the others storing away tidbits to share in gossip sessions later.

My feet falter.

This is a very bad idea.

But my father, the same man who said he didn't want to do this, lets go of my hand and forges ahead on his own. The toe of his right foot catches on a step, and he stumbles. Both Elle and I surge ahead and grab his arms, and the three of us walk out to see my mother as a linked unit after all.

The woman in the coffin looks about as much like the woman who raised me as one of those branded dolls looks like the celebrity it represents. The shape of her face is vaguely wrong, her hair styled in a way she never would have worn it.

My imagination runs away down several different rabbit holes of conspiracy theory before I realize that nobody has run off with her body. It's just the makeup and the hair.

Mom never wore makeup. Her face looks strange with brow liner and blush, her lips a little redder than they ever were in life. And she never wore her hair combed back from her forehead like that. A faint white line of a scar parallels her hairline on the right, a thing I never noticed before.

Dad sees it, too. He reaches down and tries to rearrange her hair, but it's stiff with gel and spray and isn't going anywhere. Elle stands statue still beside me, expressionless, not giving me any cues to her emotional state.

The organ reaches the end of the song again, and the organist, a small woman who has to perch on the edge of the bench to reach the pedals, glares at me directly before turning a page and going back to the beginning one more time.

"Are we done?" I whisper to Elle, and she nods.

I'm pretty sure that what we're supposed to do now is go back the way we came and then ceremoniously traipse up the central aisle, but since we've already shot the program to hell and gone, I don't see the point. We could just as easily walk around the coffin and down the steps from the platform to the front pew reserved for family.

Looking down to assess this option is almost my undoing.

The church is packed. So very many people have come to say goodbye to my mother, and all of them are now watching me. Some faces are familiar. Greg's mom is here, the critical gossip she's going to share with her friends almost visible in a cloud over her head. Tony and Mia and Mrs. Medina sit together about three rows back, and their kind faces bolster me.

"Come on," I whisper to Dad and to Elle. "Let's go this way." I take one step, and then I see Marley.

She sits right by the aisle, about halfway back on the right. Her hair is twisted up into a bun, and she wears a demure black dress. Dark glasses cover her eyes. Her feet, in sensible black pumps, remain evenly on the floor. Knees touching. Shoulders back. Chin up. She's the epitome of the perfect posture Mom tried and failed to instill in me.

Only her hands give her away. They are twisted together in her lap, instead of loosely folded, the funeral program crushed and bent between them.

Leah's Journal

I told myself that, job or no job, I would leave after the babies were born, when I was able to move again. When they could be put in a stroller or packed into the car. I believed it, too, until I was confronted with the reality of two fragile, demanding, small people.

This was a reality nobody could have prepared me for, even if there had been anybody who might have tried. They cried. Well, Marley cried; Maisey squeaked. She was smaller by half a pound. Stayed in the baby ICU two full days longer. I'd forgotten that until just now, how much I was frightened by Maisey's fragility.

I remember the day the hospital sent us home. One minute both babies were hooked up to monitors in special little temperature-controlled beds. The next they were swaddled up in blankets, and I was being patted on the head and sent out the door with all kinds of instructions. Feed them every two hours. Swab the belly buttons with alcohol. Bathe them, but don't let them get cold. Watch for jaundice.

Guilt.

Dear God, the guilt. Maybe I won't write this after all. What is the point of stirring up this muddy mess so many years later? It's not like I can go back and fix it. But it's too late for that. Pandora's box has been opened. From now until I die, I will be asking myself these questions. Why didn't I call a taxi and run away right then and there? I've always told myself that I had nowhere else to go. It's not true, God help me. My parents were still alive. They wouldn't have welcomed me and two small people into their home, but they wouldn't have shut us out.

So many things I might have done, I suppose. In fairness to myself, I'm going to remind myself of a few facts. They do not excuse me, but maybe they explain.

Fact: I was only seventeen and had never been around babies. My heart was full of love for these small creatures, but I was terrified by the amount of care they required.

Fact: I'd had a C-section. My dream that as soon as they were born, I would be light and free and have my own body back was pure fantasy. I was still heavy. My belly hurt where they'd cut me. My breasts were hot and swollen and ached. I was bleeding. Just walking down the hallway from my room to the nursery took all the energy I had. Tears were flowing nonstop. The nurses cooed over the babies, petted me, told me it was just baby blues and I would be fine.

And Boots. The nurses all adored Boots.

He would come in, golden and beautiful and unmarked by any physical change. He brought me flowers. Every day a new bouquet. Stuffed animals for the babies. Chocolate for the nurses. I should have wondered where he got the money, but I was too overwhelmed to ask questions.

"You're a wonder, Leah," he said to me. "Look what we've done, the two of us. We're a family now." He said that word, family, *with reverence. He kissed me so tenderly. Held me gently.*

I believed him.

The moment when we walked out of the hospital together, each of us carrying one baby, holding hands. The moment when I buckled Maisey into her little seat while he did the same with Marley. The moment when he opened the car door for me, all gentleman, and helped me buckle up my own seat belt.

Believing him was my greatest sin. Because in all that came after, I had so little choice.

Chapter Twenty-Two

She's here.

My sister. My Marley. She came to the funeral after all, in spite of everything.

I can't tear my eyes away from her face, and my feet, unattended, tangle up with each other. For a shattering instant, I think I'm going to fall, right there on the platform with everybody looking at me. Elle and Dad anchor me just enough to let me correct my balance.

An usher materializes and offers an arm to me and one to Dad, assisting us slowly and cautiously down the steps, Elle trailing along behind. He stops at the end of the family pew and signals me to walk in and sit.

The organist stops midsong, now that we're all seated, and shifts her pages around. A slow hymn signals Pastor McLean and Edna Carlton to come in. He approaches the pulpit and clears his throat. Edna takes a seat.

"Let us begin with a hymn," the pastor says. "We've chosen one of Leah's favorites today, 'Amazing Grace.' Let's all stand, shall we?"

The organist plays an introduction, and everybody starts to sing. At first I only mouth the words, but then memories hit me. My mother singing this song as a lullaby when I was a small child, at church on Sundays, humming it in the car, chanting it while making breakfast as if the eggs sizzling in the frying pan are an incarnation of the grace she has come to amazingly see.

Beside me, my father's quavering tenor wanders in search of the tune. I grab his hand and try to give voice to these words for my mother, who can no longer sing them herself, but my voice keeps breaking. I can't help wishing Marley stood on the other side of me, can't help wondering how it would be for the two of us to sing together.

The rest of the service inches by in a slow torment.

It's all I can do to keep my eyes forward and not look back over my shoulder for my sister.

Mrs. Carlton delivers a eulogy that seems to last for hours. A quartet sings a hymn. Pastor McLean talks about how short our lives are on this planet and the importance of living right since we never know the day or the hour.

And the whole time, the coffin is open up on the platform. My mother is in that coffin, or at least an approximation of her, a waxen effigy lacking all the endless energy and force of will that defined her. She was a believer in family sitting together, and I have never sat in a pew in this church without her beside me, ready to pinch my arm if I fidgeted too much or fell asleep.

I find myself missing her with an astonishing depth of passion.

All the years I've been away, I've rarely given her a thought outside of our regular phone calls. But then, I haven't been sitting in church with the rest of the family. Where is she now? Can she see us sitting here? Would she be glad that Marley has come, for whatever reason?

My head aches.

The minutes tick by.

At long last we all stand up to sing a final hymn and then wait as the pallbearers pick up the coffin. Our usher appears discreetly at the end of the pew, signaling that we are to get up and follow my mother down the aisle and out to the waiting hearse.

Marley is gone.

The spot she had occupied at the end of a pew is now empty. She's not in the crowd at the back of the church. She's not in the parking lot. She's nowhere to be seen at the graveside ceremony, where the sound of the first clods of dirt hitting the coffin do something to my knee joints and nearly drop me.

Dad's mind goes soft again about halfway through.

"Why are we standing here?" he whispers in my ear. "I'm thirsty. Can I get a drink?"

"It's the funeral, Daddy. This is Mom's grave."

All I want to do is take him home and put both of us to bed for a nap, but there's still the potluck to navigate.

I catch a glimpse of Tony with his mother. She stands with her head leaning against his shoulder, his arm around her waist. Mia catches my eye and smiles, a ray of light that I cling to while counting the minutes of yet another little sermon, a song, a prayer.

Greg's mom is there, in a wheelchair. She nods at me, but doesn't smile. She never did think I was good enough for her beloved son, and when I had the gall to turn down his proposal, her disapproval shifted into outright enmity. I let my eyes move away from her sanctimonious face, scanning the crowd for signs of Marley, but she's as absent as my mother, vanished just as suddenly and with as little explanation.

No warning. No good-bye. Just—poof!—gone.

~

The funeral potluck is held, not at the church, but at Edna Carlton's house. The good news about this is that it's right next door to home. The bad news, besides having to deal with Mrs. Carlton, is also that it's right next door to home. People wander in and out of both houses, as if Edna's is a buffet and ours is a museum, some sort of open-admission tribute to my mother's life.

When a breathing space presents itself between hugs and well-meant condolences, I escape to Mom's kitchen to scavenge for ibuprofen. Two women and a man, all balancing paper plates, are standing there, examining the floor by the island.

"Do you think this is where she fell?" one of the women asks in almost a whisper, eyes wide with fascination.

The man, middle-aged, short, with a monk's tonsure balding pattern, unloads his potato-salad-laden fork into his mouth and then uses the fork as a pointer. "Of course it is. You can still see bloodstains."

Both women bend their heads, peering down at the floor. "Are you sure? There's a rust color running through the tile."

"Surely the daughter has scrubbed it by now."

I have so many choices in this moment. *Leave it be, Maisey,* I tell myself. *Walk away.* As usual, I ignore my own advice.

"You'd think, wouldn't you?" I say, matching their tone. "But you know what they say about the daughter. The woman might like blood on the floor, for all we know."

All three of them stare, first at me, then back at the floor. The man's right cheek bulges with unchewed food, giving him a distorted, gnome-like expression.

None of them are wearing church-goer funeral clothes. He's in jeans and a T-shirt that proclaims he's a Budweiser man—his belly offering proof. The women are in tank tops and capris; one of them wears flip-flops.

"You think?" the flip-flop woman whispers.

The second woman sets her plate on the island, bends over, and runs a finger across the tile. "It's clean." She sounds disappointed, but then perks up. "Let's go look at the bedroom. I hear he kept her in the bed for a week."

The man laughs, as if this is a big joke. The flip-flop woman elbows him in the ribs. "Save it, Bernie. Let's go."

None of them recognize me. I could tell them to clear out of the house, that this is not a museum, but I've lost my ability for speech. I melt backward against the counter, watching them go.

They don't get far. Tony stands in the hall, blocking it. He doesn't step aside.

"Are you folks looking for something?" he asks politely enough, but his voice holds an edge.

"Just looking around," the man says.

"This isn't a museum," Tony says, his voice still deceptively pleasant. "People live here. In fact, I believe Mr. Addington might be having a little nap."

"We won't wake him."

"Of course you won't. Let me walk you to the door."

"Oh, do you live here?" Flip-flop woman puts her hand on his arm. "Could you just answer some questions? We are dying of curiosity."

"I'm afraid there's no cure for that disease," he says, still politely, then takes her arm and propels her toward the entry.

I hear the sound of the door closing and locking. Tony's footsteps. I still can't move.

"Rubberneckers," Tony says, coming back into the kitchen. "If they drive by an accident, they'll stop in the middle of the road and cause another accident, just to get a glimpse of the tragedy. I'd blame reality TV if it wasn't for history. Roman Colosseum and all that." While he's talking he grabs a glass out of the cupboard, fills it with water, and holds it out to me.

My hands are shaking again. This is getting to be a habit. I really need to get checked for all the shaking diseases. Maybe I have an aneurism, like my mom's. Would it cause these symptoms? Maybe I should call Dr. Margoni.

"Maisey," Tony says.

I blink. He's still holding out the glass of water.

"I thought they were from the funeral. Those people."

"Doubt it," he says. "Should have called the cops and had them arrested for trespassing. Drink up. Edna Carlton is asking where you got to. I'm the reconnaissance man."

"Thank you." I try to drink, but after two swallows my stomach squirms in disapproval. I set the glass on the counter. "I've never been rescued so much in my life."

"You've never been in a mess like this before. I doubt you'll make it a habit."

"I'm a little worried, frankly," I tell him.

He laughs. "You don't strike me as the damsel-in-distress sort of gal. Shall we?"

I take the arm he offers, then hesitate. "I should check on Dad . . ."

"He's actually still next door. I was just trying to instill a sense of shame in the lookie-loos."

Making sure I actually have the key, this time I lock the house door behind us. "How did they know? Those people? About what happened, about my mom?"

Tony sighs. "God. I was hoping you wouldn't ever know. There was an article in the newspaper. A little lurid in the speculation department, asking questions about your dad's mental health and talking about the way he kept your mom here."

"It was downright creepy," Mia says, coming up the sidewalk to join us. "I know better, having met your dad, and the article still gave me the chills. Whoever that reporter is should have somebody check their freezer for bodies."

"Mia!" Tony exclaims. "Not. Helpful."

But it is helpful. Mia's account takes the sting out of the encounter, helps me put it in perspective. I initiate a hug and she returns it with enthusiasm. "Mom has plans to barge into the newspaper office first thing Monday morning and give somebody a piece of her mind. You can bet your booty it won't be the calm and rational piece."

"Mia!" Tony warns again, but by now I'm actually laughing.

"Maybe I'll go with her," I say. "Maybe I'll get Greg to sue them for defamation of character or something."

"That Edna woman keeps talking about your absence. And some guy just showed up asking about you."

I sigh. It's pleasant outside, peaceful with just the three of us. The sun is warming the chill in my bones. But funerals are social events, as much as anything, and the role of grieving daughter belongs to me.

So I take Mia's hand, and the two of us brave the fortress side by side, Tony behind us as bodyguard. Once again I find myself in Mrs. Carlton's plastic-covered living room, only this time the game has morphed into something I don't even recognize.

Dad sits on the couch beside Mrs. Medina. Mrs. Carlton, ramrod straight, her mouth set all prim and prosy, her nose tilted up at an angle that signals disapproval of the highest order, presides from the armchair. And on the love seat, my daughter perches on the edge of her father's lap, chattering a mile a minute and punctuating every other word with hand gestures.

Greg.

Here.

Impossible.

I stop so short Tony runs into me from behind and grabs my shoulders to steady both of us. Mia looks from me to Greg and back again. Her mouth opens and shuts.

"Oh," she says. "I didn't . . ." Her face flushes, and she spins around and bolts out of the room.

Greg dislodges Elle and gets to his feet. "I was wondering where you'd gotten to." His words are directed at me, but his eyes are not. He's got Tony locked and loaded in his sights.

"What are you doing here?" I manage to gasp. "I just talked to you last night." All the things I said to him on the phone crash over me, a cascade of falling bricks that makes me want to hide behind Tony.

"You sounded so lost," he says, crossing the small space to pull me into his arms. "Such an incredibly difficult time for you. I thought I should be here. Sorry I couldn't make it in time for the funeral."

Greg doesn't look like a strong man. He's thin, medium height, and starting to bald. Bifocals and a precisely buttoned-up shirt and perfect tie complete his professional business look. Next to Tony he looks like the stereotypical math whiz. But his arms around me are bands of steel, nothing soft about them at all or about the way he holds me.

For one thing, he hasn't hugged me since before Elle was born. My last memory of his hands on me is of violence and shock and pain. I want to thrash against him, pull away, ask, *What the hell are you doing?*

Only there are people watching. Elle is watching. It is my mother's funeral, and I've been hugged today by people I don't even know. It's what people do when somebody dies. They hug you. They offer comfort. I'm being paranoid again.

I almost convince myself that my mother's death really is the point of Greg's appearance and his physical contact.

Almost.

I know better, and all my usually subterranean knowings seem to be surfacing today. When Greg keeps one arm around my waist, pulling me in close beside him and turning me so we're both face-to-face with Tony, memories bubble up like swamp gas, one bursting into my awareness and leaving a stench behind.

The time Greg brought Elle home after a visit and found me sharing a bottle of wine with an architect I'd been dating. A nice guy. Very cerebral, but kind and cute in a dorky sort of way.

The door opens and the two of them come in. Elle, five or six and half asleep, is snuggled up against Greg's chest.

"What's the matter? Is she sick? I thought she was spending the night with you and Linda." I get up to take her from him, but he doesn't release her.

"She said she wanted to come home. She's been crying for an hour. But if you don't want her, I can take her back."

"Of course I want her. Come here, Elle Belle. What's the matter?"

"I just missed you." She wraps her arms around my neck, and for an instant, too long, Greg continues to hold her, the three of us a human chain with Elle as the central link. I can smell the cinnamon gum Greg always chews, mixed with a hint of cologne, before I bury my face in my daughter's hair and drown out all other scents with healthy child sweat and shampoo.

Greg lets her go, and Elle wraps her legs around my hips and lays her head over my heart, too sleepy to even comment on my guest.

"Thanks for bringing her home." I beam out thought signals at him to leave now, to go back to his house and his wife, but he moves toward the table instead.

"Oh, you bought the good stuff. Mind if I have a glass?"

Yes, I mind. I mind a lot. But before I can bring myself to say anything, Lenny sets down his glass and shifts his chair.

"I should go," he says.

"No need for that." Greg goes directly to the cupboard and fetches himself a glass, as if he's the host and this is his house. He pours both for himself and my date, but not for me. "Maisey will be right back as soon as she puts our kiddo to bed."

Lenny accepts the drink, but I can see that I've lost him. He'll be out the door as soon as he can do it politely, and he won't be calling me later.

Elle is the weight of love in my arms, though, and I keep breathing in the scent of her all the way down the hallway and even after I tuck her into bed.

"I'm sorry you were sad, sweetheart," I tell her, tucking her hair behind her ear, pulling the blanket up under her chin.

"I wasn't sad," she whispers, eyes already closed.

Her eyelashes are dry. No tearstains on her cheeks, no stuffy nose. Kids recover fast, I tell myself. I wish I could be that unmarked by an hour of crying.

Walking back toward the kitchen, I hear Greg in full mansplain about my situation.

"I hope you'll make allowances for Maisey. She's a good little soul, but it's not easy being a single mother. I help where I can, of course, but the bulk of the responsibility is hers. I've always felt that was why she's not been more successful, as far as a career. Great mother, though, as you see."

"Did you save a glass for me?" I ask, pulling up the chair between them and reaching for the bottle.

Greg grabs it first, and I think he's going to pour for me, but instead he adds another splash to his own glass.

"Do you think that's wise, Maisey? You know how you get. Lenny? A refill?"

This time Lenny pushes his chair back with determination and gets to his feet. "I really do need to be going. Good night, Maisey. Thanks for the evening. Nice to meet you, Greg. Hope the little girl is okay."

He flees like a frightened bunny.

I watch him go, sadness and inevitability warring with the clear reality that the man is not exactly heroic, or at least certainly isn't interested enough in me to put up a fight.

"Oh damn. I'm sorry, Maisey. What a dick!" Greg says. "Here, have a drink. You deserve it."

He pours for me, and I catch myself feeling grateful before I remember that if he hadn't come over, I'd very possibly be naked by now and well on my way to a much-needed orgasm.

"What the hell was that?" I demand. "You couldn't just bring her home and then leave?"

"I have a responsibility to make sure my daughter is safe. If your latest boy toy isn't man enough to withstand the scrutiny, you're probably better off without him."

The fact that there is some truth to these words just drives them deeper under my skin. I take a sip, resisting the temptation to skip the glass and go straight for the bottle.

"Well, we're good and safe now. You can go home with a clear conscience."

"I'd think you'd be grateful," he says. "But never mind. Like I was telling your friend—"

"Lenny."

He rolls his eyes, as if he's an overgrown teenager. "Right. Lenny. What kind of name is that, even, for a man? I know you're trying. But you can do better."

"Tony, am I right?" Greg's voice-in-the-now cuts into my memory. "I believe we spoke on the phone. Thanks for watching out for my girls." He speaks dismissively, possessively, as if I'm a dog he's picking up from the kennel.

The pressure of his fingers between my ribs is growing into a torment. I want to tell him to stop, he's hurting me. I want to pull away. But everybody is watching, including Elle, and anything I do is going to cause a scene.

Tony extends his hand for a shake, but his blue eyes have shaded nearly to black, his face set in lines that make him look edgy and dangerous. He's dressed up for the funeral, which for him means a nice shirt and a new pair of jeans. Unlike Greg, who has every button done, Tony's got his sleeves rolled up over his forearms; the top button of his shirt is open. His hand is bigger than Greg's, his forearm about twice the size, the skin multiple shades darker.

Greg winces a few seconds into the handshake, and when they've completed that manly contest, he flexes his right hand twice before stuffing it into his coat pocket. His grip on me does not ease.

Tony rolls forward a little onto the balls of his feet, hands loose and open, his eyes never straying from Greg's.

My brain does its usual thing, diving straight into a brawl right here in Mrs. Carlton's living room. *A left hook from Tony, Greg laid out flat on the floor, me counting out the seconds like a referee.*

I need to fix this. The whole scenario is my fault, somehow, although I've forgotten what it is that I've done. If Tony hits Greg and Greg sues him, that's my fault. If Greg gets pissed off and takes Elle away from me, on grounds that I'm an incompetent mother who is exposing her to unhealthy influences, that's my fault. If the day of my mother's funeral is desecrated by a postfuneral brawl, that is definitely my fault.

But my imagination, so adept at making up stories so real I can see them unfolding in front of my eyes, is a total dud at real-life solutions. All I can seem to do is breathe past the pain of Greg's iron hand clamping down on my ribs, the looming shadow of his power play over my life, my child, this room.

Mrs. Medina breaks the tension.

"Oh, thank God, you're here," she says. "Take this plate from me, Tony. I ate so much I can't get up off this couch. Come and give me a hug, Maisey. How are you holding up, my girl? Exhausted, I am sure."

Tony doesn't move, doesn't even look at his mother. His eyes lock on mine, asking a question I'm too afraid to answer.

"I can take your plate, ma'am." Greg releases me, flashing Mrs. Medina an easy smile. "I know exactly what you mean. Edna here has orchestrated quite a feast. I think I've gained five pounds myself." He pats his flat belly and winks at Mrs. Carlton, who actually dimples.

My legs feel a little unsteady, but it's my wavering reality that makes me want to sink down onto the floor to make sure it's still solid. I watch Greg take Mrs. Medina's plate, bend down to pick up a dropped napkin, bestow another extravagant compliment on Mrs. Carlton, and then hug Elle and drop a kiss on the top of her head.

I take a deep breath. It hurts, but it's a relief and it anchors me back into my body, this room, this time and place.

Maybe I've been manufacturing drama out of nothing. Again. Greg is a good man, I tell myself. He didn't mean to hurt me. I only imagined the tension between him and Tony. Still, I find myself automatically putting distance between us, moving around the edge of the small room and scooching Elle over so I can sit on the end of the love seat with her beside me as a buffer.

The instant Greg clears the room, Mrs. Medina hefts herself up from the couch, no assistance needed. "Go hug your grandpa," she says to Elle, and then plunks down beside me. Her bulk fills the vacant space.

"I'll go look for Mia," Tony says, and vanishes. I catch myself listening to his receding footsteps, knowing they are walking not only away down the hall, but out of my world. He'll be like Lenny and all the others—poof, gone—which is just as well, really.

So why does his absence exaggerate the empty space in my belly, make me want to run after him, grab his arm, and spill a bunch of apologies and explanations and even a plea to be my knight in shining armor and fight for me?

That's an image that instigates an urge to laugh and then to cry.

A knight will fight a dragon, sure, or maybe even a cutthroat attorney, but generally for some sort of reward. The hand of a princess, say. I am far from a princess and too much of a failure to be worth fighting for.

Laughter and sadness both give way to a wave of weariness so intense that I want to lie down on the floor, right in the middle of everybody, and close my eyes. But I can't even let my head lean back, because this love seat is the most uncomfortable piece of furniture on the planet. The plastic cover is an extra diabolical touch. I keep sliding toward Mrs. Medina and the hollow her bulk has made in the seat cushion. At first I fight it, but finally give in and let my body rest up against hers.

She's more solid than she looks, muscle overlaid with padding. She pats my knee, her hand warm and steadying, and then, as if she knows what I need, guides my head down onto her shoulder and strokes my hair.

I hear footsteps in the hall and know they are Greg's. My heart lurches sideways, my eyes fly open. When I go to sit up, Mrs. Medina makes a soothing sound and weighs my head down with her hand, not so heavily that I couldn't easily break away, but just enough to encourage me to stay. I feel safe, protected, and I let my eyes close.

If I can't see him, he can't hurt me.

Maybe I'm an ostrich with my head in the sand, but at the moment I'm a very comfortable ostrich.

"How long are you staying, Daddy?" Elle chirps, and I feel my shoulders tighten, listening for the answer.

"Thought I'd stay a few days and help your mom square away some paperwork. Maybe I'll take you back with me."

"I'm staying till Mom goes." Her voice is decisive and fearless, and I feel a small burst of pride at her strength and confidence. "School's out next week already. I'm not missing anything."

"We will discuss it later," he says, and I wonder if he's already bought her a ticket. "Got an extra bed for a stray traveler, Walter?" It's a question, technically, but said rhetorically. My stomach rises, then free-falls, like a broken elevator in a high-rise.

Dad hasn't made a single decision since my arrival. Sometimes he's reasonably present and focused; sometimes he wanders where I can't follow. I'm not capable of telling Greg no. I can already see all the rational arguments he'll trot out if I should even try.

"I don't," Dad says. "No room at this particular inn, I'm afraid."

Greg laughs. "I'm sure we'll work something out."

"Well," Dad says, in a considering sort of way, "Elle has the spare room bed. Maisey's got the couch. I could offer to give up mine, I suppose."

"I wouldn't dream of taking your bed, sir," Greg says. "Elle can sleep on the floor. Right, Ellie?"

"No."

My response surprises all of us, especially me.

"Good girl," Mrs. Medina whispers, releasing my head and patting my shoulder.

I sit up, roll my shoulders back, straighten my spine. "Nobody's sleeping on the floor. Nobody's sharing beds. Wouldn't your mother be disappointed not to have you?"

"She moved into Parkview last summer. You know that. She doesn't have room for guests."

"Neither does Dad. You could get a motel, maybe, or else sleep on *her* couch."

Greg laughs again, in a doting, condescending way as if he's humoring a precocious child. "Come on, Maise. That's just silly."

My momentary courage ebbs. He's probably right. What would it hurt me to share a house with him for a couple of days? He'll need access to paperwork. We have funeral food that needs to be eaten. He can spend some time with Elle, see that she's okay, and will be more likely to let her stay with me, at least for the summer.

I'm about to acquiesce when my father speaks up. "Maisey's right. I'm afraid I can't possibly put you up with any sort of comfort. Maybe Benny's Inn? Or there's that new hotel down by the Super One. What's that called again?"

Dad and Mrs. Carlton dive into a discussion of the merits of the local motels. Greg gives me his *I know best and you'd better pay attention* stare, the one he likes to bestow on the jury during his final argument, and then seamlessly joins into the motel discussion.

"Have you eaten?" Mrs. Medina leans over to whisper in my ear.

I blink at her, finally shaking my head. I'm not sure which time frame she's talking about, but if she means today, the answer is no.

"Come with me, dear. Let's get you fed." She hoists herself up with a whoosh of expelled breath and then reaches down and pulls me up. She precedes me down the hallway, runs interference between me and anybody who presents as too weepy, too clingy, or too nosy, and makes sure my plate is filled with not only salads and veggies, but two brownies and a slice of apple pie.

"Don't you dare even think about dieting at a time like this. Comfort food all the way. I wonder where my children have got to?"

I shrug, but if Tony and Mia have any sense, they've gotten themselves well away from the train wreck that is me and my life. My sadness about this feels as inevitable as rain, and I brush it off. There's a little glimmer that keeps me afloat. With Greg here to occupy Elle and keep an eye on Dad, with Tony and Mia safely out of the way, there is nobody to interfere with my plan to drive down to the Tri-Cities and make my sister talk to me.

Chapter Twenty-Three

I use Dad as an excuse to go home.

He's clearly exhausted, his face drawn, eyes sunken. He looks like I feel. But once he's tucked into bed for a nap, I still can't rest. My nerves zing, my heartbeat won't slow down, and the internal shaking feels like it will go on forever.

Elle has gone off with Greg to see her grandmother. With Dad in bed, I have space and time to myself to read, to nap. But I feel too restless and unfocused to do either. My body aches in a million small places.

It occurs to me that a hot bath would be a luxury, and I make my way into the bathroom, where I gaze, appalled, at myself in a mirror that performs the opposite of the Snow White magic.

My mascara has smeared under my eyes; my blusher is long gone. I look pale and wretched, and the sight of myself makes me feel even less like the princess a knight would fight for. Tony was wise to flee. It's a miracle Greg still talks to me.

I give myself a mental shake, remind myself that the lighting in this bathroom made me look hideous even when I was sixteen. The walls are green, for one thing. And my parents have installed a set of harsh and unforgiving bulbs directly above the mirror.

Fortunately, what the bathroom lacks in lighting and mirror kindness, it makes up for with the bathtub. Sometime after I left home, my parents installed a huge tub with water jets. I'm not sure if either of them ever used it, but I am about to.

In some perverse spell of self-punishment, I undress in front of the mirror, forcing myself to notice every defect, every sign of aging. The soft pouch to my belly, the dimpled cellulite on the backs of my thighs, the beginning of a sag to my breasts.

And on the right side of my rib cage, four purplish oval marks, lurid against the winter pallor of my skin. I stare at them, my brain frozen and not processing, until I turn and see the fifth mark on my back.

Fingerprints.

All my rationalizations scatter like cockroaches do when the light comes on. I didn't just feel commandeered, claimed, objectified; it happened. The evidence of Greg's possessive behavior is imprinted on my flesh.

For a long time I stand there, breathing in a new reality. Realizations move through my head, clearing out debris. Memories reframe themselves. Beliefs transform. In the space of a few moments, I'm a brand-new Maisey. I even look different to myself in the mirror.

Stronger.

Braver.

More like my mother.

The tub is now full of water, but before I get in I do one last thing. Using my phone, I photograph the marks on my body from multiple angles, a reminder to myself in case I begin to forget.

I soak in the tub until the water cools to tepid, letting all my new pieces come together. When I get out, I picture emotional debris swirling down the drain.

I realize that I'm starving and think longingly of the plate I abandoned at Mrs. Carlton's house, largely untouched. There's plenty of food, though, and all I have to do is warm it up. Dad needs to be reminded to eat, and I go to his room to wake him. He's not there.

My heart starts an anxious flutter all over again. What if he's wandered off and forgets where he is? What if he's chosen to follow my mother and deliberately harmed himself?

I don't have time to get worked up very much because he's sitting at his desk in the study, sorting through papers.

"I thought you'd be sleeping," I tell him, and he swivels around to face me.

"Every time I closed my eyes I saw . . ." He swallows and stops. "Well, you know, I expect."

"I know, Daddy."

He turns back to the desk, sorting papers into perfectly even stacks. He looks better, sitting at his desk. More focused. More like himself.

"I didn't do right by you," he says. "I'm deeply sorry."

"Are you kidding? You couldn't have been a better father to me if—"

"Not that. About Greg. I didn't do right by you where it comes to Greg."

My knees do that wobbly thing. Fortunately, there's nobody to see or care, and I plop down right there in the middle of the study.

"I don't understand," I whisper.

He turns the chair to face me. "Neither did I, until today. Did he hurt you?"

My mouth opens and gets stuck that way, without any words appearing. I'm not sure what he's even asking.

"Today," my father says. "At Edna's. Come here, Maisey."

Obedience kicks in, and I get up and cross to his desk. He lifts my sweatshirt just high enough to see the marks where Greg has staked his claim. "I thought so," he says, softly. "Let me see your back."

So I show him that bruise, too, after which he says nothing, and I let myself sink back down onto the floor, legs crossed yoga style. My cheeks burn with shame and anger and even denial.

I didn't do anything. It wasn't my fault.

"I never liked him," Dad says, interrupting my self-admonishment. "From the first time you brought him home. My very first thought when he walked in that door was that he was a fine young rooster in need of a little beak snipping."

"Dad!"

"It was true, wasn't it?"

"You never said anything. I thought you liked him. Everybody loves Greg."

"Your mother loved him," Dad says, very quietly. "She thought he was good for you—steady, balanced, decisive."

I pick at the carpet, like I used to do when I was a little girl. One of the fibers comes loose, and I twist it through my fingers, wishing Mom was still here to give me a harmless smack on the back of the head and tell me to stop ruining things.

"I always thought there was something wrong with me," I finally murmur. I glance up at my father's face and then just as quickly away again. "It's something about me makes him like this. He doesn't do it to anybody else."

"Not true," Dad says, vehemently. "Don't you let him make you believe that, Maisey. Don't you believe it. What he did today, at the funeral? There was no excuse for that, even if you are sleeping with that nice young fireman."

"Dad—"

"Are you?"

"What? No!"

"Pity. Him, I like. And his mother, too. Greg's mother—let's just say I'm glad she didn't make it to the potluck. I always thought you did right, refusing to marry him. I never told you, and I wanted you to know I'm sorry."

"It's okay, Daddy."

"If I'd known—if I'd realized that he was laying hands on you—well, of course I would have said something. Your mother, too. If she had known—"

"She'd have come after him with the broomstick. Or the frying pan. She didn't know. You didn't know." I lower my voice. "I didn't even know."

"Oh, Maisey," Dad says. "I'm so sorry. I wish I could fix it. Such a helpless feeling to be an old man and not be able to do anything."

"There is something you can do."

"I can't see what. But tell me."

"Talk to me about Marley. Tell me what Mom was doing with a gun. How did she break all of those bones?"

All the clarity leaches out of him. I watch his gaze go from clear to fuzzy, his jaw slacken, his shoulders go soft. He turns the chair away from me and rests his hand on top of the papers. "I can't."

I come up on my knees and turn the chair back so he has to face me. "There's no point pretending. Marley was at the funeral. You had to have noticed. And if Mom suddenly went out and bought a gun, surely you noticed that, too."

He sighs and rubs his forehead with both hands, fretfully, like Elle does when she's been up too late and had too much sugar.

"So many secrets, Leah," he whispers. "So damned many."

I think he's drifted away from reality again, but then he drops his hands and looks at me, and I can see that he's in the here and now.

"She was only twenty when I met her. You were three. She applied for a front-desk job in my office, and I hired her on the spot." He lights up a little, remembering. "You know why I hired her, Maisey? She had no experience running an office, no education beyond a GED. You might think it was sympathy for a young single mother. Sympathy was not something I felt. I hired her because she told me I was going to. She looked me directly in the eyes—you know that look—and explained to me that she was going to be a top-notch receptionist for me, and I'd be making a mistake if I passed her over for 'the deceptive benefits of age and experience.'"

I picture my mother, young and fierce and determined. Where was I while she had this job interview? *Where was Marley?*

"She ran my office fearlessly from day one," Dad goes on. "Changed up my operating system. Found me new clients. Read books from the library about office management. My business had been okay up until then. Most of my money for the year I made during tax season. The rest of the time I skimped. I was shy and socially awkward and didn't have a clue about business. Leah changed all of that."

He falls into silence, lost in memories, and I call him back.

"Dad? How did she get from secretary to wife?"

"What?" His gaze comes around to me as if he's surprised to see me in his office, then clears again. He laughs. "She told me I was going to marry her. That's how that happened. Not that I had any objection, other than a little worry over what people would think. I was almost forty. Geeky. Reclusive. And she was beautiful and not yet twenty-one. I would never have dreamed of even asking her out.

"She was an orchestrator, your mother. She would bring in coffees for both of us, and come sit in my office while she drank hers. And we would talk. She had a way of drawing me out of my shell, getting me to tell her things about my life, my family, my thoughts on the world. Somehow I never noticed that she told me nothing about hers.

"One day I actually asked. 'My family is not worth the words it takes to discuss them,' she said. 'That part of my life no longer exists. We don't need to talk about that.'

"And that was it. I let it go, Maisey, God forgive me. I told myself she was young, and that was certainly true. She would have been seventeen when you were born. I didn't ask myself questions about her parents or her first husband or why she'd slammed the door between herself and them. She was so fierce, so determined. She could make me believe anything."

This I know to be true. My mother's word was law. If she said it, then it was true. End of story. Even if she told you that a real, living, human being—your twin sister, say—was imaginary, then that became truth.

"I came to believe," Dad says, "that I really was your father. I mean, I always knew that I couldn't be. Wasn't there for the making of you or for your birth. But somehow the meaning of that would fade out of my consciousness. So yes, I helped your mother in what I see now was a deception. Was it a bad thing, really, not knowing you had a different biological father?"

This is a question I don't yet know the answer to. I can see this lie as a protective one. What good would it have ever done me to know I had another father somewhere?

The other lie is so much more shattering.

"But you knew about Marley," I tell him, speaking the greatest betrayal of all. "You let Mom tell me I was crazy."

"I didn't," he says, shaking his head. "I didn't know then. I swear to you, Maisey. Leah didn't tell me about Marley until after the doctors found the aneurism. Looking back, there were times, in the beginning, when I should have guessed. You would go on about Marley, and she would get so irrationally distressed. 'Don't all kids have imaginary friends?' I would ask her. I couldn't understand her reaction.

"And then, in the days of shock right after the MRI results came in, Leah had a nightmare. She was screaming for Marley. When she woke up, I insisted that she tell me, and she said that Marley was her baby, and she'd lost her. And that was all. When I tried to ask her questions—Was it adoption? Did the baby die? What happened?—she said, 'That part of my life does not exist. We won't speak of this again.'

"But I was shaken, Maisey. I remembered your imaginary friend, then, and her reaction to that. I thought probably she'd had to give a child up for adoption. Curiosity got me, like it got you. I googled, never thinking I would actually find results. But I found Marley. And then I got to thinking. Leah would never revisit a decision she'd made, but surely things were different. She was going to die. She should know her daughter, or at least her daughter should have the chance to know her. I tried to tell her that, but she still wouldn't listen. I tried to tell her she should tell you. We had raging battles for the first time in our marriage. I fought her on this. In the end, I wrote to Marley. She wrote back directly to your mother. The letter wasn't . . . helpful."

"I've met her. I can imagine."

"Leah went from angry to paranoid. Maybe it was that thing in her brain, I don't know. 'You don't know what you've done,' she said.

"'Tell me, then,' I begged her. 'What's so terrible about reaching out to your children before you die?' But she refused to talk about it. She bought that gun. She got obsessive about locking doors, checking them five times before she'd go to bed, and then getting up in the middle of the night to check again.

"Something like a wrong-number phone call would send her off on a reverse number search. I didn't know what to do with her. She would tell me only that it was best if I didn't know. Best if you didn't know. And definitely best if she never, ever talked to Marley."

He falls quiet. I let him swivel the chair away from me, and he drops his head into his hands, both elbows resting on the desk. "And now I feel guilty, like I've betrayed her trust. Do you think she's haunting us, Maisey, burning holes in my back with ghostly eyes right this minute?"

I get up and stand behind him, draping my arms around his neck and pressing my cheek against the top of his head. "I think she was the luckiest woman in the world to find you and that she knew that. I think she's resting quietly in her grave. I think you and I are both going to have a hell of a time figuring out how to make our own decisions."

He sighs, deeply. "You think?"

"I know."

"God, I am so tired. I think I'm going back to bed."

"You need some dinner first."

"I'm not hungry."

"Me, either," I tell him. "But that's one of those decisions we're going to have to start making. Food. Minimum three times a day. All right?"

"If you say so."

We both laugh at that, such a tiny little moment of relief. He leans on me when he stands. I put my arm around his waist, and we walk together to the kitchen, where we both turn up our noses at casseroles and go for sugar cereal and milk, a small, shared rebellion.

I think we've left the topic of Marley behind, but when Dad sets his bowl in the sink he turns to me, serious, focused. "Leave Marley alone. It's best. We opened the door to her, and she slammed it shut. We should respect that."

"We should. Do you need a hand back to your room?"

"There are perfectly good walls to lean on. I'll manage. Where's Elle?"

"Spending the night with Greg's mom. She's not particularly happy about it."

"She'll live." He drops a kiss on the top of my head and shuffles off down the hallway.

When he's out of sight, I pick up my cereal bowl in both hands and drain the sugary milk, making slurping noises and daring my mother's ghost to come after me.

What I should do and what I will do are two different chickens, and I'm pretty sure Dad knows it.

Leah's Journal

Things got worse between me and Boots after the babies came home.

It was easy to make excuses for him. Both of us were exhausted. It took two people working around the clock to manage the feeding and diapering and crying, not to mention the house and food and all those things.

My mother was in a bout of major depression. She showed up twice in those first weeks, uncombed, gaunt, moving with exaggerated slowness. Holding her grandbabies did nothing to light a fire in her. She looked at them, dead-eyed, and began to silently weep.

"I've not done right by you, Leah," she whispered. "Not been a good mother."

"So be one now," I told her. I didn't have the energy to take care of her. I needed her to take care of me, just this once . . .

I see now that she was clinically depressed. I'm sure she needed medications and counseling. My father was a late-stage alcoholic by then, never sober. He didn't even come to see the little ones. I didn't go to him.

My mother-in-law came daily to snuggle babies, create a little order out of chaos, even restock the refrigerator.

But she had her waitress job to manage, and she wasn't young anymore. Night shifts were out of the question. And night shifts were the hardest of all.

It was 1:03 a.m. when Boots snapped the first time. The red digital numbers of the bedside clock are imprinted in my brain.

Both Maisey and Marley were crying. I don't know why. I'd fed them, changed them, rocked them. And finally, exhausted beyond caring, I put them into the crib and dropped into a milk-sodden heap on the bed.

Boots sat up when I lay down. If I'd been awake enough to care, I would have recognized that he was practically blaring outrage.

"What are you doing?" His voice was a white heat of anger, but even that wasn't enough to slice through the level of exhaustion that melted me into the bed.

"Sleeping," I mumbled, burrowing into the blankets, pulling a pillow over my head.

"Oh no, you're not." He yanked the pillow away from me. "You are going to make that noise stop, and you're going to do it now."

Adrenaline dispelled sleep enough for me to see the state he was in, but I still couldn't think straight. "Your turn," I said. "Please. I'm so tired." Tears started to flow, sideways into my ears.

"You're a shitty mother," he said. "You know that? I've been trying to help, but there's only so much I can do. Get up and make them stop crying."

"I need—"

He straddled me, knees on either side of my legs, face just visible in the light filtering in from the streetlights outside the window. "This isn't about what you need. You wanted kids. Now you've got kids. And you can fucking get up and take care of them."

I wasn't stupid. I remembered well enough the fist to my face, the boot to my belly. But I wasn't thinking straight either, and I had always had a sharp tongue. His accusations, his tone, raised my own temper.

"Maybe if you weren't such a poor excuse for a father—"

Chapter Twenty-Four

Greg walks in at precisely 9:00 a.m. No knock. No warning.

He powers into the kitchen like it's a courtroom, freshly shaven, perfectly combed, briefcase in hand. I'm lounging at the table about halfway through my second mug of coffee, my rumpled T-shirt and yoga pants a counterpoint to his impeccably ironed shirt and perfectly matching tie.

Elle flits by him, gives me a hug, and then plunks down on the floor in front of the cereal cupboard. She grabs a box of Froot Loops and hugs them to her chest.

"You've had breakfast," Greg says.

She wrinkles her nose at him. "I've had *fruit.* And *oatmeal.* A girl needs sustenance."

"Put it back. It's nothing but sugar."

"Oh good grief, Greg. Let her have some cereal."

Greg sets his briefcase on the table, a little harder than necessary. He glares, first at her, and then at me. He's justified. I've undermined his authority in front of our daughter. My hand goes involuntarily to my bruised ribs, and the haze of fatigue clears from my head. I'm awake. I'm alert. I'm hyperfocused on his eyes and his hands, every muscle in my body prepped for flight.

"Is this how she eats? No wonder she's getting chubby. Do you—"

"Her weight is perfect. Don't start. Besides, it's a funeral. Rules don't apply."

"The funeral was yesterday."

"Precisely."

I'm amazed at my own audacity. The same part of me that was slurping cereal milk last night is enjoying contradicting Greg today, even as my early warning system starts sending siren bleats of danger through my brain and body.

Be small. Be quiet. Just go along.

I've done that. I've been doing that for years.

Frankly, I'm pissed. I'm pissed at my mother for dying and for having secrets. I'm pissed that she lied to me, that she pushed and prodded and poked at me to try to make me marry Greg. And I'm royally, out-of-the-ballpark pissed at Greg for being Greg in the first place.

"Coffee?" I ask him. "There's more in the pot. Or Elle could fix you a bowl of cereal."

I brace myself for the possibility of violence, but it's not like he'd actually hit me. Not in Dad's house. Not in front of Elle. He'll take it out in other ways.

Right now, he very deliberately and precisely unlocks the briefcase and clicks it open. "We have a lot of work to do. You're not even dressed."

"I'm dressed." Maybe if he'd called ahead, I would have changed. Maybe I wouldn't have. To be fair, Elle knows where the key is hidden under the mat, and I know she opened the door for both of them. Also, if I had stopped to think about it, his behavior is perfectly predictable. Up at six, breakfast, exercise, work at nine.

His eyes flick over me with disdain, then go pointedly to the clock. He sits down at the table, but does nothing further.

It's now 9:05. I am not with the program. He fully expects me to get up from this chair and go put on some real clothes, at minimum. Comb my hair. I should have prepared. Should have had all relevant files laid out for his inspection.

The usual guilt swamps my childish rebellion. Greg's just trying to help. He wouldn't have to do a thing, and yet here he is. He's taking time away from his family, from his work, to help us out, and I am behaving badly.

Elle drags out a chair and plunks a bowl and spoon onto the table. She's mixed three different varieties of cereal. The milk is pink. My stomach takes a little spin at the thought of eating the concoction, but she makes a little hum of pleasure with the first bite.

I take another sip of coffee and go refresh my cup. "What do you need?" I ask Greg. "Maybe we should move to the study."

"I'm already set up here. I've spoken with the police, Mental Health, and Adult Protective Services. They've sort of back-burnered your dad because nobody has pressed charges. But somebody should be set up with a power of attorney. I'd like to get that squared away before I go."

I feel a little quake at the thought of all the responsibility. "What all does that entail? The power of attorney thing?"

"You would be responsible for his finances. For the estate. You could get him out of this house and into a facility."

"I don't want to do that."

Greg rolls his shoulders and sighs, patiently. "He can't stay here by himself. I think we all see that."

"I don't. He's a little muddled off and on, but what do you expect? My mom died, Greg. We buried her yesterday, in case you didn't notice."

He slows his speech down into elements of exaggerated pronunciation. "You need to face the facts, here, Maisey. I know it's not your favorite thing to do, so let me help you. Fact: Walter is an old man and is now alone. Fact: he didn't call for help when your mother suddenly collapsed. For three days, Maisey. Three days. Think about that. Her lying unconscious in that bed, and him just letting her lie there. Fact: he was burning *something* in the fireplace and made a big enough fire to warrant a call to 911."

"It wasn't that big of a fire," Elle says with her mouth full.

"Fact," Greg goes on. "He burned papers in that fire. Maybe important papers, like an advanced directive."

"Objection. Speculation. We don't know what he burned."

"I'm finding your attitude juvenile and not helpful," Greg says. "You want to pay for an attorney to do all this? Or, better stated, can you afford one?"

I squeeze my rebellious hands together in my lap and drop my eyes. "I'm sorry. Please proceed."

"Here's what I'm thinking. If the power of attorney thing seems like too much for you, I'm willing to do it myself. It makes sense to have somebody a little . . . detached . . . from the emotions. The house will need to be sold, for example."

"No!"

The mind-picture of strangers sitting at this table, working in Dad's study, drinking coffee by the fireplace in the winter, is like a knife in my gut.

"I'm not selling the house."

"See? You can't be logical about this. You need somebody who is."

"I am logical. I'll live here."

"Don't be ridiculous. I live in Kansas City. We can't share custody over that kind of a distance."

Despite his dismissive tone, there's an implicit threat behind those words that makes me bite my lower lip to keep my mouth shut.

A throat-clearing sound draws my eyes to the kitchen door. Dad stands there. He's wearing a T-shirt and a pair of pajama bottoms. His feet are bare. They look vulnerable and pathetic, the toes twisting into each other, vine-like, as if trying to grow in new and unusual directions.

"This is Leah's house," Dad says. "All her things are here."

He starts to pour himself a cup of coffee, but his hands are shaking, and he drops his half-filled cup. It splinters on the floor, and scalding coffee splatters everywhere. He continues to stand there, still pouring coffee out of the pot in his left hand, staring at the broken mug as if it's a strange occurrence completely disconnected from his control.

I knock my chair over with a clatter, leaping up to help him.

"Here, let me take that. Don't move. You'll cut your feet."

His eyes take a slow elevator trip from the floor up to meet mine. "I spilled the coffee."

"Yes, you did. We can make more." I bend down to clear away the pieces. Elle comes running with paper towels. His feet are reddened where the hot liquid splashed him, but I don't see any blisters. Greg's expression is pure *I told you so*.

I want to kiss the burns better, like I used to do for Elle when she was little. All I can do is take Dad's hand and walk with him, side by side, down the hallway to his room.

"Come on, let's find you some dry clothes, okay?"

Mom's drawers are still full of precisely folded clothes. Dad's are untidy, dirty socks and underwear stuffed in with the clean.

"Jeez, Dad, you've got a college boy system going here."

"Don't sell the house, Maisey." He drops heavily onto the bed.

"Oh, Daddy. I don't want to." I kneel on the floor in front of him and press his hands between mine. They are so cold, so stiff.

"There's money," he says. "Don't tell Greg. You can live here. I'll give you full access to all the bank accounts."

"I'm not good with money. Maybe it would be better—"

"No!" His vehemence startles me. "Don't let him. Don't let Greg do it. You have to stand up to him."

"Elle." My throat closes around her name. Everything always comes back to Elle. If I antagonize Greg, maybe he'll take her from me.

Dad pulls his hands away from me and scrubs them across his face. "It's Leah's house," he says. "She's here. She's everywhere."

"I know, Daddy."

He seems to have shrunk since my mother's death. His T-shirt hangs on him, too big. The bottoms of his pants are coffee-soaked.

"How are your feet? Do they hurt?"

"Don't have much feeling in my feet. Diabetes."

"We'll have to watch them. Make sure they heal."

It hurts too much to look at him, and I turn back to the drawers, throwing obviously dirty clothes into a pile on the floor and rummaging for clean ones.

"Laundry is definitely on the agenda. Here we go. Clean pair of jeans and a T-shirt. These socks pass the sniff test. Do you need help getting dressed?"

"I'm not a child," he says, which I choose to take as an assurance that he can dress himself.

"Okay. Holler if you need anything."

My feet drag me back to the kitchen and Greg. Elle is down on her knees, scrubbing the floor with the dishrag.

"Thanks, baby." I keep Greg in my peripheral vision while I load the filter for a fresh pot of coffee. He's bent over paperwork spread out on the table and starts in talking as if there's never been a gap in the conversation, as if the horrible meltdown with Dad never even happened.

"We've got a couple of Realtor offices to choose from. I spoke to Karen at Frontier, and she sounded like she knows what she's doing. I'll give you her number."

"We're not selling the house."

I didn't know I'd made the decision until the words came out of my mouth, but they have the ring of truth.

"Oh my God, Maisey. Really?"

"He doesn't want to."

"Of course he doesn't. But he's hardly fit to make decisions. He can't possibly take care of himself."

"He was completely clear last night." I focus my attention on the stream of water running into the coffee pot, as if it is the most important item in the universe.

"That's how dementia is when it starts. Patches of clarity and stretches of confusion and disorientation. It's going to get worse, not better."

"We don't know that, Greg. Dr. Margoni says it's possible he's just confused right now because of grief and shock."

"And maybe you're in denial." His words hang between us, harsh and uncompromising.

Unwanted tears blur my eyes, and I can barely see to pour the water into the reservoir. Some of it misses, puddling on the counter.

"Look, I'm sorry," Greg says, as I wipe up my mess. "Of course you're in denial. Your mom died suddenly. The last thing in the world you want is to lose both parents. Which is why it would be best to let me take care of things."

"No."

I turn to face him, leaning against the counter for support. "My parents. My job. I'm grateful for your advice and your help, but he wants me to take care of things, and I will."

"Maisey—"

"Let me finish, Greg. Just this once. Let me talk. There is no urgency to sell the house or make Dad move. He's better here. It makes sense for me to stay here for a bit until things settle out. I'll let my apartment go so I have no ongoing expenses elsewhere."

"And Elle?"

"I'm staying here," she chirps. "Grandpa and Mom need me."

"You have school."

"School is out next week. Do you know what happens during the last week of school? Nothing. Busywork stuff."

"This is an adult conversation, Elle. Please don't argue."

"It's a conversation about me! I think I deserve to—"

"Enough. If you can't hush and let us talk, you need to leave the room."

He doesn't yell or raise his voice, and there's nothing horribly wrong with the words. What's all kinds of wrong is the tone he uses, the same dismissive tone he uses on me, as if my opinion is a slight thing not worth his consideration. Hearing him speak like that to Elle shrivels me on the inside.

Elle, stronger than I am, plants her feet, lifts her chin, and says, "I don't like it when you talk to me like that."

The slap comes out of nowhere. No anger, no warning, delivered so rapidly I blink and doubt what I saw. But nothing else makes that same dull thwack but flesh on flesh, and an angry red splotch marks Elle's cheek.

Greg turns back to his papers as if nothing momentous has just happened. "I suggest making Walter an appointment with a psychologist for competency testing," he says, "although if we can get him to sign power of attorney papers during a period of clarity, that might be easier. Chances are good nobody will look too deeply into whether he was competent when he signed. At least, as long as the police continue to leave him alone."

As my shock dissipates, my anger increases.

Elle hasn't moved an inch. Her back is ramrod straight, her chin is still tilted up, but she sniffles, despite her attempt to blink back tears. The last thing in the world she'll want right now is sympathy or a rescuer.

"Elle, would you please go check on Grandpa?"

She accepts the option clause I've given her, dashing out of the room and down the hallway. Greg glances up, eyebrows lifting in surprise when he catches my glare.

"What?"

"Do you make a habit of hitting her?"

"Only so far as she makes a habit of sassing me."

I try to keep my voice level. "Was that sassing? It sounded like a legitimate request to me."

"Oh for God's sake, Maisey. Somebody needs to discipline that child. If it wasn't for me, she'd be spoiled rotten."

"I didn't ask about discipline. I asked if you slap her like that often."

Greg sighs, heavily, pushes back his papers, and turns to face me. "I can't believe we are having this conversation. There are more important things to worry about right now."

"Nothing is more important than my daughter."

"Which is exactly why she needs to be slapped. You're letting her get way too full of herself. She needs to be taken down a peg. And stop looking at me like that. She's not hurt. It will be good for her."

"Was it good for me the time you hit me?"

"Are you really going to bring that up, now? That was what, twelve years ago?"

"I had a root canal twelve years ago. That was good for me. I'm wondering about the therapeutic value of getting slapped by your lover. Or your father."

"If you insist on revisiting that night, let's just put it in perspective, shall we? You were pregnant. With our baby. I wanted to do the right thing and get married. You were completely delusional and incapable of rational thought."

"So you hit me."

As I say the words, understanding floods in. Somebody has turned up the volume on the sun. Light reflects off the tile floor, shines out of the walls. Everywhere, light. I can almost hear the angels singing.

It wasn't my fault that he hit me. His anger is not my fault. I am not responsible for his behavior, then or now.

"You're blowing that one supercharged moment into something it wasn't," Greg says.

"My cheek turned purple. My eye swelled up. I told people I ran into a door."

"Don't be a drama queen, Maisey. I barely tapped you."

My response is derailed by Dad shuffling back into the kitchen and over to the burbling coffee pot. He's gotten into the clothes I put out for him, but his shirt is buttoned crooked. I look behind him for Elle and am relieved to see she hasn't followed.

Greg scans my father's disheveled appearance in a slow-motion, exaggerated, top-to-bottom eyes-as-movie-camera pan meant to emphasize his point. "Can we get back to business now? This isn't something you can put off."

Dad picks up the coffee pot and a mug. I hold my breath, willing his brain and his hands to put together the process this time around. He hesitates, then sets the mug on the counter and starts to pour.

"I always wondered about Maisey's story that she walked into a door," Dad says. "It didn't fit. The bruises were all wrong." He successfully returns the pot and turns to face us, holding the mug in two uncertain hands. There's nothing uncertain about his eyes, though, or the words he now directs at Greg.

"You need to leave my house. You're not welcome here."

Greg laughs, a discordant, misfit sound in the drama-filled kitchen. "With all due respect, Walter, I don't believe you really mean that."

"I remember the night you told us you were pregnant, that you had moved out of Greg's place," Dad says, looking at me now. "Your cheek was greenish-black. You told us the door story. And you know what? I wondered. I wondered then, when you said the two of you had a fight and it was over between you. You always were precise with words. You didn't use the word *argument*. You didn't say *disagreement* or *falling-out*. A fight. That's what you said and what you meant. He hit you. We could have known. Should have known."

"Twelve years ago," Greg says. "Actually, thirteen. I made a mistake."

"And now my granddaughter is hiding in her room, and she has a bruise growing. Did she walk into a door? Or was that also a mistake?"

Greg slams down the papers he's holding. "Can we get back to what's important here? Settling your affairs and keeping you out of jail, for example?"

Dad shrugs. "I have an attorney. I have money. I don't need a man who hits women in my house."

"Maisey," Greg says. "Please speak reason to him."

There's a wildcat in my belly, hissing and spitting. My hands have claws. I want to launch myself at this man who has hit my daughter, to tear his smug face with my fingernails, to scream and shriek and watch him bleed.

Which would make me as bad as he is. I breathe. Once, twice, three times, before responding.

"You heard him. It's his house."

"You're kidding. Tell me you're kidding."

I stare him down. His eyes actually fall away from mine, and his hands start packing papers back into the briefcase.

"Fine. If you come to your senses, let me know. You have today. My flight leaves tomorrow morning, and I'm driving to Spokane tonight. I have a ticket for Elle, by the way, and will be by to pick her up tonight at seven. Please make sure she's ready."

The click of the latches sounds like finality.

"She's staying with me, Greg. I'm the custodial parent."

"Are you sure you want to play that game with me, Maisey? I'd think about that very carefully if I were you. I'll be by for her at seven."

We let him see himself out.

Dad stands by the counter, still holding a mug that has yet to make it to his mouth. I get up and take it from him, carrying it across to the table.

"Drink up," I tell him. "I need to go talk to Elle."

~

Elle sits cross-legged in the middle of the bed, scribbling furiously in a journal. When the door opens, she glances up to see who it is, then resumes writing without saying a word. Her hair screens her face, and I tuck it back behind her ear so I can see her cheek.

"I don't think that will bruise," I murmur, half to myself, letting my fingers trace the reddened skin.

"I'm fine," she says, the pen not pausing for an instant. "And I don't require a lecture."

"Why on earth would I lecture you?"

"Because I talked back, and I should learn when to keep my mouth shut and then I wouldn't get hit."

"Is that the way it works?"

She shrugs. Won't look at me.

"Does he hit you often?" I select my words with care, as if they are expensive items on display, and I can only afford a few.

The pen hesitates in its mad rushing, and she shakes her head so her hair falls free again in front of her face.

"Elle." I place my hands over hers and stop the scratching of pen on paper. She is rigid beneath my touch, and when her eyes come up to meet mine, I'm relieved to see hot rebellion burning as bright as Blake's Tyger. Greg hasn't broken her or her beautiful, extravagant self-confidence. Not yet.

"I don't care if he's my father. He didn't have the right to hit me. Not like that."

"I agree."

"Linda doesn't."

"She thinks it's okay?"

Elle drops her eyes and slams her journal closed, holding it pressed flat between her palms. "Not exactly okay. She said sometimes being a girl sucks, but you have to be smart. And if you're smart, and watch the signals and don't antagonize a man, then he won't hit you."

"That's what she told you?" I picture Greg's gentle wife, so lovely and warm toward Elle, giving this advice. The image makes me shiver. "I'm not sure she's right about that, Elle Belle."

"It's what you do," Elle says.

Touché.

The world narrows down to this single moment, to the huge responsibility of selecting the right words to set my daughter straight. Grief hits me for my own beautiful self-confidence, shattered so many years ago that I can't imagine ever putting the pieces all back together. Maybe it's too late for me, but Elle still has a chance to stay free of this broken thinking.

"I think it's like this," I say, finally. "If you were really rich, some sort of gazillionaire, some thief might come and steal your money. And then maybe people would say, 'She should have had better security. She should have put the money in a safe and hired a bodyguard.' And maybe those things are true, or maybe not. Either way, the guy who came and stole your money is a thief and a criminal. Do you see that?"

"I guess. What does that have to do with Daddy?"

"Any man who hits a woman is like that thief."

"You spanked me when I was little."

"Maybe I was wrong to do that. I don't know. You needed to learn some things, and I couldn't think how else to teach you."

Elle lies back on the bed, journal clasped over her chest, and peruses the ceiling as if it holds all the answers.

"And maybe Daddy is doing the same thing. Teaching me."

God have mercy. My mother used to say that parenting classes should be mandatory before people were allowed to reproduce. She didn't mean this to apply to herself, of course, but to the ignorant hordes whose children run wild in Walmart, pillaging candy bars and throwing tantrums. At this moment, I'm thinking there should be a mandatory university degree, which includes not only psychology but also existential philosophy.

I lie down beside my daughter and join her in staring at the ceiling. There's a water stain in the corner, but otherwise no answers I can see.

"Does that seem true to you?" I ask, finally.

"It feels—different," she says. Her voice catches as her rigid control finally breaks, her breath uneven with sobs she can't suppress.

I lie perfectly still, quelling the need to hold her. She doesn't want that, doesn't need that, and this conversation is so not about what I need.

"And how does it feel?" I ask her, or the ceiling, or maybe the universe.

"Not good," she says, and I think that's all I'm going to get. She's only twelve, for all her precocity and adult behavior. But then, as usual, she surprises me. "It makes me feel like . . . gum. Old parking lot gum. On a shoe. Inconvenient. Annoying. Disgust—"

She can't finish the word, crying now in earnest, and I have to work hard to translate what spills out of her, distorted by her weeping.

"What's wrong with me? He didn't used to look at me like that."

I roll toward her and put a hand on her shoulder. She buries her soaking face in my chest and clenches her hands in my shirt. I stroke her back, slow and steady, and rock her, until the weeping eases.

"Oh, sweetheart. Nothing is wrong with you."

Elle pulls away a little to blow her nose, then shoots the crumpled tissue at the waste basket, overhand. It falls short by six inches, a crumpled wad of snot and failure. Not one to accept defeat, she lobs the second tissue, and this time it's a slam dunk.

"See? You're even good at tissue basketball. Perfect in every way."

"You're kinda biased," she says. She laughs, just the tiniest bit, which makes my heart ache even more when she asks, with a little quaver, "Do I have to go back with him tonight?"

"You are staying right here with me."

As I say the words, a shadow Greg looms up over me, all-knowing, all-powerful. *Are you sure you want to play that game with me, Maisey?*

My answer? The thing I didn't have the guts to say? No. *No, Greg, I don't want to play. But I will. For the sake of this strong, beautiful child, I will do anything. Give anything. Confront any challenge, any obstacle, you set in my path.*

I'm just afraid that all I have will never be enough.

Leah's Journal

Pain is what I remember first. White lights in my head. A deep ache in my eye socket that made me need to vomit, only I was lying on my back and couldn't move.

Pinned, I thought, remembering Boots straddling me, only he wasn't there anymore. The weight was gone. My body didn't want to respond to my brain.

I managed to roll to the side, and the blaze of agony from moving set me to heaving. Not much in my stomach—I think I'd missed dinner—but just enough to foul my pillowcase.

Another task. That was my first conscious thought. Now I would have to do laundry.

The babies were still crying.

Boots was nowhere to be seen. His truck was not out front.

Somehow I managed to get through that night. To feed the twins. To strip the stinking pillowcase and throw it in the laundry.

The next few days were a blazing hell beyond any conscious thought. His mother, when she came over, didn't look shocked, just sad. She didn't even ask what happened to me. She fixed me an ice pack to put over my eye and my cheek. Changed the babies, held them.

"Steak is good for bruises," she said, but we both knew neither one of us could afford the luxury of steak, even for eating.

Chapter Twenty-Five

Despite all my best intentions, I'm not much of a warrior woman. I'll fight it out face-to-face with Greg if I must, but phase one in the plan to keep Elle from flying back with him is to be elsewhere when he shows up to get her. Dad and Elle both being complicit, we vacate the house in the early afternoon, in case Greg comes early.

Elle and I turn our phones off to minimize the ping of guilt that will arrive with each unanswered text message or voicemail. Dad has never carried a cell phone.

Staying occupied in Colville isn't as easy as it would be in the city, but we hit the early movie at Colville's one and only theater, which fortunately is rated PG, not R. We go for hamburgers at Ronnie D's. We pick up new socks and T-shirts for Dad at Walmart. And we go to get groceries.

We're in the cereal aisle at the Safeway—Dad, me, and Elle—having an argument about what would be acceptable for consumption, when Dad drops the bombshell.

Elle has gravitated toward the brightly colored, sugar-coated varieties. Dad mutters something about the good old days and oatmeal, and I'm really just staring at boxes and wishing there was a Make a Decision button so I wouldn't have to think.

It's 6:45 p.m., and my mind is thoroughly occupied with film clips of Greg showing up at Dad's house to find it locked up tight. Ringing the doorbell. Talking to Edna. Maybe he'll come looking for us and recognize Dad's car in the parking lot. My eyes are in constant motion, up and down the aisle.

"This one," Elle says, thrusting a garish box into my hands. "Look. Whole grain."

"And sugar is the first ingredient."

"No, it's the second ingredient. Why can't sugar be a grain?"

"Because—"

"I was wrong. I think we need to go see Marley." Dad says this as if he's read the words on the box of Raisin Bran he's peering at through his bifocals.

I take a steadying breath. "Is the Raisin Bran sending out telepathic signals now?"

Dad ignores me. "We should skip town tonight. Drive to Tri-Cities. Get a hotel. And then we'll go talk to her in the morning."

"All three of us. Just like that."

"It would solve the Dad problem," Elle says.

The box of cereal in my hands feels extraordinarily heavy. I set it back on the shelf.

"I need to get out of the house," Dad says. "What do they call it—a grief holiday?"

"A what?"

"I heard it on TV. *Oprah*. Or something. Your mother was watching it."

Elle throws her cereal box into the cart, followed by Dad's Raisin Bran, and something middle-of-the-road and boring-looking. "We need milk. And plastic bowls. We can eat cereal in the hotel room. But we need road-trip snacks. Come on."

She starts pushing the cart down the aisle.

"Elle . . ."

She keeps walking. Dad and I roll into motion like a couple of robot toys programmed to stay with the shopping cart.

Dad has totally perked up. His eyes are clearer than I've seen them since I got here, his steps steadier.

Still.

Me going to see Marley is one thing. Exposing Dad and Elle—especially Elle—to all that hostility is another.

"What if it's not safe?" I ask him. "Mom got a gun after you contacted Marley. We can't take Elle if it's dangerous."

"I'm sure it will be fine," he says. "Ask that guy to come. For protection."

"Which guy?"

"Tony!" Elle throws back over her shoulder. "That's a great idea. Hey, and can Mia come?"

"Tony and Mia have jobs, in case anybody is unaware. And most people—adults, anyway—don't just pile into the car and take off like this."

"You've never been most adults, Mom," Elle says. "Please don't start now."

"What does that even mean?" I ask, but my only answer is the uneven thud of the shopping cart wheels and the straight, unbowed spine of my still-powerful daughter leading the way to the potato chips and snack mixes.

According to Elle, who can't resist looking at her text messages when we get back to the car, Greg is still parked outside Dad's, waiting for us to show up. I've run out of places for us to hang out. Even if we head for Tri-Cities tonight—I'm still talking in terms of *if*, even though all three of us know full well we're going—there are things at the house we need. Dad's medications, for example. A change of clothes.

Visiting Mia and Tony offers refuge and a place to hang out until Greg gives up and goes back to his hotel.

I tell myself we could just go confront him. He won't physically drag our daughter, kicking and screaming, into the car. I don't think.

But the thought of facing him, planting my heels and telling him no, is daunting.

"Do you really want to do this?" he will ask me, with that indefinable edge of scorn and derision. He will manage to look lawyerly, to remind me without further words that he has connections and power and will take Elle from me. If he must, of course. For her own good. Not that he would ever want to hurt me.

My hands make the decision for me, directing the car through the turns that take me to Tony's. I drove him home the morning of the funeral; I know where he lives. Elle texts Mia to fill her in and let her know we're coming, and she meets us at the door, hugging all of us in turn once, and then again. There's no sign of Tony.

Not that I'm looking for him.

Not that I want to see him.

Not that my traitorous heart is beating a little faster at the thought of hugging him.

"Come in," Mia is saying. "We haven't had company in, like, days. I so understand you wanting to get out of the house and just get away from everything. What's this about a trip?" She takes Dad's hand as if she's known him forever, and he rewards her with a smile.

The room she leads us through is all beautiful wood and light. Skylights overhead frame rectangles of blue, letting warm golden light burnish a hardwood floor polished to a shine. The skeleton of the room is exposed, rather than hidden by the drywall; varnished logs serve as posts and pillars and beams. The wood is softened by throw rugs and furnishings in earth tones.

My feet slow, then stop, of their own volition. I have an impulse to crane my neck so I can look up to the sky, spread my arms, and spin like a child.

"Beautiful, isn't it?" Mia asks, her voice echoing my wonder. "No matter how long I live here, I always want to stop in a puddle of sunshine and curl up like a cat for a nap. But the deck is awesome, too."

I follow her out through glass doors to a wide deck. Flower baskets hang in profusion above my head. Adirondack chairs are arranged to allow an unrestricted view of the Colville valley—trees, houses, and streets all laid out below, the mountains rising up behind.

"Let me get you something to drink," Mia says. "I'll be right back."

She flits back into the house. Dad and Elle settle into chairs, but my restless feet won't let me sit, and I walk the edge of the deck and then down the steps onto an expanse of grass shaded by large trees. Around the corner, along the side of the house, a giant maple tree offers shade and privacy. Tony leans against the trunk. His face is in shadow, and I can't see his expression, but I remember the one he wore at the funeral after Greg's behavior.

My face heats with shame. I want to pretend I haven't seen him there, to flee back into the safety of Mia's chatter and my father's vagueness, but our eyes meet and it's too late. He won't want to talk to me, but I owe him an apology.

I approach the tree, conscious of the suddenness of the shift from sunlit warmth to the coolness of the spreading shadow cast by its branches.

"I'm sorry if I'm interrupting."

"What, my deep, philosophical, life-altering thoughts on the nature of the universe? Come on in. You've found my favorite spot."

His voice is light, but he keeps his arms folded over his chest, and he doesn't smile. I feel like an intruder.

"I won't stay long. I wanted to apologize."

"For what?"

"Drama."

"You're responsible for Greg's behavior?" There's an edge to Tony's voice that unsettles me. I brace myself for a deeper dig that must surely be coming, for recriminations and judgment, but he just shifts his body to lean more comfortably against the tree and reaches up to pluck a leaf, rolling it back and forth between his thumb and forefinger. Waiting.

"No. But I am sorry you got caught in the crossfire."

"I hadn't realized the two of you were still . . . together." All of Tony's attention is on the leaf, crushed now between his fingers.

"We're not together. He's Elle's father, that's all."

"That's not the way it looks." And now Tony's eyes are on me, and I wish they weren't. Assessing, questioning, probing.

"Sometimes things aren't how they look." My eyes, seeking sanctuary, turn up to the green branches above us and find a house. It is so camouflaged by leaves and branches that it looks almost part of the tree itself. A wooden ladder, stained the same color as the tree bark, leans against the trunk.

"For nieces and nephews?" I ask. "If Elle sees this, I'll never get her home."

"For me," Tony says, the tension draining from his voice. He flashes me a smile, half man, half mischievous child. "Although, yes, my sisters' kids certainly make use of it. You want to see? We can hide from the others for a minute."

My child-self dreamed of such a thing. My invisible friend Marley and I inhabited dozens of tent forts, created from an amalgam of my imagination, furniture, and blankets. We imagined some of them were in trees, way up high where nobody else could find us.

An emotion I recognize from childhood but can't put a name to creeps over me as I look up, up, into green leaves and the wooden house nestled in branches.

"Yes, I want to see."

"Go on up. Ladies first." He executes a formal bow.

I fit my toe on one of the rungs and reach for another with my hands. Each step brings me away from the earth. Up, up, into wonder.

That's the word, the label for this feeling like my heart and soul are too big for my mortal body. There is this tree, bark, leaves, a scurrying ant. The ladder. My body, hands, arms, legs, moving up, rung by rung, as if I've climbed this way a thousand times before. Up, up, all my worries and responsibilities and even my grief falling away.

My head pokes through a round opening, and I laugh out loud in sheer delight, looking around me in amazement and wonder. Floor pillows to sit on. A treasure chest, actually painted with a skull and crossbones, and above it a rough map tacked into the wood. I recognize the confluence of the Colville River with Lake Roosevelt and guess that the big white *X* lies approximately over the location of this treehouse. A stack of paperbacks, waiting to be read. A cardboard box full of snacks.

A tap on my foot and a voice from below asking, "Are you sightseeing or are you going in?" reminds me that I've stopped moving, and I climb on up to make way for Tony.

There's not room to stand upright without bumping my head on the ceiling, so I sit on one of the pillows, looking out a window into leaf-green light and a wisp of blue. Tony enters on hands and knees, crawling over to the other pillow and settling himself with a satisfied little grunt.

"Getting too old for this," he says, though he's clearly not too old at all.

"What's in the treasure chest?" I ask him.

"Arrr, if I told ye that, the pirate ghosts would come for me, sure and certain." He laughs and opens the lid, revealing more books, a length of neatly coiled rope, a radio, and a row of bottled water.

"Thirsty?"

"I am."

The water he hands me is warm, but no drink ever tasted better.

For some reason, the dim light, the slight sway, the whispering of wind in leaves all around us, relieves me of the pressure to make small talk, and we sit in silence, him cross-legged, me with my knees drawn up to my chest.

My water is gone, and so is Tony's, before either of us says a word. He's the one who breaks the silence.

"So, you and Greg."

"We're not together."

"Does he know that?" he asks, and that edge is back in his voice. "Not that it's my business."

I clasp my knees tighter against my chest, clinging to the fragile sense of safety the treehouse gives me. Tony doesn't hate me, at least, or he'd never have brought me up here. The treehouse lends itself to secrets, but still I'm quaking inside when I whisper, "I've only just realized how—things are between us. Like at the funeral. He's married to somebody else, but if he thinks I like somebody, he still pops up like a malevolent genie."

"Try *asshole* on for size. *Genie* sounds too Disney and Robin Williams."

A dry laugh turns to dust in my throat, and I cough instead. My body is damp with cold sweat, a reaction to speaking my thoughts aloud.

"Seriously, Maisey. I don't know you well, but why do you put up with a guy like that?"

"I don't. Usually. I mean, I try not to."

Tony's silence speaks for him, and I fumble my own defense.

"I only talk to him when I have to. About Elle. I didn't even know he was coming to the funeral. I certainly didn't expect him to be sitting in Mrs. Carlton's living room."

Tony shifts his weight and brings his eyes to focus on me, instead of the wall. A minute ago I wanted this. Now I squirm beneath his scrutiny, and it takes all my will to keep my chin up and meet the challenge of his gaze.

"He thinks he owns you."

"He does," I whisper, realizing. My throat constricts, an invisible chain tightening, tightening. "He does own me."

"I'm so confused." Tony leans back against the wall, and I take a deep breath as he releases me from that intense observation. "Don't take that as criticism," he quickly amends. "I get it. My mom was abused until—" The stop is as abrupt and as violent as a collision. Glass shattering, metal screeching.

When the dust settles, he starts over. "My mom was abused. She couldn't make decisions about what to do because he was mind-controlling her all the time. It's hard to make that break."

"Greg's not exactly abusive—"

It's my turn to crash into what I'm about to say. To stop. To feel the new reality strengthen around me.

Greg hit me. He slapped our daughter. He puts me down, controls my decisions, and chases away men who are interested in me.

"It's Elle," I say, very low. "I'm afraid if I stand up to him, he'll take her from me. She's the best thing in my life, and she's also my cage."

"I'm sorry." He means it. I'm not sure what he's sorry for, or if maybe he's just offering up general sympathy. It sounds more like commiseration than pity, and so it's okay. Especially when he adds, a moment later, "I've got my own cage, I suppose. My mother. My sisters."

It's my turn to put on X-ray-vision glasses and try to see through him. His turn to flush and avert his eyes.

"How?" I ask. "They're all grown up."

"I was the only boy," he answers, as if that explains everything when it's not an answer at all.

When I say nothing, he adds, "He beat them all. My mom, my sisters. So now I'm forever making it up to them, I guess. It . . . interferes."

Math has never been my friend, but even for me something doesn't add up. "They're all older than you," I say, thinking out loud. "Except for Mia. Weren't you a child? Didn't he hit you, too?"

He shivers, then scrubs both hands over his face, the way my father does when he can't think straight. "We moved here, away from Seattle, because of me. Tore the girls away from school and their friends. Because of what I—" His voice cracks. He sucks in a breath, lets it out slowly, and asks, "Why are you here? Tonight? What made you come here?"

"Hey, not so quick. It's your turn for the grilling."

"Could we talk about the weather? Or the Seahawks, maybe. That's a fine topic of conversation." His face is still in his hands.

I put my hands over his and draw them down and away. He keeps his eyes cast down. I trace the scar on his forehead with my finger. And then the bump on his nose. He shivers beneath my touch, but doesn't move.

"This," I say. "Your father did this."

"Don't." He grips my hand in one of his and pulls it away from his face, letting it rest against his chest. I can feel his heart thudding against his ribs. "This is where angels fear to tread, Maisey. You don't want to go there."

He's right. I can feel the anger crawling under his skin, the way it bunches up his muscles, speeds his breath.

"Greg slapped Elle this morning," I blurt out, as a change of subject. "For no good reason. He wasn't even angry. He did it because he could."

Tony draws in a breath. Holds it. Lets it all out in one long whoosh. "Told you he was a bastard."

"He wants to take Elle back with him, and she's not going. So we are hiding at your house. Also, we are going in search of my ever-so-pleasant sister tomorrow, and Elle was determined to ask you along as bodyguard."

"Consider me hired."

"Just like that? No lecture? No advice?" My hand is still trapped under his, the fingers splayed over his pectoral muscle, the heat of his palm almost enough to burn.

"Would you change your mind if I did lecture?" His head bends down over mine, so close his breath stirs the fine hair in front of my ear.

"Probably not."

His lips graze my cheek. I can feel the tension in his body, his muscles rock-hard. Both of us are trembling.

"This is a very bad idea, Maisey. We are—"

I silence him with my lips against his. Lightly, at first, a brush, a taste, and then his arms go around me and he pulls me in hard, our lips moving into a kiss so deep it makes me dizzy.

He's the one that breaks away, holding me by the shoulders and pushing me back to arm's length. Both of us breathe like we've been running a marathon. I think there are tears on my cheeks, but I can't quite feel my face.

"I can't do this." Tony's voice is harsh. His hands are firm, inexorable, but there are no fingers digging into me. No pain, except for what is breaking open in my heart.

"Why, exactly?"

"All the reasons," he says. "Greg being one of them."

He's right, of course. What was I thinking? Shame heats my body.

"I should go," I say, only I can't, because Tony is still holding on to my shoulders.

"When do we leave on this trip?"

"I thought you just said—"

"I can be your bodyguard," he says. Pauses. Gives me a half smile. "And you can be my long-lost pal."

It takes me a minute to catch the song reference. I run my fingers through my hair. Focus on breathing normally. He's not trying to get rid of me altogether. I can do this. "All right, Paul Simon, but don't you dare start calling me Betty."

He laughs, but there's no flash of little-boy mischief. He looks like I feel—deflated, like a punctured balloon. The treehouse isn't magical anymore. Just a box up in a tree. As I work my way down the ladder, gravity takes possession of me. My body feels heavier with every rung, so that by the time my feet touch grass, I'm not sure I'll be able to walk back to the porch.

"Come on, Betty," Tony says, and his smile is an act of courage. "There's no rule that says we can't be friends."

Leah's Journal

Boots showed up two days later, sleek and well rested and sorry. He brought grocery-store flowers. He brought me a bloody steak and held it to my cheek with his own hands.

"Poor Leah," he said. "Please don't do that again. I hate it when I hurt you." He had tears in his eyes as he said it.

In my mind, I still had all kinds of sass. Don't do what again? Get exhausted? Ask you for help? But I'd been tamed. My head hurt and the fatigue was something that mired my brain and soul in a gray fog that promised to last forever.

You will not understand this, Walter. I'm not sure that I do. But looking back at the next little space of time, Boots was my bright spot. He was still such a beautiful man. I think, twisted as it is, I came to see him as some sort of angel of mercy. Patient with my weakness. Helping me with the tasks I was incapable of performing on my own. Staying with me, even though my belly was scarred and my breasts leaked milk. Despite the baby weight I hadn't lost and my inability to do anything other than tend to the little ones and sit, blank and doing nothing, or sleep.

There was a constant litany of this. His voice a patter of toxic rain. "Not that it's your fault," he would say, "but it's a pity about those scars. Good thing you have a man who loves you anyway." That sort of thing. Always in my head, and me so tired and already believing I was ugly and ruined.

I loved him then, more than I had loved him before. Clung to him. Forgot about leaving him.

Even when he hit me again.

Chapter Twenty-Six

We can't exactly troop up to Marley's door and demand an audience, so we go the concert route again. It's not like she'll stomp off stage in the middle of a set when she sees us all sitting there.

Probably.

Maybe.

Mia and Elle together are an organizational force the military would be lucky to have. It takes them about five minutes to collect intel on Marley's upcoming gigs and to announce that we will be dining at the Emerald of Siam in Richland tomorrow night, where we will be treated to Marley's band once again.

They also locate her unlisted home address and that of her boyfriend. I know I should chastise my daughter for this stalker behavior, which goes far beyond the bounds of either family reunions or healthy fandoms, but I'm too wilted and weary to even try.

Dad has fallen asleep in a recliner in the living room, feet up, head tipped back, snoring. I'm jealous. It's been days since I've had any restful sleep, and I have no idea when, or if, it will be safe to go home tonight. I certainly don't have the energy to drive to Richland, although between Mia and Tony I'm pretty sure we can make it.

And so I sit there, half in, half out of reality, letting the conversation swirl around me and not really paying attention. When my phone goes off, it startles me half out of my chair. It's a local number, not Greg, and I manage to fumble it on just before it goes to voicemail.

"Hi, this is Karen Porter with Frontier Realty. How are you this evening?"

Tired, I want to tell her. Fucking tired. Heartsick. Despairing, maybe. Not in the mood for telemarketers.

"Look, I don't know how—"

"Greg gave me your number. He said he'd tell you I would be calling. Is this not a good time?"

I catch my breath, rein in my galloping heart. "A good time for what, exactly?"

"I've already driven by your father's property. Such a lovely home. I'm sure you're both sad about him having to leave it, but that's what happens when we get old!"

Far from sounding sad, she sounds as chirpy as the first robin with the very first worm. I don't have the energy for chirpy. "The house isn't for sale."

"Oh, are you sure? Greg said—"

"It's not Greg's house to sell. We're not selling."

I can almost hear her brain cells regrouping on the other end of the line. "Such a misunderstanding, then. I'm terribly sorry. Why don't I give you my number, and that way if you ever decide—"

I just click End and sit there, staring at my phone, daring it to ring again, this time with a psychological evaluation company offering door-to-door service. Greg has apparently made good use of his waiting time.

An idea comes to me about how to make good use of mine. Greg's wife and I need to have a little chat.

I excuse myself and step out onto the deck. Linda's voice on the other end of the line sends a fortifying bolt of adrenaline blasting through me. *All sensors go, Captain. Weapon systems armed and ready.*

"Maisey. What happened? Is Greg okay?"

"How many times has he hit Elle?"

"Oh," she says.

"How many times, Linda?"

A long silence unfolds. "He said he's bringing her back with him," she says finally, avoiding my question altogether.

"No. He's not." I bite each word off and spit it out. "Answer me, Linda. If you can't protect her, at least you can tell me the truth."

"She antagonizes him, sometimes. He corrects her. A father has a right to discipline his child."

"Does he *discipline* you, too?"

Her breathing hesitates, comes back ragged and irregular. "I need to go, Maisey. It's time to feed the baby."

Which tells me all I need to know. Linda can't help me, can't protect Elle. She's scared. I take a breath and soften my tone, coaxing her like a frightened animal.

"Wait a minute, Linda. He's not there. He'll never know we had this conversation. I won't have Elle being hit. He'll fight me in court, I know how he is. I need your help."

She laughs at that. Shaky and small, but defiant. "I've already told you he has a right—"

"You hold that thought. Now picture your son growing up. What's it going to be for him? A cheek slap and humiliation? Or fists? You think he's immune, because he's a boy. Hell, maybe you're right. But do you want him to learn that behavior? Do you really think it's okay?"

"I am *not* having this conversation. Greg is my husband. He—"

"Spare me. Do this one thing. Tell him you don't want Elle full time. You know it's the right thing to do."

"I'm sorry, Maisey. I can't."

The line goes dead, but her voice lingers in my ears, soft with what sounds like regret. Wild thoughts surge through my brain. I'll run away with my daughter. Wipe out our identities. Live in the car.

None of this is practical, and I know it. I don't have money to bankroll a getaway of that magnitude. Sooner or later I'm going to have to let Elle go back to Greg. Even if I put Dad in a care facility and go back to Kansas City, I'll still have to let her visit. Living in a car and being on the run would probably be more damaging than the occasional *discipline* from her father.

I'm in the throes of accepting reality when the slider opens and Tony comes out on the deck.

"What's the plan?" he asks. "We're game to drive tonight, if you want, only your dad looks totally done in."

I scrub my face with my hands and groan. "I know. Me, too. Just not up to fighting with Greg tonight."

"You're forgetting you have a bodyguard," he says. "Or, you could sleep here."

"Dad needs his medication. And we couldn't intrude. I'm being ridiculous, I know. I need to face up to him. It's just that I'm so damn tired."

Tony's hand rests on my shoulder. His face softens. His head lowers toward mine, and for a minute I think he's going to kiss me again. "Mia and I will go fetch the meds. I bet Elle would love to sleep in the treehouse. Maybe you, too."

I lean into this version of a plan like an illicit lover's embrace. It is warm, inviting—and wrong.

"Another time." I straighten my shoulders. "I'm not going to keep hiding from Greg. We'll go back to the house tonight. I'll tell Greg that Elle isn't going, like I'm an adult and not a frightened child. And tomorrow we'll head for the Tri-Cities if you guys are still up for that."

"Absolutely." He opens the slider for me, then pauses, hand on the door. "You can do this, Maisey. You're stronger than you think."

Marley was the strong one, I almost tell him, and then gasp as the realization hits me. All of Marley's imagined qualities: her fearlessness, her way with words, her adventurous spirit. All of them are mine. I don't remember her, not as a real child. I created her out of the fabric of my own being.

Tony's right. I can do this.

For a minute I consider leaving Elle here, safe and out of reach. And then it occurs to me that she needs to know that I will stand up for her. She needs to know that a woman can be strong against a man.

I'm not sure that I know this for myself, but I have one inner certainty. I cannot spend the rest of my life hiding from Greg.

Still, as we pull into Dad's street, I'm holding my breath with the hope that Greg's car will be gone. That he's moved on. It would be fantastic luck to have the inner credit of knowing I was ready to stand up to him without actually having to do so.

Luck is against me. Greg is against me.

Earlier, he was irritated. He is now thoroughly pissed. Rage radiates off him like heat from an inferno. He gets out of his car, sears me with a glare, and then speaks directly to Elle.

"Get in the car. Your mother will bring your things."

Elle hesitates, caught in the crossfire. I press the house key into her hand. "Go in the house, Elle. Take Grandpa and lock the door behind you."

She scuttles up the sidewalk and away.

When Dad doesn't follow, she turns back to look at us, at him, wavering.

"Please," I say to the only father I've ever known. "She doesn't need to hear this."

He nods and follows Elle up the sidewalk and into the house.

Drawing strength from the fiercely protective love I have for my father and my daughter, I turn to face the man who has been controlling my life, one way or another, for so many years.

"We are not selling the house, Greg. I already told you. So I would appreciate it if you wouldn't try to hook me up with Realtors."

"And I would appreciate it if you wouldn't undermine my authority with Elle. I've bought her a ticket. Spent money. And we need to go. It's already late, and we have an early flight."

That's the way it's going to be, then. Straight to the heart of the matter.

I draw up courage from the earth beneath my feet. "She'll come back with me. When I'm ready."

Greg draws a deep breath, snorts it out through his nose. He reins himself in, all calm control, and actually smiles. Condescending and superior and deceptively calm.

"Maisey. You aren't thinking straight. Perfectly understandable. You're grieving. It's been a difficult week. *Our* daughter needs to return to her normal routine. She needs to get back to school. All this chaos isn't good for her."

"She wants to stay."

"She's a child, Maisey. She doesn't get to make decisions."

"But I do, Greg." I say it gently, surprising myself, as if he, Greg, is a child in the middle of a tantrum and needs soothing. "I'm the custodial parent. I'm actually pretty good at knowing what she needs. School is not an issue. There's absolutely no reason why she can't stay here."

"Except that I'm taking her."

"No. You're not. Good night, Greg. Go home. And stop with the Realtors. If I want one, I know where to find one."

I turn my back on him and start up the sidewalk.

"What the hell has gotten into you?" Greg calls after me. "This isn't like you."

My feet grow roots that stop me short. I can't run away from this. From him. I take a breath and turn back to face him.

"You. You are what got into me. You hurt me, Greg."

He opens his mouth, but I keep talking. "Don't start with the whole bit about how long it's been since you hit me. You still put me down, every opportunity you get. You always make me feel stupid. You've followed me around the country, interfered with my relationships. I've put up with it, tolerated it, sometimes didn't even notice it. Why? Because of Elle. And now—" My voice breaks, and the traitorous tears come in a rush.

Greg takes my emotion for weakness and starts up the sidewalk toward me. "Is that what this is about?" he asks, oh so gently. "You think I hurt Elle?"

My breath comes in gasps. I can't stop the tears, don't trust my voice.

Greg holds his hand out to me, palm up. Takes a step closer. "Come on, Maisey. You know better than that. I'd never harm her."

"I saw you. You can't—"

"Oh, Maisey." He sounds sorrowful now. "I don't know what you think you saw, but discipline is necessary. Does she act like an abused child to you? Think about it."

Elle. Beautiful, confident, irrepressible Elle. Maybe he's right. I know full well how my imagination can run away with me, make things seem real when they are only figments. Only Marley is real. Was real. Not a figment at all, no matter what my mother and the counselors drilled into me.

I wrap my arms around my chest, holding myself together.

And wince as my fingers press against the bruised place on my ribs. I press the sore place harder, deliberately invoking the pain and the memory that comes with it. Greg claiming possession of me, antagonizing Tony. The look on Elle's face after he slapped her. His casual nonchalance.

I hold out both palms toward him, not in surrender but to ward him off.

"Stop."

He doesn't. His confident, patient steps bring him up the sidewalk to me. His chest against my hands. Mostly bone. I'm surprised by the relative slightness of him, compared to Tony.

I plant my heels and lean my weight against him, shoving him back. He staggers a little, rights himself.

His shock gives me space to square my chin. Level my voice. Look him in the eye.

"Maybe you believe what you're saying. That's the most positive spin I can find. But this is the truth. You hurt me then. You hurt me at Mom's funeral dinner. I have bruises, Greg."

"Because you were with that—"

"See? That's an excuse. There is no excuse for that behavior, just like there's no excuse for slapping Elle. I'm done. I'm not going to argue with you or try to explain. Go home to your wife. Try not to take this out on her."

"Maisey. You can't—"

"I can. And leave Dad alone while you're at it." This time, when I turn to walk away, I am not running from anything. Every step feels solid and right. My body feels more like it belongs to me, instead of a puppet dancing on invisible strings.

"You can expect legal papers in the immediate future."

My smooth steps hitch. My right toe dips a little too far and catches on the sidewalk. A slow-motion recovery goes into play. Thigh muscles tightening. Brain zeroing in on balance.

I get myself back upright and keep walking. Don't turn around or acknowledge his words. Dad is waiting on the other side of the door and opens it for me. When I walk through, Elle is standing there beside him. Nobody moves for a minute, or says anything.

Elle has a different expression in her eyes when she looks at me. I'm not precisely sure, but I think maybe it might be respect.

Leah's Journal

I forgot all about leaving.

My life was Boots and the babies. I became grateful for being allowed to have this life. Grateful that he tolerated me. Grateful that he didn't hit the girls. I took my beatings when they came to me. Took the time my husband deigned to share with me.

Of course there were other women. Why wouldn't there be? I was damaged goods, no longer beautiful. Nobody else would want me, and yet he continued to love me. I believed this. Sitting here, thinking back on my years with you, Walter, it occurs to me that I should find a way to tell you how you have healed and restored me. Given me back my soul and a sense of myself as having worth. But these are things I can never bring myself to say. That part of me will always be broken, I guess.

It's funny how life spins, how we go on for long stretches of time and nothing changes, and then all at once, in a single moment, everything is altered.

Things had gotten a little easier. The twins were two. They were sleeping through the night, potty-trained, able to feed themselves. I was sleeping at night. No longer breastfeeding. And as my body returned to being my own, as the haze of fatigue cleared from my head, I grew restless. I had glimmers of understanding that my relationship with Boots was wrong.

Those were dangerous glimmers. It was like he could see them in my eyes and immediately felt the need to take me down. It was during that time that he started breaking bones. My collarbone. My ribs. Both casualties of a brand-new pair of shiny boots and his brand-new addiction to cocaine.

Where he got the money to use, I don't know. He never held a job for longer than a few months at a time. Maybe he was dealing. I didn't ask those kinds of questions. But while he was away doing whatever it was he did, I began to do things. I got my GED, for one.

And then I landed a job, almost by accident, answering phones in an office for a female attorney.

Boots wasn't happy about me working. What about the babies? What about him? Did I really think he couldn't bring in enough money to support his own family? Maybe he knew in his head the answer to that one, because I kept the job and all I suffered in payment was a black eye.

My new boss was a woman, novelty number one. She was a lawyer. She dressed in power skirts and jackets, and nobody was beating her, that's sure and certain. Her name was Hetty Johnson, and she became my idol. Thanks to Hetty I came to understand some truths.

Not all women are beaten. They can be smart and independent and make their own decisions. They can live in this world without a man.

Of course I didn't believe that woman could be me. I never did come to believe that, Walter. I found my way to you instead. And I don't regret it. I never wanted to go to college or run a business. But she made me think.

It wasn't Hetty that set me free, for all that. It was one of her clients.

Chapter Twenty-Seven

Tony sits in his pickup in the dim, predawn light, wrestling with his conscience and his courage. The entire fabric of his careful control, the balance of penance and duty and family, is coming unraveled, and Maisey Addington is the unraveler.

What he wants to do is start up his truck and drive directly to her house, be sitting on the doorstep when she wakes, like a stray cat asking to come in. He's tired, not just from lack of sleep, but from his constant vigilance.

Remember who you are, Tony.

Remember what you've done.

But that remembrance is fading around the edges. He keeps seeing himself in a different light these days, as if maybe he's the sort of man who could be with a woman like Maisey. As if he might even be good for her.

He's been to the shooting range twice this week, but his ritual with the gun is apparently not enough to keep him on the straight and narrow.

So he's come to create a new level in his own private circles of hell.

The sun hasn't cleared the mountains yet, and in the dim light, the graveyard looks bleak and otherworldly. He's not given to fears of ghosts, but a little shiver tracks its fingers up his spine. If there were a time for ghosts to walk, this would be it.

"Coward," he mutters to himself. "Do what you came here to do."

The morning air is cool enough to raise goose bumps on his bare arms, and the mosquitoes are hungry and find him in seconds. He ignores both cold and insects and marches himself between the rows of headstones until he finds one that looks right.

It's not his father's, of course. That grave is across the mountains in Seattle. But he chooses a headstone that looks similar, and when he closes his eyes, it's easy enough to see the inscription that reads:

ANTHONY MEDINA
BORN 1945
DIED 1990

And that's it. No *Beloved husband and father*. Not even *May he rest in peace*. Not so much as a clue carved into the granite about the man who was Tony's father.

But Tony's body remembers. Twenty-seven years since his father's grave was dug. Twenty-seven years since the last time Anthony Medina Senior let a bottle fuel his always-simmering rage. And still, Tony can feel the blow that broke his nose. Can taste the warm salt of blood filling his mouth, pouring down his throat, remembers gagging and choking on it. He can hear the sound of fists on his mother's flesh, hear his sisters screaming, taste the sharp smell of gunpowder.

This is why he came here, to make himself remember.

Who he is. Where he came from. All the times he failed to protect his mother and his sisters. All the anger that built up in him during the years both before and after his father's death. Holes punched into walls. Fights with boys at school. Endless hours chopping wood and hammering nails into building projects, his mother's solution to managing his rages.

He wants to run away now, as if he is twelve again and about to be beaten, but his legs don't seem to belong to him. His hands are shaking.

And his heart, oh, his heart is definitely his, beating out fear and pain and regret against his ribs.

The pain is physical, a deep ache that nearly doubles him over.

Not a heart attack, he reminds himself over and over again. *Just panic. Just memory. It will pass.*

But there's a new intensity to the familiar pain. He's already let Maisey under his skin. He's tired of his rituals and rules, and holding the barrier is so hard. Years ago, he swore he would never risk becoming his father, would never risk exposing a woman to that sort of treatment.

He'll hold to his vow. If he can help Maisey, he'll do it. Protect her, support her, the way he protects and supports his mother and his sisters. But nothing more. No matter what his traitorous heart tells him. No matter that his body responds to thoughts of her, even now, with desire.

"I am the son of my father," he whispers. "I swear on his grave that I will not forget it."

Chapter Twenty-Eight

No hiding this time.

We have a table at the Emerald of Siam, right out front and center, where Marley can't help but see us. Once again we show up plenty early to claim our table and order our food.

The waiting is purgatory for me, but everybody else seems contented.

Mia and Elle sit across from me, heads together, chattering. The two of them are dangerous, and I don't want to know what they're planning this time. I'm sandwiched into a bench seat between Dad and Tony, my heart rivaling the rapid tempo of the music playing through the speakers.

Dad is vague and confused tonight.

"Long way to come for Thai food," he says, trying to navigate chopsticks with moderate success. "Why didn't we eat in Spokane?"

"Marley," I tell him. I like to say her name. It makes me feel sorrowful, but also real. Not my imagination. Not a thing I made up. "We're here to listen to Marley sing."

And to make it up to her for being left behind, if we can. But that I keep to myself.

Tony's bulk beside me doesn't help much. A little shiver of fear runs through my body. Not a shiver. A frisson. Such a wonderful little word. So underused.

A frisson of fear. And a big old bucket of nausea.

Normally the smell of lemongrass and curry makes me ravenous, but tonight it turns my stomach to acid. I sip at a glass of house wine, white, and wait, wait, wait, for what seems an eternity. By the time the band finally troops onto the stage, it's all I can do to stay in my seat, fingers white-knuckled around the chair.

Marley doesn't see us at first. She's busy assessing the crowd as she launches into the first song. But her eyes, inevitably, find us. Her gaze lingers on the small blue bear sitting on a pink blanket. The taped-together photograph of our mother, a pink bundle cradled in each arm. Just for an instant, the hard shell cracks, and her face goes soft.

I hold my breath, realizing too late that springing this on her in the middle of a concert might seem like an emotional ambush. I will her to keep singing, not to fall apart here in front of an audience. So far, the sins she holds against me are my mother's, but if I mess up her song, she'll never forgive me for that.

I needn't have worried. Her voice doesn't falter. Her professional persona slides back into place, and she redirects her focus to other parts of the room. For the rest of her set, she avoids even a glance at our table.

Her sound guy, on the other hand, glares at me pretty much nonstop.

When the band takes a break, Marley comes over.

"Are you going to make a habit of this sort of thing, now? Groupies?" Her right hand, as if it has a life of its own, reaches toward the blue bear, stops, and falls back to her side.

"We need to talk." I hear my mother's tone coming out of my voice, and soften it. "Please."

"I don't understand what you want," she says.

"You look like her," Dad says. His eyes fill with tears. "Like Leah. I thought you would look like Maisey. I didn't think—"

"None of you thought," Marley snaps. "Or you wouldn't be here. What is it going to take to convince you that I don't want this?"

"You came to the funeral," I protest. "If you don't want anything to do with us, then why did you bother?"

Marley shifts her weight, one foot to the other. "Honestly, I wanted to know. What kind of woman abandons her child? That has always been the question." Her eyes settle on me. "I used to worry about you, taken away by a mother who could forget her own baby. Can you imagine? Me, worrying about you. And all the time there you were with your awesome new dad and your beautiful life—"

"She told me you were a figment of my imagination! She sent me to counselors who told me I made you up. How did I know to look for you? To worry about you? You have to give me a chance."

Her lips part. Her eyes soften. She strokes the bear's ears with her fingertips. And then she shakes her head, more as if to ward off flies than to say no, but the meaning is the same.

"It's too late. Not your fault. I see that. But I can't do this now. You're just going to have to accept that."

"Marley—"

"Tell you what. You want to know this side of the family? I'll introduce you to our father. And then you will leave me alone. Deal?"

"I don't know if that's wise," Dad whispers.

It occurs to me that this must be hard for him on so many levels. He's the only father I've ever known. Now Mom is gone, and I'm meeting this other shadow family. Maybe he thinks I won't need him anymore. Of course I need him, will always need him.

But the need to know the secrets my mother has been keeping has become a driving force. Besides, I need just one more chance at Marley. One more opportunity to get her to agree to try to be sisters again.

So, wise or not, I nod. Yes. "Deal."

She scribbles an address on a napkin. "Be there at eleven tomorrow. I'll make the introductions."

Without another word, she turns her back on me. I have been dismissed.

Leah's Journal

She walked into the office with three solemn children trailing behind her. At a signal of her hand, they arranged themselves on the waiting room chairs while she came to speak with me at the reception desk. The oldest, a girl not more than ten, took the toddler on her lap and rocked her.

The fading bruise on the woman's cheek was all too familiar, and I knew what her problem was going to be without asking. Still, I followed the professional script Hetty had taught me. "How can I help you?"

"I need to leave my husband," she said. "I need help with the divorce."

Hetty swept her away into the office and left me with those children. Not a one of them would smile. The littlest, safe in her sister's lap, stared at me out of wide eyes and sucked her thumb. None of them fidgeted or fussed.

I could hear fragments of conversation through the closed door. Two of those fragments caught in my head.

The first was about a safety plan. "Where will you go, where will you stay, how badly will he hurt you when he knows you want to leave?"

These words, rather than weighing me down, sang to me, in that way it is when a bit of a tune gets stuck in your head. Over and over, all the rest of that day, into the night, and the days that followed.

Where will you go, where will you stay, how badly will he hurt you when he knows you want to leave?

Maybe those questions would have been enough to set me free, but it was the next bit about the children that changed everything. There they sat, unnatural in their silent watchfulness, like small animals, hoping they won't be seen if they don't move.

And in the office Hetty asked her, "Does he hit the children?"

And she answered, "No. I've taught them how to keep from being hit."

Those were the words that took my breath as surely as a punch to my gut. Three pairs of watchful eyes on me, aware of my every movement. Three pairs of watchful eyes in a home where it was their responsibility to avoid getting hit.

I was so enmeshed in my own nightmare, I still might not have dared a break for freedom, but Boots, in perfect timing, chose that evening to come home, high and edgy. Probably he hadn't slept since the last time I saw him. Certainly there was a craziness in his eyes.

The girls were tired. I'd been leaving them with Boots's mom while I worked, and she hadn't given them a nap. They smelled of stale cigarettes, and they were cranky and difficult. Dinner wasn't quite ready when he walked in. Marley was whining, Maisey was crying.

"This is ridiculous," Boots said. "You are not going back to that job."

The world slowed down.

I watched both of my little girls respond to his tone. They went quiet and still. The tears stopped. The whining hiccuped once, then trailed away. They froze. And in that moment, even before the first blow came at me, I saw again the children waiting in the office, and I knew—knew—I had to get the girls away from him.

Chapter Twenty-Nine

We follow GPS directions, Tony driving slower and slower as we get closer to our destination.

"This can't be right," Mia says, when the too-cheerful GPS voice informs us we have arrived. "Maybe she wrote it down wrong."

Elle consults the napkin where Marley had written the address. "This is what it says, all right."

Tony pulls the car over to the edge of the road, and we all stare at a run-down single-wide trailer occupying a lot where weeds and garbage compete for space. The trailer itself is beat-up and faded. One of the windows is boarded over.

Two cars are parked in the rutted dirt driveway. One is burgundy with one black door and a rear bumper hanging at a crazy angle. The other is a nondescript hatchback, far from new but at least all one color and not looking like a kindergarten kid's crazy drawing.

All of us stare at the trailer. I can feel Tony assessing the rest of the neighborhood. We're out of the city, but here it isn't suburbs. We've passed grassy lots with horses, goats, chickens. Even a small herd of sheep. Plenty of mobile homes, many of them well kept up, the yards clean, the animals healthy. If we were in a movie, this lot would house the psychotic murderer.

"Looks about right," Dad says. "Are we going in?"

He has an expression on his face that I haven't seen there before. It's almost like Mom left her iron will lying around, and he's picked it up and put it on. His mild features set in those lines of determination make him look foreign and strange. I feel adrift again, without anchor, but before I can restore my equilibrium, he's opened the door and started unfolding himself out of the car.

"Wait," I call after him, getting out of my own door. "Maybe we don't all have to go in. You and Elle could wait—"

"Oh, I'm going in," he says.

"Elle, you stay here with Mia," I call back over my shoulder, taking a few running steps to catch up with Dad, who is moving faster than I've seen him since I got home.

Tony is right behind me, which should be comforting, but the responsibility of his presence weighs heavy on me. As for Elle, once again she doesn't listen, and she and Mia troop up behind us.

The door opens as Dad steps up onto the pallet that serves as a porch.

Marley stands there, looking even more like a younger version of Mom now that she's not dressed for a performance. No makeup, her hair drawn back into a loose ponytail. She's wearing faded jeans and a western shirt, sleeves rolled up to the elbows.

She steps out and closes the door behind her. A wave of stale tobacco accompanies her, along with the blare of the television.

"This really isn't a good idea," she says. "I'm sorry. Maybe—"

"I want to talk to him," Dad says.

"He's not fit to talk to. Usually he's better at this time of the day. Tomorrow?"

"Now." Dad again. I can't think what's gotten into him, but I'm grateful. Now that we're so close, I can't bear to walk away without meeting my birth father, without knowing the other side of where I came from.

"Please, Marley. We had a deal."

She shrugs. "Fine, then. It's on you. Don't say I didn't warn you."

She opens the door and steps aside to let us troop in.

There are too many people for the space, that's immediately clear, and we all stand in an awkward huddle, exchanging curious stares with an old man propped up in a recliner. He's got a can of beer in one hand and a half-smoked cigarette in the other. Two empties sit on a cluttered end table beside him, next to an overflowing ashtray.

"Who is this, then?" he demands. "Did you let some church group in, Marley?" His voice competes with a laugh track on the TV.

She crosses to him, picks up the remote from the arm of the chair, and presses Mute.

"This is your daughter—the other one. Maisey. She wanted to meet you."

He squints in our direction. "Well, I'll be a rat's ass. Never expected to see your face, that's certain. Come over here and let me get a look at you."

He botches his first attempt to adjust the recliner so he can sit up, obviously confused by the problem of his occupied hands. He finally sets down the beer, takes another drag of the cigarette, and pushes the lever that brings him to sit upright.

His arms are thin and bony, his belly bloated. He reminds me of a spider.

I approach him the way I might something dead and stinking that needs to be attended to. There's a sharp, bitter taste in the back of my throat. Up close I can smell beer and smoke and an infrequently washed body. He looks old. Much older than Dad. He's bald on top, what's left of his hair uncombed and lying in greasy strands. His front teeth are missing. Gray beard stubble sprouts from his jaw.

"You don't look like her," he says. "Marley favors Leah. You look more like me."

It's revolting but true. I can see the shape of my features in his wrinkled face. And his eyes, reddened and sunken as they are, still are the color of my eyes and Marley's.

"Cat got your tongue?" he asks. "Seems like you must have had a reason for coming here."

"Have a chair," Marley interjects. "Sit down. I'll bring more from the kitchen."

I don't want to sit. I want to bounce right out the door. But I perch on the edge of a ratty old couch, picking up a newspaper to make room. Dad sinks down beside me. Tony stays standing, and I can tell he's on high alert.

"I didn't know about you," I say. "I did some digging after Mom died."

"She's truly dead, then." He stubs his cigarette into the ashtray, but it doesn't go out. Smoke continues to curl up, blue and sinuous.

"I told you, Boots," Marley says. "You never listen."

"Thought maybe you were making it up," he says, dismissively. "Females." He directs this at Tony. "Anybody want a beer? A cigarette? What can I do you for?"

I can't think of anything to say. My imagination, generally so quick to jump in, completely fails to put this man together with my mother, even if I picture him young and possibly handsome. He's tawdry and cheap and mean.

"You beat her," Dad says, in a conversational tone of voice. "Frequently."

Boots laughs. "Is that what she told you? Had a good imagination, did Leah. Passed it on to Marley. What about you, Maisey? You got an imagination?"

"Actually, Leah never mentioned you," Dad goes on. His flat tone makes my spine prickle. Old and frail or not, there's something menacing in the way he's talking. "Damn close to forty years of marriage. Never mentioned you. Not one word."

The old spider—I can't think of him as my father—levels a look at Dad that is pure venom. "I had the juice of her," he says. "You got the leavings. How was she? Still to your taste, I'd say, if you stuck with her so long."

I'm going to vomit. Right here, in the middle of this sordid room in front of this horrible man and the sister who hates me. I press a hand over my mouth to hold it back, but then I have to breathe through my nose, and that does nothing to ease my nausea.

Dad is made of tougher stuff. "We found the broken bones when she was dying," he says. "Ribs. A collarbone. A cheekbone. Did you break them all at once? Or one at a time?"

Boots takes a long swig of beer. "I'm empty. Fetch me another, Marley."

Marley doesn't move. She stands across the room, hands on hips, looking at him as if he's as much a stranger to her as he is to me. "You beat her?" she asks.

He slams the can down on the table and raises his voice. "I asked you for a beer!"

She doesn't budge. "And I asked you a question."

"Don't you turn this on me," he says. He levels a finger at Dad. "You. Coming here into my house, turning my daughter against me. Get out. The lot of you."

None of us move.

I've got both hands cupped over my nose and mouth now, trying to use them like a mask.

Marley crosses the floor, only a few steps, each one taken with precision, to stand directly in front of Boots. "Nobody ever told me that you beat her."

"She left us," he says. "Walked away from me and you when you were just a bit of a thing. Not a second thought for either of us. Don't you let these people make you forget that."

"I'm not likely to forget," Marley says.

"What kind of mother leaves a child behind?" Boots smiles a gap-toothed smile at her.

Silence descends. Every one of us can see that there is no excuse for abandoning a child. Mom took me with her. Why not Marley?

In this moment I understand my sister's anger. How would I feel if I'd been left behind? Not just left, but left with this old asshole of a man. I wonder how often Marley has been beaten. I can't help picturing fists smacking against my mother's flesh hard enough to break bones.

God.

My stomach erupts into heaving I can no longer control. I struggle up toward my feet, one hand over my mouth, the other pushing against the arm of the sagging couch for leverage. I can taste the acid. I'm not going to make it.

But then Tony is there, just in time, with a plastic grocery bag he grabbed up off the cluttered floor. When I take it from him, he holds back my hair. His hands are so gentle; his presence feels like a fortress of protection. When the spasm ends, he takes the bag, knots it, and sets it outside the door. Marley brings me a glass of water, silently, wordlessly, an act of grace.

Boots wheezes laughter. He taps a cigarette out of a half-empty pack and lights it.

"I remember that day like it was a painting on my wall," he says, blowing a stream of smoke out in a cloud around his head. "It was about this time of year. Blue sky. The whole world turning green with promise, but what does she do? Can she enjoy it? Of course not. Nothing was ever good enough for her.

"'I'm leaving,' she told me. Just like that. No by-your-leave, no warning. 'I'm leaving and I'm taking Maisey.'

"'How am I supposed to raise a child?' I asked her. 'A man's got to work and such.'

"'You'll figure it out,' she said. 'You've got your mother to help you. I can't manage both of them on my own.'

"She didn't even kiss Marley good-bye. I know this is a sore spot with my daughter, but let me tell you this. I raised her, and she turned out good and strong, so good riddance to Leah, I've always said."

His words fill the room with finality.

I sit with the enormity of it. My mother did this thing. She was justified in leaving him. I can see that. He's a heinous example of a human being. But leaving a baby. I try to imagine leaving Elle behind and can't do it. I'll go back to Kansas City with her, if I have to. I'll put up with Greg for the rest of my life, if that's what I need to do to keep her safe.

I wish she wasn't here now, though. She's too young for this. I'm too young for this.

And then Dad leans forward, puts both hands on his thighs, and says, "Enough with the lies. How about if you tell them what really happened?"

Leah's Journal

And here we are, at last, at the moment I've been dreading and avoiding and talking circles around since I started writing this story. The moment that has cast its wide shadow over the rest of my life, and your life, Maisey's, and Marley's. And I suppose even over Boots.

If we were Catholic, maybe I'd go to confession, but I don't think I could speak this aloud. I've always told myself I did the only thing I could. Truth? Or a comforting lie that helps me maintain my distance from the past?

I don't know. I'll never know. So here are the facts as I remember them.

It was a Sunday morning, just past dawn. Boots was out all night, partying.

I didn't sleep that night. I spent it packing. Very carefully, knowing that I would have to carry everything with us in one battered old suitcase. I packed their favorite blankets and their blue bears, the one good thing Boots ever gave them. I took the little stash of money I'd been hoarding from what I coaxed out of him for groceries and rent.

We had moved into an apartment in Pasco, not far from the Greyhound station. I'd already bought the tickets. All I had to do was get us there. It wasn't a long walk, not more than half a mile, but with the way my ribs were hurting, the weight of the suitcase, and trying to coax the girls to walk, it stretched out ahead of me like a marathon.

All the while, there was the fear that Boots would come home before we left the house or would drive down the wrong street at the wrong time and see us walking. I told myself over and over this wouldn't happen. It was way too early for him to come home after a party. He'd be sleeping until noon; it was only 6:00 a.m.

I told the girls it was a game and that I would buy them ice cream when we finished our walk. They were only two, but bright enough to capture cause and effect. They didn't get ice cream often, and they loved it. We started out, me with the suitcase in one hand, holding Maisey's hand with the other. Marley held on to Maisey, and so we went, down the sidewalk, a small human train headed for freedom.

It didn't work out that way. Boots had found a woman who sourced his fondness for cocaine. Instead of lying on a couch somewhere, sleeping off too much alcohol, he was wide awake and supercharged.

He found us before we'd made it more than a few hundred feet.

That moment, when his pickup truck nosed up to the curb on the wrong side of the street and he stepped out to stand on the sidewalk, blocking our path, has played out in nightmares over and over again. He had the mean look on his face. He stood like one of those western gunfighters, legs spread wide, hand on his hip.

I thought he was just posturing. My fear was solely around another beating. And then he pulled something out of his pocket, and I saw that he had a gun. When he got it, where he got it, I'll never know, but I will never forget the instant I realized what he held in his hand. The terror of knowing what power he had in that moment to end me, to end all three of us.

"And what exactly is this?" he asked. His voice was too calm. It didn't match the crazed look in his eyes. There was a little too much white around them. His hair was uncombed. He needed a shave. He looked like he belonged on a street corner.

I set down the suitcase, knelt on the sidewalk, right there, and gathered both girls into my arms. There was no point making up a lie. It would only make things worse.

"I'm leaving," I told him. "I'm taking the girls."

"Is that right," he said. It wasn't a question. He turned that gun in his hands, pointed it at Marley first, and then at Maisey, before aiming it at me. "I thought it was you and me forever, Leah. Things changed after the girls came along. Maybe it could go back to how it was if they were gone."

Showing him fear would have been the worst thing I could do. I knew that, but what do you do when a madman has the lives of your children in his hands? I didn't care about my own at that point. I knew I was going to have to go back. Going to spend the rest of my life in his prison, because I wouldn't have the nerve to try again.

So it was the girls I was thinking of, their safety. Their lives. If it was just me, I would rather he shot me and got it over with. But for the little ones I was willing to grovel.

"I'm sorry," I told him. "I was being stupid. Don't hurt the girls. I'll go right back home. I'll never do it again."

"What makes you think I still want you?" He spat on the sidewalk, as if he had a bad taste in his mouth. "You're ruined, in case you hadn't noticed. Stretch marks and fat and useless in bed. No fun anymore. I've got a new woman who's actually worth fucking. So don't bother ever trying to come home."

He stepped off the sidewalk, down the curb, and into the street.

I stared at him. At the gun. At the open sidewalk. I got to my feet. Picked up the suitcase. Took Maisey by the hand. Both of the girls were whimpering, but they already knew better than to cry outright when he got like this.

He still stood there, the gun at his side.

I took a step.

"Course, there's always a price for freedom," he said. "I'm not about to let you treat me this way and walk off without me having something to show for it."

"What do you want?" My mangled hope died a sudden, misbegotten death right then. I knew that what he wanted wasn't going to be simple like money or my suitcase or a final purchased kiss.

But I never could have imagined the sort of devil's bargain he was about to offer me.

Chapter Thirty

"You calling me a liar?" Boots shouts. "In my own house. In front of my daughters. You can get out. All of you. Just get out!"

"Sure," Dad says, very quietly. "We can go outside. It's easier to breathe out there, anyway. Did you want to come, Marley? And I'll finish telling you what your father did."

He makes a move to get up, but Boots isn't having any of it.

"If you're going to tell lies about me, I want to hear them. You stay right where you are."

Dad shrugs. "Have it your way, then." His eyes seek out Marley, and he talks as if she's the only person in the room who matters. "She meant to take you both. First thing you need to know, she was hurt. He'd battered at her sense of self for years already. First time he hit her, she was pregnant with the two of you. And only sixteen. No parents effective enough to intervene.

"So on that day—the day she left you behind, Marley, there are things you have to know about her. She raised both of you pretty much by herself, sleep-deprived and hurt half the time, while your father went out partying.

"On the day she managed to get away, she had broken ribs—he'd kicked her after he knocked her down. There were two of you, and she couldn't carry you both."

"Now, Marley," Boots protests. "Don't you listen to this pack of lies. Not a word of it is true. If Leah had broken bones, then he's the one who gave them to her."

"The journal," I say, the lights coming on all at once. "You read the journal. I thought you burned it."

"God help me, I had to read it first," Dad says. "I know she trusted me to destroy it, but I wondered, too. How could the strong woman I knew have left a baby behind? I couldn't reconcile it in my head. And so I read everything she wrote."

"Do you still have it?" I lean forward, hoping. I want to read it for myself. Maybe it would help Marley in some way.

Dad shakes his head. "I burned it. After the shredder jammed, I threw it on the fire."

For the first time since I've met her, Marley's control cracks. "So she chose Maisey." Tears flow down her cheeks, and she scrubs them away, roughly. "I can see why she left. But you're not helping. How could a mother leave her child with a . . . a . . . monster?"

"She didn't have a choice," Dad says, and his voice has gone so cold, a shiver skates up my spine and settles at the base of my skull.

Leah's Journal

"You can go," Boots said, "but you have to leave one of the girls."

Horror crawled all over me. Like ants, it felt. Ants in my belly and my heart and crawling in and out of my lungs.

"You're crazy. What would you do with a child?"

"That's my business, isn't it?" he said. "You were leaving. Anything that happens here is of no concern to you."

"I can't—how could I do that?"

"Should have thought about that a little sooner. Pick one."

"No. Please." I actually clasped my hands to him. I let go of the girls and crawled to him on my knees. "Don't do this, Boots. I'll do anything you want. Just let me come back."

He loved that. Made him feel powerful and godlike. I could see it on his face. But he was not a benevolent god.

A kick to the side of my head knocked me over onto the sidewalk. I lay there, the world spinning, pain blazing, and I couldn't think. His words kept hammering at me.

"Pick one, Leah. Do it before I count to ten, or I get both of them."

I couldn't even see straight, Walter, let alone think. I was afraid he'd just shoot us all, he was so crazy in that moment.

He started counting, his voice bludgeoning my brain, my emotions, my heart. Every number leading up to the absolute disaster. I was paralyzed.

But then he got to eight. Nine.

"Maisey," I said. "I choose Maisey." She wasn't as strong as Marley. That was what did it in the end. She was sick a lot. She was sensitive. I guess I figured that if one of them was likely to survive life with Boots, it would be Marley.

I also told myself I'd come back for her. It wasn't forever. Only just right now. Today. I'd go to the police. I'd find money somewhere and get a lawyer. I'd get her back.

"Perfect," he says. "So like you. You get the runt, I get the strong one. Marley, come here."

I'd managed to sit up by then. She didn't want to go to him. She locked her arms around my neck and half strangled me, holding on. Marley never was much of a crier, but she started wailing at the top of her lungs. I thought he might hit her to shut her up, but it seemed like maybe he liked to hear her cry, or at least enjoyed the effect it was having on me.

He came over to us and grabbed her around the middle. She screamed and kicked and held on, but he yanked her off me.

I'll never forget that moment when her little hands let go, the sudden coolness on my neck, my face, the sound of her screaming. He held her tight, and then he put that gun against the side of her head.

People talk about slow motion, but I'm telling you this: In that moment, all the world went still. Nothing moved. Everything was a series of snapshots.

Boots holding Marley. Her tear-streaked face. The gun pressed to her head. Maisey sitting on the sidewalk, wailing.

"If you come looking for her, I'll kill her," Boots said. "If you talk to the cops or hire an attorney, I'll kill her. You will not make contact with her or me or your parents or anybody in this town. If you do, after I kill Marley, I'll come looking for you and Maisey. Do you understand?"

I couldn't even begin to breathe. It still feels like a nightmare, writing this. Every day since it happened I've tried to wake up, to change the way the dream ends. Back then, kneeling in the street, I thought maybe I could appeal to his better self somehow.

"You don't mean that," I said. "You're her father."

"Do I look like a man who doesn't mean it?"

He looked like the devil himself. There was a grin on his face. The sun came out just then and turned his hair gold. He was beautiful and evil and all the reason had been burned out of him by the drugs and alcohol.

I wanted to kill him. I think I would have, if I'd been the one holding a gun.

But the gun was aimed at my baby. I was sick with pain and terror, and I believed him. I believed he had the power to know if I was following his instructions. I believed he would do what he said.

And so I managed to get up onto my feet, the world spinning, every breath an agony because of my ribs. I picked up the suitcase. I picked up Maisey. And I walked away from him and from my beautiful Marley still screaming in his arms.

Chapter Thirty-One

Dad's voice falters into silence as he chokes on his own emotions.

Even Boots looks subdued, smaller. He's not one to give up easily, though. "It's not true," he says. "Don't you listen to him, Marley. Don't you believe a word he says. These people are trying to poison you against me."

Marley doesn't seem to hear him. She stands like a statue in the middle of the room. And then, "I remember," she whispers.

"Oh, that's just ridiculous," Boots scoffs. "You were barely more than a baby."

She turns, slowly, as if just waking from a trance, to face him. "I've always remembered. I just thought it must be a dream. A nightmare. I still dream it sometimes, but I only remember flashes. A woman on the ground. A boot kicking her in the head. A gun. Me screaming, screaming, screaming, trying to hold on to something that is torn away. It all happened, didn't it? It's real."

Elle buries her face in Mia's shoulder and starts to sob. Tony gets up and turns his back to us, staring out the window. Dad looks exhausted.

As for me, I feel like my heart has swollen so big that it's occupying all my insides. I want to hug the child that Marley was and the woman that she is now. I want to hug my father—not the devil father, Boots, but the man who raised me as his own, the man who helped to heal my mother.

I want, more than anything, for my mother to be alive so that I can tell her that I understand now. I can see why she pushed me so hard to be better, to do more, why nothing I did was ever enough for her. She needed me to make up for Marley, to be enough for two girls even though I was only one.

For me, it's too big for tears.

I get out of my chair and cross the room to Marley. "I have the same dream," I tell her. "The woman on the ground. The flash of a gun. Me, screaming. Only in my dream, it's you I'm being torn away from."

We stand there, face-to-face, looking at each other, and then the barrier between us shatters. We both move at the same time, arms around each other, cheeks pressed together, holding on for dear life to what feels like the missing half of what I've always needed to be whole.

"I hate to interrupt this fairy tale," Boots says, his voice dripping sarcasm, "but would you all mind clearing out of my house?"

Marley's body stiffens at the sound of his voice. She moves out of our embrace, but her hand finds mine, and our fingers clasp, joining us together as we both turn to face him.

"That's all you have to say for yourself?"

"I see no point. You've judged me. Anything I can say that will change that?"

His gaze moves from my face to hers and back again. "I thought not. Get me another beer before you go, will you? And be sure to close the door behind you."

"You can get your own beer," Marley says. "You're on your own. You might think about getting up off your ass and finding somebody to buy your groceries. I won't be back."

She tugs at my hand and leads me out of that smoke-filled cesspit and into the light of a beautiful spring afternoon.

Chapter Thirty-Two

It's three days shy of a month after Mom's funeral when a teenager walks up the sidewalk to the front door. I open the door with a smile, expecting some sort of pitch for a school fund-raiser.

"Maisey Addington?" she asks.

"That's me," I say, before I can wonder how she knows my name. She holds out a manila envelope, and I take it before I register that there is no catalogue full of chocolate or popcorn. As soon as it's in my hand, she trots down the driveway and takes off on her bicycle without looking back.

I know what's going to be inside that envelope before I tear it open.

Greg has drawn the case up himself. He is suing for full custody of Elle. He takes several pages to lay out my unfitness to be a parent. By the time I'm done reading the accusations against me, I'm inclined to put Elle on a bus and refrain from even visiting.

But Greg hasn't counted on my family. Or his timing. The revelation of what Boots did to my mother, and to Marley, and to me, is still fresh, and we're all full of fight in need of an outlet.

"What happened?"

Marley comes out onto the porch and plops down beside me. She's got this sixth sense that tells her when I'm upset about something. I've got the same thing about her. It's fascinating how this works, given how we didn't cultivate some special twin radar growing up. But it's there anyway.

I hand her the papers, and she starts reading through them, cursing all the way.

"What an absolute piece-of-shit asshole," she says.

"Who is a piece-of-shit asshole?" Elle asks, behind us.

Marley and I exchange a glance made up of chagrin on her part and panic on mine. The language isn't the issue. I don't want Elle to know about this. She can't know.

But Marley turns around and says, quite calmly, "Your father, honey."

Elle drops onto the step below me, where she can look up at both of us. "What's he done now?" she asks, with deceptive calm.

"She's going to have to know sooner or later," Marley says. "Might as well get it over with."

This is the problem with logical, decision-making people. I would have run off with the papers, made up a lie. Protected my daughter as long as I could. But it's too late for any of that now, so I let her read the papers.

Meanwhile, Marley is busy laying out battle strategy. "Of course we'll fight this. Doesn't Walter have an attorney? Maybe that Tony guy has some connections. He's a firefighter, right? They're tight with the cops. We need a judge we can corrupt. Or—"

"Don't I get any say in this?"

Elle's voice stops us cold. She lays the envelope on the step and the papers on top of it, squaring them all precisely before she looks up at me.

Her face looks remote, her eyes cold, and my heart freezes. What if I've been delusional all this time? What if the things Greg says about me as a parent are true, and Elle would rather live with him?

"You might," I tell her, tuned to her reaction. "I'm sure the judge will ask. But that's probably not the deciding factor."

"Well that's just stupid," she says. "This whole thing is stupid."

"Elle. He's your father."

She stares at me. "What the hell? You're going to give me the respect-your-father lecture now, when he's pulled this shit? Then you're just stupid, too."

I freeze, mouth hanging open, not sure whether I should begin with the swearing or the disrespect to her father or her disrespect to me.

Marley, on the other hand, applauds her. "Attagirl," she says. "No abusive asshole is ever going to hoodwink you." Before I can remonstrate, she puts her hand on my shoulder. "Maisey, go easy. You think the girl doesn't know any swear words? If there was ever a time to say them, this is it. Also, if you believe one word of that trash he wrote about you, then Elle is right. You are stupid."

Between the two of them, on top of what I've just read, I'm pretty much incapacitated. Elle comes to sit beside me. "I'm sorry," she says. "I shouldn't have called you stupid."

I put an arm around her, and she leans her head on my shoulder. "I love him," she says. "But I don't understand him. And I want to stay with you."

Her words thaw the frozen place inside me. I plant a kiss on top of her sun-warm hair, breathe in the smell of her—shampoo and soap and cotton. In that moment, all my rationalizations flee. To hell with the notion that a girl needs her father. If he's going to behave himself, sure. But she doesn't need to grow up believing it's okay to be discounted, belittled, slapped for having opinions.

I'll run away with her, if I have to.

~

Dad, as it happens, has an attorney and invites him over for battle planning. Geoff Jenkins is about my father's age, but there's nothing of softness in his eyes or his face. He carries himself erect and with confidence and declines the slice of pizza Elle offers him.

"This is not a social call," he says. "If you don't mind, I'd like to get right to business."

"Hang on a sec," I say. "Marley?" She understands what I'm asking without me saying the words.

"Come on, Elle. Pizza is better outside."

Elle looks torn. "Maybe I should stay here."

"You need to go," I tell her. "Please, Elle." I say please, but she knows I mean it and will insist. To my relief she doesn't push the issue. Maybe she doesn't want to be caught in the middle any more than I want her to be there.

"All right," she says, finally. "But don't try to pretend you're not just getting rid of me. You sure you don't want any, Mr. Jenkins?"

"I'm sure. Thank you."

As soon as the door closes, Dad turns to him. "Well? What do you think, Geoff?"

"I think we have a good case. Custody tends to favor the mother, and Maisey has been the custodial parent from the beginning. The parents are not and never have been married. In addition, I took the liberty of pulling the original parenting plan. It was filed here. So we'll start with the request that the venue be here in Colville."

"Is that likely?" I ask. "Greg is an attorney and has connections."

"And I am an attorney and also have connections," Geoff says drily. "I also have the advantage of older and deeper connections than his. I suspect the judge will not be interested in a change of venue."

I absorb this information with the first real glimmer of hope I've felt since being served the court order.

Geoff continues. "Your job is to collect written statements from teachers and friends who are likely to feel you've done a good job parenting your daughter. Is his name on the birth certificate?"

"No."

"Good," he says, scribbling. "Any chance she might be someone else's child?" He peers up at me over his glasses.

"What? No. God, no. Greg is her father."

"This is not about morality," he says. "In this case, we could wish you had been promiscuous. However, he will have to prove paternity. Anything else?"

"Violence," Dad says. "Tell him, Maisey."

Geoff's face lights up. "He hits you? Domestic violence can play in the mother's favor, at least if you have protected the child."

"He only hit me once. Before Elle was even born."

"Still," he says, making notes. "Now, what about the child?"

"He's slapped her. He'll say it's discipline."

The old man's eyes soften. "I was wondering what she would want to do and whether she will testify. But if he's been violent with her, then that makes our job easier."

All my beliefs about Greg go swirling through my head. *A child needs a father. He's been a good father to her. Discipline is a good thing. When she was little, he spanked her. Now he slaps her face. It's not that big a deal, if she gets lots of love the rest of the time.*

Is it?

I remember that moment. It wasn't the blow that did the damage. It was the way he dismissed her, demeaned her, discounted her. Maybe an occasional dose of that on weekends won't do too much harm, but I cringe at the thought of her subjected to him full time.

Still.

"He's her father and she loves him. I don't want her put in the middle. It's not fair to pit a child against her parents like that."

Geoff looks up at me over his reading glasses and nods. "That may not help your case, but I approve of the parenting decision, young lady. Noted. I would like to have a chat with her in private though, if that's all right. Just to see what she would like to do."

"All right."

"My office, then." He scrolls through the calendar on his phone. "I have an opening at three p.m. on Monday. Will that do?"

"That will do fine."

"Well, then. It was a pleasure to meet you." He gets up from his chair and shakes hands with my father. "You take care, Walter."

"Thanks for coming over, Geoff. Especially on short notice."

"Oh, I'll send you a bill."

"How about I buy you a drink?"

"Make it three."

They walk out of the room together, two old friends, Geoff's hand on Dad's shoulder. I sit in the chair where my mother used to sit, sometimes, while Dad worked. She was always busy. Writing letters, knitting blankets for unwanted babies, giving Dad advice about a business he knew and understood perfectly well.

My hands are empty and still. I close my eyes and try to put myself inside my mother's body, to feel that force, that drive, that allowed her to re-create an entirely new life out of the ashes of something that would have destroyed me. I need her now, after all the years of tuning her out and avoiding her.

What would she do about Greg?

Whatever it takes. And that's what I, too, am prepared to do.

Chapter Thirty-Three

Tony's nightmares are out of control. Every night now, not just once a month or once a week, he wakes up in a sweat-drenched bed, breathing hard, pulse pounding. Half the time he doesn't even remember what he dreamed, but the sound of gunshots is in his head, in his ears, vibrating through his body. Sometimes he can smell gunpowder.

The last few nights, it has been so real, he's had to get out of bed and walk through the house, turning on lights, checking doors and windows.

Playing Whisper Me This with Maisey triggered a new intensity in his flashbacks. The visit to the evil old man who fathered her completely unhinged him.

On that day, in that dingy, smoke-filled room, listening to Walter tell the story of exactly what Boots had done, Tony had wanted to kill. He'd stared out the window, breathing, working his system of getting calm but the whole time all he wanted was a gun in his hand. The smooth glide of the trigger. The recoil.

The old bastard's blood.

For Leah. For Marley. But mostly for Maisey.

He hasn't seen her since that day, but his avoidance tactic is getting increasingly difficult to maintain, thanks to Mia. And his mother. The two of them have adopted the entire Addington family. Elle runs in a pack with Tony's nieces and nephews and is in and out of his house with them on a regular basis. Tony has worked extra shifts to avoid dinners at his mother's house when he knows Maisey will be present.

If he wasn't a coward, he could handle this situation better. But he's afraid that when he takes one look at Maisey's face, he'll kiss her again. He can't do this. Won't do this.

She's called him and left voicemail, once to say thank you, once to ask him if everything is okay. He hasn't called her back. She doesn't need a man like him in her life. She doesn't even need a bodyguard anymore. Maybe Boots was dangerous once, but he's toothless now.

On this particular day, the problem has intensified to the point of being intolerable. Mia's chatter has been full of Greg and his legal quest for custody of Elle, so Tony's well up on the situation. His protective instincts are running high, and there's no outlet for them. He's exhausted and useless and literally pacing the living room, one side to the other, when the door opens and his family traipses in.

Mia. His mother. All his sisters. None of the husbands or kids, and they all have that expression on their faces that means he's in for some kind of lecture. They are also far too quiet. No laughter. No chatter.

"God have mercy," he says, watching them arrange themselves on chairs around the room. "What is this?"

Mia stands in the doorway and folds her arms over her chest like a bouncer on duty. "This," she says, "is an intervention."

"Sit down, Tony," his mother says. "We need to talk to you."

"I think I'll stand." He leans his back against a wall, surveying the forces arrayed against him. He loves them all, but knows full well that when they unite in a common mission, they are formidable. His mother. His oldest sister, Theresa, fourteen years older and in many ways more mother than sister. He's a foot taller than she is now, and has about a hundred pounds of muscle on her, but inside he still quakes when she looks at him like she is looking now.

Vanessa and Jess, only one year apart and always attached at the hip. As little kids, they shared everything and even had a special language for a while that the rest of the family couldn't interpret. They married brothers and live on the same street, sharing kids and household chores. Between them, they manage school fund-raisers, community blood drives, two husbands, and seven kids. There is no project they won't tackle, and right now that project would appear to be Tony.

Barb, quiet and thoughtful. Generally she minds her own business, and he knows it's a busy time of year for her. She'll be working horses, keeping an eye on the cattle, helping to get the fields planted on the ranch. The fact that she is now sitting in his house, with her hair braided to stay out of her way and mud on her boots, is possibly the most ominous sign of all.

"I'm frightened," Tony says, lightly. "You are all far too serious for my own good."

And he is frightened, although he hates himself for this fear. The blood is loud in his ears. His breath keeps catching in his throat. His knees are even a little wobbly, and he wishes he'd opted to sit down.

"It's time we had a little talk about your father," his mother says. "Well past time, really."

Tony's throat constricts. "And if I politely decline?"

"Not an option." Theresa leans forward in her chair and sets both of her capable hands on her knees, bracing herself. "This isn't easy for any of us, Tonio. But there are things that need to be said."

"Why now?" he asks. "We've managed not to talk about it for, what, twenty-seven years? Seems like there should be a statute of limitations on certain topics of conversation."

"You're having nightmares," Mia says. "You think I don't hear you talking in your sleep? That I don't notice you getting up and checking doors?"

"My sleep problems are my own business," he says. "Please. I know you all mean well, but this isn't going to help me."

"There's also Maisey," Mia says.

"What does she have to do with any of this?"

"Tony. Look at me." His mother is so incredibly calm. She reminds him of the maple out back that holds his treehouse. Her roots run deep into the earth. She sways with the wind but never breaks.

And yet, it's her voice he hears screaming in his flashbacks and his nightmares. Hers. Theresa's. Vanessa. Jess. Barb. Mia. All of them were there that night. All of them know what he did. The thing they've never talked about. The thing they inexplicably want to talk about now.

"I was too broken to talk to you right after," his mother says now. "I sent you to the counselor to do what I should have done myself. I am sorry for that."

"You have nothing to be sorry for," he says. His voice is rough in his throat, sandpaper. The words hurt him. His breathing hurts him. All their eyes on him, the weight of their collective memory, hurts him.

Vanessa and Jess wrap their arms around each other. Mia's face is wet with tears. Even Barb's sun-weathered face is creased with grief.

But his mother continues, perfectly calm. "It never occurred to me to ask you what you remember about that night. What you believe. You were only a child, Tony. I'm not sure if you realize that."

"I was twelve!" His voice sounds angry, the rage he feels at himself breaking through his reserves. "Old enough to know what I was about."

"Same age as Elle is now," Mia says, very softly. "Think on that, Tony."

"Not even a big twelve," Barb agrees. "I could still take you in a fight."

"We were all bigger than you," Vanessa says, "except for Mia."

Tony closes his eyes. In his memory, in his dreams, he's always the size he is now. Six foot two, two hundred pounds of highly capable muscle. With their words, he has a sudden flash of himself at twelve, a skinny kid. Bookish. Shy.

It's too much of a shift for him. He shakes his head. "Old enough to think of something else."

Theresa gets up and crosses the room to him, takes his hands. He lets her, surprised to discover that hers have age spots. She's fifty-three and was twenty-six the night it happened.

Which is another trick his memory has played. He always sees her as a terrified child, huddled in the corner with the rest of his sisters. She was home for Thanksgiving, he remembers now. Had moved out the day after she graduated from high school.

"I've always felt guilty," Theresa says. "I took off as soon as I was legal and left the rest of you in that house. I didn't have the guts to do what you did. I wish to God I had been the one to pull the trigger."

Her words carry him back to the cramped living room of the run-down house in Seattle. His sisters are all weeping silently, huddled in a little knot at the end of the sofa, as far away from his father as they can get.

The TV is blaring, but it can't shut out his mother's voice, pleading, or his father's, threatening.

She's on her knees, and her eye is swelling shut from where he punched her.

Tony, man-size and powerful, holds a gun in his hands. He aims it, a deadly marksman, at his father's chest and pulls the trigger. The recoil. The blood. The smell of gunpowder.

But Theresa keeps talking, and her words change the picture.

"You were such a stringy little kid," she says. "Even at twelve. You hadn't hit your growth spurt yet."

"And those glasses!" Barb's voice adds in. "Too big for his face. Like Harry Potter."

"You couldn't see properly that night because he'd blackened your eye and broken your nose before he started in on Mom. Your nose was pouring blood all down your shirt."

"No," Tony says. "No, it wasn't like that at all."

"It was exactly like that," Vanessa and Jess say together.

"Defiant," Barb says. "All of us girls were trying to hide. But not you. You marched out of the room, a little wobbly from the head punches, and came back with the gun."

Flashes of memory come at Tony from all directions. He can't look at any of them very long, they're like a strobe light. Pain in his eye.

Blurred vision. Blood gushing from his nose down the front of his shirt. Nausea twisting in his belly.

And the blurred image of his father, yanking his mother's head back by the hair.

Tony gasps, leans back against the wall behind him. "He had a knife," he says. "I'd forgotten the knife."

"You saved me," his mother says, her calm voice cutting through the haze of his growing panic. "Maybe all of us. He was crazy drunk and into some kind of drugs, I think. I don't know, but he was worse that night than he'd ever been. Paranoid. He said I'd been cheating on him. He said he would kill me first, and then all of you, one by one."

Tony's knees give way, and he slides down the wall, letting the floor and the wall hold muscles that don't know what to do anymore. He is weeping in a way he didn't know was possible, as if something lodged deep inside his gut is trying to tear itself loose.

And then Theresa is on the floor beside him, with her arms around him, and she is weeping also. And then all of his sisters pile on, one after the other, like it's a football game and he's the quarterback. He's buried in a pile of soft arms and hair and perfume and tears, but it's all right. They are there because they love him.

A long time later, when the tears stop and the girls are all sitting on the floor around him, he says, "I remember it all so different."

"I wish I had asked," his mother says. "You don't owe us anything, my son. You saved us. We owe you."

"I don't know what that means," he answers.

"It means," Mia says, irrepressible and already laughing through her tears, "that you can stop being such an idiot of a martyr and take Maisey out on a date."

"You're a crazy girl," Tony says. But in his heart, he begins to think that maybe, possibly, he might do exactly that.

Chapter Thirty-Four

One day flows into another, and we flow with them.

Marley and JB have moved into a house just outside of town, one with a couple of acres and their own small, personal forest. She says she can breathe out there and is working on clearing away too many years of ugly. Turns out JB is more teddy bear than bouncer, unless something is a threat to Marley.

As for the rest of her band, they weren't too excited about Colville. She says they can suck it up. She can find new people either here or in Spokane. It's not like she even wants to be big-time; she just likes to make music. She's teaching guitar lessons and waitressing for now, but she is talking about going back to school. She says she doesn't care what she studies, as long as she studies something. She always wanted a college degree.

Geoff succeeded in his bid to have Greg's custody suit heard here in Colville. He's also managed to get the date set for the first week of October. That way, he says, the best interests of the child are more likely to have her continue the school year here, especially if things are going well.

We are now two weeks in, and so far Elle is happy. She says school is still boring, and she still wants to homeschool, but she gets that it will be better for the court thing if she's enrolled in regular classes for now. She's making friends, and she's in band and choir and drama.

As for me, I'm still at loose ends. Dad's cognitive state is pretty good, in general, although he never has gone back to work. He reads a lot, sleeps a lot, takes long walks around the neighborhood. So he doesn't require much care from me, apart from cleaning the house and making meals.

Sooner or later, I'm going to have to do something to earn my keep, but for right now I feel like we're both blessed to have time to reset and recover.

I've started seeing a counselor to help me work through a lifetime of beliefs that need changing. It's an amazing process to begin to understand that I couldn't possibly have ever been enough for my mother, no matter what I'd managed to accomplish. Even if I'd gone into politics and managed to be the first woman in the White House, she would have still needed me to be more.

So right now I'm working on being enough for me.

I'm sitting on the front porch with my journal, breathing in afternoon sunshine that still smells of last night's frost. The sky is cloudless and blue beyond imagining. The maple on the front lawn is scarlet, and I've forgotten about writing down my thoughts because I'm lost in the contrast between the scarlet and the blue and how beautiful it all is. How quiet.

And then a pickup truck pulls into the driveway.

Tony.

My heart does a sideways lurch one direction and then the other. A flock of butterflies that has apparently been roosting in my belly bursts up in a flight pattern that would be the envy of the Blue Angels.

The last time I saw Tony was that day when Walter told us the story of how my mother came to leave Marley behind. Mia and Mrs. Medina have been in and out of our house on a regular basis, and I've been to Mrs. Medina's house for dinner more than once, but Tony has always been working. He hasn't called to check in or offer any commentary on Boots or any words of support over Greg's attempt to take Elle away from me.

He hasn't returned my calls.

I watch him walk up the sidewalk and can't think of anything to say.

"So this is awkward," he says. Sun picks out highlights in his hair, makes his eyes shine as blue as the sky. Despite how gorgeous he is, he makes me think of junior high dances, like both of us have too many hands and feet and not enough by way of words.

"You could sit, if you want," I tell him. "Chairs are free."

He settles himself into the Adirondack beside mine, and that's better because we can both look at the tree and the sky instead of at each other. The silence stretches taut between us, until it reaches a point where it's pulling at my lungs and my heart and I have to say something, anything.

My mouth opens, but before any words come out Tony says, "Would you—I mean, could I take you out for dinner?"

I stare at him in what would be a pin-drop silence if it weren't for rustling leaves overhead and a car driving down the street. My mouth stays open. This totally unexpected question has incapacitated my brain circuits.

An exploratory drop of drool creeps up over my bottom lip, and that jolts me back to my senses enough to make me close my mouth and swallow.

Tony gives me a smile that's equal parts charm and apology. "I'm sorry. You can call me Mr. Suave."

"Does this mean we're not Betty and Al anymore?" I ask.

He grins, his whole face coming alive in a way that melts my heart. "I thought you'd be mad."

"I am mad," I tell him, but my voice doesn't sound mad, and there's a smile nudging at the edges of my lips. "Some bodyguard you turned out to be."

His face darkens, and he turns his head to look out into the street so that all I can see is his profile.

I want him to smile again, to look at me again, but he's got some explaining to do.

"It's not that I didn't want to be here," he says, finally. "I didn't feel like you . . . like I . . . the last thing I thought you needed was a guy hanging around who has the kind of baggage I do."

"Seems like maybe that would be my decision to make. If you wanted to be here, that is."

"You're right. I'm sorry. But that's the thing. As hard as I try to not be like my father, the next thing I do turns out to be just like him. Assuming a woman can't make her own decisions, for example."

"Tony."

He turns his head to look at me, and I can see it takes an effort.

"I need to tell you some things I've been too much of a coward to tell you," he says. "That's why I haven't been here. Couldn't bring myself to do it. I didn't want to see the way you were going to look at me after. Especially with how Boots turned out to be. And then Greg."

I lay my hand over his arm. It's rigid and unyielding beneath my touch. "You are nothing like your father. Or Boots."

He takes the sort of breath Elle takes when something hurts her. A burn. A slap.

"I've been to juvie," he says.

"I know."

"I"—he holds his breath, and when he releases it the words ride along with it, all in a rush—"killed my father."

"I know that, too."

The muscle beneath my hand softens ever so slightly. When he speaks again, it sounds like a question. "I have nightmares?"

"Know it."

His head drops into his hands, and his shoulders quake. I'm not sure if he's laughing or crying, or both. "And you know all these things about me, how?" His voice comes out sounding all muffled.

"Mia."

"Of course, Mia. My God. Nothing is sacred." He draws in a shaky breath and drops his hands, but he still doesn't look at me.

"Mia casts you as a hero. Don't let it go to your head or anything."

"Mia is . . . special. I don't expect the rest of the world to see it that way." What he means is that he doesn't expect me to see it that way.

I do, though. Ever since Mia told me about Tony, and how he saved them all from their dad the night he decided to kill them, I can't help wondering how things would have been if somebody had just put a bullet in Boots's forehead. Maybe then my mother would have been able to accept me for just me, instead of needing me to also be Marley. Maybe Marley would have gone to college and achieved some amazing degree and been a brilliant lawyer. Or maybe she could have played in a famous band that toured the world. Maybe I would have written novels or painted pictures.

Or maybe none of those things would have happened.

Maybe I never would have had Elle, and that is beyond imagining.

"Yes," I say, looking up at the sky.

"Yes, what?"

"Yes to dinner. Yes, I would like to go out with you."

I'm still looking at the sky, but I hear him draw in a deep breath and breathe it out in a whoosh. And then his hand finds mine. Our fingers intertwine and we sit there, separate but together, both of us looking up at the sky, and even though I'm not looking at him, I know his face wears a smile that matches the one on mine.

Leah's Journal

Are you judging me yet, my Walter? I am judging myself, and find myself wanting. Not for what I did that day, the day I limped down the street with Maisey and that heavy old suitcase. Even now, looking back from this viewpoint, I don't know what I could have done differently.

I didn't trust the police would protect me or that a restraining order would do me any good. And I believed then, and still believe, that Boots would have done as he said. I could have gone back to my life with him and taught my children that it is okay to be beaten into subjection and submission by a man who is nothing—nothing—compared to you in terms of intelligence and decency and worth.

Or I could rescue one of them and teach her that a woman can do anything, be anything she wants to be.

I'm proud that I left him. Proud of the life I built here in this house with you.

I'm proud of my Maisey and what she has turned out to be, even though I know she could have done so much more.

But I see now that I should have gone back.

I should have left Maisey here, safe with you, and tried to rescue my Marley. Only I believed—I can't tell you how fervently I believed—that if I so much as whispered this story to anybody, Boots would do as he had promised. That he would know if I spoke of him, that I had broken my part of the bargain, and he would kill my baby.

I believed he would come after us here. That he would kill you, Walter. And Maisey. And then me.

And so I have kept silent and stayed away for all of these years.

When you told me you had contacted Marley, I was terrified. I understand why you did what you did. I know you wanted to help. And I hadn't told you anything about Boots. I was terrified that he would know and come after me or the girls. And Marley was still there with him.

What should I do? I waited in dread to hear of her murder. I hoped he wouldn't find Maisey, since she carries your last name. I hoped he wouldn't find me—or you—but I bought that gun, just in case.

And I began searching the internet, looking for news of my Marley. And I saw what she has become, despite her father and the upbringing she must have had. She makes music, Walter. She did more than just survive.

You want me to reach out to her, to try to talk to her. It is too late for that. Better to leave things as they are. If I were able to explain, if she were able to bring herself to forgive me for leaving her, it would be for what? To watch me die?

Death is a difficult companion. It is with me always now, demanding more attention than Boots ever did. This time I can't run away. And I have no attention to spare for building new relationships or repairing old ones.

I have loved my daughters—both of them, the one I brought away with me and the one I left behind. I have loved you. And I've tried to make amends as I can for the places I went wrong, for the decisions I wish that I could change.

Was it worth it, to write out my story? To force myself back through the heartbreak and the fear and the guilt? I think so. I feel something that is very close to peace. Not with death, mind you. He'll drag me from this life kicking. Neither have I come to any compassion or forgiveness for Boots.

But I can see my own choices from this new place, and that will make the dying a little easier.

Tomorrow I will shred these pages, to save you the pain of that task. The last wish of my heart is that I could make this easier for you. But I can't. I suppose my death is part of your own journey and the choices you have made, and that, my dear Walter, is as close to wisdom as I am ever going to get.

Leah

Epilogue

One year after my mother's death, the three of us—Marley, Elle, and I—go together to visit her grave. Dad comes here regularly, I know, but when we asked if he wanted to come today, he just smiled and shook his head.

I'm not much for graveside visiting—I don't see the point.

My mother is present in every room of the house. She's always in my head. Her grave is the last place in the world I feel close to her. But today is about some kind of symbolic gesture, as Elle puts it. And this was Elle's idea.

The three of us stand in a row, spring sun on our bent heads, staring down at a grassy mound that is meant to represent, somehow, a woman who was never still, who never rested.

I feel awkward and self-conscious. All my grief and whatever else I'm supposed to be feeling is hanging out at some other grave, I guess. After I lay down my bouquet of flowers, I have nothing to do with my hands. I watch a parade of ants marching over the corner of her tombstone. Shift my weight to ease a sudden random pain in my right calf. Barely restrain myself from taking out my phone to see if Tony has messaged me.

As usual, Marley is the one to speak up first.

"Are we supposed to do something?" she asks. "Because if the idea was to stand here and look at the grave, we've done that. Can we go now?"

Elle glares at her. "It won't hurt you to stand here for a few minutes." Her gaze shifts to me. "Or you, either."

Marley rolls her eyes at me. I grin back. All at once it feels like we're the ones who are thirteen, being lectured by an adult.

But then the tears fill my daughter's eyes and spill over and my heart twists in my chest.

"Aw, shit," Marley says. "Shoot, I mean. What's the matter, baby?"

Elle doesn't answer, her face all screwed up tight with the effort to hold back tears.

I don't need her to tell us. I am smart enough to figure it out.

"I'm sorry, Elle Belle," I tell her, reaching for her hand. "Aunt Marley and I aren't so good with emotions and symbolic gestures. We'll behave. Only you need to tell us what we're doing."

Elle sniffles. "It's just—I thought Grandma should know. That we found Aunt Marley. And that you're with Tony. And that Dad didn't win the court case."

All at once it dawns on me what Elle is trying to get to.

Marley's face mirrors my thoughts, and I know she sees it, too.

My mother—our mother—somehow found the strength to break free of the chains of her own family. Her mother, her grandmother, her mother-in-law, all were suppressed and beaten down by life and their husbands. Love for her daughters gave Mom the strength to break free from indoctrination and violence, to create a reality in which her daughters and her granddaughter stand free and independent today at her graveside.

Marley has cut all ties with Boots. And I am finally done with Greg.

The judge in our custody hearing chose not to change the parenting plan, which means I keep Elle. Greg can have her on weekends, but since she lives with me, he'd have to get her back to Kansas somehow. The judge says that's his problem. She also says that if she ever hears a case presented to her again with evidence that Greg has hit Elle even once, she'll deny him visitation.

He says she can't do that, but she said, literally, word for word, "Watch me, Mr. Loftis. Go ahead, make my day."

Elle will be going to see him this summer for a couple of weeks, but she says that's okay. She wants to see Linda and her baby brother. She wants to see Greg.

And she wants her grandma to know all these things, only it's weird standing over a grave talking to a dead person, especially when your mom and your aunt are acting like stupid teenagers. I'm trying to think how to fix it, prepared to go so far as to start talking out loud to my mother, even though I know she'd be more likely to hear me in her kitchen, when Marley solves the problem.

Right there in the middle of the empty graveyard on a Tuesday morning in June, she starts to sing.

Amazing grace, how sweet the sound

That saved a wretch like me . . .

Her voice floats up, up into the blue sky, strong and true. I join in with harmony on the next lines.

I once was lost, but now am found

Was blind, but now I see.

And then Elle, who has seldom been to a church but has managed to learn this song somewhere, somehow, despite all that, joins in. We link hands, standing in a circle, like maybe we're performing a sacred rite.

And maybe we are, because it feels like we've summoned Mom to stand in the space between us.

With my eyes closed, I can see her, wearing the same sort of triumphant smile she wore every time I actually brought home an *A* on a school report card, the day I graduated from high school, from college, when my very first article was published in a newspaper.

All three of our voices rise triumphantly on the next verse, and if I didn't know better I'd swear my mother's voice is with us, adding a faint counterpoint.

Through many dangers, toils, and snares
I have already come
'Tis grace hath brought me safe thus far
And grace will lead me home.

The sound of our singing drifts off into the breeze, but we still stand there in the silence, linked by our hands and our hearts: three strong women with our lives ahead of us, one strong woman in the ground. I feel weirdly like we are trees, rooted in the soil my mother composted with her life.

"Are we good now?" Marley asks. Her voice sounds abrasive, so I know she's just as moved by what happened as I am.

"Perfect," Elle replies, letting go of my hand. "Anybody want ice cream?"

"Is ice cream your recipe for fixing everything? Like the Brits are with tea?"

"Pretty much. Don't try and tell me you don't eat ice cream when you're mad or whatever. I saw you."

I hear their feet swishing through grass as they move away from me, their voices already fading into background noise.

"You coming, Mom?" Elle calls.

"Give me a sec!" I holler back.

There is something I need to say to my mother, something for her ears alone. Maybe I was wrong about this place, because in this moment, anyway, I feel like she can hear me fine.

"Whisper me truth, whisper me lies," I murmur, Tony's melody drifting through my mind. "All the things you did wrong, you did exactly right."

She doesn't answer me, of course. Even if she hears me, she'd have no idea what I mean.

Sunlight shines warm on my face. A cool breeze touches my hair. Elle's laughter floats back to me. I hear forgiveness in all these things, and love, and I'm able to let go of this moment and take a step toward the rest of my life.

ACKNOWLEDGMENTS

This book grew out of a discussion the Viking and I were having about an acquaintance who is trapped in an abusive relationship. The Viking asked this question: What does it take for somebody to get free from something like that? Is it a flash of inspiration? A sudden knowing? An event? What?

Right then and there, the seed for *Whisper Me This* was planted.

Only the book wasn't called *Whisper Me This*. In fact, it was still being referred to as *That Book That Still Doesn't Have a Title* when I turned it in. The lyrics for the little song "Whisper Me This" came to me while I was mulling comments from Jodi, who is the crème de la crème of editors, and I knew at once that this would be the title of the novel.

My son Brandon took the magic further by writing music to go with the "Whisper Me This" lyrics and sang them to me at my release party for my previous book, *I Wish You Happy*. This is one of the most beautiful gifts I have ever received.

I had so much help along the way in other departments, as well. So much gratitude to my critique partner, Susan Spann, for reading and giving valuable feedback, and again to the Viking for providing the all-important continuity read.

Thanks to orthopedic surgeon Dr. William MaGee for answering my questions about the ins and outs of the forensic dating of healed fractures, to Adult Protective Services worker Monty Jones for helping me work out the details of Walter's legal situation, and to Chuck Harrelson for talking to me about firefighter protocols.

Last, a resounding and heartfelt thank-you to the many good men in my life, beginning with my father and my brother. Because of you, I grew up without ever knowing what it was to fear a man because I was a woman. I'm only just beginning to realize what an exceptional gift that is.

BOOK CLUB QUESTIONS

1. Elle seems wise beyond her years—what do you think has contributed to that?

2. Do you think Maisey is as scattered and flighty as she appears to be? Or is our perception as readers colored by her own mistaken beliefs about herself?

3. Tony and Maisey experienced very different childhoods, but both of them have been affected by family violence. In what ways has this shaped their adult lives?

4. Marley presents as cold and resentful toward Maisey, even though what happened to her is clearly not Maisey's fault. Do you blame her, or do you understand why she would feel this way?

5. The relationship between Elle and Maisey is very different from the relationship between Maisey and Leah. Do you think this is just a consequence of personalities, or is there more going on?

6. Leah was forced into a decision that haunted her for the rest of her life. How do you think you might react in a similar situation?

7. Walter accepted Leah's reluctance to share her history and never pushed for any details of her past. Why do you think this might be?

8. Tony fears that he will become a man like his father. Do you think this is a realistic concern for him? If not, then what evidence is there in the book that he's broken the cycle of violence in his family?

9. Leah stayed with Boots for a long time, even after the violence started. Why do you think it took so long for her to try to leave him?

10. Do you think there is hope that when Elle grows up she will be able to escape the cycle of domestic violence in her own relationships? Why or why not?

11. Secrets play a significant role in this novel. Have you ever kept a family secret that could cause significant harm—or even good—from a family member? If so, what did it cost you personally to keep that secret?

ABOUT THE AUTHOR

Photo © 2012 Diane Maehl

Kerry Anne King is the author of the international bestselling novels *Closer Home* and *I Wish You Happy*. Licensed both as an RN and a mental-health counselor, she draws on her experience working in the medical and mental-health fields to explore themes of loss, grief, and transformation—but always with a dose of hope and humor. Kerry lives in a little house in the big woods of the Inland Northwest with her Viking, three cats, a dog, and a yard full of wild turkeys and deer. She also writes fantasy and mystery novels as Kerry Schafer. Visit Kerry at her website, www.kerryanneking.com, or follow her on Twitter (@Kerry_Anne_King).